Cataclysm: Return of the Gods

Third Edition

by Stephen H. King

(TOSK – The Other Stephen King)

ACKNOWLEDGMENTS

There's simply no way this novel would have happened were I left to my own devices. Thus, more than a few acknowledgements are in order.

First and foremost, to my beloved, the family's creative yin to my yang, the undisputed expert on strong women and their reactions to husbands' hijinks, and my most avid reader and chief supporter—my wife, Heidelinde—a great big, warm thank you from the bottom of my heart.

To my editor, Debra Ginsberg, I send thanks for pressing through a first manuscript at a record pace. She made such a huge difference in the work with her comments and suggestions.

To all my readers, who gave me a smattering of some of the best advice I've ever received: Jaime, Doug, Lisa, Rebecca, Broog, and Elena. You guys rock!

To my daughter Jessa, thank you for your unquestioned support despite being banished from the living room for months while I needed space to write.

Finally, to Tom Gehrke, thank you for the use of Ares on the cover, as well as your understanding for the incident that occurred. You're a great artist and a great person as well.

TABLE OF CONTENTS

The Coming Storm

Crystal braved a glance at the chaos that surrounded her. She was past the initial *we're all going to die* panic and was now curious to see if the others were experiencing the same wondrous and terrifying sensations that filled her.

To either side, and facing north also, stood John and Birch, both good friends but from different places in her life. Birch, the druidic practitioner and expert on all things mythological, she'd known for years, while John was a new acquaintance. Both men, though, appeared as she thought she must, enraptured expressions molding their faces as magical powers they'd never felt before coursed through their bodies and minds.

Crystal could barely hear the incantation the twelve people recited in unison over the wind that whipped both inside and outside the protective bubble they had created with the new-found power they wielded. The words were being supplied telepathically somehow by Matthew, in a language that had started as English but now seemed to be Latin—"seemed to be" because the conjugations and sentence structures didn't fit with what Crystal had learned in the one Latin class she'd taken. She doubted they had any meaning at all, in fact, in part because she could see that the multi-colored energy flows that melded into the protective hemisphere weren't affected at all by the chanting. Mostly, though, she knew her husband well enough to sense the ironic lilt in his telepathic compulsion.

Matt was *playing* with them.

While, that is, he was saving their lives, a conflict that she put aside to worry through later. For the time being, she continued wrestling with magical forces and participating mindlessly in the chant, whatever it was, while she watched the cataclysm in the form of plunging temperatures and a great tidal wave slam across the world she had known, turning structures both man-made and natural into shredded mockeries of what they had been. The raw power of the earth's forces—wave, wind, and temperature—crushed and dominated, destroying everything the people in the circle had ever known.

Everything was gone, or would be very soon.

But they were all going to live. It seemed.

It had taken so little time to upend Crystal's world. She'd been sitting calmly in her craft room just minutes ago when the lights had gone out and it had become strangely dark for the middle of a pleasant spring day. Suddenly a light, round and brilliant, had shown through a portal that opened in the center of the room. Her husband's voice called to her through it, inviting her to come to the light.

Weird, that. And it just got weirder after.

The day had started so—so normally.

****

Crystal bustled about getting breakfast and lunches ready for the day. It was a task she'd cherished every morning of the thirteen years of her twin daughters' lives. Today, it served to take her mind briefly off of her husband's strange brooding.

"Hi, Mom!" Heidi, always the happier of the girls in the morning, said as she skipped into the kitchen. Crystal finished depositing their lunches into the insulated carriers and then closed the bags and her thoughts off. She forced a smile as Heidi and her sister Linda each took a plate and a glass of juice from the counter to the table and sat down to eat.

"Mornin', girls," Matt said from behind his cup of coffee. "Sleep well?"

The twins acknowledged their father's morning ritual with a

nod. His habits, he always claimed, were what made him successful. It was an assumed personality trait rather than a natural one, Crystal knew. Back when they had met, and later on vacations and weekend excursions, Matt was charming, funny, irreverent, and sometimes downright chaotic. On work days, though, her husband seemed to toss on a cloaked disguise, switching from her fun-loving mate to Dean Vincent with the deft twist of a Windsor knot.

Dean Vincent's regularity, in fact, was what made this morning's difference noticeable, having so far run along a subtly changed script. Matt still looked the same, his copper-colored hair styled just so and his black business suit and pastel tie carefully plucked clean of the white hairs from Yuki, their Chihuahua, that tended to find their way to every article of clothing in the house. This morning, though, the normally talkative man said nothing of consequence to her when he walked in to the dining room, and he also ignored the newspaper that she had placed in its usual spot on the table. His own breakfast sandwich lay uneaten beside the mug of coffee that he was sipping.

"Is everything all right, Dad?" Linda asked. So Linda picked up on it, too, Crystal noted. Heidi laid claim to all of the youthful impishness in the twins, while Linda had been blessed with an attentiveness that belied her age.

"Fine, Linda," Matt said. "Sorry. I—I had a bad dream last night that's still bothering me. There was a disaster. You two stay close together at school today, okay?"

Heidi snorted and said, "Dad, it's been decades since there was a major earthquake here."

Matt's eyes stared at a point far away for several moments, and then snapped back to focus on each of the girls in turn. He rose and opened a cabinet door above the refrigerator, reaching in to where emergency supplies had been stocked ever since they had moved in.

"I didn't say earthquake. Even so, you're probably right, Heidi. Still, it would make me feel better if you each tossed a flashlight into your backpack for today. Please? For me?" He placed a small emergency flashlight beside each girl and then headed upstairs.

Crystal broke out of her own routine and followed him up the stairs. "A bad dream, Matt?" she asked as he brushed his teeth. "Matt, you've said that you don't have any dreams, much less bad ones. So now your first dream happens to consist of a disaster scene scary enough to inflict on the girls and me?"

"Mm hmm," Matt said around his toothbrush, shrugging as his eyes met hers. He rinsed his mouth before continuing, "Look, I can't explain it. I feel like something disastrous is likely to happen today. I can't know for certain, but I—well, I sense it coming. There's a flashlight in the cabinet for you, too. Just do me a favor and keep it close. You're not going anywhere, are you?"

"No. Ms. Evans doesn't need me to volunteer in her classroom today. I'm just dropping the girls off at school and coming home. I'd planned to spend the day cleaning up and organizing the craft room, but if we're all going down in a deadly disaster of doom, maybe I won't bother." She stuck her tongue out at him.

Chuckling, her husband flicked his towel at her. She dodged to the side, and he took advantage of her off-balance moment to dart to her, enfolding her in his arms. His eyes held hers, his expression turning playful for a moment.

"I love you, Crystal," he said. "That's why I worry. Look, I could be wrong. Everything's probably going to be fine; I'll just be a little bit embarrassed over predicting a disaster that didn't happen. Just keep the flashlight close by, okay? For me?" He kissed her and then left the bathroom.

"And with that," he called over his shoulder, "I bid you good day."

"Drive carefully!" Crystal yelled after him, watching her husband, his form still muscular despite his age, slip his suit coat back on and step purposely out of the room. She listened to his footsteps descend the stairs, and then turned to look in the mirror. She smiled to reassure herself. Crystal had never seen that look in her husband's eyes, but all this over a dream? Really, now....

The College

O'Suaird College of Business occupied an entire sprawling two-story building in the rear of a commercial area located in a section of the city that was known for its zoning's aimless wandering from commercial to residential and back. From that building it had served its small but elite student body for dozens of years.

Unpretentious double glass doors opened into the main reception area for the building, a single hall leading back from the front desk to the bulk of the administrative offices of the college. One office stood separate; Dean Vincent's had been carved from space in the student lounge upstairs. From the dean's lair, as some students referred to it, he presided over the academics as well as the student lounge with sharp efficiency. He was known to be both tough and fair, wrapped into a combination that some called mean. Most of the students respected him and some even feared him, but those who attempted to see around the façade learned to enjoy the dean's subtle humor that he sometimes allowed to break through. Those few students would shock their peers by visiting him in his office occasionally, a practice he neither encouraged nor banned.

Sometimes new students approached RJ, the president, regarding an academic crisis real or imagined. The encounter always proceeded in the same manner: RJ would thank them for taking the time to—he would usually pick a fine business word like *collaborate*—with him, wish them luck in their studies, offer an inspirational quote from the industry giants who had come before, and then firmly tell them to see the dean.

The day's weekly management meeting crawled quietly

through its agenda despite the energizing Bay Area springtime that unfolded outside. The topics were routine, which helped play into the somber mood. The eight men and women sitting around the table in well-starched business attire had worked together as a team for a long time—the newest had joined over four years previously—and the weekly meetings were typically viewed as an opportunity to lighten the burden of running an academic institution with a touch of humor, whether the president felt it appropriate or not.

RJ sat in his usual location at the head of the table. At the other end sat Matt, the dean's frown darkening the whole room. The rest of the seats were taken by the other directors, who had spent most of the meeting muttering quietly, absorbing and then echoing Matt's tense mood.

"I'm sorry, what was that you asked?" Matt replied to a question from RJ, turning some of the heads at the conference table. Tuning out the president was rare for Matt, as he seemed to relish the management meetings as an opportunity to get in his weekly quota of wisecracks.

RJ looked surprised, too. "I asked about your department's readiness for the upcoming accreditation visit. How's it coming along?"

"Oh. Fine. " Matt shrugged.

"Fine? That's not very specific."

Matt shrugged again. "When I get back to my desk, I'll e-mail you an update that's specific. Everybody's working on the files. It should be a great visit, with no findings." A couple of the other managers coughed in surprise. A visit with no findings, the term for citations issued for being out of regulation, was almost unheard of due to the sheer volume of the documents a college had to be in compliance with.

RJ, apparently sensing that the update was the best he would get, shrugged also. He said, "I look forward to a perfect visit then. You know what will happen if it's *not* perfect, right?"

"Hmm? Oh, sure. Fifty lashes, right?"

RJ's chuckle held little humor. "Yeah, I think it's a hundred now. More, if you don't start paying attention."

Matt nodded, sat forward, and looked directly at RJ. "Not sure how much attention I can afford to pay on my salary, but I'll try," he quipped with a grin.

Everyone except RJ chuckled, glad to see the normal Matt back for the moment.

RJ looked down at his agenda to move to the next item. As he opened his mouth to speak, though, the room went dark. Silence descended, hanging for several long moments as people adjusted.

"Damn," RJ said as the others in the room started whispering to each other, each wondering what could have caused the outage. Suddenly a light flared up, and as everyone shook the spots from their vision they saw the light was not coming from the fluorescent bulbs in the ceiling, but rather from a glowing ball that floated above Matt's outstretched left hand.

"Well, we probably won't get that visit after all," Matt said and stood up.

"What do you mean?" said Mary, the college's financial aid director.

"How did you do that?" asked Sue, director of human resources, her question echoed by several at the table.

"What the hell is this?" RJ said, finger punctuating his question in a jab at the table.

Matt smiled, standing quietly for a moment, his gaze sweeping the room. Finally he spoke, his voice energized, coming in staccato commands. "Okay, look, we need to get everybody out of the building, and none of the emergency indicators are going to work. Bob, you evacuate downstairs on the south side. Sue, downstairs on the north. Mary, upstairs south, and Jennifer, upstairs north. RJ, you get the hall cleared out. Take some of this light with you, and everyone meet in the front parking lot." As he spoke, Matt walked rapidly around the table, waving his left hand over the left hand of each of the other people in the room. Their hands made contact, causing smaller balls of light to separate from the one Matt held and take a position levitating over the palms of their new owners. RJ shook his head and opened his mouth to argue against receiving his ball of light.

"Shut it, RJ," Matt said with a force behind his words strong enough to surprise and silence everyone at the table. Matt continued, his voice softer in volume but equal in intensity, "I'll explain, but right now the students and staff need your help evacuating from total darkness."

Matt waved his hand and the door across the room opened, allowing the noises of shuffling and muted panic from outside in to the room.

"They need you. Go now," Matt ordered. Heeding the urgency in his voice, the administrators walked out, obeying in stunned silence while they examined the balls of light that were attached over their hands through no force they could identify.

RJ headed into the pitch blackness of the administrative hall, noting that the only light was the one he held in his hand. No—the one that somehow hovered over his hand, he corrected. The battery-powered emergency lights at each end of the hall should have been glowing brightly, but all was black except for the feeble gleam from the globe Matt had given him. He went to the far end and called to his executive assistant.

"Tracey, are you okay?"

"Yes." He heard Tracey's irritation in her voice as she replied. "Yes, I am. But I'm going to have to retype the report I was working on for you."

RJ groaned softly, knowing the report she was referring to was a long one. "Bummer," he said. "Well, there's plenty of time for retyping this weekend. Now, though, we need to get out into the daylight, so follow me. And I saw that."

"Saw what?"

"You waved your middle finger at me." RJ hadn't been able to see a thing, since the globe's light only extended a few feet, but he knew that Tracey's middle finger was her favorite means of expression when she didn't like something she heard.

RJ continued down the administrative hallway, calling for the occupants of the offices he passed to follow him. He stepped out into the lobby, a cluster of staff stepping close behind him. He noticed that the lobby was dark and quiet, though shuffles and muttered conversation could be heard down the halls. A grunt and exclamation alerted RJ to hold the light higher and look toward the sound. The front desk temp—RJ wished he could remember her name—was picking herself up off the floor.

"Tripped over the planter. I'm fine," she explained, giving the planter a light retaliatory kick.

"Wonder what happened to the emergency lights," Tracey muttered.

RJ nodded in agreement. "Me, too," he said.

Matt was already in the lobby, holding up a now-larger ball of light for all to see. "Out to the parking lot," Matt ordered before marching quickly out the double glass doors.

Cataclysm

As the workers filed out, they could see Matt standing by the side wall working quickly. He drew a rectangular area onto the brick wall with his finger. Once the rectangle was complete, he stepped away and called out, "Crystal?"

The rectangular area stood out from the rest of the wall in the strange glow of RJ's and Matt's levitating spheres of light. Instead of reflecting the meager illumination, the rectangle simply framed darkness. From the muttering behind him, RJ could tell others were as curious as he to determine the secret of the dark shapes.

"Matt? Is that you?" RJ recognized the voice as belonging to Matt's wife.

"Yes, Crystal. I'm here. Come toward the light. Bring Yuki."

Moments later, a woman's figure stepped out of the portal and onto the college's grounds holding a small white dog in one hand and a flashlight that was off in the other. RJ stared at her in disbelief.

Matt moved a few feet over and repeated his motions, drawing another doorway with his finger. This time he called, "Heidi? Linda? Come to the light, girls." Two pretty teenage girls stepped out.

RJ found himself standing, staring. He had been able to ignore his confusion over seeing the bubble of light appear in Matt's hand and spread to his own and the hands of those in the room due to the urgent need to evacuate. The scene unfolding, though, was beyond that. Doorways through space? Impossible.

"Matt," he said, "What is going on?"

Matt ignored RJ's question and started drawing on the wall

again.

"Dad, the flashlights are dead," one of the twin girls said. RJ wished he could remember how to tell which was which.

"I know. Go with your mom over to where RJ is."

"But if you knew they were dead, why'd you make us carry them?"

Matt stopped what he was doing, turned, and tousled his daughter's hair. "It's a long story, dear. I knew you'd be okay, even with those, if you remembered that today was going to be different. Now please go, Heidi. I have a lot I still need to do."

In the next doorway he created, Matt called for Krista. RJ's heart jumped as he heard his own wife's voice respond, and he rushed to the doorway to meet her. "Bring the puppies!" RJ called out. His wife, a statuesque blonde carrying two pugs, stepped through and ran to him. RJ's son Clint, a boy of ten, and his seven-year-old daughter Amanda sprinted from the next doorway, joining their father and mother in a family embrace.

The crowd all began talking at once, asking Matt how he was doing whatever it was he was doing. Finally Matt turned around. His suddenly-amplified and commanding voice shook the nearby windows as he said, "There is no time. Get to the middle of the parking lot. I will explain, later. I promise I will, but there is no time now, so go. Now."

Matt turned back to the wall and repeated the drawing process over and over, calling out names, while those behind RJ hastened to obey the very loud new version of Matt.

As the sides of the entryway began to fill with the people Matt was bringing in, RJ heard a growing rumbling behind him. He turned and saw that the students from the college were out of the building, ambling toward the parking lot in a disorganized gaggle. Not wanting to interrupt Matt, though he desperately wanted to know how Matt was doing whatever it was, and seeing a traffic jam building up with students watching Matt work, RJ started directing and pushing the rest of the students toward the evacuation area across the lot. While he pushed the students, he called out the teachers' names that he knew, asking if they had all their students with them.

Once at the parking lot, RJ could hear the muttered complaints of the staff and students. It was cold! He'd always enjoyed the Bay Area springtime because of the warmer air that came with it, but the temperature this afternoon reminded him of when he'd stepped off an airplane in Alaska in the winter on the way to a conference. Students moved to stand closer to each other, their breath fogging icily in the eerie glow of his and the other administrators' balls of light.

Tracey stomped up. "Why won't my car start?"

RJ looked at her in confusion, the reporting process interrupted. "What?"

Tracey said, "My car. It's parked right there. I turned the key, and—nothing. Won't start. Won't even make a noise like it's trying to start."

"You sure you had the right car?"

"Yes. I'm not stupid," she said, crossing her arms. "The key let me in."

Wanda, the full-time receptionist, walked up and said, "Mine won't start either."

RJ asked, "Why are you trying to start your cars? The power's just out. It'll probably be back on in a few minutes."

Matt, who had come up behind RJ, said, "No, the power's not just out. Your cars won't start, not for a long while to come. A couple of thousand years, in fact. By then, they'll probably have some rust issues."

"What?" Tracey said, turning an incredulous look toward Matt. "You're crazy. That's crazy talk. This isn't happening"

Matt shook his head and smiled gently. "No, not crazy, though you're justified in wishing that I were. No time to explain now, though—it's on its way. Please head toward the group there in the middle of the lot, and move everybody away from the vehicles that are parked here."

"Wait. What's on its way?" Tracey asked in a high, intense voice.

"Just go. I've already spent too much time saying I'll explain. If you want to live, you have to get over there."

RJ moved obediently toward the gaggle in the middle of the parking lot, shivering in the unseasonal cold, dragging Krista and Tracey along behind.

Suddenly the white ball of light in Matt's hand grew much larger, lighting up the entire group overhead, and Matt's voice boomed across the parking lot, loud enough to overrule any possible opposition, "Let me have your attention." Obediently, everyone turned toward him and stopped talking. Matt turned toward his wife and daughters, who were clinging to each other and looking at him with terrified faces. He smiled and winked, and they relaxed visibly. Watching this, the tension in the rest of the crowd relaxed as well.

"Okay," Matt said in his impossibly-loud voice, "look. I still don't have time to explain what's going on. I will have time in the near future, and then I will explain to all of your satisfaction, but for now just take my word that the world as you have known it is about to end. You have two choices, really. You can stay here and very likely die or you can come with me and live."

Out of the rumble that erupted, a few voices questioned Matt directly.

"What about my wife?" shouted a business professor.

"Where's my daughter?" yelled a student.

"I have brought all that I can here. I would bring more, but it is impossible. I can only open tunnels to destinations I know, unfortunately. For me to toss them out without knowing the location I send them to is asking for trouble, for people to be sliced in half or buildings destroyed." His voice took on a new intensity as he continued over the rumbling of concerned voices around him, "Everyone, please listen to me. Now, please. A massive tsunami is on its way, and it will be here soon. The city will be wiped clean, and those who survive the wave will have to live through temperatures close to a hundred degrees below zero. I have an estate that is protected from the cataclysm, and after the destruction has run its course you can help rebuild civilization and live happily ever after, and all that. But to get to there from here, you need to survive."

"Why won't my car start?" Tracey asked loudly. "I want to go be with my boyfriend!"

Matt sighed. "You won't give up, will you? Okay, fine. Electrons no longer exist."

"But my car isn't electric. It's gas."

"Even internal combustion engines require electricity. Every time the shaft turns, it is powered by explosions of gas caused by the spark plugs. And guess what spark plugs cannot function without."

"Oh," Tracey replied quietly and then stepped back with an embarrassed expression.

"We now have one less minute until the wave gets here, folks. I need all of you to decide right now between life and death. If you choose to go with me, get close together there in the center of the open area of the parking lot."

"But my boyfriend!" Tracey said, bouncing on her heels, conflicting expressions warring on her face.

"Can't help him," Matt replied. "Go, or stay, but decide now."

Several people walked away, but after a few strides some of them shook their heads and reversed course to rejoin the group.

Tracey turned and walked toward the road. RJ called after her, "Tracey, come back!" He sprinted over to her and grabbed her arm, spinning her to face him. "Look, if Matt is right, there's no point in both you and Bill staying here and suffering through it. If he's wrong, then when the power comes back on you can go see Bill and be glad it's over. Either way, you need to come with us. I'm ordering you to come back to the group."

Tracey considered RJ's words for several long moments and then nodded and returned to the center of the lot.

"Good. Now, we can begin. Please let me have your silence unless I ask you to speak, so that this can be completed in time," Matt said as Tracey stepped back into the group.

"How do you know what's coming?" Krista asked, hands cupped around her mouth. It was becoming harder to be heard through the strong wind that had come up from the west.

Matt said, "I've been through this before. It always happens the same way, except that there aren't always nuclear power plants just a few hundred miles south of here. Now, can you please hold your questions till I can get you to safety?"

Striding into the center of the group of people, Matt motioned for the space's occupants to clear it for him. Warily, those closest to him moved away, pushing others out too. Matt looked in the direction of a lone car that was in the way of the throng of people on the east side of the group. He made a small wiping gesture, and the car flew several dozen feet away from the group, turning upside down in the air. Those who were looking that way gasped and turned awed expressions toward Matt.

"*Crystal, John, and Birch, to the north. Phoenix, Mary, and Claudia, to the east. Krista, Ryan, and Richelle to the south. Leonard, Carol, and Michelle, to the west.*" Matt's words were carried telepathically to the crowd, causing many of the people to start muttering and look at Matt quizzically.

"*Quiet!*" Matt's mental command rolled over everyone's talking, and the crowd obeyed.

The light over Matt's hand bathing the whole circle in its radiance, Matt began chanting. All twelve who had been called to the edges of the circle joined in as though they were reading scripts.

****

Crystal stood at the edge of the circle, right in the spot into which her husband's mental command had pushed her. Her head reeled; this morning the love of her life had laughed off the warning, pulled on his coat and strode out pleasantly. Now, she hardly recognized the man in the center of the circle. She'd occasionally seen the dean come out of her husband at events where he needed to be in charge, but that was nothing compared to the being who towered before her now. She could see tendrils of multicolored power whipping around him, each one only barely visible as it glowed transparently against the darkness. The large ball of light supported above him by a yellowish, writhing column of energy illuminated a face that belonged to her husband in shape but bore a primal expression of what looked like glee.

She realized suddenly that she was speaking, reciting the same words her good friends John and Birch beside her were saying, the phrases pushed into her head by telepathic command that could only be coming from her husband. She recognized the ritual: "Guardians of the East, watch over our circle. Let the power of Air support us and help carry us where we need to go.

"Guardians of the South, watch over our circle. Let the power of Fire support us and keep us warm as we travel.

"Guardians of the West, watch over our circle. Let the power of Water flow through our beings and strengthen our protective shields.

"Guardians of the North, watch over our circle. Earth power, be our shield against the coming wave."

As she and her fellow chanters completed each post in the watchtowers sequence she had come to know through her dabbling in Wicca, Crystal saw and felt that sector of the circle surrounding them blazed to colorful life with elemental energy. Twin Crystals seemed to be watching as to the east, yellow energy sprang to life representing the fundamental power—the watchtower—of air. Fire was red, water blue, and earth a dull bluish-purple. The analytical Crystal was pleased that the energies were the colors she had learned, that the magic was unfolding much as she would have imagined it. The other Crystal, meanwhile, exulted in the raw power she felt; she'd always dreamed of seeing real magical powers in her younger years, and now she was touching those very elements. She wanted to run, giggling, out to touch the bubble, but she didn't dare. The analytical Crystal took over once again as she checked over her shoulder, making certain her daughters were still standing near their—well, near the man whom she'd known as their father.

The power was getting stronger, she could tell. As each direction was called out, the wind had died down more, warmth spread around, and now a shimmering bubble coalesced around the entire group. A calm silence settled in once the hemisphere was complete, within the confines of what could only be a protective shield, and inside it felt warm again.

Shielding ritual complete, Crystal felt herself compelled along with John and Birch to turn inward to look toward Matt, who was now holding a silver dagger up toward the sky.

"Mother. Gaia. Join our work and bless us with your presence," Matt said alone.

Crystal joined others in a collective gasp as a woman's form shimmered into view beside Matt. "Ares, it's nice to see you again," the newcomer said. Crystal gawked at her beauty. Her delicate frame was clad in a simple verdant dress tied at the waist with a leather cord, her gray hair braided and woven with dozens of brightly colored flowers. High cheekbones and a soft chin framed a smile so warm that Crystal felt giddy when she met her eyes with it. Gaia slowly turned a full circle to examine the assembled crowd.

"Mother," Matt said, bowing slightly. Crystal thought back to the story of Matt's parents dying in a car crash when he was young. Another question, then, for later.

"Up to your usual tricks, I see. Pulling the forces through humans? Is that really necessary?" Gaia said.

Matt shrugged. "Of course not, Mother. But it's useful to start my battle mages out early by having them experience a flow of power. I figured I'd try something new this time."

"You're not worried it might kill them?"

"No. I'll be gentle,"

Gaia shrugged, matching Matt's expression of ambivalence. "Alright, then. It's time, anyway. Shall we—as in you—get started, or should we break out the tea and cookies first?" The goddess looked to her left, where Tracey was reaching out tentatively to touch her. Tracey's hand made contact with Gaia's left sleeve, and then yanked back. Gaia beamed a pleasant smile at the executive assistant and inclined her head. "Child," she greeted Tracey gently.

Several others close by also reached toward the goddess, emboldened by Tracey's success. As over a dozen hands snaked toward her, Gaia's smile vanished. Her lips parted and from between them came a ferocious lion's roar. Everyone but Matt took a surprised step back, the reaching hands snapping to their owners' sides. Crystal felt the hair on the back of her neck rise at the sound.

"Mother," Matt admonished, "Be nice, please. You were a myth to my humans just a few minutes ago."

"So?" Gaia said, directing a flat expression toward Matt. "They could at least ask politely."

Matt met her stare for several moments. Finally he shrugged. "You're right," he said simply, and then turned westward. His hands rose slowly from his sides. Crystal drew in a sharp breath of surprise and heard both John and Birch do the same as she felt a river of elemental power flow through her from her feet up through the crown of her head. The new flux of power through the twelve chosen caused the shimmering half-sphere to brighten as a muted roar rose from the west.

"Don't look down," Matt cautioned everyone in the group, prompting many to look down to see the parking lot dropping slowly away. Crystal heard sharp breaths taken in around her as people adjusted to a new feeling of vertigo, and some sat down heavily on the now-solid air beneath them.

"Clearly, we'll need to work on this obedience thing," Matt said, a sarcastic lilt to his voice, as the half-sphere continued to rise and the roar from the west grew louder. They rose to level with and then above the treetops, giving them all a view of a towering wall of water rushing toward them over the city that lay unprotected below their feet. The roar coming from it, though muffled, shook the crowd on their platform of air.

"Brace yourselves," Matt called out, and everyone in the crowd set themselves to meet the wave.

Gaia chortled and wiggled a finger at a couple of people close to her. "He meant the humans at the watchtowers, silly," she said. "You can relax. And you should. Relax."

Then the wave was upon them. Its power passed around the hemisphere with a calm that belied the fury with which it hit everything outside the bubble. The students and staff watched the college building explode as the force of the wave hit it, and the cars in the parking lot were picked up and tossed into the trees like plastic toys. Trees were uprooted and snapped like matchsticks. Limbs, fish, and parts of what appeared to be buildings hit the bubble and bounced away as the crowd inside the bubble exclaimed in shock and terror.

"Was that a whale?" one student asked the group around her, her question met with awe-struck silence.

Crystal watched in amazement, enraptured tears running down her face as her focus remained on the flows of the magical bubble they were in. She could see the individual strands of elemental power course through the shield, each piece doing its part in holding rushing water at bay. As items hit the bubble, the magic strengthened and flexed at the site of impact. Even more, she could feel it, could sense the ebb and flow of power—Matt's power, her power, she wasn't sure—as the bubble worked to keep everyone safe from the torrent outside.

Crystal finally heard the gasps and looked around as the bubble kept rising through the water that was surging about it. In a moment her focus on the colors was lost, instead drawn helplessly to watching the important landmarks and buildings fall beneath the wall's onrushing power. She saw large groups of people in the distance turn and flee to no avail. The water took pity on nothing in its path. "A ship!" a student to her right yelled, causing her to snap her head that direction just in time to see half of a military ship twist past in the turbulently flowing deluge. She idly wondered where the ship parts would end up as she wrenched her attention back to the more pleasant consideration of the fluidity of the twisting powers in front of her.

Finally reaching a safe height, the hemispheric shield passed through the top of the maelstrom, emerging into a darkness that now seemed serenely calm after the turmoil inside the wave. Crystal relaxed and breathed deeply as the hemisphere itself seemed to wane in intensity.

Matt smiled and said, "See, Mother? All alive and well." Gaia's chuckle chimed in response.

Matt raised his amplified voice again and said, "It's travel time, folks. The trip from here to my estate would take too long just flying, so we're going to be a little unconventional." Again, Gaia chuckled, causing several around her to cast glances of concern.

Matt said, "Don't be alarmed. You will feel a little weird at first, kind of like if your stomachs were trying to leave your bodies through your big toes, but all will be well. I've taken lots of humans traveling like this in the past, and very few have died."

"You are joking, as usual, right?" RJ demanded.

Matt smiled. "You'll see."

Matt raised his arms, and the world *bent*. Crystal gasped at the sensation and a few inside the circle shrieked as everyone inside the bubble seemed to simultaneously flatten into nothingness and stretch into infinity. The sensation left as quickly as it had come. Everyone shuddered, and most went down onto one knee or two.

As their outward senses slowly returned, Gaia's crystal-clear voice cut through. "Well, aren't you good. They all lived."

Rising, RJ glared at Matt and said, "Don't ever do that again."

Matt snorted. "It's okay. We're there." He pointed to a huge compound with a mansion and several buildings in a green valley surrounded by towering mountains. Daylight now surrounded them, and they noticed that the bubble had vanished. The flying group was slowly coming to land on a hillside. As they touched down, they could see hundreds of figures leaving the compound and walking toward them.

"Where's there?" RJ said.

"My home," Matt said. "Estate, actually. It's my own little sheltered retreat up here in the mountains, away from what remains of human civilization. You technically stand on the Asian continent now. You would actually be able to see Mount Everest on a clear day from those hills over there. It's quite a beautiful little strip of land, don't you agree?" Matt pointed around with both hands, smiling.

The Estate of Mars

Turning to Gaia, Matt repeated his half-bow and said, "Mother, thank you for your presence. It is always delightful to be near you. Stay if you will, or go if you must."

Without a word Gaia smiled and disappeared.

Matt's voice infiltrated the crowd's minds again. *"Welcome to my estate. You are safe here through the cataclysm and thereafter. I am sure many of you still have unanswered questions, but first we all need to rest and recover from the trip. In the meantime, those coming to meet us are my servants. My servants, not yours. They will be polite to you and help you become accustomed to your new home, and will happily share this space with you, but don't be foolish. The thrakkoni are not human. They look like you, but any one of them is stronger than the entire group of you. They are very, very slow to anger, but if you succeed in angering them you will very likely die from it, and with my blessings to them. Do not mess with them. Got it?"*

As the thrakkoni came closer, several of the students and staff whistled softly in admiration. Each of them was nearly a perfect replica of the others. The two aspects differentiating them from one another were gender—approximately half were male, and half female—and hair color. Otherwise, their angular faces featured round eyes sitting across the bridge of a sharp nose. Long necks led down to lean, muscled torsos that were clad in simple wraparound tunics over breeches and sandals. Each one alone could be mistaken for a slender and fit human being, but together they looked like a mobile army of porcelain dolls. Their gait was lithe and smooth, and their long strides quickly brought them to the group surrounding Matt. They all stopped, kneeled, and bowed as one, foreheads touching the soft billowing grass on the hillside.

The thrakkon in the front, one of the females, rose, her long shining silver-colored hair falling back to frame her face as she said in a voice like a wind chime, "Master, welcome back. We have kept your estate as you desire, and we are overjoyed at your return."

Matt strode forward and, in his amplified voice, said, "Thank you, Sorscha. Thank you, all. I, too, am overjoyed at returning in this new age of magic. I bring a group of human friends, and would appreciate your help at getting them into guest rooms and making them as comfortable as possible. They have just traveled, so be especially gentle as what was in their stomachs may not remain there long and may need to be replaced with some gentle fare later this evening." At that, several thrakkoni made nasal chortling sounds that struck Crystal as a type of laughter. "Rise, and let's get down to the house to relax and recover." Matt walked to his wife, took and kissed her hand. Motioning for his daughters to follow, he started down the hill at a brisk pace, Sorscha falling in behind the family.

He completed his speech over his shoulder, "Get some rest, folks, and we'll talk over dinner this evening." The other thrakkoni moved as if by unheard command, each walking to one of the humans, bowing, and leading the people down the hill toward their new home.

Crystal wasn't certain what word fit her emotional state best as they walked. She was exhausted from her suddenly-imposed participation in the ritual of power. She was queasy from the sudden jolt of transporting. She tried to remember what Matt had called it: teleporting? Traveling? She was more than a bit lost; her husband was clearly the master of this manor yet she had no idea what her own status was. She was relieved that her daughters and some of her friends had made the trip, yet she couldn't help thinking briefly of the friends left behind. She was amazed at and in awe of Matt for his sudden display of raw power in getting here. And she was jealous—insanely, unexplainably, and totally jealous—over the beautiful argent-haired woman leading them to the manor, genuflecting to Crystal's husband, and acting as though she had known him forever.

So Crystal walked, following "the master", holding her girls' hands, trying to hold back the tide of emotions and get a grip on what she was feeling while she observed what she guessed was her new home.

Stunning. That was the only word she could find to describe the entryway into the estate which confronted her with both opulence and incredible beauty. Flawless landscaping and sweeping marble stairs led up to massive mahogany doors that opened into an entry rotunda that was floored in fine marble. Above, the domed ceiling appeared to mimic the night sky, with clouds drifting across the stars. She gasped as what had to be a shooting star shot across the dome, not following the circular surface but rather crossing the space in the middle. She'd always known her husband had rich tastes, and had occasionally wondered where he had acquired his appreciation of lavish décor. His world, if this was it, was unutterably amazing, she thought as she followed him and his servant through hallways lined with statues of marble, alabaster, copper, and other materials, vases carved of stone or formed from fine porcelain and accented in gold, and artwork, some of which she recognized and some she did not. It was beautiful. It was amazing. It was—his. Was it hers? Right now, all she really wanted was a comfortable bed; there would be time for that question for later on. There would have to be time for many questions later on. For the time being, though, she filed it away and continued walking, mutely taking in the splendor.

As she walked, her mind inventoried and catalogued the people who had survived the cataclysm with her today. The college staff and faculty she knew from all of the events she had attended with Matt over the years. She considered many of them to be friendly, but none really fit into the category of friends. They were—or had been, anyway—Matt's co-workers or subordinates, and she knew them most vibrantly from the stories he told over the dinner table. The students, too, were recognizable for the uniform blazers they all wore; the adoption of the uniform had been one of Matt's prouder moments, she recalled. The uniformity of the thrakkoni fit right in to that mental picture she had of her husband at work. He had always been one of the most martial of the men in her life, a trait she had admired balanced as it was by love and—humanity? Was that the right word to use now? Gaia, if that really *had* been the earth mother, had called him Ares, the Greek name for the god of war. Was he—could he be—*that* Ares? Based on the power she had seen in the past several minutes she wasn't sure she could continue doubting it. If so, he had also been Mars to the Romans, right? In that case, *martial* made sense; the word was based on his name, after all.

Setting the word games with her husband's supposed names aside, Crystal considered those Matt had teleported in immediately after her. They were all pagans. Growing up, Crystal's parents had been Methodists, sort of. At least, they had attended service on Christmas and Easter and on whatever days in-between that they had really felt a need to be holy. She had, herself, been involved in youth programs occasionally throughout junior high and high school, whenever the youth programs were doing something cool that her parents could afford to let her attend.

When she and Matt had started dating, then, she had enjoyed experimenting with him in what she saw as alternative options: New age, Wicca, druidism, and Asatru, the Norse thing she'd never been able to understand. They had all been popular diversions on the campus where Crystal had obtained her teaching degree. The couple had continued their involvement, mostly in Wicca, over the years since, participating in whatever ceremonies she could pull Matt out of the house for. It was in those circles that she had met most of the people whom Matt had invited through the same type of doorway she had come through to be saved from the cataclysm.

"Why Wicca, Matt?" she asked as they walked, hoping the connection would bring some sense to an otherwise senseless day so far.

Matt stopped walking and turned toward her. "The cataclysm you saw today marked a transition, my love. Tonight at dinner we'll get more detail, but in short it was a transition from a two thousand year long technology era to a two thousand year long magic era. Those who will be rulers and shapers of the civilizations to come will be the ones who can successfully shape the flows of magic. I've known it was coming, though I didn't know its actual date and time of arrival. Remember my unease this morning? I could sense the cataclysm's approach, though I was being honest when I said I wasn't sure it would arrive today."

Well, Crystal thought, *at least Matt was honest about something*. The timing of the cataclysm aside, he still had some explaining to do.

"To answer your question, though, for the past several years I've been trying to find people with latent magical abilities so that when the cataclysm happened, I could pull them through and teach them to be my battle mages. What fun is the god of war, after all, without battle mages? The practice of paganism has done me a favor, really, in concentrating a group of people who tend to have strong latent magical power. Each of you whom I put at a watchtower tested well. You each survived the flow I directed through you, and Phoenix was even able to manage it a bit."

"So I'm just your little pagan lover, your little battle mage?"

Crystal asked, not sure if she really wanted him to answer.

"No, absolutely not," Matt said, catching her tone. "You're my wife, a status that transcends magical ability or anything else. In fact, I hadn't meant to send you to a watchtower. One of the mages—remember Chris?—didn't respond to the summons. You did well, though. Very well. Regardless, you're safely here, and now we can go back to being husband and wife."

Crystal caught what she thought was a disapproving expression from Sorscha as they continued down the hall. *Oh great, competition from the flawless one.*

Finally they reached an ornate mahogany door. Sorscha stepped aside, bowing, as Matt opened the door and beamed a huge grin toward Crystal. "Welcome to your new home," he said as he motioned them all through.

Stunning, again. The room they entered seemed carved to her specific tastes, as though it had been built with her in mind. Lapis lazuli tiles lined the floor, grouted with what appeared to be solid gold. The walls were covered with translucent blue sheets, each sheet somehow rippling with some sort of visual effect that reminded Crystal of waves at the beach. Looking up, she was amazed to see a chandelier of blown glass that seemed alive. Each arm was rotating around the center, apparently moving of its own volition. Meanwhile, the ceiling, like that in the entryway, appeared to be an actual slice of the heavens, except that this one contained a central feature. She recognized it as the red planet, Mars.

She'd always wanted to believe that her husband was a god. What woman didn't? Now, though, that the reality was slithering out to resemble the fantasy, she wasn't sure she wanted it. Godlike, yes. But an actual god? Was he immortal? What did that mean for her? What did that mean for her daughters? Were they demigods? Had he been lying to her over the years? She went over her memories, looking for questions that might have been answered untruthfully, not finding many obvious ones. Granted, she hadn't ever asked him, "So, Matt, are you a god?" She supposed that the *till death do us part* bit was a stretch for an immortal, but there wasn't actually a lie there.

She had to admit that she couldn't recall one instance of him saying something that wasn't true, save perhaps the bit about his parents' death. It didn't seem to matter. At the moment, she felt like her whole life had been a lie.

Crystal realized she was still holding her breath over the beauty of the room when she heard the twins release theirs. Looking back at them, she smiled at their awed expressions, happy for the moment at least that her daughters shared her sense of wonderment. Even if she wasn't certain who her husband was anymore, her daughters were still her little girls, her foundation.

She turned to Matt when he cleared his throat. He and Sorscha were looking at her, him smiling and the—what was she again, a thrakkona?—with a guarded expression. "What do you think?" Matt asked.

"It's amazing," she said. "Unbelievable, in fact. I might just pinch myself, except that it would wake me up if I'm asleep, and it would hurt if I'm not. This room looks like it was made for me. Was it?"

"Actually, it was made for me, but since you and I share so many tastes, made for you is close enough. Do you like the ceiling?"

"It's incredible. It can't be real, though, can it?"

"By real, do you mean a real view of the heavens?" Matt said. "If so, then yes. Sort of, anyway. The ceiling is indeed a transmitted view of the night skies above, just with my favorite planet centered and closed in on. You know what planet that is?"

"Yes, I do."

"You sound disappointed. Or.... Something strange."

"No! Not disappointed at all! I'm married to Mars, the God of War, it seems, and I'm sure I'll eventually figure out what all that means. I'm just taking it all in, really I am. And I'm so tired. That—what did you call it, traveling? That was exhausting."

"Ah, of course." Matt opened a door into a beautiful bedroom and said to Crystal with a grand flourish, "Entrez-vous s'il vous plaît!"

Matt's poorly done French brought a brief smile to Crystal's face. His answer to nearly every down mood of hers was to clown around, but then again, it always worked. She looked around; solid oak columns stood at each of the four corners of what must have been more than a king sized bed. Gossamer cloth draped from each column, fluttering over the bed in a luxurious canopy. The walls were the same translucent blue, and the floor the same lapis lazuli exhibited in the entry. Unlike the ceiling in the entry, though, this room's overhead presentation was a more peaceful picture of a night sky, painted shades of blue and gold. A gentle breeze somehow gusted through the room, reminding Crystal of laying, dozing on the beach during their travels, and she found herself even more tired.

"I think I need to sleep," she said, walking toward the bed without looking at either her husband or the creature by his side.

"Of course," Matt said. "Get some rest, and I'll put the girls to their room, too, and then after I've caught up on affairs of the manor, I'll come get you in time for dinner." With that, they closed the door and left her in silence.

Crystal looked around, sighing. Today was a disaster. Or, perhaps, a great success? Her husband was a god. Whatever that meant. And he had just left her alone in her bedroom—their bedroom?—and walked away with the most beautiful silver-haired bombshell she had ever seen. But he loved her, she was sure. She *was* sure, she reminded herself. She knew it in her heart, and she only had to keep telling herself that as she prepared to get the sleep that she desperately needed. She was exhausted down to her toes, and she sighed as she laid down in what she thought must be the softest bed she had ever been in. She was tired, and needed sleep, and she was sure all would be fine when she rose.

A New Life

Crystal jumped slightly when she woke to a kiss, but opened her eyes to see Matt smiling down at her. "Feeling any better?" She nodded, hoping that the bed she was in was actually a hotel bed, and that she would rise to find out they had gone on vacation and that what had happened so far was just a dream.

Basking in her husband's smiling embrace, she moved her arms and legs between the covers, enjoying the luxurious feel of fine linen. Yes, her organs that had seemed so twisted now were feeling normal. Legs work—check. Arms also—check. Try to make lips smile—yep. Check. All was good.

Then she heard the twinkling voice, raised her head, and looked across the room at the too-perfect creature known as Sorscha. It wasn't a dream, after all.

"Crystal?" her husband interrupted her rising irritation, "Dinner is happening soon. Do you want a shower, or a change of clothes?"

"I'm fine."

"Okay. Sure. I'll let you get ready, then. Sorscha, would you stay and help Crystal get ready for dinner?"

Crystal could think of nothing she'd like to do less than spend time with the argent-haired beauty, but her husband's words seemed to be orders to this *Sorscha*, who smiled, nodded, and glided sinuously across the floor to the bed as Matt left the room.

"I'm quite capable of getting myself ready for dinner," Crystal told her, ignoring the outstretched hand.

"You have no reason to be jealous," Sorscha said through a tight smile. "I'm here to help you, and to serve the master."

Crystal looked up at Sorscha for a long moment before rising on her own. "You're probably right. But I'm still tired, and I've had a long, long day, so just let me deal, okay? And—where's my dog?" Crystal realized that her feisty long-haired Chihuahua hadn't greeted her awakening by sticking its tongue in any of her facial openings, and while most days that proved annoying, this evening she missed it.

"She was fed and watered and now awaits you in the sitting room."

"Well, get her, please. I want my Yuki." Crystal's normally unshakably polite manner was cracking; she was trying to be civil but she heard the petulance rising in her own voice.

"Right away," Sorscha said and made her words good as she opened the door and the Chihuahua bounded in and leaped into Crystal's arms. Crystal held Yuki tight for several minutes, savoring the time with the one being she absolutely knew still loved her.

"Dinner will be served soon, and I believe the master wants you there," Sorscha said.

Crystal put Yuki down, holding her temper carefully in check until her puppy was safely perched on the soft cushions of the bed, and then she turned toward Sorscha and let her ire bubble over the top. Moving up close to the thrakkon, she screamed as she wagged her finger in Sorscha's face, "I don't care if he wants me there," punctuating each word with a finger point.

Sorscha took the screaming solidly, her face alive with an understanding expression, her strange round cat-like eyes never flinching. After Crystal's flare-up was spent, she smiled slightly and said, "I understand it is difficult. The master does what he does, and always for a reason. But he loves you. Also, I know that he plans to discuss what has happened over dinner. Please, do him and yourself a favor. Go to the dining hall and join him."

Crystal glared at her opponent. Sorscha was right, no matter how much Crystal wanted to hate her for it. Finally, she nodded. "Could I at least get some clean clothes? These feel—bad. Dirty."

Sorscha's face erupted in a warm smile. "Certainly. This is your closet," she said, leading the way to a closet that was bigger than Crystal's bedroom had been in her home. "Anything that is here is yours, and if you do not find anything that suits your desires you have but to let me know."

Crystal looked through the finery in the closet in awe. There were kimonos of the finest silk, tunics of every imaginable cut, and robes that felt like a quiet waterfall gliding over her. After trying on a few options, she settled on a rustic linen tunic over tan leather leggings.

"Okay, I'm ready. Lead on," she said, and followed Sorscha out into the waiting room of their suite where she found her daughters already dressed and ready. The twins were both clad in the same cut of tunic and leggings as she had chosen. Their hair was neatly done in an intricate style wrapping a French braid around the sides of their heads. "I *love* your hair. Did you do it yourselves?" Crystal asked, and was gripped with jealousy when the girls pointed to Sorscha, each exclaiming how the thrakkon had worked magic. "Oh. Well, it's very pretty," she said, pushing her green monster back down. "So, girls, how are your rooms?"

"Wonderful, Mom!" Heidi said. "We each have our own room, with everything right there, and they're so pretty. Wanna see?"

Crystal did want to see, so she followed the girls into their rooms, curious over where her daughters were staying. Both rooms were set up nearly identically, each with white four-poster beds and matching furniture very similar to what they had had at home. Heidi's room was her favorite shade of lavender, and Linda's room her favorite, was a muted shade of teal. Heidi's room was decorated in pictures of unicorns, her favorite mythical creature. Linda's room, on the other hand, was decorated with forest landscapes.

"Alright, how did you know how to decorate these two rooms?" Crystal leaned over and asked Sorscha, her voice low. "They're too perfect for the girls."

Sorscha turned another maddeningly sweet smile to Crystal and said, "I didn't. Yesterday these two rooms were actually part of a different suite. The master has moved entire mountains and seas before with magic, though, and so moving a couple of doors and re-coloring walls is fairly trivial to one of his power."

"Of course. Matt redecorated on the way for us. Quite un-derstandable," Crystal said, realizing by the thrakkon's expres-sion that her intended sarcasm was either missed or ignored. She sighed and turned to the twins. "Ready for dinner, girls?" she asked, and was reminded of what mattered most to her when they giggled and each held one of her hands. The trio walked out and down the hallway together.

Explanations

The Grand Hall was aptly named. Huge chandeliers cascaded their twinkling light from a ceiling painted to resemble cherry trees blossoming overhead. Stained glass windows filled the walls, beaming colored swatches of light onto a pearlescent floor. Rectangular mahogany tables, each large enough for ten or twelve diners, filled the hall in orderly rows. Around the walls were white statues from seemingly every era and region of mankind, some in the classic Greek form, others resembling the statues she had seen on her travels through Rome and Naples, and others the multi-armed and animal-based statuary of the Asian continent. A marble fountain behind the long head table seemed impossibly alive with birds and fish.

The bell had summoned everyone, it seemed, and hundreds of freshly-washed faces lined into the hall. The thrakkoni placed everyone efficiently while exhorting them to not sit until the master arrived and sat down. At the head table, Crystal and the girls were joined by RJ and Krista and the ten others who had participated in the ritual.

Crystal introduced everyone at the head table to RJ and Krista, since everyone but those two already knew each other from various get-togethers in the past. Krista asked where they had met, and Crystal explained that they had been a loose grouping of friends before the cataclysm, brought together by various levels of interest in paganism.

A soft popping sound interrupted conversation, as Matt suddenly appeared behind his seat at the center of the head table. Crystal jumped. Matt put his hand on Crystal's arm and said, "Sorry to startle you."

She shrugged. "Your flair for theatrics seems appropriate now."

Matt chuckled then turned to Krista, standing to his left. "I hope your rest was good." Smiling, they shared a few lines of banter before Matt turned to the assembled group of humans at the tables before him. Loudly enough for all to hear, he said, "Welcome to my home. Please, be seated. We will soon work out a schedule where domestic duties will be shared, but for the time being the thrakkoni are gracious to serve us all."

As the humans sat, Krista asked, "Do they not eat?"

"Oh, they do," Matt said. "They prefer a different fare, though. They have their own dining and food preparation areas as a result."

On cue, Sorscha and other thrakkoni appeared behind the head table, and others came out in the dining room, all carrying stacks of plates and pitchers of ale, wine, and juice. Crystal noticed that while all the thrakkoni were polite, the only one showing a hint of servitude was Sorscha, and she only served Matt.

The meal was well done. Crystal thought briefly that roast beef and vegetables made a good choice for a large group, and a quick count of tables told her that there were several hundred people. "I hate to bother you," she said politely to the thrakkon putting a plate in front of her, "but I am celiac. Do you know what that means?" When the thrakkon looked at her blankly, she sighed and continued, "Is there any wheat in this?"

Matt smiled and put his hand on Crystal's arm. "You need not worry about your former allergy here."

"Former? What—how....?" Crystal sputtered. Her food allergies had dogged her eating habits for most of her adult life. Every time her family had eaten out she had been forced to ask the food servers about the ingredient list, and over the years she'd come to the conclusion that food servers in general either needed more education or more motivation, or good-sized helpings of both in some cases. There had been plenty of times when she'd told the staff that she was allergic to wheat only to be assured that the restaurant had white bread as well, and once at a restaurant that bragged of their celiac service she had been served a salad covered with garlic bread croutons. "What are croutons made from?" she had asked the server with as much kindness in her voice as she could find for someone who had almost sent her to the hospital in his ignorance. Hearing, now, that her allergy was a thing of the past felt too good to be true.

"It's my protective shell around the estate. It cleanses such things from people. Purifies your bodies, so to speak. Oh, you're still mortal, but you have no need to worry about food allergies, or such things as thyroid or liver disease. You won't even be bothered by mundane things like colds, flu, or sinuses."

"So I can have pizza?" *That* would definitely tip the scales into news that was too good to be true, as she'd craved a good piece of pizza for years.

Matt grinned. "Well, sure. If you can find the ingredients, anyway. The closest grocery store is another teleport away."

Crystal's intestines seemed to flinch at the thought of another teleport, while Birch's wife Frieta asked, "Does that mean I don't have to worry about my diabetes anymore? I was wondering how I was going to get insulin here."

"Absolutely," Matt said. "Look, folks, you're still humans. You can still die from all sorts of causes, including the trauma to your body that would be inflicted by a thrakkon deciding he was angry enough at you to throw you against a wall. But what my shell does is refresh the workings of your bodies so that your glands, organs, and other mechanisms work properly. I may be known as the god of war, but I can heal a fair amount too."

Once she'd digested the good news about her allergies, Crystal continued to poke at her food, distracted by the rough day's events. As perfectly-cooked as it was, she still wasn't certain her stomach had recovered from the teleport, and the barrage of feelings she been assaulted with after the transport hadn't helped. She settled her attention instead on the thrakkoni who were moving about the room serving steaming dishes to hungry humans. None of them spoke to each other, she realized as she watched them work. Each one glided through a delicate dance of food service seemingly without cues of any sort. The only communications she observed were glances and occasional nods.

"Do they practice this, Matt?" she asked.

"Practice what, Crystal?" Matt must have been watching her watch the thrakkoni.

"Serving large dinners like this."

"No, thrakkoni almost never do this sort of thing. Why do you ask?"

"They seem to know exactly who's going to do what, when, and where, without anyone in charge giving directions."

"Oh, right. They communicate telepathically. When we made them, we added that ability in to enhance their capacity to serve us."

"We," Crystal said, looking directly at Matt. She chuckled, a manic tone creeping into her voice. After a long breath in, she said, "You know, it's not too difficult to accept whatever creation myth I feel like, whether it involves the heavens and the firmament, a bunch of titans, the great spirit, a big bang, or even a large sea turtle named Fem Wa Woo with the world perched on its shell, when the myth isn't sitting here beside me. I suppose, though, that when you say *we* made them, you mean you, personally. Am I right?"

"Indeed you are," Matt said. "Each god or goddess makes his or her own servants. Thrakkoni are kind of the accepted standard, because they have a lot of physical advantages and yet they're immune to the flows of magic, which keeps them from being magically subverted from their role as servants. And there is no sea turtle named Fem Wa Woo, you know."

Crystal shot Matt a withering look. Glancing around, she saw that she and Matt were the only ones who seemed to be lacking appetite; everyone else was attacking the food with vigor.

"Not hungry, Matt?" RJ asked, apparently sensing a lull in the discussion.

Shrugging, Matt said, "I don't have to eat. I've never had to eat, really. I enjoy it for the flavor, and this roast is very good. Before the transition I tried to keep up a show of being a normal human—if you'd heard me suggest that I was a god before today, you would've had me committed, right? But now it's not so important. So, anyway, I guess you're right that I'm not hungry."

With that, Sorscha appeared and removed Matt's plate. Briefly nodding thanks, Matt turned back to the assembly of humans, rose, and began to speak in his amplified voice. "My friends, I promised you some explanations when we had time. Now seems that time. I'll tell you what has happened, and then I will take your questions and answer them as I may."

As the hall became quiet, Matt said, "You all have grown up in a world where physical laws were relatively constant, where the fundamental particles joined together to create fairly well behaved electrons and protons. In your world, the 'magic' of, say, the aurora borealis is caused by physically explainable activity of electrons. Well, I'll change that to mostly physically explainable, a paradox your quantum physicists were struggling to overcome, but by and large everyone at least accepted, if not understood, the basic laws of electromagnetic dynamics. Oh, the fundamental particles also bound together to form things that controlled gravity and other forces, but your physicists just hadn't quite figured that part out yet. I think you'll all agree, anyway, that electricity and magnetism were very well understood and, more importantly, controlled.

"But see, there are many different ways to combine the fundamental particles, and a long, long, long time ago they were programmed to shift combinations every so often. Specifically, they shift every two thousand years, which was what happened today. Thus, what was an electron yesterday and for the previous two thousand years is now a completely different particle and will be that for the next two thousand years. The world effectively rebooted from a technology age into a magical age, and in two thousand years it will reboot back to technology, only to continue the cycle. Electrons took a while in the last cycle to be identified and named, and similarly the particle for magic hasn't been named yet in this cycle. Civilizations in previous magical cycles have called it many different things, in many different languages. I'd call it a 'magicon' now but that just sounds silly, doesn't it? Regardless, the new particles are just as controllable once you figure out how. In fact, I'm going to teach those of you who have some latent skill in it, specifically, those of you here at the front table. We'll work at it, and some of you will become the first in this era to earn the title of battle mage.

"The cataclysm we have just undergone is temporary. It's part of the attempt by Gaia and the rest of us to, well, *reset* the world. The tidal wave you saw, which managed to destroy the entire western coast of the continent from Baja California up to Anchorage, as well as the hugely populated east coast of Asia, was the result of a massive island resurfacing. You probably felt the cold, as well, which was a result of a change in the atmosphere that resulted from the loss of electrons in the universe, which temporarily wiped out the earth's magnetic field. The electrical charge in the planet's atmosphere combined with its magnetic field kept many of the gases in place surrounding the planet, and these gases in turn regulated and stored the sun's heat. Scientists called them greenhouse gases for this reason. The realignment of elementary particles caused a loss of these gases, and it also caused a sudden realignment of the earth's core, so suddenly the spot we were on wasn't facing the sun any longer, and the atmospheric blanket was removed, which caused temperatures to plummet. I wasn't kidding when I said the temperatures would reach one hundred degrees below zero. Those who survived the tidal wave will have to find a way—without electricity, or the ability to pump any other fuels—to stay alive in temperatures that cold. Some will. Most won't, in part because the human race has become a bit lazy that way. On the other side of the planet, meanwhile, it's the opposite problem as the direct rays of the sun try to cook every flesh-covered creature.

"Within a few days, the planet will regain its atmosphere, this time magically rather than electromagnetically. Temperatures will return to normal, and the animals will for the most part—well, those who survive the floods and the nuclear meltdowns and such—be fine. The hundredth of a percent of the human race that survived will have to adapt to a world that doesn't contain the same tools it once did, but many of them will, and your race will go on even outside the protection of the estates of the gods."

A lady stood up from her table and interrupted Matt's speech. She said, "What about our friends and family? This morning my husband kissed me on his way to work, and now here I am looking to go home to him tonight or tomorrow. You're telling me he's dead? Mary here has kids at her mom's babysitting while she's at school—are they dead? All of our friends? This can't be." Most heads in the room nodded in agreement, and the angry buzz of hundreds of conversations rose through the hall.

"Silence!" Matt said, again adopting his amplified voice to cut through the talk, and then he said in his regular speaking voice, "Please, silence. Look, I know this is difficult for you all. The cataclysm is a disaster for all humans, planet-wide. The short answer to your question is that I don't know whether your husband is alive or dead, nor do I know whether Mary's kids are still with us. Most humans perished, but...." Matt clinked his knife against his glass to get everyone's attention as the assembly again burst into murmurs. "*but* there are always many who find suitable shelter and adapt to their circumstances and thus survive the transition. Once the cataclysm is over, and the outside atmosphere becomes survivable for a human, you will all have transport available back to your homes to check on your loved ones and bring them back here. Until then, going outside the protective bubble of my estate is suicidal. Only the gods can walk the earth for the next few days.

"So speaking of gods—you must be wondering who I am, yes? Most of you have known me as Matt, the dean of your college or as Matt, a personal friend. In truth, I am one of the immortals that your race normally refers to as gods. I'm one of the oldest and most powerful, and those of you who are up on your mythology will recognize some of my former names of Mars, Ares, Tyr, and Monthu."

A movement down the head table caught Matt's eye, and he turned. "Birch, do you have a question?"

"Well, yeah," the slight man with a huge beard replied. "If you were Tyr, how can you have two hands?"

If anyone could question Matt's relation of the ancient myths, it would be Birch, Crystal thought. His wife, Frieta, a dear friend of Crystal's from elementary school through graduation and beyond, had practiced paganism for as long as Crystal could remember, and she had met her soulmate in the body of Birch. The two together had formed the core of one of the circles Crystal and Matt had attended most often, and they had even taken up the mantle of leadership. Birch had devoted much of his life to studying paganism, focusing mostly on Norse deities, and now his attention to his studies showed.

Matt smiled and held up his right arm, hand suddenly missing. "You mean this stub, where my hand was bitten off by the wolf-god Fenrir?

Birch, looking perplexed, managed a soft, "Yeah."

Matt's smile deepened as his hand reappeared, and then he turned to address everyone. "Many of you have read at least some mythology. Keep in mind that all mythology, be it Greek, Roman, or Biblical, was written long after the fact by people who weren't there. There is a touch of truth to nearly all the myths, but the details are often, well, muddied.

"In the case of Tyr and Fenrir, that story comes from the Gylfaginning. I walked the lands of the great north as Tyr about a thousand years before the last cataclysm, but the Prose Edda containing that story was written over two thousand years later. I knew Snorri, its author. In fact, I helped him with some of the stories he wrote. He insisted that Tyr lost his hand in the story. Who was I to argue? Besides having been Tyr, of course, but how could I convince him of that? I did ask, of course, how it was that a god wouldn't be able to grow back his own hand, but he brushed off the question and I didn't press it. Snorri was intent in his belief, one shared by many historians, that the gods only exist because they—we, I should say—arise simply out of human storytelling. In this belief system, powerful chieftains and warriors become godlike over many years and many retellings of the old stories. In other words, to him, I was actually a powerful warrior who became a god in the stories only."

A girl—Crystal didn't recognize her, so she assumed she was from the college's student body—rose from a table near the front and said, "I hope you'll understand, Dean Vincent, or Tyr, or whoever you are, why we're having a hard time with this. We've seen your power, to be sure. But you're a god, you say, and yet you're telling us that you're not the Christ. The church's teachings tell us that you then must be evil. Are you telling us the church is wrong, or are you evil?"

"Which church, dear?" Matt replied. "I've seen the rise and fall of thousands of churches in my time." He paused with a warm smile on his face for several seconds before continuing, "Oh, I'm sure you're talking about the Christian church, but I had to make the point that yours isn't the first religion on the planet to convince its followers that it's right and that every other alternative is lying and evil and wrong. As to your question, well, there's a lot of truth to the writings. First, Yahweh is real. He, also, has gone by several names to several groups. He hasn't been around for a while, to be sure, but you're welcome to go try to find him. As to the exclusivity of godhood, he never said that he was the only god, did he? He said that he wanted to be the Hebrew's only god, and that he was a jealous god, but not once did he deny the existence of the rest of us.

"Many of the Old Testament stories come from ancient manuscripts, and while the details of those stories can be a little strange, the stories themselves are largely true. There was a flood, for example. Granted, you all saw one again today, so at this point the occurrence of a flood wiping out much of humanity shouldn't seem all that unique any more. Meanwhile, some of the stories didn't actually happen but are meant to metaphorically stand for a greater truth. For example, humans never really tried to build a tower to the heavens in Shinar, but the reality that the metaphor was based in, specifically of humans' attempts to usurp the domain of the gods, is—has been for a long, long time—alive and well. The problem with that isn't so much that we care much about our turf versus yours, but for some reason when humans become powerful you start trying to destroy stuff. In fact, the story that is told of gods' response to the Tower of Babel is grounded solidly in truth; it's actually the reason for the periodic cataclysm you saw today."

With that pronouncement, murmurs erupted around the hall. Matt stood passively, watching, letting people come to terms with his revelations. As the murmurs died down, he said, "You saw, toward the end of your own technology age, how close your race came to destroying the planet. It's like that every technology cycle, really. You start off with copper and bronze and sticks and rocks and you end up with some very destructive firepower. Nuclear, in your case. That destructive knowledge base is all stored electronically somehow, whether that be in computer mainframes or in pyramids. So, to keep Gaia safe, after your race is allowed to build and grow for long enough, the electrons just go away, taking the knowledge bases as well as the destructive weaponry with them, and the world gets rebooted."

Matt took a breath and then continued his lecture, "The ages of magic are no smarter, really. You start out with a few sets of people who can toss rocks at each other using flows of air, and end up with guilds of mighty sorcerers able to bring city walls down. A couple times humans have even become so powerful—and destructive, of course—with magic that they blasted entire land masses clean."

A former student near the front of the room challenged Matt, "So, different topic. Are you that Ba'al guy who Yahweh fought in the early days of the Bible?"

"Sort of, but not really," he said with a shrug, and Crystal grinned at his characteristically Matt-like response. "First of all, Yahweh never fought any gods. There was only one time that I know of when two gods actually fought each other, and that was millions of years ago. It was epic, believe me. I was there. Hermes, or the god that the Greeks knew as Hermes, anyway, and I got into it over—well, never mind that part. But we really got a raging battle on. You've not seen the full power of an angry god, and you're not really likely to in the future, but take my word for it that it's immense. The battle lasted day and night for a long, long time, thanks mostly to our inability to harm each other. It finally ended with a stalemate where we sat down together at the edge of an immense new canyon that had opened up in the earth. We surveyed the damage we had done, which included the extinction of an entire family of animal species, and then we went back to Olympus and got everyone to agree not to have any more god-on-god fights. That truce has lasted ever since."

As Matt stopped for a breath, a voice from the middle of the room asked in an incredulous tone, "Are you saying you killed the dinosaurs?"

Matt smiled toward the voice's source, shrugged and spread his hands in front of him and said, "Guilty?" Crystal was both fascinated and horrified at the flippancy of his response.

"Anyway, back to the question of whether I'm Ba'al," Matt pressed on. "Sure, yeah, we all are, including Yahweh. The people of that region used the honorific Ba'al to refer to any male leader, which of course includes us gods." Matt punctuated his sentence with a playful flex of his arm muscles, causing a few chuckles in the dining room. "Further, the folks back in that time who lived in the Canaan region were specifically forbidden by their priests to say the actual names of their gods, so we all came to be called just Ba'al. It's like in Spanish, where if you don't know their honorific, you think that Quixote's first name was Don. All Spanish noblemen were called Don, and for the same reason all gods in the Middle East were called Ba'al."

As Matt took a few breaths, one of the college's former business instructors stood up from his table near the front. "I have a question," he said. "Was the lady we saw today really Gaia, the titan?"

The question brought a chortle from Matt as he replied, "Well, yes, but again, sort of. That was Gaia, the mother goddess. Through all the millennia she is one of us who is nearly always called the same thing. But I'm glad you mentioned titans. The distinction between them and gods is a bit contrived. It served the Greeks well, certainly, as they sought to describe and understand the creation of the world, in the same way that all creation stories do. The whole thing about Uranus being castrated by his son, who was in turn led by a frustrated Gaia, made for an engaging story to tell, but like I said before, the myths are stories that are at best only partly true. You have to take them with a grain of salt, so to speak. The Creation was a momentous event, of course, but since the Greeks weren't there, they got it wrong, as did all the other world religions of your age."

"So was that a pagan ritual you led today, and why did you do it that way?" RJ asked. Crystal could hear the frustration in RJ's voice and guessed that the topic had been bothering him for some time.

Matt looked at the former college president for several moments before responding, "Yes, it was pagan. Sort of, anyway. The pagans themselves took a lot of their rituals from previous philosophies. Did you know that the Ionic School in Greece actually looked at the elements of earth, air, fire, and water as more important than the gods? It was funny, in fact, that they used what they considered natural elements to explain how the world didn't need gods, not even realizing that they were describing the parts of magic as their natural elements, and thus they were explaining the power of the gods while saying that the gods didn't exist. Then they spent the rest of their time arguing over which element of the gods' power was most important. I spent an evening buying wine for Thales of Miletus himself, having him explain to me how I didn't exist, and I got a lot of perverse pleasure from that.

"Anyway, I digress. See, to me, a ritual is a ritual is a ritual. We could have been just as effective had everyone faced the center, kneeled, crossed themselves, and completed the rites in Latin. Or, for another option, had everyone just stood there and watched me do all the work. It's all the same to a god, but a human being needs a structured approach to magic. I chose the pagan style because most of the people I called to my side to participate," Matt punctuated his explanation with a glance up and down the head table, "were practicing Wiccans and druids and pagans prior to today. It's familiar to you, though frankly up to now all you've done is what I call fluffy bunny stuff." Taking on a playful tone, Matt waved his hands and said, "Ooh, let's all say some magical sounding words and jump over this big fire pit and pretend like it's going to help spring come faster." Some people chortled; several at the front table looked offended. Matt continued, "But seriously, those of you at the front table, with the exception of our dear campus president here, have been playing at magic, and starting tomorrow you'll begin learning to actually use it."

Crystal had to admit the explanation made sense, but RJ shook his head. "Why Krista, then?" he asked. "She hasn't ever even seen a pagan ritual." The president's wife had always seemed steady and down-to-earth, and it surprised Crystal also that she had been identified as a potential magic-user.

Matt said, "She's got latent power, RJ. A lot of it, actually. I can sense those around me who will be able to touch the elemental flows of magic given some training in it. Over the past several years, I've gathered this group together, knowing this day was coming."

"How did you know today was the day?" RJ asked.

"I didn't, not at first. Gaia's timer isn't set for exactly two thousand years. When it runs down, I can feel the elemental forces gaining a sort of tension. I've known for a few days that it was imminent. When the change actually flips, it's an exhilarating rush."

"So what are your plans for us?" a middle aged woman rose and asked from a table near the back.

Matt spread his hands. "For the moment, while the cataclysm rages out there, I have no plans. Eat, drink, and be merry. In fact, we have a concert right after this that I'd like all of you to attend, though you're certainly free instead to seek your own entertainment this evening. You readers will find my library extensive, and there are horses to ride on the grounds as well as other activities to keep you busy. Pretend it's a grand vacation, if you will. As I said before, within a few days the changes will be complete and the planet will have regained her axis and atmosphere, and then? I don't really care, honestly. Stay if you wish, or go out into the world as you desire. You'll find that there is now a great new land for the taking, though you'll also find limited tools available to make your living easy. Those of you with the power to learn to wield magic will have far greater tools to work with, but you'll have to practice for a while before you're proficient in their use."

The questioner interrupted him, "But must we worship you?"

Matt's belly laugh echoed through the grand hall. "Worship? What for? I'm a god. What do you think I'd need your human platitudes for? Oh, some of my fellows get off on that sort of thing. I mean, if you were with Apollo, for example, or Aphrodite, you'd have to be falling over them whenever they swished by. But me? Eh, whatever. I like your company, and I certainly wasn't going to leave you there at the college. Worship if you want, or don't if you don't. But now, it is time for the concert."

Adopting the grand tone of a stadium announcer, Matt bellowed, "Ladies and gentlemen, the thrakkoni have been practicing for centuries to bring us the musical entertainment they feature this evening. Some may seem familiar, as they have based some songs on human musical efforts, and some will not. But I assure you that it will be grand, and you are all invited to join me on the amphitheater just outside those doors."

Concert

Matt moved to the right and clasped Crystal's hand with one of his and Linda's with the other, motioning with his chin for Crystal to hold Heidi's hand also. As soon as their hands made contact, Matt nodded and—blinked. The sensation reminded Crystal of teleporting earlier that day, though it had less intensity this time as the family was only transported from the head table to the side of the dining hall. Crystal's stomach protested briefly and then quieted down.

"Could you warn me next time, please?" she asked Matt, not certain if he would respond as her husband or as an angry god.

A twinkle in his eye answered her concern as he responded, "Of course. Sorry, I'm just really enjoying having the magic back. To me, it's an old friend I haven't seen in thousands of years, but I know it's a new thing to you." Releasing her hand, he caressed the back of her head as he pulled her face to his for a soft kiss.

Giving in to the kiss for a moment, she closed her eyes and imagined that nothing had changed. But it was a short kiss, more loving than romantic, and the sensation was fleeting. Opening her eyes again, she stared in Matt's eyes, inches away from her own. Her voice a mere whisper, she said, "Strange. I feel like I don't know my best friend any more. Are you still the man I married?"

The pained look in Matt's eyes reassured her; for a moment, she had Matt the husband and father at her side. "I understand," Matt breathed an answer to her unspoken question. "It's been a tumultuous day, and it's set your world completely on its head, hasn't it? Come, enjoy the concert with me, and then we can talk more deeply tonight. All right?"

The twinkle in his eyes gave her a split second of warning to what was coming, but he had always been faster than she, so his first and second fingers closed rapidly on her nose in a gently playful squeeze as he said, "Honk, honk." He danced away playfully, his grin the impish expression she had come to love years before. When she couldn't keep from smiling, he took her hand and led the family—walking, this time—to the center front row of the amphitheater.

Crystal took her seat and then looked back at all of their former friends, co-workers, and the rest of the people filing into the amphitheater. RJ and Krista and their children sat down just behind, and Crystal wondered idly how they were doing adjusting to their new reality. Before she could figure out how to ask the question, though, the musicians filed out onto the stage.

The amphitheater seemed stereotypically Grecian, though she thought that the basic design would have to be universal. True to its name, both the stage and the seats were open to the elements. For a moment, she wondered if the estate's protective dome ever allowed it to rain. The back of the stage was built right into a cliff behind it, but the cliff face was lined with marble up to a spot some thirty feet high, where it curved back over the stage in an attempt to broadcast more sound toward the audience. The stage was well lit with more of Matt's glowing balls of light. The chairs on stage were fairly substantial, far more so than the folding chairs she had often seen on stages.

Crystal turned her attention to the audience. The god and his family, apparently, had special seating in stone chairs that, though unpadded, were proving to be surprisingly comfortable. Their backs supported their occupants without being high enough to restrict the views of the rows behind. Other seats— benches, really, with imprinted spaces for seats and low backs— weren't as ornately carved, yet their occupants seemed as comfortable as Crystal.

"You sure do like statues, don't you?" Crystal murmured to Matt, noting the array of low statues set in front of the stage and the taller ones surrounding the seating area, setting it off from the rest of the estate. He smiled and nodded in response, but any comment he might have been ready to make was cut off by the flourished entrance of a thrakkon dressed in the style of a symphony conductor. Striding purposefully to the center of the stage, he bowed to the audience and then turned and ascended the central dais.

As the conductor raised his hands, the musicians readied their instruments. Crystal took the opportunity to look at what they held. Most were familiar. A group on the left held what looked like traditional violins, and some behind had enlarged versions what she took to be cellos and bases. Or was it violas? She really wished she had paid more attention in music classes way back when. The clarinets looked similar to what she had seen before too. Some of the musicians held what looked like should have been bugles or trumpets, except that they were made of wood instead of metal. Flutes similarly seemed to have been fashioned from tree branches instead of metal sheets, and there were several sizes. Toward the back on the right, she recognized many of the various percussion instruments—drums, tympani, xylophones—but some were constructed differently than anything she had seen before, and all were wood or, even stranger, marble or other stone. There didn't appear to be a piece of metal anywhere on the stage.

Leaning closer, Crystal whispered into Matt's ear, "Why don't they have any metal instruments?"

Matt looked at Crystal and smiled. "There aren't any smelting or forging facilities on the estate," he whispered. "Besides, the thrakkoni craftsmen do such wonderful work with wood and stone that metalwork would be redundant."

Waving his arms, the conductor launched the musicians into

what quickly became a medley of top hits from recent years. Crystal found it strange at first, but the music was really well done. She was surprised when Sorscha walked out on stage and added a stunningly bright vocal performance to Rhythm of the Night and then other similar songs. She couldn't recall who had originally sung it, but the song about La Isla Bonita was truly beautiful, and somehow the combination of the instruments with Sorscha's clear voice and perfect pitch made Crystal hate her and fall in love with her at the same time. The music seemed to transport Crystal to the beach, with palm trees and a warm breeze blowing.

With a start, Crystal realized that she was actually seeing palm trees and feeling a warm breeze. Looking around briefly, she saw her fellow audience members seemingly as enthralled as she had been. Matt's hand squeezed hers, and she turned to see him wink at her. His impish expression was all she needed to realize that somehow, this was his doing.

The concert continued through several phases. After the pop medley, the audience was treated to a few well-known classics as well as a selection of songs that Crystal couldn't recall ever hearing before. All the offerings were beautiful, and all were accompanied by their own sensory treats. The Flight of the Bumblebee was actually accompanied by bumblebees, though the bees were well-behaved enough to not come near the audience members. The Ride of the Valkyries was accompanied by warlike women borne on flying horses, real to every sense including smell.

The concert came to an end with what Crystal recognized as the crescendo of the 1812 Overture, complete with booming fire from cannons that could not really have been there, and even more inexplicably, a big brass sound from a collection of instruments that weren't made of any metal at all, much less brass. But the fireworks were spectacular, lighting up the entire sky in perfect synchronization to the cannons and the tympani.

As the last chord and cannon peal echoed off the distant hills, slowly closing the concert, Crystal heard and felt her fellow audience members sighing sadly along with her. She had never felt music as completely as she felt it tonight, with every sense alternately teased and assaulted by some sort of stimulation. She had never realized how much music could be enjoyed. It had been beautiful, and it brought her to tears that it was over as she and the rest of the audience rose to their feet in thunderous applause.

"Do they do concerts often?" Crystal asked Matt, yelling over the crowd's noise. He nodded and grinned, saying directly into her mind that she did not need to yell.

"Once a week, or once every other week. The thrakkoni love music, and love to perform it. Their long lifespan gives them lots of time to perfect their instruments, and in many cases several instruments," he informed her. "The concerts are beautiful without my enhancements, but I think you'll agree that adding the other sensations to the experience heightens it a bit."

"That was you?" Crystal asked, realizing before she'd finished what a silly question it seemed. "Never mind. You're a god, I know. Why can't they do the same thing, though?"

"The thrakkoni can't use magic. Everything they do, they do physically."

"What?" Somehow Crystal had imagined that these perfect beings she had come to dearly despise would also be master magi. What else couldn't they do, she wondered?

Matt chuckled. "Let's talk more inside. I need to finish off the concert and send everyone home." With that, he hopped up onto the stage and shook the conductor's hand, then turned back toward the audience and acknowledged the musicians with a flourish. A new wave of applause broke out while the musicians quietly filed off stage.

A Lovers' Spat

Crystal was as taken by her new quarters this time as she had been earlier. It was beautiful. "Stunning," she said softly to herself, standing just inside the door and looking all around.

"I'm glad you like it," Matt murmured in her ear, closing the door softly behind. "Would you like for me to draw you a bath before bed?"

"Um—sure," Crystal said, not certain what would be best, though she knew that a bath would feel good. "Hey, how do you have running water?"

Matt smiled. "Magic."

Well, duh. Magic. Just yesterday, he had responded the same way when she'd asked how he'd finished the dishes so quickly, and she had known at the time that he was kidding. How things had changed!

When she had met Matt, they were both just embarking on their new careers, or so she had thought. He was a newly-minted Ph.D. in business heading to a small community college nearby to be their science and business teacher, while she was just about to finish her teaching certification classes. Crystal remembered her friend's graduation party where they had been introduced. She had been drawn to his looks, true, but his good-natured wit had captured her heart. She had always thought she knew what he had found enticing in her, as well, but the revelations of the day cast everything into doubt. She wasn't certain, though, how much doubt she was free to communicate. On the one hand, this was Matt, her husband, but on the other, she was coming to grips with his existence as the god of war. Would he react to her doubts and questioning as he'd always done, or would he just wiggle his nose and blast her out of existence? Should she trust him, worship him, or fear him, or a combination of all that?

Still deeply mired in contemplation, she followed him into the cavernous bath and stood mutely while he turned the knobs on the faucet and checked the temperature of the water with his hand. Once satisfied it was just right, her husband moved over to a cabinet and pulled out a neatly folded towel and a wash cloth, then retrieved a bar of soap and a stoppered bottle of shampoo from another. Laying them out beside the tub, he walked over to her. For the first time today, their eyes connected, plunging as they so often had to the depths of each others' souls.

"Long day, huh?"

She knew what he was doing: deliberately saying something pithy to provoke an angry outburst so that they could get the emotion out of the way and really start talking. She knew it, and didn't want to play along, but her emotions bypassed her capacity for rational choice all at once and started flowing directly out of her mouth.

"Long day? Long day! Yeah, long day. We've lived together for fifteen years now, and I'm just now finding out that, what? You're a god? I've had your children. Oh my God, are they gods too? And now here we are, in this huge manor house with your beautiful servant. And I'm—I'm just an intruder here, aren't I? Your pet human? How much of what I've known about you is real? What don't I know?"

Her tirade continued for several long minutes, the rational part of her ducked inside her head and listening in dismay as she laid into her husband with every ounce of verbal force she had in her. Matt waited patiently through the flurry till she ran herself down, and then he moved forward, enfolding her in a tight hug. His voice was as soft as a breath as he said, "I love you, Crystal. I really do. Okay? I love you. Still, and always. I've never lied about that; I promise. I love you."

Stepping back, he held her shoulders and gazed into her eyes. "I wish I could have told you before," he said, his voice growing strong again. "But what would you have said to, 'Honey, guess what? I'm a god. No godlike powers right now, but just wait.' What would you have said to that? You'd've called me nuts, right?"

She nodded slowly, acknowledging, a little grudgingly, that he had a point.

He said, "I'm sorry to have left you here all afternoon by yourself. I could tell you were tired, though, and I hadn't been back to the estate in many years. I had a lot to check on, and a lot of thrakkoni to speak with and get updates from."

"How many years?" she asked, incredulous.

"Well, remember the teleporting I did to get here? In the technology cycles it's a little harder. In the magic cycles, I can just wrap myself in the right flows of magic and pop in anywhere anytime, but when there are no magic flows I have to use unified fields to transport myself, and it's not possible to go as far instantaneously. Last time I was here was several decades ago."

"Several decades, huh? That's nothing, I guess, compared to cycles of two thousand years, right? I'm still having trouble with that, though. How old *are* you?"

"Um—old. I came to exist shortly after this universe began. So, millions of years. Hundreds of millions. I'm immortal."

Her eyes narrowed and her arms crossed over her chest, an implication of his latest admission bothering her. "And how many wives have you had in these hundreds of millions of years?"

"You really don't want to know the answer to that, do you?"

"When we married, you told me you'd had a wife. It had been a young college marriage that didn't last more than a year. Was that a lie, then?"

Matt looked her in the eye for several long moments before answering. "Well, yeah, I guess that was a bit of a lie. I'm sorry!" he interjected as her fist contacted his chest, making a loud thump but having no other apparent affect. She continued to swing at him, but his hands caught hers and held on.

"I've been married, on and off, for millions of years," Matt continued. "Single men aren't well received in society these days, nor have they ever been. Problem is, I can't grow old. I can't. I can appear to be old, but that only works to a certain extent, and even that only with stupid people. As I'm sure you know, I can't marry a stupid person. So while the technology phase is going on, I can't stay married. I can't grow old with anybody."

Crystal's flare of anger dissipated. Matt looked over his shoulder as the tub water level reached the top. Moving impossibly fast, he turned off the water. "Oops," he said, "that might have been bad." He looked at the drain lever. Crystal saw a flow of something yellow, something she'd never directly seen before, surround the drain lever, and suddenly it flicked open to let out some of the excess water that had overfilled the tub.

Matt rose and returned to Crystal. "Bottom line is that you're my wife right now. I love you, and I have loved you ever since we met. It didn't bother you before that you weren't my first wife. Now that everyone knows I'm a god, I don't have to worry about not getting older. Now we can live the rest of your life together, and I can make sure you're the best kept woman in the world. Heck, the best kept in the universe."

"So what do I call you?" she asked. "People have called you by all sorts of names, and frankly, Matthew is sounding a bit plain comparatively. What's your real name?"

"Matthew is, actually. That's the name I've gone by for hundreds of millions of years in the technology eras, and at times in the magical eras as well. It's my original name. I would be pleased if you would continue calling me that, or your husband, or your love."

As he spoke, he gently removed her tunic and pants and then led her by the hand to the tub. He looked down, and she saw the drain lever, surrounded by the same yellow energy, switch back to its closed position. He helped her step into the oversized tub. "Take a bath, my love. Relax. Enjoy."

She slipped down and loved the feeling of the warm water caressing her skin. Sinking into it, she relaxed for the first time that day, closing her eyes and stretching out.

Several minutes later, Crystal sensed someone in the room with her again. Turning her head, she saw Matt had come back in and was now holding an exquisite robe in front of him. "Do you like?" he asked.

"Yes, it's very beautiful," she said. The deep purple hues were perfectly offset by the gold cords used as accent, as well as by the gold thread used to hem the robe. It looked like silk, but the cloth shimmered in an almost iridescent way. "What's it made of?"

"Silk. A special silk, actually, hand drawn and handmade by nagas. A robe this fine would have been impossible to find yesterday."

"What's a naga?" Crystal asked, confused over a term she'd heard before in her dalliances into popular computer games but had never expected to hear referencing a real being.

"Inhabitants of the island that erupted back into the world today. We'll go there sometime soon, as I have some business to attend to, and I look forward to showing you to some of the best shopping on Earth. For now, though, you need to finish your bath and dry off before your whole body shrivels away into nothing."

Crystal chuckled. "I'm not done yet, but okay, fine. Whatever you wish, hon." With that, she rose, started the tub draining, and began toweling off. Once her body was dry, she walked over to Matt, prancing with her naked body, and was pleased to see him respond with his normal leer. Maybe things hadn't changed that much. Turning, she let him drape the robe over her and wrap the tie around her waist, and then she followed him into the bedroom.

"The girls aren't gods," Matt said as they each took their spots in the bed.

"What? Oh," Crystal said, remembering having asked the question earlier. "Why not?"

"It doesn't work that way. Sometimes the kids of gods are mages, but neither of the twins seems to have the ability to manipulate the magical flows. It's a little surprising, really, considering that I'm a god and you have a strong latent ability. But no, the whole demigod thing is contrived."

"Like Perseus and Achilles?" Crystal said.

"Exactly. There weren't many genetic tests back then, so somebody who was particularly strong, brave, or lucky could claim to be the son of a god or goddess and be worshipped as a demigod. In reality there's no such thing. You're either a god or you're not."

"So I don't have to worry about some day waking up to a strange pronouncement from my children?"

"Oh, I'm sure they'll have their share of strange pronouncements for us, but not that one."

Crystal smiled and snuggled in to her husband. Suddenly a question occurred to her, and she pulled away slightly to ask it. "So, now that you're a god, I have to ask—what is making love to a god like? I mean, is it any different? Does it kill the human? Or does the lovely human lady wake up in the morning alone but with a new set of armor by the bed and silk treasures in her closet?"

Matt chuckled and pulled her back in close. "Well," he said, "that's a lot of questions. I can arrange for the armor and the silk, but I suspect you'd rather go shop for them yourself. As for the death thing, I'm pretty sure you'll be safe. Now, is it any different? Well, I do have a couple of magical tricks up my sleeve, so I'm betting you'll find it a little more stimulating, but there's only one way to know for sure."

Matt's right hand stroked down the side of Crystal's head, along the outline of her ear, and then down her neck, coming to rest gently in the hollow by her collarbone. His left hand cupped the back of her head, pulling her mouth to his for a deep, passionate kiss. Other hands were added, shocking Crystal at first. "Relax, it's just magic," Matt said, his voice purring in her ear and then his mouth finding hers once again. Crystal felt the flows of magic wrap around her breasts, their warm touch caressing her skin, curling around and around up to the nipples, and then snaking back down to the base of her breasts. She glanced with a short-lived curiosity and saw the same yellow energy she had seen before, but this time orange, purple, and green were mixed in. Curiosity satisfied, she closed her eyes and relaxed again into the sensations. She felt a gentle gliding touch on her pubic area as it wrapped around the curves of her thighs and down into the lips of her womanhood. She felt the caress travel up, then, getting to the very point of her passion. Suddenly her arousal blossomed both inside and out, and she was taken to the highest peak of orgasm she had ever felt. Matt held her close, their mouths still joined in a kiss, as her body convulsed in pleasure.

"Wow," she said, barely able to form the word out of the breath she exhaled. "That was...."

"Different?" Matt said, pulling away enough for her to see his impish grin. "Magic can reach places that hands can't."

"I was about to say amazing, but yes, different is true too." Crystal relaxed in his arms.

"Well, I'm not done with you yet," Matt said, and once again he demonstrated his skill in stimulating Crystal's erotic areas, this time using his own hands and mouth. The foreplay lasted much longer this time, and the buildup added to the heights she reached when he finally entered her.

"You didn't use magic that time," Crystal said between breaths once her power to speak returned.

"No. I guess it may not be all that different," Matt said, a wide grin on his face. He pulled her to him and they snuggled as Crystal drifted off to sleep.

An Unwelcome Visitor

The next morning came much too early for Crystal, who still wasn't sure she should be getting out of bed considering the twisting her stomach had taken in the teleporting yesterday. The decision was taken from her though, as the sound of curtains being thrown aside hit her ears at the same time a gleaming beam of sunshine hit her eyes. Yelping, she raised her head and looked, but she was blinded by the brightness. She searched frantically for her enemy till her eyes adjusted and fell on the beautiful thrakkon from the day before, Sorscha.

Growling, she put her head back down onto the pillow and closed her eyes. "I hate you," she murmured out loud.

Crystal was irritated further by Sorscha's pealing laughter in response. "Yes. But the master awaits your appearance in his chamber. It is his first day back in a long time, and business calls. He's requested your presence, though I am sure he would understand if you did not feel up to attending him."

"Of course I feel up to attending him. I am his wife, after all," she bit back at Sorscha, giving special venom to the word that indicated her special position with "the master." The thrakkon merely nodded, holding the door open to the massive closet that was now Crystal's.

Crystal climbed out of bed, not certain whether she was succeeding at looking like the wife of a god or a more like a petulant lady awakened too early. She was used to being the calm, loving one, but the events of yesterday had thrown her so far out of sorts that she couldn't help behaving as the latter. She looked in the closet at the hundreds of outfits displayed, and then said to Sorscha, "I suppose you have an outfit to suggest for me, don't you?"

"Of course," Sorscha replied with a smile.

"Tell me, then. What should the human wife of a god wear to his court on the first day back?"

"Well, it's morning court, so nothing too fancy. But you *are* the first lady of the manor, so something befitting that station would be appropriate. May I suggest this?" Sorscha asked, reaching into the room and coming out carrying a green silk tunic embroidered in tulip patterns with what appeared to be spun metallic red and yellow thread. In her other hand, she bore a pair of tan pants embroidered down the side in gold thread.

Crystal gasped. "That is lovely. Thank you," she said, and then watched as Sorscha carried the outfit over to the bed and reached out to help her get out of her nightgown. "Are you, um— I thought you were the master's—my husband's servant?"

Sorscha nodded patiently. "I have been helping the master with all domestic matters for a long time. Right now, that includes assisting his lady with getting ready for court."

"How—how long of a time?" Crystal asked, not sure if she wanted an answer.

Sorscha shrugged in response, and then added, "A long time. We thrakkoni live nearly as long as the gods do. We don't count years, though, so I really don't know."

"You are quite beautiful, then, for one who is that old," Crystal replied, allowing Sorscha to tug the tunic over her head.

Sorscha looked Crystal in the eye. Her gaze was flat, steely, and entirely without emotion, Crystal realized, and she couldn't tell whether the thrakkon had caught the snide insult hidden in the compliment. Inwardly, Crystal cursed herself for taking the petulance too far; it really was beneath her to behave this way. After several moments, Crystal looked away, disturbed at the way she was almost mesmerized.

"My kind is not like yours," Sorscha finally stated. "Beauty in this form is not the same to us."

"I'd love to learn what it is to you, then," Crystal said quickly, hoping to finally break through the barrier between them. "Will you share it with me?"

Sorscha shook her head. "We have no time for a discussion now. Please, come with me to attend the master."

Frustrated, Crystal followed Sorscha to the corner of the room. She hadn't noticed the doorway earlier, but now Sorscha held it open for her. "Up these stairs, please."

They climbed a short circular stairway that was obviously constructed for the sole purpose of allowing the ruler of the manor special unobserved access to his chambers. Darkness met them at the top, along with a curtain that Crystal ran into and would have fallen through had Sorscha not caught her from behind. Without a word, Sorscha's hands steered Crystal to the left, along the stone wall and through a break in the curtain to a better-lit chamber, which itself was walled by a curtain. On the other side of the curtain, Crystal heard Matt's voice.

She started to walk forward but stopped herself, looking back at Sorscha for guidance. The thrakkon nodded, and so Crystal pushed the curtain out of the way and walked in. On her entry, talk ceased and Matt looked at her, smiling.

" Crystal!" he exclaimed. "Good to see you up and about. Our chief administrator Rellgll here was enlightening me on the status of food stocks at the manor."

To that, another thrakkon in the room bowed and, turning back to Matt, continued listing quantities of livestock at the manor. After a few minutes, Crystal decided to placate her boredom by surveying the room and its inhabitants. The first thing she noticed was the room's comparative blandness. The floor consisted of a marble inlaid tile, grand in comparison to most floors she had seen, but pedestrian if set aside other floorings in Matt's estate. The god—her husband—sat in a simply-carved wooden throne that looked like mahogany. His chair at the dinner table was fancier, she thought. No other furniture existed in the windowless room, which was oval in shape with the throne along one of the longer sides. The curtain Crystal had entered through was at one end narrow, and the other narrow end widened slightly into an alcove containing a single bell mounted to the wall a bit over head-height, and a bright circle on the floor inlaid with gold. Several thrakkoni whom she had not met were standing around the room, in addition to Birch, RJ and Krista, Tracey from the college, and a few other humans. Crystal wondered why the non-magical and magical humans were there, but now didn't seem the time to ask.

The report droned on. Apparently the manor kept a sizeable stock of food animals tucked somewhere in a clearing near the manor. As the report included numbers of births, Crystal assumed the thrakkoni maintained the stock through animal husbandry techniques rather than somehow transporting them up from markets elsewhere. The animal population was huge, she realized. Sure, there were a lot of people at dinner last night, but a couple thousand cattle sounded like a bit much to Crystal. Matt seemed to have unlimited resources, though, so the number of cattle probably didn't matter much to him.

Crystal's musing, as well as Rellgll's droning voice, were interrupted by the bell in the alcove as it rang once and then twice more quickly. Matt sighed quietly, a sound that brought all eyes to him in the otherwise deep silence. Mentally, he projected to Crystal, and from their expressions she saw he was projecting to the rest of the room as well, a rapid fire set of instructions. *Stand relaxed, but guard your expressions. Our visitor can be a bit unstable. I can protect you, but I shouldn't need to. Stand silently; do not react. Do not let on who you are. Especially do not let on which of you is my wife.* The last instruction made Crystal both uncomfortable and curious.

"Come," Matt said out loud. A female form shimmered into being on the gold circle in the alcove, and then stepped out into the room. Crystal heard RJ and Birch both gasp, and she felt her irritation and petulance rising unbidden again. Here was the second, in as many days, woman whose mere presence redefined the word "beauty." Instinctively she hated the newcomer even more than she had hated Sorscha at first, as the newcomer's beauty was different. Sorscha was perfect, flawless, the personification of a fine porcelain doll with no defects whatsoever. Crystal was certain that Sorscha would be just as beautiful wearing a garbage sack.

The newcomer, though, exuded beauty as a fire's burning coals exuded heat. Her features were just as flawlessly composed as Sorscha's, but this woman went the extra distance of advertising her sexuality. Long legs, flat stomach, and ample breasts were clearly displayed within a skin-tight tunic and bikini bottom that would more appropriately be called lingerie. Her cascading strawberry blonde hair framed an oval face that featured high well-accented cheekbones, lush red lips, and piercing blue eyes.

It suddenly occurred to Crystal that she recognized this woman. Something—she wasn't sure what, exactly—in the way the newcomer held herself reminded Crystal of a statue she had seen years before, an unusual one that had caught her eye in a museum in Naples. As often as she toured with Matt, she was used to seeing ancient men, women, and gods portrayed in heroic poses or noble poses, but this one had been of a beautiful lady peering over her shoulder, admiring her own rear end. "Matt, this one's kind of funny," she had called to her husband.

Matt had walked over from where he had been eyeing a portrait and said, "Ah, yes. Aphrodite Kallipygos is a funny one."

"Aphrodite who? *The* Aphrodite? Wasn't she the goddess of beauty and love? Why is she looking at her own butt like that?"

"The goddess of beauty and love is pretty much right. Most mythology looks at Venus, or Aphrodite, depending on whether you're Roman or Greek, as the most beautiful of the goddesses, and the goddess of all things love, beauty, and sexuality. *This* one, though, actually is kind of a funny tale. Want to hear it?"

Crystal had nodded, but Heidi had just walked up and asked, "Could you shorten it a little this time, Dad?"

"You think my stories are boring?" Matt had asked with a mock pout, his blue eyes twinkling beneath his red bangs.

"Not boring, Dad. Too long. There's a difference."

"Okay, then," Matt had said with a laugh. "Shorter version coming right up! So—way back, many hundreds of years ago, two young and rich men down in Sicily were walking through the fields," he paused and looked at Heidi, who had crossed her arms in impatience. "Right, short. So the rich men met and fell in love with two daughters of a farmer. Of course, you know that wealthy men weren't supposed to marry poor girls, but these girls were amazingly pretty. They were so pretty, in fact, that the new brides became famous among the upper crust for their—well, their butts. Which were their prettiest features, I guess, or maybe people back then liked butts more than other parts. Regardless, later, after the rich brothers had become richer, their wives founded a temple to Aphrodite in their town of Syracuse. They now knew, of course, how important having a pretty butt could be, so they named their temple Aphrodite Kallipygos, which is Greek for Aphrodite of the Pretty Buttocks. And, well, what you see is how that works out in a statue."

Now, the newcomer—was it really Aphrodite?— said in a voice that reminded Crystal of warm water running over silk, "Hiya, Matthew. I spent all night last night with the magic back and no one to play with. No time to swing by my place yet?"

Looking at her husband, Crystal was relieved to see the newcomer's presence wasn't having the same effect on the god that it was on the human men. His face twisting into a half-smile, Matt said, "Hiya, Kallipygos. Always a pleasure to see you again too." Crystal saw the goddess narrow her eyes, and Matt continued, "I'm afraid I've been quite busy here. Surely you have enough pets at your own manor to slake your thirst?"

The woman's lips curled into a sneer. "Oh, my my, my darling Matthew. Yes, I do have a lot of pets back home. You should see some of the fine specimens I brought back with me through the cataclysm. But compared to a handsome and strong god of war, they're just—pets." The goddess' pout with her last word made Crystal want to retch, but she remembered his instructions and didn't move.

Crystal watched warily as the woman sauntered toward the throne, licking her lips as suggestively as Crystal had ever seen done. She was beside herself, nearly ready to spring and hurt this—this woman—no matter what Matt had said, when his hand went up and the woman stopped in her tracks. Crystal could see, if she didn't try to look very hard, a shimmering force field between the two. Rising, Matt said sternly, "Kallipygos, no. This handsome and strong god of war isn't interested. Not today, and not ever. Got it?"

Crystal wondered whether the goddess could have broken through Matt's force field, but she was relieved that it wasn't attempted. Leering, the woman looked around the room. "New pets, yourself, Mars? Which one is your new little plaything? Is it that one over there?" she said, pointing at Krista, who looked terrified. "No, a quivering blondie isn't your type. I'll bet it's her," she said, pointing directly at Crystal, who responded with a glare.

Matt gave one dry snort. "Why do you think I'd put my—ah, *pet*—on parade for you? Do you really think yourself that important to me? No, I think you need to leave now, Kallipygos."

Turning, the woman blew Matt a kiss, her lips curling into a parody of the gesture that could only be intended as sarcasm. "Fine. Later, then, Matthew," she said, winking out of the room.

The release of tension was palpable. Krista dropped to a knee and breathed heavily, her fists clenching and unclenching, and RJ kneeled beside with a protective arm around her. Crystal found herself slumping back against the wall. "Who was *that*?" RJ asked.

Matt kept standing, glaring at the alcove. "That was Aphrodite. Venus, if you'd prefer her Roman name. The goddess of love, and beauty. And sex. Can't forget the sex. She won't let you."

Birch, who seemed least affected by the encounter, asked, "Wasn't she supposed to be a consort of yours, Mars?"

Matt's head snapped around, eyes glaring at Birch. "Get out. Now."

Birch looked shocked. "What did I...? Huh?"

"Just. Leave," Matt said, and suddenly a flaming red sword appeared in his right hand.

Birch rapidly disappeared behind the curtain in the opposite long wall. Matt sat heavily on his throne, a scowl on his face, as the sword disappeared. "I'm done. We're done. Rellgll, we can pick this up tomorrow. Everyone, please leave me in private for the moment."

Crystal felt Sorscha's hand pluck at her sleeve in a gesture to depart, but she wasn't ready to go yet. This was her husband, god or no, and she needed to be here. Shaking away Sorscha's hand, Crystal walked over to Matt. "Hon?" she said, her voice coming out a little weaker than she had intended it to. It was nearly a squeak.

Matt turned fierce eyes to her. "You are not a pet," he said.

"I know."

Matt sighed a long and deep breath. "I've been alive millions of years. In that time, I've done many things that sounded good at the time, but weren't so great in hindsight."

"I'll bet."

"Gods can do many powerful things, but we can't see the future any more than humans can."

"Of course not."

With that, Matt's hand reached up from the arm of his throne, and Crystal extended her own hand to meet it. She said, "Matt? Husband? Let's get out of here. Show me around your manor. Okay?"

Matt rose and said, "No, love, not now. We have something important to attend to. Sorscha, please round up the potential magi and bring them to the sorcerer's chamber."

Sorscha nodded and left.

Matt turned to Crystal as Sorscha departed. "I will show you around later, but we have something important to do now."

Crystal nodded once. "I'm holding you to that promise for a tour. I'm curious about something, though, something you might be about to explain to all the magi. Before, when you were flicking the drain in the tub, you used yellow magic. When we made love, you used a lot of different colors. Your force field, though, was just a shimmery, gauzy thing. Was it a different kind of magic?"

Matt's face froze in an expression that appeared to be panic, although Crystal couldn't think of any possible reason for it. "You saw the field?" he asked slowly.

"Yes, I did. Why? Wasn't I supposed to?"

"Well, um, no, you weren't. But...." Matt sighed deeply and continued, "Well, I'll try to explain later. We need to get down to the sorcerer's chamber now."

Matt closed his arms around her, hugging her tightly for several seconds before leading her through the curtain out into the manor.

The Sorcerer's Chamber

Matt entered the circular room he called the sorcerer's chamber, followed closely by Crystal. The eleven other potential magi were already there. "Thank you, Sorscha," he said, looking around at the people in the room. Crystal looked around also, but she was drawn in by the plainness of the room. Nearly every room in the estate that she had seen thus far contained an opulent display of wealth, and even the simple throne room had held a mahogany chair, but this room was spartan. A simple rough stone floor was inscribed with two concentric circles as its only decoration. The stone wall was bare except for sconces holding glowing globes of light. The only furniture in the room was a simple pine desk with an equally simple pine chair.

"Stay here with Sorscha, my love," Matt ordered Crystal and then walked purposefully into the center of the room. Crystal was surprised by her exclusion; what was Matt doing? She started to ask him why she should stand back away from him, but the stony seriousness in his expression stopped her. She stood silently, watching closely.

The eleven moved toward him in the room. "Are we here to become battle mages?" Phoenix asked.

Phoenix had always been abrupt. Crystal had met her in one of the classes they had shared back in college, and she had been attracted to the woman because of her charming and sometimes overstated differences. She was a Wiccan, a fact that everyone who met her knew within minutes of the introductions. In fact, Phoenix was a priestess of the third order or third circle or some such designation; Crystal forgot the specifics but had been too scared to ask again. She had an actual legal name—Crystal knew better than to call it a normal name—but few knew it. Her Magickal name—Crystal and Matt both enjoyed poking fun at the humorously peculiar way in which Phoenix inserted the 'k' into the word Magical both in writing and somehow in speaking—was chosen in reference to her rebirth as a priestess, a leader of her coven. A bit of a strange bird, then, both Crystal and her husband thought. But at least she was consistent and sincere in her beliefs and her ever-present spirituality, which was more than Crystal could say for many of her other friends of varying religions. She was a good, and solid, friend to have.

Matt snorted in what might have been amusement and motioned for all to stand in a semi-circle around him. "We'll see," he said. "The title of battle mage is quite some distance in your future, if you're able get there at all. I will try to teach you a small part of the craft for now, but you'll need to agree to some pretty strict requirements first."

"Name them," several of the initiates said in unison. Each seemed to be trying to out-do the others in broadcasting seriousness of purpose. Crystal found it entertaining to watch the interplay. Some of the new trainees, like Phoenix and Birch, seemed completely absorbed by the prospect of learning, while others, like Leonard and Carol and Michelle, were detached. Those three surprised Crystal more by their presence than by their detachment. They had been Matt's friends primarily, though Crystal had come to know them through occasional social get-togethers. They had gotten to know one another through a circle Matt had participated in before he'd met Crystal. All three worked in an accounting firm downtown and occasionally had social events that carried a hint of paganism at their various homes. She'd always felt that that group was more interested in coming together for social events than for anything related to mysticism or paganism or magic.

Matt looked around the group slowly, meeting each of their

eyes for several seconds. Once his eyes had made the circuit he grinned, clasped his hands together, and then pitched a softball-sized ball of yellow energy at the center of the crowd. The assembled humans dove away as the glimmering ball stopped and then exploded in a soft "pop." Those who dove too slowly were pushed away in mid-air, and came back to their feet rubbing heads and shoulders that would be bruised tomorrow.

"What was that for?" Leonard, a towering man and former Marine, started to protest, but Matt cut him off.

"That was a sonic energy ball. It uses air pressure to do its bidding at its destination, which some of you have already figured out. Do you have any questions, or want to see it again?" Matt asked, the last part with a toothy grin making it clear that further demonstrations would likely cause more pain.

"I want to see fire," Birch said, prompting a snarl from both Leonard and Carol.

"Fire. Yes, one of the more useful of elements. You can use fire to light a candle, or a torch, or a fireball," Matt said. "It's a different element, though, and quite powerful. Are you sure you want to see it?"

The group nodded, most of them warily. Matt shrugged. "Here goes." He held out his hand at shoulder level, palm facing up, and grinned as a tongue of flame sprang from the center of his palm, rising nearly a foot before settling back into a steady six inch high fire. Several in the group jumped and then relaxed as they realized that the demonstration wasn't aimed directly at them.

"Fire," Matt stated. He gazed at the flickering for several seconds quietly and then allowed the flame to wink out. "Anybody need to see it again?"

Everyone nodded again eagerly, and then dove sideways as a softball-sized ball of flame sped from Matt's hands toward the group. Rubbing elbows, knees, and palms that had taken the brunt of their dives onto the hard stone floor, they rose and glared at the god.

"So, requirement number one," Matt said with a smug grin on his face. "Magic kills humans, and has even seriously injured a god or two in my time. You *will* respect it each moment you interact with it. Never let your guard down or you will die. Got it?"

Matt made an obvious point of looking each initiate in the eyes and waiting for an acknowledgement before continuing. "Requirement number two. You will respect me when I teach you. Also, Sorscha is the only thrakkon who enters this room, and while she is here you will respect her as though she were me. Got it?"

After again receiving acknowledgements from each of the humans, Matt said, "Okay, requirement number three, the last. Until I give you permission otherwise, if I ever give you permission otherwise, you will only practice the magic I show you, and you will only do so here in this chamber. You may have noticed this chamber is different from the rest of the rooms in my estate. First, the stone it is made from has been strengthened and is fire-proof, sonic-proof, air-proof, and—well, pretty much magic-proof. Magic can be a very destructive force, and it won't do to have my estate blown apart by an apprentice. That would make me angry. The room is also shielded from teleport in or out by any but me, and it's that way on purpose. As future magic-users, you are something other deities are interested in. As future magic-users being taught by the god of war, you are even more valuable to certain other deities. That's why it's important to not practice anywhere but here."

"But," Krista interjected, and then seemed to recall the third requirement. Blanching, she said, "um, if I may ask a question?" When Matt nodded, she said, "Aphrodite rang a bell before she teleported in today. Right? Are you saying she could have just popped in?"

Matt's eyes twinkled as a large smile spread across his face. "An excellent question! Please, all of you, take this to heart. If you're going to succeed as a mage of any caliber, you have to always observe what happens around you and attempt to connect the dots, as Krista just did. To answer your question, Krista, Aphrodite did ring the bell in my chamber with her signature ring to let me know she wanted to visit, and she waited for my response before teleporting in. Any of the gods or goddesses can easily teleport into any part of this estate that's not shielded at any time, but that would be rude. Even though we don't always like each other, we do try to respect boundaries."

Matt walked over to the desk. "Now, another special thing about this room. See this book?" He pointed to a large leather-bound book on the table.

"Where did that come from?" Crystal asked. The desk had been completely bare earlier.

Matt opened the book to the first page, ignoring the question. "This is a spell book. It's a special one, as you have probably already guessed. Once you've mastered your control over magical flows, if of course you ever master them, you'll want your own spell book. For now, this book is attuned to each of you and will contain the notes you've written when you look into it. Whenever you look for it, it will be here, and to protect itself, it disappears when it's not needed. It can't be removed from this room, or even from this desk, though."

Opening a drawer in the desk, Matt retrieved a small sack. "Now, let's begin. First, does anyone wish to bow out? You may feel free to stop at any time, and each of you should honestly consider the option. The path of a mage is dangerous to yourself and to others around you, and I assure you that you will not be able to master anything beyond a pitifully small fireball, if that, in your lifetimes. If you're here for the glory, in other words, forget about it. The only advantage you'll have as a mage is unlimited access to this room, anytime day or night, and exemption from the chore list that every other human will participate in. So, if you wish to just say no, now is a fine time to walk out."

Matt waited several long moments as no one took him up on his offer to leave. "Yeah, didn't think so. Fine. Catch," he said, tossing a small round object at each initiate except Crystal in a rapid-fire fashion. Some caught the small river rocks that he tossed at them while others dove away, scurrying after their rocks red-faced as they realized that the flying objects were just normal rocks.

Matt said, "Remember the second requirement? When I tell you to catch, you catch. Next time you don't do what I tell you to, you'll very likely die."

Everyone rejoined the circle clutching rocks in their hands. Matt held his own right hand out, palm up, with a rock in the middle, and the initiates copied. "Air is the safest element to start with. It will eventually give you the ability to throw sonic balls, but for now just concentrate on lifting the rock. Watch." In silence, everyone watched the rock slowly levitate out of Matt's hand, hovering on a column of yellow-colored, air-based energy several inches above his palm. "Can everyone see the flow?" he asked, and everyone nodded. Crystal watched from a distance, annoyed at being left out but pleased that she could see the flows. "Good. Remember what I said earlier about rituals. If you can't just connect with it mentally, try making up a rhyming phrase and repeating it, concentrating on the energy you see me working with now. Trust me, it's in front of all of you, and you do have the power to touch it, but the ability doesn't come easily. You'll have to work on it. When you can do this, let me know and we'll move on to lesson two." The rock fell back into Matt's hand and he turned wordlessly and strode out of the room, motioning for Crystal and Sorscha to follow.

Matt closed the door and walked several dozen steps up the

slowly-spiraling hallway before uttering a sound, and then laughed aloud. "What's funny?" Crystal asked.

"They have no idea what a difficult exercise they're in for."

"I don't get it. You're such a wonderful teacher. Why be rough on them?"

"Because magic is rough on them. It's very, very, very difficult to control. I wasn't kidding that a sloppily crafted spell will kill. The simple activity of raising rocks is the exercise that will separate the true magi from those who just think it's cool to shoot fireballs, and will hopefully leave the failures in the group alive and in one piece."

"Oh. Well, that makes sense. When am I going to learn magic, by the way?"

Matt stopped and turned. "You? Hadn't thought you'd want to. It's hard, Crystal. Really hard. And you're the wife of a god. Why would you want to learn magic?"

Crystal shrugged, not sure how best to respond to the question, uncertain as she still was regarding her new standing in her marriage to the God of War. "I—I don't know. Probably best not to, as you suggest. But I see the flows, and when we teleported here I was thrilled at being able to touch them. And you did include me in the twelve people at the watchtowers in your ritual. And I've seen them when you used them on me, and want to return the favor. In any event, I don't want to just hang around being the wife of a god. I want to participate, to be your equal partner as we've always been."

Matt caressed her face lovingly. "You are my equal partner, magic or no. What sets you apart from any and all of my previous wives, in fact, is that you are so much my equal in character and intelligence. Everyone in the estate will respect and follow you as though your words were mine. It feels foreign now, I'm sure, but over time you'll come to understand and enjoy the intricacies of running the estate. Isn't that enough?"

She wasn't sure. "Oh, I don't know," she heard herself say, giving in to him as she often did, trusting that her willingness to give in would eventually yield a corresponding willingness in Matt's stance, as it often had in the past. "It probably is. There's still just so much going on in my brain. Anyway, is it finally time for that tour?"

Phobos and Lady

Matt nodded, then took her hand and continued up the hall. The tour started with the pair stopping back by their chambers to collect the twins. Linda was excited, but Heidi moped.

"What's wrong, Heidi?" Crystal asked.

"There are no boys here," the young teenager replied.

"Sure there are!" Crystal answered, trying to inject a cheerfulness into her voice that she didn't really feel. "There's—um—Matt? Are there any boys here?"

"Heidi and Linda's age? One. RJ's son," Matt replied.

Heidi's face twisted in visible disgust. "He's not even a teenager yet, Dad. He doesn't count."

Matt shrugged and said, "Well, then, I guess the correct question is 'Are there any boys here who are teenagers like Heidi and Linda, now that they've reached the exalted and wizened age of thirteen?' The answer to that, of course, is zero. Sorry, girls."

"So how are they going to be social over the next few decades if they have nobody to hang out with?" Crystal asked, Heidi nodding in agreement with the implied accusation.

Shrugging again, Matt replied, "We'll find some. You heard me last night when I said that very few humans will survive the cataclysm going on right now, right? But some will. We'll go looking for survivors before too long. Plus there's Atlantis and other magical places, as well as human survivors at the other gods' estates. You shouldn't worry about the future much."

"Atlantis?" all three women asked at the same time. "Isn't that a myth—oh, wait, stupid question alert," Linda said. Matt glared at her, and she continued, "I know, I know, there's no such thing as a stupid question. But gods are myths, too, and you're standing here in front of us."

Matt tousled his daughter's hair. "Yes. I am real, and so is Atlantis, dear. In fact, remember the wave that destroyed the West Coast as we were leaving? It was caused by Atlantis resurfacing."

"Wait," Linda challenged her father. "Atlantis is in the Atlantic Ocean. How did it drown the Pacific Coast?"

"Atlantis was believed to be in the Atlantic Ocean according to Plato, and then by everybody else who bought into that story," Matt said. "The Greeks really had no idea there was a Pacific Ocean. Remember, nobody in Europe knew the Atlantic Ocean had another side until they started crossing it about a thousand years ago. Plato had no way of knowing that Atlantis was actually a huge island on the opposite side of another continent that he didn't know existed."

"Oh, right. No maps. That was silly." Heidi said, earning a glare from her sister.

"So, let's go tour." Matt said. "Let's start with the grounds, since it's such a beautiful day outside, and after that we can look around the inside." The family followed him out of their suite and down a new hallway that opened to a side courtyard. A fountain stood in the center, four unicorn statues pushing water through their upturned horns in the four cardinal directions. A circular path of flat polished stones went around the fountain, with an arch-covered bench seat on either of the two sides of the courtyard just off the stone path. A bush in each corner of the yard was artfully trimmed into the shape of a creature that Crystal had once considered mythical: a hydra, a dragon, a gryphon, and a mermaid.

"Do unicorns exist?" Crystal asked Matt, her eyes on the fountain. Each unicorn had features that made it uniquely different from its stone companions.

"Hmm?" Matt asked, looking back at Crystal then following

her eyes. "Oh. Well, sort of. Horses exist. Unicorns are just magically-modified horses."

"So you can make me a unicorn, Daddy?" Heidi asked, using the tone and title she always used when she wanted something from Matt.

Matt turned toward the more precocious of the twins with a twinkle in his eyes. Inhaling deeply, he brought his arms up and hummed for several moments, squeezing his eyes shut. His entire body started quivering, hands clenching and unclenching. With a great exhalation, he brought his arms down to rest his hands on her head and said in a deep, booming voice, "Abracadabra! You're a unicorn!" Opening one eye slightly, he asked quietly, "Did it work?"

Heidi glared at him while Crystal stifled a chuckle. Linda's loud guffaw caused Heidi's face to redden as she stomped her foot. "That wasn't funny."

Smiling tenderly, Matt caressed the side of her face. "Well, I enjoyed it. To make it up to you, some day, I will turn a horse into a unicorn for you. But you have to promise me in turn to respect the creatures of the estate, magical or not. Okay?"

Smiling through her own glare, Heidi nodded. "Okay, deal. And don't think I'll forget, Dad."

"You never do, kiddo. You never do," he said as he led them around the unicorn fountain and through a gap in the tall hedge that set off the courtyard from the surrounding estate and finally out onto an expansive lawn.

For the first time, Crystal looked around at the beauty surrounding the estate. When they had landed—how could it have been just yesterday, she wondered—she had felt too nauseous and shocked to take in the surroundings, and she had been indoors since except for her time in the darkened amphitheater last night. Now she realized that the estate matched exactly the picture she and Matt had built in their discussions of what they would look for when they retired some day. He had probably known all along that she would be living here, she realized, and she wasn't sure if her mental image came from her own desires or his descriptions. She really didn't care.

Towering mountains flanked the lush green valley in which they were walking. Looking in all directions, she noticed that there probably wasn't a path through the mountain peaks to reach the estate by foot. That revelation made sense based on his probable desire to keep the estate undiscovered through the technology eras. "Matt, are the mountains passable on foot?" she asked.

"No, they're not," Matt said. "There are only two ways to get here, by teleportation and by flying. But you have to know where the estate is to fly to it."

"Why don't the airplanes see it and land here, Dad?" Heidi asked.

"Well, first, because we're in a very mountainous region that planes rarely fly over. Second, the protective shield around us also deflects the light from outside and makes it look like a mound of rock."

Crystal's eyes followed the base of the mountains. The oval-shaped valley was ringed by thick forest, some evergreen and some not, and the inner part seemed to be manicured lawn. She didn't know how big the lawn was, but it was bigger than she had ever seen. Ten acres? A hundred? She wasn't sure.

The estate's buildings sat to one side of the valley, on a plateau slightly above the valley floor that ran all the way up to the base of the mountains on one side. Looking across the valley she thought she recognized the spot they had set down on yesterday. Turning back to the direction they were walking, she saw they were approaching stables. Linda, who had always had a love for horses, began clapping her hands. "Horses? Horses! We get to ride horses!" Matt turned and smiled at his daughter before physically hefting a large door to the side and motioning the family in.

Two thrakkoni bowed as they entered. One asked Matt, "Which horses should I ready, master?"

"Get Lady ready for Crystal, and two of the ponies for the girls. I'll go see if Phobos is up for a ride."

As the thrakkoni walked toward the stalls, Linda looked hurt and Heidi said, "Dad, I think we're old enough to ride real horses."

Matt chuckled and patted her on the shoulder. "Easy, killer. In the stables of the god of war, the ponies are actually pretty big. You three stay here while I go get my steed. The thrakkoni will bring yours pretty quickly."

Within minutes the thrakkoni returned, having made fast work of saddling the horses. One led a huge dappled white and tan mare to Crystal. "Lady has the calmest manner of any of our steeds, ma'am. Still, she may take a little extra effort to get up onto. May I help?" When Crystal nodded, the thrakkon helped hoist her easily onto the horse's saddle. Looking down she wondered if the horse really was as big as a Clydesdale or just seemed that tall from Crystal's perch on her back.

Both Heidi and Linda oohed and ahhed over the horses chosen for them. Matt had been correct; a pony in these stables was as large as the regular riding horses they had rented on their vacations. The mare chosen for Heidi was a spirited solid chestnut with a white star and strip on the face that she now turned toward Heidi as if to express disapproval for being saddled. Linda, in turn, was helped onto a brindled chestnut mare that seemed more docile than Heidi's mount. "Vera and Belle," a thrakkon said, pointing to the chestnut and the brindle in turn, then led the two out of the front of the stables as the other led Lady out.

Outside, Matt smiled at them from the top of a beautiful black stallion that towered over all the other horses. Crystal couldn't be certain from her vantage point, but she estimated the stallion's height at nearly eight feet—nearly twenty-four hands high! As the rest of the family approached, Matt's warhorse turned its head and snorted disapprovingly. "We're not charging into battle today, Phobos," Matt said. "This is a nice friendly ride around the estate so that the women can see everything. Got it?"

The horse gazed back at its rider, and Crystal got the uneasy feeling that the horse actually understood Matt's words. "Phobos is his name?" she asked, then continued, "He's an amazing steed."

Matt nodded, not breaking eye contact with his horse, and said, "Yes. Phobos is what he's been called since last we were together. It's Greek for terror, which is—well, appropriate," he punctuated the last by raising his eyebrows and glaring even more intensely at Phobos. "He's one of the four immortal steeds of the god of war, of course, and can be a little intimidating. But he'll be nice and sweet for this ride, today. Won't you, Phobos?"

With that, the black stallion threw his head forward and snorted. Crystal and the girls all jumped as flame shot out of his mouth and nose. "Oh, and he can snort fire," Matt said. "Only a few inches, anyway. Which is, of course, more useful for inducing terror than for actually setting anything ablaze, but it makes him happy."

The stallion kicked the earth. "Okay, then, let's getty up and go!" Matt said, and Phobos responded by rearing onto his hind legs, screaming an equine war cry, and leaping over a fence that Crystal guessed was about eight feet tall. "Wait. For. Them," they heard Matt say, punctuating every word.

The three women nudged their horses on the sides, and all three trotted out of the yard. Around the side of the enclosure they found Matt waiting for them on Phobos, who seemed to be laughing. "Never mind him. He's a bit impatient," Matt said. "We're going to ride around the valley, and you'll get a chance to see the trails and some of the hidden gardens. Most importantly, you'll get to be out in the open air with your favorite Dad."

Heidi's eyes hadn't left Phobos. "Daddy, can I ride your horse sometime?"

"Um—no. Sorry, Heidi, but there's just no way. He barely allows me to ride him usually, and I could pick him up and throw him over the mountain to his doom if I wanted. You and your sister can ride any horse on the estate you wish at any time, but you can't ride any of the four immortals. It's obvious which ones they are, and the thrakkoni won't—well, can't—touch them, and you need to stay away from them too, clear?"

Heidi sighed with disappointment. "Right, Dad. I'll stay away."

Matt, who had heard that tone before, turned to face her directly. "Really, Heidi. I need you to really stay away from them. This isn't a joke, and it's not like the BB gun that—well, it's not like that. If you try to touch Phobos or any other immortal, you will die. Promise me."

Heidi smiled at him. "I promise." Suddenly her face brightened, "But can you make him into a unicorn for me sometime?"

Phobos reared, clearly angry, then pawed the ground and shot fire out both nostrils for several seconds. "Easy, Phobos, easy," Matt calmed him. "Heidi, Phobos understands our speech, and what you just said appalled him." Phobos, still breathing heavily, glared at her as Matt explained. Crystal, though, could tell that despite Matt's stern voice, he was barely holding back laughter.

"Oh. Um, sorry, Mister Phobos. I like unicorns is all."

Phobos snorted and turned back toward the woods. "Let's go," said Matt, and the family set off toward the wood line at a trot that became a canter, the horses all showing a desire to run. Crystal urged Lady up beside Matt and was shocked to see Phobos leering toward the mare. "Matt, I didn't know a horse could leer, but yours is at mine."

Chortling, Matt replied, "There's a lot that people don't realize Phobos can do. He's sort of a god, after all, in his own way. I've seen him cause earthquakes with his footsteps before."

Crystal blanched at that revelation. "Oh, okay. Wow. Anyway, I was curious. Do the thrakkoni from the estate ride the horses while you're away?"

"Absolutely not. A thrakkon would never get on a horse's back, and a horse would never let one ride it. Except, that is, for the two in the stables, whose job is to break the horses to the bit while I'm gone. Why do you ask?"

"I just noticed that the horses really seem to want to run. I guess some time without riding would make them that way."

Matt looked down at Lady, who was keeping up with Phobos while gamefully ignoring his leers. "I guess. I think it's time to oblige them." He looked back at the twins, who were doing fine, and then accelerated to a gallop.

The family's ride took them on a path around the perimeter of the valley, a trip Crystal guessed was a few miles total. A good bit north of the estate they stopped and dismounted at a clearing hidden in the trees that held a small cottage landscaped to appear as an English countryside home. Made entirely of stone and mortar, the single-room home was well furnished for living but didn't appear to have been occupied in a while. "Sometimes I like to get away from the estate," Matt explained. "You are all welcome to come here whenever you'd like, of course, as a home away from home. It's protected from unwanted entry, but the wards are now attuned to all of us."

Crystal admired the flowering landscape as the twins walked into the cottage, asking "how do all these flowers stay so well kept?" She recognized flowers and herbs of all sorts, including daffodils, mint plants, and even the columbine flowers that she knew to be Matt's favorite. Matt walked up beside her and shrugged, smiling. "The wards maintain them. Really, it's simple. They need to stay watered and not be choked out by weeds, and just like I keep unwanted people out, I also keep unwanted plants out."

A soft popping sound behind warned them of a magical arrival. "Well, don't you have the cutest family, Matthew?" The same strawberry blonde who had so angered Matt this morning, stood with her hand on her hip. This time instead of lingerie Aphrodite was wearing the more modest attire of a huntsman, except that she made it look every bit as sexual as the lingerie had. Looking at Crystal, Aphrodite asked, "How are you digging being married to the great god of war, dear?" She coyly turned over a pebble on the ground with a foot clad in a skin-tight leather boot.

Crystal sneered but said nothing in reply due to Matt's gentle grasp on her hand. Instead, she turned to him and asked in her sweetest voice, "Honey, I thought you said your wards keep unwanted people out. Could they be going stale?"

Aphrodite erupted in laughter, both hands in relaxed fists resting on either side of her waist. "That was good," she acknowledged, a slight dip of the head. "Matthew, your taste for well-built redheads with a sharp wit is obviously still strong."

"What are you doing here, Kallipygos?" Matt asked with a level, dangerous voice. "I've asked you not to pop in like this. Your tasteless abandonment of manners is obviously still one of your most redeeming qualities."

Aphrodite shrugged and blew a kiss Matt's direction. Lips pouting, she replied "And your sarcasm is one of your least redeeming qualities. I just wanted to see what you were up to, loverboy." As she spoke, the twins walked out of the cabin, their appearance sending a wave of alarm through Crystal. "Ah, what a quaint little family unit," Aphrodite finished, sarcasm dripping from her words.

"Linda, Heidi, come over here," Matt said.

"Oh, don't order the kids around on my behalf. I'm afraid I can't stick around, much as we'd all like that. Just wanted to pay my kindest respects. Ta-ta!" Aphrodite said, her voice like a wind chime, and just as quickly as she had appeared, she popped back out of existence.

Crystal spent a few moments breathing, allowing herself to calm down. She turned to the twins and wordlessly beckoned them over. They were recovering from seeing the goddess disappear, so they began walking slowly but then sprinted over to their mother's arms.

"Who was she, Mom? She looked dangerous," Heidi said, her voice finding its way out from her the spot where her face was buried in Crystal's bosom. Crystal kept both girls wrapped tightly in her arms, using alternate hands to stroke each girl's hair, and turned her head toward Matt.

"Matt, I was serious. Are your wards intact? How did she get in?"

Matt shrugged, his face still awash with anger. "She's a goddess. No ward will keep her out. I'd hoped she would follow convention, but clearly that's not going to happen. I'm going to have to set them up to warn me of her arrival."

"But you said the chamber we saw earlier was warded against even a god's teleporting in and out," Crystal objected.

"Yes, I did, and it is. But the dense stone surrounding the room helps in the warding process there."

Moving over to comfort the twins, Matt put his arms around the three women. "It's safe, though. She's gone. I know she is, because gods can sense each other, so I could tell if she wasn't. Let's just continue our rides, all right?" The family remounted in silence, somber expressions not giving way to returning smiles till they covered several miles of playful gallop along paths through the trees and foliage dressed out for springtime.

At the extreme south end of the elongated valley, they came to another opening in the tree line. Crystal and the girls reined in and crinkled their noses at the smell of cattle. "Your livestock is through there, I take it?" Crystal asked.

"Indeed. Tucked back in between the mountains is a holding area for the several thousand head of cattle as well as many smaller animals."

"Who comes all the way out here to take care of the herds? Do the thrakkoni do that for you?"

"For us," Matt corrected gently, "And yes. The thrakkoni are in charge of all livestock management. They do it quite well."

They turned their horses back to the north and galloped toward the estate, and after they had followed some of the rest of the perimeter they came upon another clearing. Crystal's stomach began fluttering as it came into sight, and by the time they were within several yards she felt sick. Holding out his hands, Matt announced, "That's close enough."

Lady needed no encouragement to back away a few steps, prompting what could only be a sneer from Phobos. "What is that?" Crystal asked at the same time as the twins, who were also backing away.

Matt turned his back to the clearing and looked at all three. "This is an area you must never enter. There are plants used in times of war and strife, and this is where I cultivate them. Some can kill a human, while others put you to sleep for a long, long time. Others permanently or temporarily remove your ability to reason. You'll know you're close to it when you feel the wards making you queasy. Never, ever, push your way through the wards."

Crystal nodded. "Sure, but why?" she asked.

"Why what? Why does the god of war cultivate plants of war, you mean?" Matt asked, bemused.

"Never mind."

"Let's get back to the estate," Matt said, turning Phobos toward the complex. Crystal noticed that the buildings were starting to cast longer shadows.

They arrived back at the stables without further incident, Matt taking Phobos around back while the two thrakkoni helped the ladies dismount. Matt walked in as the horses were being led away, and Linda asked, "Can I go help rub Belle down? She's such a pretty horse."

"Another time, yes, but we have lots more to see inside. Follow me!" he said and walked out, retracing their steps earlier to enter the main building through the side door.

"This valley looks like it was created just to be your estate, Dad," Heidi said as they walked.

"It was, Dear." Matt replied. Looking back at her and smiling, he flexed a bicep and pointed to it.

"My Daddy, the mountain mover," Heidi said in return. Matt nodded, pleased.

As they walked down another hall Crystal hadn't seen before, she asked, "How many rooms are there, total?"

Matt cocked his head to the side slightly in his usual *I'm thinking* pose. "I suppose I've never added them up," he said. "Counting bathrooms and all, but not counting closets, I think there are four or five thousand. Or so."

Crystal gasped. "I had no idea. Where are they all?"

"Well, here. You were asking about this complex, and not my others, right?"

"Others? What others—oh, wait, I'll get to that. Yes, I meant here, but where do you hide them all? The estate didn't look that big."

"You've only been in the main mansion. This building alone has three floors with four hundred sixty-three living quarters, and since they're all in the main mansion most of those have between two and five rooms. Plus there's the dining room and the other rooms we're headed to see now, and there's the magic rooms in the basement. And, oh, I guess I wasn't counting the wine cellars beneath the main building. So add five."

"Wait," Crystal said, trying to keep up physically as well as mentally. "Magic rooms? Plural? Why haven't you shown us the others?"

"The magi are still effectively children, so they get the room that is set up like a crib. As they get better, they will have other areas revealed to them."

"Will I be able to practice in one of them?"

"Why would you do that?"

Crystal groaned, but Matt ignored her and opened the huge oak doors they had come to. "The library, my love," he announced as the aroma she had come to associate with age-old tomes—a scent that as a result of her association gave her an immediate case of extreme sublime happiness—wafted out to greet the family.

Crystal filled her lungs with the smell of books and then slowly exhaled, and then opened her eyes and gasped. Her daughters echoed the sound. All of them had a great love for books, and the library was huge for a private collection. The circular room was nearly fifty feet in width and three stories tall, the unending wall covered entirely with shelves lined with rows of mismatched books of all shapes, sizes, and covers. The ceiling was domed stained glass that covered the polished mahogany floor with fancy colored patterns. Two swiveling ladders were attached to tracks on the wall for easy book access. Simple wooden tables were spaced at uneven intervals around the room, each supplied with between four and six simple wooden chairs, and many of these had books or scrolls set neatly on them. Crystal saw that an entire section of the shelves appeared devoted to scrolls. There must be hundreds of thousands of manuscripts here, Crystal thought.

"Don't get too excited," Matt said. "The majority of these manuscripts are not in English. Remember that I haven't been back much since English was invented, and my agents can only do so much. But once the cataclysm is over and we can start traveling, I will beef up my English language collection. In the meantime, Erszie over there will be pleased to translate nearly any language into English for you." Matt pointed to a thrakkon sitting at the only desk in the room. Erszie looked up and smiled at them. "She is an expert in linguistics, and can even translate the lost languages that are here."

Linda moved over to one shelf and removed a book. Opening it, she said, "This looks like a construction book." She pointed to a detailed diagram showing stone work being joined together, and her fingers played over the delicate script on the page. Crystal, looking over Linda's shoulder, couldn't tell what language it was written in but loved the script's uniform slanted lines.

Matt nodded. "It is a construction manual. It's written in Atlantean, and details the building methodology for pyramids and the differences between the ones found in the north of the African continent and the ones found in Central and South America. It's a wonderful work, and it cost me a fair amount to acquire."

Crystal looked at Matt with a quizzical expression. "How old are these books, anyway?"

"Some of them are nearly as old as me," Matt said. "Millions of years. This room is magically treated to ensure the books don't disintegrate, and Erszie also has a treatment for each book to prevent the oils from our hands from harming the pages. I like to collect some from each cycle. Each magic cycle will generate spell books and books on the magical powers of the elements, and I try to save some of them from the marauders of the technology cycle who invariably claim that magic is evil hocus pocus from some sort of devil. Each technology cycle, meanwhile, generates tomes on whatever they manage to discover in their time, whether it be nuclear power, pyramid-generated calculations, whatever, and I try to collect some of that as well to save it from the mages who consider technical manuals to be rubbish."

"I would have thought that the god of war would collect books on, you know, war," Crystal said.

Matt caught the sarcastic tone in Crystal's voice and smirked at her. He pointed to one area of library, waving his arm to include many of the manuscripts. "Books on, you know, war, are right over there. Well, and scrolls, too. I am the god of war, you know, even if I have other interests from time to time," he said.

Crystal left the library reluctantly after Matt's observation that if they didn't hurry up they would miss dinner. The family walked back down the hall, and she asked, "What about all these other hallways going off to the sides?"

"Living quarters. This building can house four hundred and sixty-three families, so most of what you see in the wings are just where people are staying, or where some might stay if they were occupied. The population of the estate will increase over time."

They reached a room Crystal had seen before, and she gasped once again at the beauty of the welcome chamber. Matt smiled and stopped, letting her take in its grandeur as they stood hand in hand. He then pulled her up the curved stairs to the second floor, where they followed another hall in a path that ended in a circular stairway up to the third floor. Matt palmed a spot on the wall and opened a hidden door on the wall of third-floor landing. The chamber they entered contained more stairs; Crystal saw them and mentally apologized to her burning thighs. "Why can't you just make an elevator?" she asked, expecting and receiving a sardonic look from Matt in reply.

The family walked up two more floors and then exited the top of the stairs into a round glass chamber that commanded a three hundred sixty degree view of the estate. Looking down to the roof below, Crystal could see at last how massive the main mansion was. She looked out behind the primary building and counted the number of other structures, whistling. Matt said, "That's where all the other rooms are, most of them built smaller for single residents. This estate was constructed to hold several thousand people comfortably. There," he said, pointing to the left," is the courtyard we walked out into today, and over there are the stables." Motioning to the right, he said, "There is the amphitheater in which we had our concert last night."

"It's beautiful," Crystal said, turning to face him. "Amazing." They shared a warm kiss as the light from outside dimmed.

Heidi cleared her throat. "Mom? Dad? It's getting dark in here. Shouldn't we go back down now?"

Matt answered with a soft *Harrumph* and said, "Okay, sure. The stairs are lit, but getting to them in the dark can be tricky, I guess."

"This is so beautiful, Matt. Thank you for showing it to us. When are you going to start teaching me magic?" Crystal asked in her prettiest-sounding voice.

"I'm not," Matt said, and then smiled at her warmly as he herded his family down the stairs.

"Dad, can we learn magic?" Heidi asked on the walk back to the suite.

"You and your sister? Unfortunately, no, dear, you can't," Matt said. "Most humans aren't born with the ability to see or touch the elemental flows that make up the practice of magic. It's not really genetic, either. You were born to two parents who have some strong potential, but I've never detected the potential in either of you. That's not unusual, mind you. It might skip a generation, so your children will be strong mages, or it might not appear at all."

"Could it be something we might grow into later?" Linda asked.

"Probably not. You're thirteen now. Most of what you can do has been programmed into you already. I mean, it's always possible, but don't sit around pining for the ability to do magic."

"So what good is it to be the daughter of a god?" Heidi asked, crossing her arms.

Matt sighed, stopped, and turned toward Heidi. "Well," he said, "you get your pick of horses to ride anytime you want. You get the best rooms in the place to live in, and the best thrakkon to serve you. Several years, once you're grown and on your own, all you'll have to do is bat your eyelashes at me and say, 'Daddy, I want that land over there,' and you'll get it. What more could a little girl want?"

"Immortality." Heidi cocked her head to the side in her way of emphasizing the point, and Linda, standing behind, nodded vigorously.

"You're not going to believe me if I tell you that immortality sucks sometimes, are you?"

The twins both leveled a flat stare at Matt, their answer clear.

Matt sighed again. "Okay, look. I don't expect you to understand everything I have to say right now. If nothing else, accept it, catalog it, and come back for further explanation in a few decades if you don't understand it then. First of all, I can't grant you immortality no matter how much I might want to. It can't be done. I'm powerful, yes; I'm considered by my peers to be the third most powerful being in the universe, in fact. Not even I, though, can bend the rules of that universe. It can't happen, whether you still want it at the end of our talk or not.

"Now, let me talk a bit about this immortality thing. When you're human, you are born, and then you learn, and you grow, you love, and you experience. And then you finish your life the better for having done all of that. When you're immortal, none of that seems to matter anymore. We roll through cycle after cycle, and I see hundreds of generations of humans going through all that while I stay the same. Nothing changes; nothing grows except my frustration over the human race's inability to learn from its mistakes. It, well—it just isn't a status I'd wish on anybody. And I mean that, girls."

Matt turned and started toward the dining hall again. "Let's eat. It's getting late," he said, the smile on his face not touching his eyes.

****

"Why do you want to learn magic?" Matt asked as the couple undressed for bed.

Crystal froze, taken aback by the question. It had been over an hour since her request to learn magic had been summarily dismissed, and she hadn't expected him to bring it up again, at least not tonight. She recovered, summoned as much logical tone as she found available, and said, "I have several reasons, Matt. First, you've already said I have a strong capacity for manipulating the flows of magic. It seems wasteful to not utilize that god-given capacity." Matt grunted at her choice of words, but she pressed on, "Second, I've always dreamed of being a spiritual healer, which is what kept me interested in the paganism, honestly. With magic, I would be able to do that, and fulfill a dream. Third, I feel like I'm a third wheel in this room. You've got your powers, and Sorscha has her strength, and I have—nothing. I want to feel like I'm half of this relationship, and I don't right now."

She left her answer hanging on the air for several long moments. Finally he looked her in the eyes and spoke. "I understand your inability with magic is bothering you in your relationship with me. If being my equal in all things is vital to your happiness in our relationship, though, we have a problem. Please trust me when I say that I love you for your spirit, for your courage, for your intellect, for your sense of humor, and for hundreds of other aspects of your personality I consider important that were evident long before you knew that magic really existed. But you'll never be my equal in magic. If we started working on learning magic tomorrow, and you did nothing but practice for the remainder of your life, you wouldn't stand equal to my power or magical knowledge. It would be impossible. That's not a big deal to me. Please, accept your own worth. You're every bit my equal in this relationship as far as every important facet of it goes. You don't need to learn magic to have my love, Crystal."

Yuki the Therapuppy

Activity over the next couple of days rapidly settled into routines. The humans without magical abilities easily slipped into a pattern of labor sequenced by the scheduling efficiency that was Rellgll's hallmark. It surprised Crystal at first how readily a group that was comprised mostly of college students fell into a manual lifestyle, but Matt reminded her that the regular physical activity presented by the work was therapeutic in a way, helping them focus on something other than what they had lost in the cataclysm.

Crystal was brought up short by Matt's comment. Her life was wrecked, it had seemed. Everything she had known about life was now topsy-turvy. Her husband was a god, for God's sake, or—well, however that phrase needed to go. Matt's comment about the others' losses, though, brought to focus that she really hadn't lost much of anything, comparatively. Her husband—whoever he was—was here with her, as were her daughters and her puppy. She had never been particularly close with her aunts and cousins and distant relations of some nature that she could never recall, and it had been years since her parents had passed away, and of course Matt's family was nonexistent. Most of the people wandering the halls, meanwhile, had lost someone important in their lives, and many had lost everyone to whom they were close. Crystal felt a twinge of shame when she considered her initial reaction, and set out to make it right somehow.

She found the trick in taking Yuki with her. After visiting a few people who broke into inconsolable sobs when approached, Crystal recalled from somewhere back in her years of teacher training reading a report about animals' immense positive effects upon humans when recovering or learning. Acting on a hunch, she took the white Chihuahua with her when she visited with the former director of financial aid for the college. Mary had been a close work friend of Matt's, but never to the point of meeting her family other than the occasional quick greeting at the office Christmas parties, and Matt had explained to her that that was the key. Where he had gotten to know people before the cataclysm, he'd been able to sense their presence strongly enough in the moments just after it to send them a portal from the college, but Mary's family he hadn't gotten to know well enough to connect with.

Crystal attached the thin pink leash to Yuki's collar and walked out the door. Mary's apartment was right around the corner from her own in an area all the college's directors had been moved into. Matt had been able, in the moments after they landed, to communicate telepathically with the thrakkoni guides who had met them on the hill and lay out the room assignments for several hundred new guests simultaneously. He'd described the logic underlying his placements to her over breakfast, but it had seemed such a huge and largely administrative undertaking that she hadn't paid much attention except for a few important details. The suite across from theirs, for example, was the only other suite on the wing, and it was reserved for visiting deities or heads of state, he'd explained. Around to the left, though, was another long hall that he called his "hall of friends." It was along that hall that his peers at the college and most of the magic-users' rooms were found. RJ's quarters, meanwhile, were right below her own in the "noble's hall," down a path that was currently deserted by all but the former college president, his mage wife, and their children. Once, they'd had a brief chance at lunchtime to connect woman-to-woman, and Krista had spoken proudly of their well-appointed rooms. Crystal, though, suspected that Matt had other motives in mind when he'd assigned

RJ to a spot downstairs and down a long hallway from everyone else.

Crystal knocked on Mary's door. The stout brunette opened the door partially, looking out through a not-quite-human-width opening,

at Crystal. It was obvious from her puffy face and red eyes that she had been crying, and her initial expression clearly indicated that she intended to deal with her visitor and return to that activity as soon as possible.

Then she saw Yuki. The small white dog made herself impossible to miss, prancing up to Mary's feet with her white long-haired tail waving like a banner and enunciating one clear *Yip* in greeting. Yuki stood, head swiveled up and cocked slightly to the right to gaze directly into Mary's downturned face, big soft Chihuahua ears with their long tufts of white hair perked up into the air, weight evenly distributed across all four legs, waiting for Mary's response.

Mary's breath escaped in a half-sob, half-chortle. She wiped a tear that seemed left over from earlier, and then reached down. Yuki leaped easily into the woman's arms and, as Mary straightened back up, began licking her face in earnest.

Mary, her expression now one of amazement, met Crystal's eyes. "Thank you," she said simply, and then, "please, come in."

Crystal entered the apartment, saying, "Yuki was telling me she was lonely, just playing with me and the girls, so I was hoping you wouldn't mind giving her a change of routine today." She sat down on a comfortable couch, reached into her pocket, and pulled out a tiny stuffed unicorn that she handed to Mary. "She loves to chase Uni," she said. Mary gently set Yuki down on the floor and tossed the unicorn several feet away. The Chihuahua dashed after, growled and shook the unicorn, and pranced back over to Mary, her catch proudly displayed. Mary took the unicorn from her and threw it again several times, with similar results on each toss.

For the first time since they had arrived, Mary's face brightened in a true smile. She jumped down from her chair onto all fours on the rug, growling at and playing with Yuki. When Yuki dropped into her playful pouncing position with her belly on the ground, front legs splayed out in front, and head and ears and tail erect, Mary copied as closely as possible. Crystal imagined, from her vantage point on the couch, that if Mary had been graced with a tail it would be wagging as rapidly as Yuki's.

Together the young adult dog and the middle-aged adult woman tussled their way around the living room, Mary alternating between playful grows and laughter. Crystal watched, overjoyed at the change.

Breathing heavily, Mary finally drew up onto her knees. Still laughing, she picked up and hugged Yuki, the tiny dog wrapping her front paws over Mary's left shoulder, head wedged against her neck. Mary walked over to Crystal and sat beside her, throwing her right arm around and pulling Crystal into a three-way hug.

"Thank you."

"You're welcome, Mary. Yuki needs the exercise, and you needed the smile. I'll come by again if that's okay."

"Whenever you'd like, Crystal, and not just with Therapuppy there. This apartment gets big and lonely and mean after a while."

"Don't let it, Mary. Get out of it and walk around some. Come by my apartment sometime. The kids and I don't bite, and neither does Sorscha. I think she doesn't, anyway." Mary chuckled. Crystal asked, "Do you like to read?" When Mary nodded, she said, "Matt showed me to the library yesterday. It seems like a great place to sit and read, quiet but not alone. There's even a little thrakkoni librarian to shush you if you get too loud. Also, if you like to ride horses, the stables are right back behind the main mansion. Tell them I said to give you a spirited horse to ride around and explore on."

After an extended session of farewells and thank yous, Crystal returned to her own quarters with Therapuppy. Therapuppy—the title sounded right. She looked down at her companion trotting proudly beside her, head and tail both held high, tufts of ear and tail hair streaming proudly behind. Yuki was aware of how much she had helped Mary, she knew, and she loved the little long-haired Chihuahua all the more for it.

The girls were gone when she walked in. Matt had assured her it was safe to let them run around on their own, so she did. They were probably out riding again; both girls loved horses. Crystal thought briefly about riding Lady again, too, but her curiosity over magic drew her in. She refocused her gaze, sensing rather than actually seeing the flows of elemental energy that surrounded her. The air was full of prismatic energies, it appeared, and by looking for specific colors she could pick them out from the others. They weren't physically there enough to touch or to gaze at, but by reaching out with some strange sixth sense she had never known she had, she could cause eddies in the flow, bending the elements around. She tried yellow, and then she tried red, recalling Matt's lessons from the day before, and just as suddenly she recalled his prohibition against practicing magic outside of the chamber they had been in. She wasn't really practicing, though—was she? She was touching, fluffing, plucking at the flows, but she wasn't really doing anything with them. Nothing useful, anyway. Surely he wouldn't be mad over that, would he?

With a start, she realized that this was the first time since she had known him that she had even considered whether or not he might become mad. Other emotions, certainly; she always considered how he felt in making her decisions. But—anger? *Stop it*, she told herself. He was her husband, and she his wife, and that was that.

Resolved to learn more about magic, and to set the example for the others by doing it the proper way, in the room where her husband had said it must be practiced, Crystal left Yuki curled up in her bed and walked down to the chamber of sorcery. All eleven new magi were there, standing and sitting in various places around the room staring angrily at the rocks that sat, unmoving, in the palms of their hands.

Matt looked over from where he stood beside Birch, the mentoring moment suspended in mid-sentence. He said nothing, but Crystal easily read his expression, with one eyebrow quirked above the other, for the challenge it was. *What are you doing here?* he was asking without deigning to verbalize.

Once again feeling unsure of herself and her relationship, Crystal returned a half-smile to Matt, shrugged docilely, and sat on the floor against one wall to watch. Satisfied, the God of War turned back to Birch and continued his quiet discussion. Crystal smiled gamely at everyone who was paying attention to her, and then realized that no one was. Other than Matt, no one had even turned their eyes away from their rocks. Crystal sat and watched, emotions at war, her false smile barely holding tears of frustration at bay. Why was he excluding her from learning magic so thoroughly, so coldly? Why was she putting up with it? She still loved him with all of her heart, but for the first time ever she found herself fearing him.

"Screw this," a gruff voice cut through the room, drawing everyone's attention to Leonard. "I guess I'll never be a battle mage. I can't do this," he said, marching resolutely to the desk and smacking the river rock down on its surface. As he walked out of the chamber, Carol shrugged and followed, running to catch up. Matt's eyes followed them without expression.

"Hmmph." Matt's grunt was the only sound he made before he returned to his conversation with Birch. Crystal saw that

Matt didn't even look up as Michelle also rose, placed her rock quietly on the desk, and followed Leonard and Carol out the door.

Not long after, she got bored and left. Watching people stare at rocks was not exciting in the slightest, and she still had to sort through, categorize, and figure out her feelings toward Matt and who he had become. She couldn't do all that, she knew, while staring at him. Crystal wandered, mind idly skipping from one thought on her relationship to another, neither feet nor mental process taking on any sort of direction.

"May I help you, Crystal?"

She realized with a start that she had wandered into the library. The question had come from Erszie, the thrakkon Matt had introduced them to yesterday. "Magic," Crystal stammered slightly, saying the first thing that came to her mind. "I'm looking to read up on the use of magic."

"Any particular type of magic?" the thrakkon asked. "I have books on the magic of healing, the use of magic for both utility and war...."

"How about just basic magic?" Crystal said, cutting Erszie off. "I don't know enough about the basics to understand any of the more specialized uses."

"Ah, of course. Have a seat there, and I'll get you a couple of books that you might find useful." Erszie showed Crystal to a nearby seat and then rolled a ladder around the shelves till she found whatever she was looking for. She climbed several feet up and pulled two books from their spots. She returned to the table and laid the books, both leather-bound tomes that appeared to be old from the wear on the edges, in front of Crystal separately.

"Neither one is in English," Crystal objected, seeing that both covers were covered by marks that she couldn't interpret.

"There aren't any books on magic written in English, Crystal. The language hasn't been around in an age of magic till now.

Would you prefer a book in English, or a book on magic?"

Crystal looked at Erszie's expression suspiciously, trying to determine if the librarian's question had been sarcastic. It was indecipherable, though, so Crystal decided to assume that the thrakkon was being earnest.

"I'm here to learn about magic, but I can only read English."

The librarian's face brightened into a smile. "That's no problem, Crystal. I am fluent in a great many languages, including both Atlantean," she pointed to the book that was bound in a square shape nearly a foot across, "and Amiotrian," she said, pointing to the other book that was only a few inches wide but over a foot high. "It's my job, and my pleasure, to provide translation services."

"I appreciate that, but I'm not sure I can ask you to sit here and read to me."

"I'd be happy to do that as well, but it wasn't what I was offering. We have translating devices. The master created them magically, and I program them with the appropriate translation heuristics for each new language brought to the collection. Here," she said, pulling a thin block with a window in its center from the middle of the table, "is one. They are easy to use, see?" The thrakkon demonstrated by setting the device on top of the book she had indicated as Atlantean with the linear slanted lines on the front cover showing through the window. It appeared to Crystal to just be a thick piece of plastic, several inches tall and about a foot wide, larger than but similar to the learning aids she had used to help dyslexic children focus on a single line at a time while reading. Erszie said, enunciating clearly, "Translate Atlantean to English." Suddenly the linear script came to life, morphing instantly from a set of delicate parallel lines into the words "Elemental Flows: A Primer on Magic." Crystal gasped.

"That's amazing," Crystal said, turning to grin at Erszie. "How does it do that?"

"Magic."

"Thanks."

"That's all I know, Crystal. I can't do magic, myself. I can't even see the flows. None of my race can."

"Yes, I know that. I shouldn't have asked the question. This is just really incredible to me. How do you program them?"

"Once I determine how a new language is structured and as many of its exceptions as I can find, I draw out the logic and program it into that machine over on my desk," Erszie said, indicating what Crystal had assumed was a variation of a basic typewriter. "Then I put all the translators in, one at a time. The programming is fairly simple. The hard part is doing the linguistic analysis."

"I'll bet. Some day I'd love to learn more about how you do that analysis."

"But first," Erszie said, completing Crystal's thought for her, "you should read what you came to read. The Atlanteans are the recognized experts in magic, second only to the gods themselves in its use. The book in front of you is the primer that they begin with to teach all their new mages. The Amiotrites were an ancient civilization that was quite thoroughly wiped out when they became far too confident and aggressive in their power. They left behind some seminal works, though, on the use of and training in battlefield magic. The master himself adopted some of their practices. I think you will find both books quite useful in your study."

Crystal thanked the librarian and opened the Atlantean book. She stared at it for several minutes, admiring the writing, before thinking of putting the translator over it. It was beautiful script, she thought. It seemed to be written by a hand that flowed from left to right, with short horizontal lines joining the slanting vertical marks. She didn't see any rounded letters; alphabetic distinctions seemed to exist only in the height of the vertical marks and the point at which they were joined by the horizontal lines. When she asked, Erszie confirmed her conclusions. Individual letters didn't exist in Atlantean, the thrakkon explained. Syllabic sounds were indicated by combinations of between one and four vertical marks, and were differentiated mainly by the number and heights of the marks. The positioning of the horizontal connectors clarified whether the vertical lines were to be in the same symbol or separate ones as well as the proper enunciation of the syllable.

With a start, Crystal realized how much the colored lights from the glass roof had shifted. She'd been sitting there admiring the text for a long while and hadn't yet actually read the material. She flipped back from the section she was admiring that was liberally enhanced with beautifully drawn illustrations to the first page, one that looked like a table of contents. The translator, she found, was still set on "Translate Atlantean to English" mode—maybe it stayed there till it was reset by another command?—and it confirmed her assumption about the page with which she was presented. The simple table of contents referred to a few chapters on the harnessing of basic elemental flows, and then a chapter each on the fundamentals of healing magic, war magic, utility magic—she flipped to it, curious, to find that utility magic referred to such mundane tasks as shoring up a building's foundation and providing a purified source of flowing water—and then something that was simply called "ka."

She tried skipping immediately to the chapter on ka, but she couldn't understand much beyond the fact that ka seemed to be the fundamental force underlying all of the elements. It was alternatively referred to as both a force of great creation and a force of great destruction. The one thing the author seemed to be able to clearly enunciate was that this force was beyond normal mortals' reach. Don't even try, the confusing chapter seemed to be telling its poor readers, to touch the province of the gods, because you'll be wasting your time if you do so.

Disappointed, she turned back to the first chapter and started reading through the window of the translator. It was a well-written book in the beginning, she thought, but beyond the first few pages it lapsed into presenting more of a workbook approach to magic. It seemed the author's desire to present each concept as briefly and generally as possible, and then lead the readers through practical exercises that illustrated the concepts. *Must have been presenting mostly to kinesthetic learners*, she thought to herself, thinking back to the classes she'd taken on educational theory. Of the three types of learners, kinesthetic relied most heavily on practice and practical examples. She wasn't a kinesthetic learner, she knew, and on top of that, Matt's prohibition against practice outside of his precious sorcerer's chamber kept this book from being useful to her. She set it aside with a frown.

It was a good time for a break, she thought. Maybe Thera-puppy would help her by taking her mind off of the argument with Matt while she was helping some of the other residents. She went and got Yuki and started looking for others to be with.

An Assault on Mars's Estate

Over the next several days Therapuppy and her human friend Crystal were extremely busy. Frustrated over her inability to progress toward her dream of learning to use magic, Crystal spent nearly every spare minute visiting with people and discussing the nature of their losses. Yuki somehow always knew the right thing to do, whether it was a playful outburst of energy or a tender moment of cuddling. At night, then, Crystal shared the stories she had experienced with Matt and was glad to see that he responded with feeling, the core of the warm loving man she had known apparently still in him. They were both pleased at how effectively Crystal and Yuki were able to console so many people.

In the sorcerer's chamber the efforts weren't nearly as successful. Some of Crystal's friends were nearly always there, even in the dim hours after midnight, but others had joined the first three in becoming frustrated and leaving. Birch progressed rapidly, making his rock levitate for a full second several times. Phoenix achieved the same, while Krista, bereft of success at moving the rock, still exerted a single-minded focus on the task. She even brought RJ with her when he wasn't working, having him sit and watch, offering his support as she practiced with the rock over and over.

Phoenix, Birch, Krista, and RJ were in the stone room after lunch when Crystal walked in by herself. Looking up from his rock, Birch greeted her. "How's life, being married to a god and all?"

"Fine," Crystal said, her voice icy as she walked toward the desk. She reached into the drawer and pulled a rock out of the sack, and then sat down and stared at the rock in her open palm for several long moments.

"Mars tell you to come check on the peons?" Phoenix asked. Crystal winced, though she knew that the biting tone was most likely just Phoenix's misplaced attempt at humor.

"No. I'm here because I want to figure out how to throw rocks around with magic."

Krista smiled. "Must be frustrating sometimes, being married to, yet stuck in the shadow of, a god."

Crystal's only response was a shrug. Eyebrows furrowed, she stared at the stone intensely. She could see the clear yellow magical energy surrounding the rock; the trick was grabbing hold of it. Crystal had touched the flows, fluffing them up some, before, but bundling them into a physical force great enough to lift the rock was a task of an entirely different level. Crystal remembered, though, a class she had taken once on meditation, and so she calmed her breathing and her mind as they had taught her. She reached out to the energy in her now-calm state. Suddenly the rock leaped out of her hand and flew across the room, clattering as it hit the opposite wall and fell to the floor. Krista jumped, and Birch yelped softly.

A smug smile on her face, Crystal stood and slowly walked over to her rock. She picked it up, held in for a moment in her palm, and once again threw it across the room using only a flow of elemental force. This time it hit the opposite wall even harder than before, bouncing back toward the center of the room and coming to rest inside the inner circle engraved on the floor.

Crystal beamed her smile around the room. "How—how did you—how did you do that?" Krista stuttered as Crystal walked into the center of the room and picked her rock up again.

"It seemed easy, actually, once I relaxed," Crystal replied. "Can't you see the air energy around the rock?"

"The slight shimmering? Yes. But I can't get it to do anything," Krista said.

Their discussion was suddenly cut off as a loud alarm sounded. The door flew open and Sorscha glided into the room moments later. "Birch, Phoenix, the master has need of you now in the main courtyard," she said, and then turned abruptly and walked out. Birch and Phoenix followed closely, with Krista, RJ, and Crystal on their heels.

The hall curved upward then ended at ground level, a door leading to a courtyard and another into the main halls. Walking into the courtyard, the group saw Matt in the center surrounded by at least two dozen thrakkoni. Matt looked at the mage trainees and said, "Oh, good, you're here," and waved his hand, turning off the klaxons. "We're under attack. Time for you to be battle mages."

Birch had time to sputter, "Attack? What? Who?...." before he and the rest of the humans, who by then had been joined by RJ and several others, all gasped as they watched the thrakkoni shrug their tunics and pants to the ground and begin transforming. The first to do so was a blonde male toward the front of what Crystal recognized as a sort of formation. The thrakkon bent over to touch the ground with his hands, except that by the time his hands hit the ground they were claws. His entire body expanded while his arms and neck grew in length. Within a second what had been his back was towering twelve feet above the ground and his six-foot-long neck supported a scaly serpent-shaped head. A newly formed tail swished ten feet behind him, and the gathered humans shielded their eyes slightly to protect them from the reflections from thousands of new gold scales. Bellowing a triumphant battle cry, the dragon charged into the air on huge gold wings and circled while the other thrakkoni in the courtyard transformed in turns.

"Ohmygod ohmygod ohmygod," Phoenix said, shrinking away from the dragons. "Are we supposed to transform somehow too?"

Matt turned to her, an enraptured expression lighting his face up. "No, of course not," he said with a chuckle. All the thrakkoni except Sorscha and two others had transformed, and these three looked at Matt, Birch, and Phoenix. Matt said, "You are to ride these two," he pointed to the other two thrakkoni, "into battle."

With that introduction, the other two thrakkoni transformed. Crystal noticed that the thrakkoni always transformed into dragons covered in scales the same color as their hair. Blondes transformed into gold dragons, and the two redhead thrakkoni transformed into crimson dragons. "Pretty," she said, and walked quickly to one of the dragons in order to stroke its side.

"There will be plenty of time for that later," Matt said with a smile still warped by battle lust. "The time will come, Phoenix and Birch, when you will ride into battle casting massive balls of flame. For now—well, just don't fall off." One at a time, he grabbed the two humans and leaped onto one dragon's back and then the other depositing the new riders. "You'll find that their scales shift to form saddles, sort of, and if you reach down to the bases of their necks there are strips of sinew to hold onto."

Phoenix reached right for the dragon's neck, quickly finding a hold. Her red dragon assaulted the air with ferocity as she shrieked in terror. Her scream seemed to strike fear into Birch, who sat and looked at the dragon's neck.

"Grab hold, Birch. It's really rather fun," Matt ordered. Birch complied and then yelped as his dragon, too, took to the sky.

Matt turned to Sorscha. "It's time," he said, excitement floating on his words. She nodded and walked several meters away from Crystal. Dropping her own clothing, she transformed into a massive silver-scaled dragon, the largest in the company. Matt turned and winked at Crystal, then lightly vaulted the twenty feet onto the dragon's back. Sorscha, at the same time, turned her massive newly-serpentine head to Crystal, blinked both eyes in apparent salute, and took to the air with a grace belying her bulk.

Crystal watched with the rest of the humans as the huge silver spot that Sorscha had become beat its wings, powering itself away from them and toward the rest of the dots in the air above. As a mass, the dots wheeled and headed toward a separate group of dots that had appeared in the sky. Crystal wondered why, if the other group was attacking, they didn't approach any of the defenseless people or structures on the ground, and then that pondering slipped away as battle was joined and the two sets of dots charged toward each other in the skies above.

The battle itself reminded Crystal of the lightning storms she had watched growing up in her visits to relatives in the South. First she would see a sizzling bolt of energy, though they were too far away to see what type, and seconds later she would hear the peal of thunder that resulted from the air being split. The energy would strike against an invisible shield of some type, and then another bolt of energy would erupt from the opposite side. The energy bolts seemed to be coming from two dots in the air, while the other dots that were dragons from each side joined together and grappled in the sky.

Crystal watched the far-away battle, nearly missing the soft popping noise behind her. She sighed, though, when she heard Aphrodite's voice in her ear. "I sense your magical powers, little human," the goddess's silky voice taunted. "No doubt your lover-boy can too. Be careful. He doesn't like his women to have powers. Get too strong, and you'll end up like me, popping in and out and wishing he were still around."

"I don't think I could ever end up like you," Crystal replied out of the corner of her mouth, unwilling to take her eyes off the battle scene unfolding above.

Aphrodite let out a deep, throaty chuckle. "We'll see, joven," somehow choosing one of the few Spanish words Crystal understood before disappearing with a pop.

In less than a minute, the battle was over. Crystal saw lightning hit one of the dots, heard a human scream, and then saw the dot fall toward the earth spinning. Halfway down the dot separated, the larger part flying back toward a now-retreating formation, and the smaller part continuing to plummet unevenly toward the earth. The remaining dots flew back toward the manor, slowly resolving themselves into the dragons, Sorscha and Matt, and finally Phoenix and Birch and their dragons.

As the legion landed, each wave of dragons nimbly set their weight upon the earth with their claws and transformed back to thrakkoni quickly. Shaped again in their human forms, they grabbed and pulled on their clothes quickly while running toward the side of the courtyard, making room for other landing drakes. The last four riderless drakes transformed and waited for Birch and Phoenix's mounts to land, and then helped the pair to the ground gracefully as their crimson drakes transformed as well. They pulled the humans out of the way as Sorscha's immense wingspan covered the entire courtyard, bringing her airspeed down so that she landed softly. The silver dragon transformed back, quickly pulling her own clothing up and over her lithe form.

Mars, who had leaped to Crystal's side as Sorscha landed, beamed with joy and excitement. "Great job! Great job, all! Though Helepatus is a lesser god, he was the first to challenge the god of war, and we have soundly defeated him. We shall feast tonight to celebrate our victory!"

The thrakkoni cheered. Birch looked less amused, but he waited till Matt turned to pluck at his sleeve. "Um—Matt? Mars? How did we win that one?"

Matt motioned for the humans to follow him back into the

hall leading to the sorcerer's chamber, and they did, with Sorscha trailing. "Helepatus suffered the first loss, so he left the field. Why do you ask?" he responded, continuing walking toward the chamber.

"Well, it seems like the battle was just him and you shooting bolts at each other. We just kinda watched until a human died. Is that all?" Birch said.

Matt smiled at Birch. "Yes, that is correct," he said, continuing down the hall.

"Are we just the pawns?" Birch asked, stubbornly standing in the hallway now, arms crossed defiantly.

Matt turned and looked at Birch. "Well, yeah, I guess so, if you want to say it that way." Matt seemed to reconsider briefly, and then moved back up the hall toward Birch. "Lookit. There were two gods there, and we're immortal, right? We can't die." Matt shrugged. "And the thrakkoni cannot be affected by magic, and they hold their own species' lives to be sacred, so unless one of us gods is threatened they won't kill each other. So the only possible outcome to the battles, really, is the death of a mage. That's why I shielded you two fully, and why all the attacks seeming to come from you were directed at Helepatus's magi. Once one dies, the battle is over."

Birch wasn't mollified. "So you're saying that the death of a human is the deciding point in a battle."

Matt seemed to be getting frustrated with the conversation as he said, "Yes, I am."

Birch folded his arms and said, "I'm not sure I like participating in a battle where I'm the chief target yet I'm not able to deal damage."

Matt shrugged. "Well, I have two answers for you. First, it's a good thing that you're a mage to the God of War, since no other god can protect his magi as well as I can, and my status as third in the hierarchy, behind only Yahweh and Gaia, make attacks against me rare. Second, you really ought to start learning faster so that you *can* deal damage."

Matt turned and continued walking down the hall. Birch seemed to consider the comments briefly and then ran after the group. Phoenix stopped and asked, "Wait—are you telling us that Helepatus sacrificed a mage, knowing you were the more powerful god?"

Matt stopped again and looked back, this time directing his gaze at Phoenix. "Your understanding of strategy makes up for your lack of ability with magic, Phoenix, at least for now" he said, earning a glare from her. "Yes," he said, "Helepatus knew what he was sacrificing, but probably wanted to see if I was building up strength as I always have. Mages right now are—forgive the use of a clichéd phrase, but you're a dime a dozen. None of you really has any significant power yet, so none of you is particularly valuable yet. In chess terms, you don't quite rank pawns. It shouldn't surprise anyone that a god of the third tier should attack a god of the first in order to gain a little information."

With that, Matt spun around and continued toward the chamber. Crystal stamped after him, wondering what the tiers he referred to really meant. At the same time, she kept stewing over the most recent encounter with Aphrodite.

Discipline in the Ranks

The group filed back into the sorcerer's chamber. Matt motioned for all to stand in the middle of the room, and then walked up to Crystal. Smiling, he held his hand out to her, looking down at her hand that she now realized was still clenched around the river rock. She palmed the rock into his hand with a blush. Still smiling, he clenched his fist and crushed the rock as though it were made of sand, letting the tiny fragments fall through his fingers.

Crystal's face clenched in anger as she realized the meaning behind Matt's gesture. Aphrodite had been right. He did know what she had done, and he didn't like it. Unable to bring voice to the words she wanted to say, she spun on her heels and walked out, slamming the door behind her.

Krista watched Crystal storm out, and then turned on Matt. "What did you do that for?" she asked. "She was good, better than any of us might have gotten in a long time."

Matt shrugged, still smiling. "It's none of your concern. We need to continue your lessons."

RJ rose, angry over Matt's tone. "Don't talk to my wife that way. We just saw you kill someone up in the sky, using your vaunted battle mages as mere pawns, and then you said the mages should learn faster, and then you play all smug and coy when you stop your wife from helping. It's disgusting and arrogant, man. Who the hell do you think you are?" During the diatribe, RJ had approached Matt, entering the inner circle and punctuating the last question by crossing his arms.

Still smiling, Matt replied in a calm, smooth voice, "You should keep in mind that I'm the god, and you're not. It's none of your concern either. My reasons and motivations are not up for public debate."

RJ kept going, hitting one open palm with the other fist for emphasis, ignoring Krista's pleas to be quiet. "Well, why not? This affects us all, doesn't it? This isn't your own selfish little time. Those were our friends up there pretending to cast fireballs to protect you and this estate of yours. The least you could do is give them ammunition, not piss off the one who can use the magic the best. You're being stupid, man. Stupid and arrogant."

Matt's smile disappeared, morphing into an angry expression. Eyebrow quirked in irritation, he looked RJ up and down silently, and then snorted. The magi standing to the side couldn't see exactly what happened, but they sensed as the elemental energy moved from Matt to RJ despite a complete lack of motion or sound on Matt's part.

RJ toppled, motionless, features already going pale. Silence gripped the room's inhabitants as his body just stopped living in front of them. Matt towered over RJ, arms crossed.

Krista rushed to RJ's corpse. "RJ! RJ!" Futilely she beat on RJ with her fists, trying to revive her husband. She felt his throat for a pulse. Letting out a loud cry of anguish, she rose and charged at Matt, pounding her fists on his chest by way of punctuating her cries. "You monster! You killed him! What kind of god are you to kill a helpless man?"

The humans gasped as Matt's body suddenly changed. Instead of a six-foot tall man wearing a plain tunic and pants, the god in the center of the room became nearly ten feet tall, his clothes changing to Greek armor with a bronze sword that flamed as he brandished it over his head. Judging by her expression of terror, Krista realized what she had done and that she was likely to die next. "Go ahead! Kill me too. I don't care anymore. Just—if you kill me, too, take care of my children. Please?" she said, her voice suddenly quiet and her expression defeated.

Sobs wracked her chest as she continued to speak unintelligibly, her head bowed over and face pressed into her husband's lifeless body.

Mars lowered the sword and the flame flickered out. "I'm not going to kill you. You're a mage in training, good one or not," he said, changing back into himself. "But the fact remains that you're a human, and I'm a god. You're in my estate. I will try to play nice with all of you out of courtesy, but you will not approach me or speak with me disrespectfully. Got it? Not now, not ever. Women have been killed just for walking close to my temples at the wrong time of the month. Were you a citizen in the streets of Egypt or Rome or Hermonthis, I wouldn't have given you the second to apologize. Your body would already be dead on the floor."

Krista looked up and nodded, and then looked back down on RJ's lifeless corpse and continued weeping.

"Oh, get up, both of you," Matt said, irritation in his voice. As Krista's face shot up she mouthed the word *both*. RJ's chest moved. Matt continued in a biting tone, "I didn't actually kill him, though I did come close. Take note of this, my magi," he stopped briefly to help RJ back to his feet, the man still looking pale and shaken but otherwise functional. "There are many ways to kill a human. With a sword is the easiest. Of course, most magical ways to kill a human are also far outside the powers you may at some point hope to acquire. That said, you all know where a human's heart is, right? A small flicker of air at the right spot will stop it cold. The human heart is to the body what the main circuit breaker used to be to buildings. Flip the switch off, the body goes into dying mode and the person will die pretty rapidly after that. Flip it back on, as I just did, and if it hasn't been too long the person will recover with just a pretty severe headache to show for it. I'm not going to teach you how to do this yet, but I eventually will, and keep it in mind because it's a far,

far easier way to kill a foe than trying to wield some sort of magical burnburn at them." He demonstrated the meaning of *burnburn* by waving his hands and wiggling his fingers randomly in front of him with a comical parody of concentration on his face.

As Krista helped RJ onto a bench to rest, Matt continued in a more serious tone, "Of course, that's assuming you want to kill them. I don't think any of you would normally want to cause pain without death, but sometimes there's a call for it. For that, it's best to melt their faces. A little earth mixed with a little water to make it stick, and then mixed with a lot of elemental fire, applied evenly over a person's face, melts it quite satisfactorily. Need me to demonstrate?" His biting tone on the last sentence made it clear that he was perfectly willing to if needed.

All shook their heads, horrified expressions on their faces. Matt looked around, his face softening. "Oh, come now. Don't tell me it occurred to none of you that the God of War might have a little bit of a violent streak."

Birch stepped forward, wringing his hands together. "Matt," he said, a tremor audible in his voice, "you know I've always looked up to you as a friend. But I think I speak for everyone that we're feeling a little bit used, and scared too." Birch looked around at the group, the expression on his face begging for backup.

"I think what Birch is trying timidly to say, Oh Mister Great and Powerful God, is that right now we're given to thinking that you're an asshole," Phoenix said. "Go ahead, kill me too if you must," she said as Matt cocked an eyebrow and crossed his arms. "Kill us all; why would you care? We're just pawns to bow and scrape and then play target to fireballs in your games, right?"

"How many times have you bowed and scraped to me since we arrived?" Matt asked, his voice soft but cutting.

"Well, none, but...."

"Right," Matt cut her off. "And you've been fed well, yes?

And are any of your quarters uncomfortable or insufficient to your needs?"

"Look, we appreciate the hospitality, Matt, but...." Phoenix started, only to be cut off again.

"Hospitality? The Apocalypse just occurred. The date that nearly all the major religions on the planet feared came to pass. I could have easily teleported back to my estate and left you all to die. Why do you think I shielded you from that?"

A few of the mages in training shuffled their feet in the silence that ensued. Matt let it hang for a long moment and finally continued in a softer voice, "Look, folks, I like humans. I like having you around. I brought you here because I want to share this space, this life, with you. I have to be hard on you, though. First of all, I have to establish with all of you what my being a god means. Second, and more importantly, some day in the reasonably near future the magnificent changes that have occurred as a result of the cataclysm will come to fruition, and there will be a great big and largely empty world out there for you to repopulate. You're welcome to stay here, of course, but it's not in your nature to do so. At that point, you'll find that your own power is your most vital quality. The practicing in this dark room, the aerial jousting, all of it is designed to improve your power."

Matt smiled at each of the mages in training before continuing, "Besides, I'm certainly not holding you against your will. You can each quit at any time you like, with no hard feelings. I've chosen each one of you specifically because I think a grand future awaits you, but I'm not forcing you to accept your destiny."

Matt let the last word reverberate around the room and then held up his hands, producing a fireball that he turned and threw across the room at an empty space on the wall. After it hit and exploded against the stone, he returned to a lecturing voice and said, "Now, fireballs are the most commonly used offensive weapon of mages. Some will consider you unsophisticated for using them, while at the same time they really are the easiest strike to deflect, but they're simple to cast and don't require much effort. Thus, we will learn them first."

Looking around to be clear that his pupils were watching him attentively, Mars then held up his hands again and a fireball blossomed. Holding it, massaging it as though it were a thin-walled balloon he was trying to keep afloat, the god continued his lecture. "The fire is the easy part, really. The element of fire, the red energy, already exists all around you, and all you have to do is concentrate it into a little ball here. See it? Of course not. That's because fire by itself rapidly dissipates. Keeping a fireball as a fire*ball*—now, that's the tough part. It takes just the right application of air all around it, gently pushing the fire back into shape when it starts to bulge out, but not pushing too hard. Ever made one of those great big bubbles out of soap and water? It's kind of the same trick. Be very, very gentle with the air flow surrounding the fire, else you'll squish your bubble."

Matt tossed the fireball at the opposite side of the room again and then continued, now meeting his students' eyes with an excited gleam, "Once you get the fireball to remain a fireball, you need to consider getting it to wherever you want it to go. That takes air again, and it's just as tricky as holding it. You have to apply air to push the ball toward the target, but carefully. Push it too hard, and the fireball dissipates. Don't push it hard enough, and it doesn't go anywhere. And you have to stay focused, since the ball of fire can easily fall apart at any point on its path. Keep it surrounded in its cushion of air right up to the target. Like this, see?" He summoned another ball of flame and threw it high, making the fireball turn at the last moment and do a lap around the room over their heads.

Letting the ball of flame dissipate, Matt continued, "At the target is the trickiest spot of all. If you just get the fireball there and keep it enclosed in air, you've provided a nice heating source for your victim. Not very scary, is that? If you get it there and let it go, it just dissipates into the wind, which causes your target to laugh at you. Which then causes you to get angry and toss more useless fireballs. It denigrates quickly into a silly little cycle after that, see. So the trick to making your fireball explode satisfactorily is more air. Oxygen, really, but air is the trick. At the last split second, open your protective cushion of air holding the fireball together, but only in one small spot. Smack it with a column of air, and watch it explode. Like this." With that, the god raised a large ball of flame between his hands, threw it against the wall, and laughed as it exploded into a bright, hot, and loud inferno.

"I think you melted my face," Birch said, wiping his beard ends that really did look to be singed.

Matt nodded once, and then turned on his heels and left abruptly, calling over his shoulder that he expected them to be working on both rock raising and fireball tossing.

Matt marched to his chambers and went straight to his room, where he was met by his wife, her red hair snapping around her face as she glared at him.

"Hello, my love," he greeted her. She continued to glare at him.

The silence continued for several minutes, both halves of the pair staring at each other across the room. Finally Crystal appeared to give up on winning the silence battle, demanding in a cutting voice, "Tell me about you and Aphrodite."

Matt's surprise showed on his face. "Okay," he said, surprise turning to a gentle smile as he moved to one of the chairs. "It's a long story, though, so I'm going to sit down. You should consider doing that also," he added, pointing to the other chair in the room. The chairs didn't face each other directly, each instead facing toward the bed with a coffee table between them. Crystal spun her chair around to face him and then sat down without breaking her glare.

"Right," he said. "Aphrodite. She wasn't always called that, of course. There was a time when she called herself my wife, and stood beside me with every bit of love and loyalty as you have through the years. It's true, in fact, what Birch said about the Greek and Roman legends involving the two of us being consorts. We were, though not in that cycle. Still, story writers love a good romance, and this made for a divine one, in more ways than one. I loved her, and I thought she loved me. But it all changed. She got into magic. Got *really* good at magic, in fact, rising to where she was nearly as powerful as me. I thought, at the time, that it was wonderful, that the two of us could stand as equals in the future that I built for us in my mind. She apparently thought otherwise. As soon as she could, she dumped me. Said I no longer excited her now that she was my equal. Went and made herself her own thrakkoni, and her own estate, and collected some human toys."

"So that's it? You just make thrakkoni?" Crystal interjected, curious over the implications.

"Well, yes," Matt replied. "The gods, as a whole, came up with both humans and thrakkoni. The thrakkoni specifically are manufactured to be our servants. You didn't know? They have to be made. They have no reproductive system."

Crystal mulled over this new revelation, quietly pondering its implication with her relationship with Sorscha. "Wow. No, I didn't check up her skirt when I walked in, if that's what you mean," she joked, realizing that Matt had succeeded in his clever ploy to defuse her anger.

"So," she said, "when did all this happen?"

Matt shrugged and answered softly, "I really can't tell you. I lose track. Many cycles ago, I know that. Millions of years ago, I guess. Like I said, it started much like this. She was my wife at the beginning of a magic cycle. My human wife. Don't take this wrong, but she was very much like you. Super intelligent, great sense of humor, absolutely gorgeous—the physical and mental traits I've come to love in you I also saw in her. She didn't want kids, though, because she thought it would make her ugly, despite the fact that human medical science in that cycle was more advanced than what we had at the end of the last one. I guess I should have seen something from that." Matt paused to shrug again. "I don't know. I've never claimed to have all the answers. I just saw what magic and the quest after the power it brings did to her, and to our relationship, and...." his voice trailed off momentarily. "I know this sounds silly coming from a Greek god, but I'm afraid. I love you, and I don't want magic to come between us."

Crystal rose from her chair and sauntered over to her husband, sitting down in his lap with an arm around him. She kissed his ear, then bit it gently for good measure, and said, "I'll never leave you, Matt. You're my love, and my life, and the father of the two most beautiful girls I've ever imagined. I absolutely can't even consider what life would be like without you."

The couple snuggled for several long minutes, happily embraced in the armchair. Finally Matt picked Crystal up and carried her over to the bed. As he laid her down, she whispered in his ear, "So can I start learning magic tomorrow?" and turned an impish grin at him.

Chuckling, Matt tweaked her nose. "Well, we'll see. But if you do, no more being good at it, right?"

Crystal nodded her assent, still grinning as Matt first removed her clothes, and then his own.

Atlantis

Crystal's eyes opened to another beautiful day. As she raised her head, the warm lump of Chihuahua at her feet realized she was awake and scrambled up to perch on her bosom to begin her daily task of cleaning the sleep out of Crystal's face. As always, Crystal tried to get irritated but was too charmed to do so, so she just chuckled. "Stop it!" she said, pushing Yuki away. Yuki obeyed the order with her normal pained expression that spoke wordlessly of betrayal, unrequited love, and the general stupidity of the human race.

Hearing a laugh that she recognized, Crystal peered past the sad Chihuahua to see her husband sitting in an armchair, looking out the tall bay windows at the estate. He turned his head toward her with a broad smile. "Good morning, love!" he said, happiness evident in his voice. "Such a beautiful day, and we're going to make good use of it. The cataclysm is now over, and the atmosphere has returned to normal. Let's take a trip."

Emotions still aglow over the post-argument lovemaking from the night before, Crystal clapped her hands in excitement. "Yay! A trip! To where?"

Matt walked over to the bed, smiling as he bent down to kiss his wife. "It's a surprise," he said, winking at her. "You'll likely be the first human in this age to see it."

"Any chance we can go back by our old neighborhood?" Crystal asked. She wasn't sure she wanted to, but she was very curious to see how the house had fared. Her biggest fear, she knew, was that it had been vandalized, and that the stuff she had previously counted valuable had fallen prey to the huge roving gangs of marauders that she imagined were ranging the post-apocalyptic streets in their home town of Half Moon Bay. It was kind of ridiculous as a fear, of course. Her town was hard to get to on foot from the greater San Francisco metropolis, and she couldn't imagine any locals forming roving gangs of anything.

"We can go back there," Matt said, "but I'd rather leave that for later and just go have fun today. Is that all right?"

"Sure," Crystal said, leaping out of bed over her startled puppy. "Are we bringing the girls, or leaving them here with Sorscha?"

"Actually, Sorscha is going to be our transportation. She always is when I need or want to travel a distance. We can leave the girls here with someone else. Or just let them enjoy the day here. I think they're old enough to not get in much trouble, and as you've already noticed, there are no teenage boys around to help prove me wrong."

Crystal nodded and then asked, "So what do I wear? Should I dress up like a noblewoman, or put on simple traveling clothes?"

"Traveling clothes, I'd say," Matt answered. "Not sure if the people there will know me by face immediately, but we didn't exactly part on great terms last cycle, and there's no point asking for their attention now."

Crystal cocked an eyebrow and asked, "Are we going somewhere dangerous?"

"Not really. I've flattened the whole place once, and I can do it again. I'd just rather spend the day shopping than flattening, if you know what I mean."

"But what do we spend? Wherever it is, I kinda doubt they take Visa anymore."

Matt's smile broadened as he replied, "I got it covered. You just get dressed and then plan on enjoying the trip."

Crystal disappeared into the cavernous closet, coming back out several minutes later dressed in a simple green linen tunic, exquisitely embroidered along the hems in gold thread with a leaf pattern, and brown leather pants. Heidi, who had entered the now-open doorway to the sitting room, walked up to her mother as Matt continued speaking with Sorscha just outside. "Mom," Heidi said, "Can't we go with you?"

Hugging her daughter, Crystal shook her head and replied, "No, dear. Dad and I are going on a date trip, and you know how those are, with all the hugging and kissing and stuff."

"That doesn't gross me out anymore, Mom. I'm thirteen, not six."

"That's good. Someday I hope you have a man to do all that hugging and kissing with whom you love as much as I love your father, and it won't gross you out then, either. But for today, your father and I are going alone. It's a special trip. You two can find stuff to do, okay?"

Matt came up and put his hand lovingly on Heidi's head. "Sorscha will have one of the thrakkoni watch after you and make sure you don't get too bored. Why don't you ride your horses, or go to the library?"

Heidi's pout disappeared when Matt mentioned the horses, and she grinned and walked back to her room.

Matt took his wife's hand and led her and Sorscha from the room and down a hallway to the main courtyard. A few humans were out in the courtyard, and Matt cautioned them to move away from the middle as Sorscha disrobed and transformed into her argent-scaled dragon shape. Smiling, Matt put his arms around Crystal's waist from behind and leaped up onto the dragon's back, still holding her in front of him as he reached for the sinew she had heard him describe to the riders yesterday. "Let's go," he called out loud, and Sorscha's massive wings expanded upward and then came down as her powerful body left the ground behind.

Crystal peered over the side at the receding valley, marveling at its beauty. Sorscha seemed to sense Crystal's admiration as she wheeled around the massive estate once and then twice, gaining altitude with each pass. Soon Crystal could see that the mountain range in which the estate sat was what kept humans out of the estate, as un-scalable peaks rose and fell for hundreds of miles in each direction. "How many estates like this are there?" she wondered aloud, sure that Matt wouldn't hear over the gusting wind whipping by them as the dragon accelerated in her climb.

Many, her husband replied directly to her mind, causing her to jump a little. *Sorry for the surprise, but I can hear very well, and I can speak to you telepathically, so all you have to do is barely mouth the words and we can still talk.*

Like this? Crystal said through her mind, having observed Matt's telepathic communication enough to figure out the combination of strange elemental powers—yellow, orange, and green—that her husband was using and thus attempt to control them herself.

Um—well, yes. Just like that, Matt responded telepathically. *You are even more gifted than I gave you credit for, and I had already put a lot of credit into the 'Crystal is gifted' column. Telepathy isn't something I teach to novices, or even most experts. I'm very, very, impressed that you figured it out on your own. But anyway, as I was saying, there are many enclaves like this around the world. Some are as large as mine, and some aren't. We'll likely visit some of the other gods sometime soon, and I'll have to take you to one of my other, smaller, retreats sometime also.*

Sorscha turned her massive head back toward the couple, and after a moment Matt said, *Time to teleport. It would take us all day to fly there without teleporting. You're stronger in magic than you were before, plus you've already been through a teleport once, plus it will feel much smoother with me just teleporting you than it did me teleporting hundreds. So don't worry, but do hold on tight. It wouldn't do to teleport you just to have you fall off and take a swim in the ocean.*

She nodded, trying to come up with a snarky reply. She lost interest in replying when the world blinked. She still felt a little queasy, she noticed, but the sensation wasn't nearly as gut-wrenching as it had been several days ago. *You're right,* she thought, *that was easier than before. I don't feel like vomiting on you this time. Hey...,* she added, an implication of something he'd said just catching up to her, *what do you mean about teleporting me? How did Sorscha get here?*

Dragons are just as immune to elemental flow manipulation as thrakkoni are. I mean, they're not immune to the effects. Put up a wall of solid air, for instance, and the dragon would be stopped. But they can't be touched by the actual flows. I can teleport a house, a mountain, a large group of people, or the love of my life, but I can't teleport a dragon.

Yet clearly she's here with us, Crystal said. *That must mean dragons can teleport themselves.*

Exactly! We anticipated this problem, and to be honest, we also wanted the thrakkoni to be able to teleport to meet our needs faster, so we built into them a different means of them teleporting. It's the one magical ability they have. Well, that, and a different method of telepathy, which is how she and I often communicate as well as how she manages to run the estate so well.

I don't get it, Crystal said.

Well, it's complicated, Matt said. *I'm not sure if you saw the flows I pulled together to teleport, and if you did, please don't try it yourself yet. But dragons teleport by a mass acceleration exchange. The particles that make up a dragon literally lose all their mass, and they're able to reach any distance in the universe instantaneously at an infinite velocity. Same effect, really, as our magical teleporting, and after many centuries together Sorscha and I pull it off by materializing in or near the same spot. But the two are different mechanisms entirely in the magic age. In the technology age, they're actually very similar. Does that make sense?*

Pretty much. I didn't see the elemental components, so I'll just leave that stuff to you for the time being. I promise not to try teleporting myself.

Great news, that, Matt said, a touch of sarcasm behind his projected thought. "Hey!" he said aloud, "there's our destination." He pointed through the clouds at a large island rising from the sea they were flying over.

"Is that—is that Atlantis?" Crystal asked, actually speaking the words out loud in her shock. She was amazed. The island was huge, covering easily as much land as any of the major cities she had flown into. The city itself covered the whole island, buildings rising within a few hundred yards of the beach on all sides. The north quadrant of the city was obviously a palace, seated atop the highest spot and surrounded by thick walls. The south central area of the city was an enlarged open area filled with colors. As they got closer, she could make out many people moving in the streets below.

"Yes. It's a wondrous place, you'll see. Keep in mind, though, that as a human you'll be distrusted, since normal humans won't have found a way to the island yet, and they have an eons-old dislike for us western style gods. They have a strong sense of duty to visitors, though, being the folks who invented the concept of 'face', so if we smile a lot and play nice and just be tourists, nothing bad will happen."

Crystal smirked. "Anything else I should know, master?" she said aloud, imitating Sorscha's tone. Through her legs she felt the dragon's snort in response and was glad to know that Sorscha had a sense of humor as powerful as her sense of hearing.

"Well, they're not like us, but that should be obvious. For one thing, they're not humans. They're naga."

"Okay, I'll bite. What are naga?" Crystal asked, peering harder at the creatures wandering in the streets below in the hopes that her eyes would soon be close enough to make out the details.

"Naga are naga. They're bipedal like us, but a few feet taller than humans. Their bodies are cold blooded and scaly like reptiles. They have tails, which can get awfully challenging to deal with in a wrestling match. Speaking of which, they're strong, since not being warm blooded more of their body mass can be utilized for motive muscles. Many of them are innate magic users. They're also a little grumpy usually when they wake up from their 2000-year hibernations, kind of like you before you experience the joy of coffee in the morning, but most of them have probably been awake long enough to get over the grump a little."

"You're really not doing a good job convincing me that this will be a fun visit," Crystal said as Sorscha gently set down on the beach behind a hill that separated their landing from the city. "Is she coming with?" Crystal asked, happy to be able to hear again.

"No, she'll probably go hunting for some food for herself, won't you, Sorscha?" The huge dragon's head managed a grin. Her bulk lifted off the beach with a powerful beat of her wings, and she flew off again.

"What do dragons eat?" Crystal asked, and then corrected herself, "No, wait, I already know the answer to that, and I don't want to hear it."

Matt nodded. "Yeah, they're carnivores. Omnivores, actually, just like us but with bigger stomachs. Why do you think I have to keep such huge herds of livestock on hand at the estate?"

Starting to walk around the hill toward the city, Matt added, "Much bigger stomachs" and chuckled.

The Battle Chamber of Mars

Heidi and Linda stood in the main balcony of their living quarters watching their parents fly away on Sorscha's back. "I wish we could go with them," Linda said.

Heidi grinned at her sister. "Nah. C'mon, we need to explore!"

Linda turned toward her sister, an accusatory expression on her face. "Remember last time we went 'exploring.' Mom and Dad were pissed at us for weeks."

Shrugging, Heidi smiled and said, "Yeah, but they got us out of that jail no problem. And there are no jails here, right? C'mon!"

"Wait," Linda said.

"Wait for what? Come on!"

"No, wait a minute. Did you hear that?"

Both girls stood silently for several moments until the sound repeated itself. Recognizing the soft mewling of a cat somewhere outside the suite's entry door, Heidi sprang toward the entry, motioning for Linda to follow. The twins reached the door at nearly the same time, opening it and stepping into the hall.

"There it went!" Heidi said, excitement coloring her voice as she pointed down the hall, the corner of which she had just seen the small creature dart around. "Here, kitty kitty!"

Heidi waited a few seconds to see if the cat would come to her call. When it didn't, she started to dart down the hall after it. Linda stopped her by grabbing the back of her collar. "We're supposed to have a thrakkoni guide to watch us, Dad said. We can't just run off like that!" Linda said.

"Oh, come on," Heidi said, wiggling her shirt free from Linda's grasp. "We don't *need* a guide to go after a lost kitty, Linda. The poor thing is probably starving, and you're keeping us from helping it. It's just a cat, anyway, and it's inside the estate house. How dangerous can it be?" She slipped down the hall stealthily, trying to be as quiet as possible so as to not frighten the cat any further.

She peeked around the corner as Linda caught up, the other twin also getting into the game of moving stealthily. "See anything?" Linda whispered.

"No," Heidi said just as softly. Just then another quiet mewl sounded from the direction of the entry hall. The girls took off, balancing stealth with speed, slipping along the hall to the entry as quietly as they could. They emerged onto the second floor landing, looked down to the right, and saw the cat on the main floor to the right of the entry doors gazing up at them.

"Here, kitty k-oof" Linda called, stopping short from a lack of breath caused by Heidi's elbow in her solar plexus. "What'd you do that for?"

"You scared her! She ran down that hall as soon as you raised your voice," Heidi said.

"Yeah, well I'd run from an elbow-tossing brat too. Hey, wait for me!" Linda sped up to catch up to Heidi. The girls, stealth abandoned for the moment, sprinted down the stairs to the spot where they'd seen the black and white tuxedo cat. They continued around the corner, slipping back into their stealthy creep, heading toward the doorway out to where they had watched the thrakkoni transform to dragons for flight.

"I wonder if the dragons will eat her," Heidi fretted.

"Shhh!" Linda hissed. Heidi turned her head to glare at her sister; she did not like being shushed. The glare only lasted for a moment, though, because the cat mewled again in the distance causing Heidi's head to swivel back around and focus to the front. The twins picked up the pace ever so slightly.

When they reached the door to the courtyard, they found it closed. Knowing the cat couldn't have opened and closed the door, they continued down the curved hallway, following it below ground level. A heavy oak door, closed at the end of the hallway, came into sight just as a black and white animal streaked across in front of it and through an opening in the wall to its right.

Seeing the cat move quickly, the girls once again abandoned stealth and sprinted down the hall and around the corner through the opening they had seen the cat run into. Both skidded to a halt at the same time as they saw a closed door on the other end of a thirty-foot-long hall. The opening in the wall behind then closed with a smooth grinding of stone on stone.

"I—I'm not sure we should be here," Heidi said.

"Oh, come on. You were the one who wanted to find the kitty," Linda reminded her sister. "The cat probably ran through the other door. Dad's house is magical, right?"

"And dusty?" Heidi said, leaning down to run her finger through the thick layer of dust on the floor. "Lin, I don't see paw prints in the dust. Shouldn't we see paw prints?"

"Down there," Linda said, pointing down the hall where some prints could just barely be seen.

"Those weren't there," Heidi objected.

"Quit trying to scare me," Linda said. "This is Dad's estate. What's there to be scared of? Come on, let's find your kitty and get back." Linda tromped down the hall deliberately, raising some dust with her steps that made Heidi sneeze as she followed. She reached for the door at the end and then paused. "That was weird," she said.

"What?" Heidi said. "Can we just go now?"

"No, it's not dangerous. It just clicked," Linda said. "And I saw—something. It was a weird white smoky stuff that flowed into the door."

"What do you mean it just clicked, and you saw white smoky

stuff? I didn't see or hear anything."

Linda didn't answer. Instead, she pushed the door open with one hand, standing back a pace in preparation for whatever might leap out at them. There was nothing. The door swung open silently, revealing a single large square chamber within.

Linda walked through the doorway. The room *was* cool. Scrolls lined one wall, laying flat in hundreds of small square receptacles. On the opposite side of the square room, racks of weapons stood ready. Two concentric circles were carved into what looked to Linda like an ancient granite floor similar to what was in some of the abbeys she had seen in their tours of Europe. Hanging on the walls were tapestries depicting grand battles, the tapestry on the wall opposite the entry showing an armor-clad man and woman pair standing over a pile of dead bodies, with smaller people around kneeling. On a desk in the corner rested an open book and several jade, ebony and ivory figurines.

"Wow," Heidi said, having followed her sister into the room.

"Is that Dad?" Linda asked, pointing at the tapestry.

"I think it is," Heidi agreed, and then moved closer to observe, "And the woman next to him—that's the woman from the cottage yesterday, isn't it?"

Linda, walking toward the tapestry, looked down as she stepped on a darker spot on the granite floor, and then paused. "Is this—a blood stain?" she asked.

Heidi walked over and looked down. "I think it is. Where's that kitty? We need to find it and go; I don't feel good about this room."

A soft mewl came from behind the wooden desk in the corner. Both girls ran over, hoping to finally corner the feline, but when they reached it the corner was empty. In her haste to get around and see, Linda bumped the desk, causing one of the figurines to fall over into another one.

The room suddenly sparkled as a lizard-like warrior and a human mage appeared in front of the girls. The warrior and the mage circled each other, each one clearly getting the measure of his opponent. The twins jumped as the mage formed a ball of fire in his hands and threw it at the warrior. The warrior's quick reflexes avoided it as he leaped to his left, hissing, and then charged the mage, who yelped and threw something the twins couldn't see at the warrior's face. The warrior, apparently blinded, missed his strike with the trident and went down clutching his eyes as the mage threw another fireball at the warrior. Again the warrior leaped sideways, his stout tail giving him additional leverage to somersault to the side and take up a defensive posture while still rubbing his eyes with his free hand.

The mage gathered two handfuls of what seemed to just be air and threw them at the warrior. This ball, unlike the fireball, didn't hiss or pop on its way to the warrior, and so the target didn't know it was coming at him till it went off on his chest. The explosion shook Heidi and Linda, hurting their ears. Eyes watering from the blast, they almost didn't see the mage pull a dagger from his belt. Taking advantage of the warrior's momentary stun, the mage jumped closer and plunged the dagger through an opening in the plate mail in the warrior's armpit. The warrior roared in pain and twisted his tail violently around, slashing the feet out from under his opponent, who grunted loudly as his body crashed heavily to the granite floor. Hearing the cry, the warrior brought his trident around and down, plunging it into the mage's chest. Still standing, the warrior pulled the dagger from his side, and then both warrior and mage disappeared.

"Wow," Heidi said quietly, looking at the two figurines on the desk. "Yeah, wow," Linda agreed, nodding at her sister and looking at the figurines, carefully putting down the one she had picked up. Both girls tried to rub the pain from the mage's sonic blast out of their ears.

Suddenly the desk shook violently, heaving back and forth which caused figurines to topple into one another. The twins watched, horrified, as figure after figure popped into existence on the stone combat arena. "Did you touch it?" Linda said, fear causing her voice to rise in pitch.

"No, I didn't touch it!" Heidi said, panic evident in her voice as well.

"Who did?"

"I don't know, but let's get out of here," Heidi said. She started along the wall toward the door they had entered. It stood open mere yards away, inviting her toward its safety, but well over a dozen fully-armed and armored combat figures already stood between her and it. The number was still growing, and many of the men had already leapt into battle.

"What about the cat?" Linda said, ducking down behind the desk.

"The cat can—eeee!" Heidi squealed and jumped backwards to join her sister as a barbarian slammed into the wall right in front of her. Shaking his head to clear it, the fighting figure unfolded his nearly-seven-foot-tall frame, bellowed a challenge to his opponent, and charged back into the fray swinging his flail.

"I think we know where the blood stains on the floor came from," Heidi said to her sister.

"Well, duh. Got any good ideas, like how to get out of here without getting killed?"

A fighter in the middle of the room growled and brought his claymore around in a powerful arc. The huge sword cleaved halfway through the body of a mage who was trying feverishly to get a spell off, and the carry-through of the swing sent the failed caster's slight body flying into the desk, spraying it, the floor, and the walls with his blood. Heidi, who had been watching with rapt attention, ducked back behind the desk and looked at her sister, horrified.

"Ewww, blood—on your forehead!" Linda said, pulling her tunic sleeve out and reaching to wipe her sister's face clean. She wasn't given the opportunity, though, as the blood dwindled away and disappeared as the mage's body vanished.

Linda's frozen expression caused Heidi to wipe her own forehead. "What? What are you staring at?" she asked.

"The blood—it—it disappeared."

"Well, good. That was...." Heidi's voice trailed off as the implication dawned on her. "I wonder whose blood it is in the floor, then."

One of the combatants—neither girl could see which from their crouches—slammed into the desk, scooting it back onto them and, from the clinking sound on its surface, rattling more figurines into each other. The crash was followed immediately by a powerful fireball that exploded against the wall behind, giving the air an aroma that combined the smell of ozone with the acrid smell of some of the girls' hair melting. The din in the room became louder as more martial weapon bearers joined the melee and elemental forces were tossed around by numerous magi seemingly without any attempt toward accuracy, and Heidi shouted over it, "We've got to get out of here!"

Both girls squealed in panic as another combatant in scales fell backward and slammed into the wall beside them, closing off their escape path once again. As the twins watched the dazed fighter attempt to rise, a helmet flew over the desk, ricocheted off the wall behind, and hit Heidi's right arm. The ragged edge of metal from where it had been smashed away from its former wearer's torso opened a gash in her sleeve, and blood ran down her arm. As the helmet came to a rest under the desk, its former occupant's head rolled out, his dead eyes gazing past the girls to the wall as it slowly vanished from sight.

"Stop."

The command, issued both physically and telepathically, cut

through and instantly ended the tumultuous clamor. After a few moments of peace, the twins felt it safe enough to raise their eyes over the surface of the desk to see who the woman was who had saved them.

"You're…." Linda started, and was interrupted by her sister.

"…the woman from the cottage the other day," Heidi said. "And the one in the wall hanging here, right?"

"Guilty!" the woman said, her voice ringing like a bell. "Though I really am not sure what I'm still so guilty of. We haven't been properly introduced. Come on out from there so we can be. Don't worry. It's safe now; I banished all those fighters. You were lucky I came by when I did."

Heidi and Linda crept cautiously from behind the safety of the desk. "Who are you, then?" Linda asked, arms crossed.

"You probably already know me from your mythology classes as the goddess Aphrodite. Long ago your father and I fought alongside each other. We were allies. That tapestry was created in remembrance of one of the great battles we fought together, in fact. I'm not sure what happened, but later on he turned against me, leaving me to wander his estate. Oh, your arm is hurt," Aphrodite said, crossing the room to Heidi. The goddess waved her hand over the cut on Heidi's arm and it closed, leaving drying blood and the rip in the shirt sleeve as reminders of the injury. "There, it'll be all right now." Aphrodite looked around furtively. "I really need to be going, though. No telling what he'll do if he catches me here talking to you. He is the god of war, after all. I'm just glad you're safe. You two need to get out of here too, or he'll be pissed. Run!"

Aphrodite ran out through the door. Heidi chased her, hoping for an opportunity to talk more, but as soon as Aphrodite's body cleared the doorway she disappeared.

The sisters looked at each other, uncertainty playing across their faces. "Do you believe her?" Heidi asked.

"Not entirely, but—I'm not sure," Linda said. "Let's get out of here to where it's safe, though."

The cat forgotten, the sisters ran through the dusty hallway and back up to the family's chambers, where they brought out a chess board and began playing while quietly discussing the events of the afternoon and planning the questions that they held in store for their father.

Aftermath of a Visit

Crystal and Matt walked into the city. She was surprised at first at the city's abrupt edge, its first buildings simply rising out of the rock of the island while the road, made of cobblestone, sprang to existence between the first buildings. Considering the little bit that she knew of Atlantis, though, it made sense. A city submerged beneath the ocean for two thousand years had no need of walls or protections, and she didn't see how they would need roads connecting to anywhere else. Still, it was disconcerting to be walking on beach one moment and paved city street the next.

The Atlanteans they encountered eyed them as though expecting a fight. Crystal believed what Matt had told her about their concept of face, but they still seemed hostile. Physically they looked exactly as Matt had described, and Crystal abruptly realized that their mental conversation had held much more exactness of meaning than any normal vocal conversation could. When Matt had transmitted the mental message about the naga being taller and much denser than humans and with scales and heavy tails that dragged the ground behind, he had actually sent a vibrant picture that Crystal was now seeing played out in front of her. She was glad he had shown her what naga eyes looked like before she was confronted with them in person; the gaze from the wide-set snakelike eyes was, when met directly, every bit as immobilizing as she'd heard the gaze of a normal snake could be to its natural prey. *This telepathy thing has its advantages, I guess*, she thought to Matt after she'd redirected her gaze for the third time to avoid being frozen in place.

Hmm? Matt thought back to her, clearly paying close attention to maintaining a peaceful disposition, with shoulders relaxed and hands joined naturally in front of him, while winding their way through the city.

If you'd said that the naga are physically imposing that wouldn't have done the real facts justice, she said.

Indeed, Matt said. *They've played the role of conquering civilization many times, and I don't recall a single time when they've been conquered. In most magic cycles, the only reason there are continents that don't end up belonging to them is that they don't like to go far from the water. The good news is that they're just now awakening from their hibernation, and thus still sluggish. The few you see out on the streets are the early risers.*

Are they immune to magic, like dragons?

Nope, Matt said. *And thank goodness for that. However, because of their long life spans, their magi wake up with millennia of practice under their belt, and are thus way ahead of any human sorcerers that might happen along. There aren't many naga mages, but those who exist sure are powerful.*

Their eyes are dangerous, Crystal observed.

Only if you look into them, Matt said. *There are charms for human warriors that can disrupt their gaze, by the way.*

That's good news. What manner of magic creates the effect their gaze has?

'S'not magic. It's psychology, actually. Deep inside your psyche, there's an urge to run away from the big bad snake that's going to eat you. Higher up, there's a need to stand and fight. As the elements of your subconscious battle, you stand frozen in place.

Through the discourse Matt continued leading her at a steady pace, lending credence to his claim that he knew where he was going despite the circuitous route they were taking. As they walked, Crystal paid greater attention to the architecture, having spent hours in each city they had visited in Europe, the Middle East, and the United States on their travels wandering the streets to observe the differences. She was no trained architect, but she loved looking at the ways cultures asserted themselves in their building accents and styles.

Eclectic was the closest Crystal could come to encapsulating the Atlantean sense of architecture. On one building she saw what she thought were classical Greek-style columns, and right next to it sat a building that looked like a pagoda. Down the street a building sported a grand façade reminding her of a merchant's house she had seen in Rome. Another dwelling on the same thoroughfare might have been transported directly from London. Perplexed, she shook her head.

Matt caught her mood and chuckled out loud, causing several naga on the street to stare and look at them. Holding up his hands in peace, Matt bowed to each, smiling pleasantly, and they continued on whatever their business had been. *Love,* Matt's bemused voice tickled Crystal's noetic presence, *you're wasting your time trying to figure the Atlanteans out by their architecture. They spend two thousand years at a time beneath the ocean, and the next several weeks just cleaning sea garbage off of their homes. Then they spend the next couple thousand years ruling much or all of the world, and the true Atlanteans who live here, in the very center of their empire, during that time either copy their homes into the areas they conquer, or vice versa. This really is a meta-culture, a mélange of the best and worst worldwide.*

Crystal attempted to send a mental nod to Matt, thinking she knew how to do it and wanting to try something new. It apparently succeeded as Matt chortled once and then continued on his navigational quest.

They walked down several streets, Crystal knowing only that she was following Matt into what she thought was the center of a large and seemingly hostile city. Suddenly Matt turned to the left and knocked on a red door that marked the entrance to one of the larger homes on the street.

Matt's knock, Crystal noticed, seemed a rhythmic signal, and it was answered quickly by the door opening partway and a naga motioning them impatiently inside. Matt stepped in and yanked Crystal behind him, and then the naga shut the door just as impatiently. Crystal jumped at the sound of the door snapping shut, but as her eyes adjusted to the dimmer indoor lighting she relaxed. The naga led them up a flight of stairs to a study that was exactly as Crystal expected to see, a smoking room for gentlemen except for the seating. Instead of brown leather armchairs, this room held brown cushioned stools that Crystal supposed made more sense for a race that was blessed with thick tails. The room also contained a simple mahogany desk and walls covered with glassed-in bookcases.

"Welcome!" A naga bustled into the study and spoke to Matt. At least, that was how Matt's voice inside Crystal's head translated the greeting. The naga's language seemed to consist mainly of clicks and hisses, and Crystal was glad that her husband was capable of letting her know what was being said. He continued translating as the naga spoke, "Matthew, how great it is to see you again. Forgive the inferior lighting and our lack of refreshments, please, as we have just recently come out of our long sleep. You and your guest, though, are a sight for sore eyes!"

Crystal examined the naga with interest. What Matt had said about the architecture seemed to apply to the attire as well. The naga in the street had been dressed in various outfits that included western style pants and button-down shirts, kimonos, and even togas. It had seemed as though everyone just picked something they thought interesting for the day and went with it. This naga, at least, seemed to be more contemporarily dressed in breeches, boots, and a buttoned tunic with wide collars, all in black except for gold buckles holding the laces on his boots.

Matt grinned and motioned toward the naga, saying, "Crystal, this is Prince Dhritarashtra, brother of the king and ruler of the naga of Atlantis. Dhri, this is Crystal, my wife." She noted that Matt spoke in English, and wondered if he was in turn translating to Dhri's mind.

The naga prince bowed at the introduction. "It brings me pleasure to meet the wife of one of my favorite western gods," Matt translated the clicks and hisses as Dhri bowed with both hands together, palms touching.

Matt chuckled. "Oh, come on, old friend. One of your favorites? How about the only one you would even open your door to?"

The sides of Dhri's mouth turned up slightly, and Crystal assumed it was what passed for a naga grin. "That is true, Matthew," the naga replied. "By the way, are you still going by Mars?"

Matt held up his hands in a gesture of ambivalence. "Not really. The humans I brought back to my estate needed to hear that I was Mars to put perspective on their reality, but my beloved here knows me as Matt."

"So what is the purpose of your visit today, my old friend?" Dhri asked.

"Shopping for my lady," Matt replied. "She was impressed by some of the silk work from your craftsmen that was housed in her closet, so I figured our first stop after the cataclysm should be a visit to your cheerful city to enjoy the wit of your merchants."

"Not here to visit with my brother, then?"

Matt chuckled as he replied, "If I recall correctly, the last time he and I visited I had to prove that your tridents still won't penetrate the hide of a god. At least, not permanently. He probably still hasn't forgiven me the broken trident, or the broken wall, that resulted. No, I don't think I'll visit him this time."

As Matt spoke, he walked over to a small globe on the desk.

It was a simple black piece covered in various astrology symbols. He idly spun it, and as it rotated Crystal saw a white gauzy energy coalesce around it.

"Well," Dhri replied, "your trip is well timed, I think. The merchants are mostly still getting their wares back out for view, and are pretty sluggish as of yet. As far as I know, the king hasn't emerged from his own slumber. Odds are good that your shopping trip will be entirely without incident."

"Great news," Matt said. "I will not keep you long, then, as I know you have much work to do now that you have awakened. It was good seeing you, my eternal friend. Namaskar." With the last word, Matt placed his palms together in front of his chest and inclined his head toward Dhri. Crystal realized she had seen the gesture but not heard the word before, in the few yoga classes she had attended while trying it out.

"Namaskar, friend," Dhri responded, giving the same gesture.

Crystal repeated the gesture and word that she had seen Matt and Dhri use, and both of them looked at her with a bemused grin. Self-consciously wondering what she had done wrong, she turned and headed for the door, stopping when the same naga who had let them in stood in front of it.

Out of the corner of her eye she saw Matt and Dhri exchange a vigorous handshake, and then Matt followed her toward the door. Once both were there the naga looked carefully through the viewing hole and after a few seconds swung the door open. Matt grabbed her hand and pulled her through quickly.

Once back out in the street, Crystal followed Matt a few steps and then in a fit of impatience asked in her newly-discovered mental voice, *So what did I do wrong back there?*

Wrong? Back where? Matt asked, replying too quickly.

Don't do that, she shot back.

Sorry. It's not a big deal, really. Remember what I said about the naga at various points in time ruling the entire eastern hemisphere, including Asia and India? Dhri, in the previous cycle, ruled over much of the Ganges area in India, and so he participated in that social framework. Or he created it, one of the two. I'm not sure which, honestly. Regardless, in the culture he knew for hundreds of years before going to sleep, the women didn't take much part in social interactions. Namaskar is the formal version of Namaste, which you've heard used as a farewell, yes? It was appropriate between a human god and a naga prince, but for his culture it was a little—um, presumptuous, I guess would be the best word—for any woman to depart the prince's company using it.

As Crystal's expression turned to horror, she received a mental version of a chuckle from Matt, who said, *Like I said, don't worry. It's really not a big deal. Yes, you're a woman, but you're also the wife of a western god. Screw presumptuous—your status is high enough that you could have done pretty much anything. Your formally greeting your way out of the conversation wasn't offensive at all. It was just unusual to him.*

Relieved, Crystal thought back to the other unusual aspect of the visit. *That's the second time I've seen you using a white-colored flow of energy, Matt. What were you doing, and what kind of magic is it?*

Matt sighed out loud, causing a few naga heads to turn toward them. He smiled and nodded politely and they continued on their way, and then he replied, *You weren't supposed to see that, obviously, but what I was doing was refreshing the communication spell on the globe I gave him a long time ago.*

Communication with—you? Crystal said.

Well, yes, of course.

So the prince is your spy? Crystal asked, incredulous.

Matt grinned and said, *Nothing so cloak and dagger-ish, love. We have a mutual arrangement. He keeps me apprised of what his brother the king is up to, and in turn I spare his house when I have to flatten Atlantis.*

You're right, Crystal agreed. *It's too outright forceful to be cloak and dagger-ish.*

Matt sent her a mental image of a shrug and said, *Hey, I'm Tyr, not Loki. Besides, there's more to it. I make sure the Prince is well taken care of as only a god can. I've helped him visit other gods, for example, and once I helped him broker a truce that would have been impossible for a mortal working alone.*

Crystal had been absorbed in the task of following in Matt's footsteps to the point that she was surprised when she realized that they had entered a busy bazaar. Naga headed every direction, some at a leisurely pace and others in a hurry. As the pair slowly made their way around the outside loop, Crystal estimated that the shopping area was a hundred feet long and a couple of hundred feet wide. Booths lined the perimeter, and down the middle ran two additional rows of shops. The scene reminded Crystal of many markets she had visited around the world, except that both the market and the booths seemed larger than usual. Each booth was nearly twenty feet wide at its face, and many seemed to be set up in a short storefront with a larger curtained off area behind.

Several merchants didn't seem quite ready to open yet. Matt made telepathic comments to Crystal regarding some of the slower merchants. It seemed to Crystal that he knew this bazaar well, as often as he was able to comment. "Been here often?" Crystal asked, shifting to speaking aloud in the relative safety of the noise of the bazaar.

"Define often," Matt said. "They only come out of hibernation at the beginning of the magic cycles, once every four thousand years. I've probably been here every time they've come out thanks to the cool stuff you can find now, and that adds up to a lot of times being here, but I'm not sure any sane person would say that once every four thousand years is 'often.'"

Crystal conceded the point to Matt. "You're right," she said. "Honestly, I guess I'm just getting tired of making a loop around the place. These booths look magnificent, and I really want to shop."

Matt chuckled and said, "Well, then, it's time we did so. But before you do, there are a couple of things to keep in mind." He shifted back to telepathy and said, *First, never, ever buy an item for the first price mentioned. It's expected that you'll haggle a bit, and if you don't haggle with any one merchant, every other one will know about it before you leave the first merchant's shop.*

Crystal nodded. *Got it. Haggle for everything. You know I'm pretty good at that. What's the second thing?*

What second thing?

You said there were a couple of things to keep in mind. What's the second one?

Oh. I did, didn't I? Okay, then, have fun, Matt said.

That's not a second thing, Crystal admonished Matt.

I said it second, didn't I?

Yes, but—okay, smart aleck, you win for now. You can celebrate your winnings if you'd like by showing me to the vendor where you bought those incredible silk kimonos, Crystal said.

Hmm, Matt huffed. *Okay, let's celebrate together, then,* he said, and then picked up his pace walking down the aisle between the vendors. Crystal followed closely, thinking to herself how much she loved being able to exercise her own unique sense of humor with the man—no, the god, she reminded herself—in front of her.

Matt slowed down after a few minutes, drifting to the right toward the booths on the outside. Crystal saw that he slowed down significantly as he approached one of the several dozen tailor shops in that section of the bazaar. Curious, she mimicked his carefree saunter into the shop, looking idly left and right, unsure why he had picked this shop out of several. The walls were wooded with gauzy silk draped over them, and every spare foot of space was lined with racks containing outfits, mostly cut in the style of kimonos, made of serviceable but unremarkable cuts of silk cloth. Crystal eyed several outfits she wouldn't mind owning, but she saw nothing special about this collection.

The proprietor appeared to recognize Matt and smiled, speaking in the same serpentine tongue as Dhri. "It is good to see my favorite customer again," Matt passed the translation mentally. "You have come to buy a lovely dress for your lovely lady, yes?"

Matt shrugged in response, still looking around at the merchandise and not meeting the merchant's eyes. "Lovely lady, yes," he replied. "Lovely dress is still to be seen. You don't seem to have much decent inventory out yet."

The merchant smiled, moved closer to Matt, and said in a soft voice, "Oh, but I do, Sir. I have just the right dresses for your lady, but I wouldn't put them out here where anyone could touch them. Please, come look at my finer examples." He pulled the curtain blocking the back of the shop to the side slightly and motioned Matt and Crystal in. As he followed the pair, another naga stepped out into the shop area and took the original merchant's place.

Crystal gasped as she entered the inner chamber of the shop, seeing an amazing display of finery inside that had been absent in front. The kimonos that lined one wall caught her eye first; Crystal had always loved the look and feel when they were well made. She started to dart to the closest rack to see the kimonos up close, but stopped before her move began and looked at Matt with a quizzical expression. Was his cool look coming up to the booth for the benefit of other merchants, or this one? Had she already given away too much? To her relief, though, Matt smiled, inclined his head toward the rack, and mentally said, *Go ahead. Your enthusiasm is a compliment to our host, and I think he deserves the compliment. Don't you?*

Crystal turned back to the displayed garments, giving in to her passion for fine clothing. She breathed, "Oh, my, yes," without really caring that the merchant couldn't know the question to which she was responding. She ran her fingers delicately over the first gown she touched, noting the masterwork of tiny pearls delicately embroidered onto the finest purple silk she had ever touched. "This is—amazing," she breathed again, enamored by how smooth it felt as well as how its iridescent shimmer caught her eye.

The merchant barked a pleasant chuckle. "Why, my lady, I see your tastes are as exquisite as your beauty. The dress you are admiring was created to enhance the beauty of a high queen, but I believe it is sufficient to fit well the form of Mars' lady."

Crystal kept her hand on the dress as her head whipped around to face Matt, another quizzical look on her face. Matt laughed and said aloud in English, "Yes, my love, this is Alcor. He and I have been doing business for a long, long time. He sold me much of the silk that currently exists in your closet, in fact, and some of it is—well, rather old."

Two more naga walked in from behind the inner chamber. One of the females appeared older to Crystal than the other. Matt bowed and spoke in the clicking hissing language from before, translating mentally. "Crystal, this is Alcor's wife, Srensha, and their lovely daughter Zhan-tzing. Ladies, it is my pleasure to have you meet my wife, Crystal."

Crystal and the female naga bowed simultaneously, and then the two naga moved closer to Crystal and began examining her hair and her skin, chittering in their strange language. Crystal looked at Matt, hoping for either a translation or an explanation.

"They're talking between themselves about how beautiful

your hair and skin tone are," Matt said aloud in English. "You've got a couple of ardent admirers there, it appears. Which is a good thing, since they're the ones who will be measuring and fitting you into whatever you end up with."

Crystal nodded and smiled at the two admirers, who each smiled and nodded in response and then resumed their sinuous speech in their own language. Finally Alcor said something in the same tongue, and both of the female naga nodded and exited.

Alcor said, "My apologies, my lady. My wife and daughter do not usually behave such, but they were captivated by your beauty. They had already begun fitting your perfect figure."

Crystal blushed at the compliment in spite of her doubts regarding his sincerity in general. There being nothing to gain through challenging Alcor, though, she played along and said, "Thank you for your most gracious compliments. My husband says that your silk is the finest, and that statement is obviously true. Where do you get the silk that you use in your garments, if I may ask?"

Alcor's face glowed with pride as Matt translated. "My lady," he replied, "It is a top secret operation, and I couldn't possibly let you in on the details. I can, perhaps, give you some information, though, since your husband is one of my best clients. Are you already aware of the basic tenets of sericulture?"

Crystal nodded, having visited a silk production facility once on a trip to India. "The basics, yes. The worms create cocoons which in turn are unraveled to make silk, correct?"

Alcor smiled. "Indeed. We've found that if we keep the worms in a special cavern, and then treat the silk filaments to a soak in a pond in that cavern, a better luster of silk, of more consistent quality is produced. Please, though, my lady, do not tell anyone I have spoken of this, as it is a highly guarded secret that many would be angry over my revealing to you."

Crystal waited for Matt to finish the translation, and then

said, "Thank you, Alcor, I am honored that you've answered my curiosity. This dress, then," she pointed to the ornate purple dress that had caught her attention earlier, "is made from silk harvested from that procedure, I assume?"

"Yes, my lady. That dress seems to have caught your eye; would you like to have it fitted?"

Crystal started to reply, but she saw Matt's eyes widen as his telepathic translation trailed off, and then intense concentration claimed his facial expression as his eyes bored into the opposite wall of the shop.

Crystal looked out of reflex toward the spot where Matt was staring, but nothing was evident. Assuming Matt was communicating telepathically with someone important, Crystal maintained the silence for several minutes, looking at the gown and her hand on it while feeling self-conscious due to her inability to communicate on her own. Alcor, too, stayed silent, a tense smile on his face and his arms crossed over his burly linen-clad chest.

Finally Matt's attention snapped back to Crystal. "That was strange. We need to get back soon," Matt said in a matter-of-fact voice.

"What's wrong?" Crystal asked.

"I'm not sure. Somebody at the estate did something that wasn't supposed to have been done. The thr—the servants—can't find anything amiss. That actually bothers me more than the initial alarm."

Crystal nodded. "This is a beautiful dress, Alcor. It would brighten my closet amazingly well, I am certain. Unfortunately I do not believe this to be the time to get into fitting," she said and noted Matt's approving smile from the corner of her eye. "We must come back, though, and have it fitted later."

Alcor's smile was warm and understanding. "Of course. I will look forward to your return, and will set the gown aside for whenever that time might be." Alcor finished with a grand flourish that Crystal thought might have done service in any court in the west, and then he held the curtain aside again for the pair to leave.

Crystal found at first that she had difficulty keeping up with Matt, whose walking pace seemed faster than any running she had ever done. She managed, though, and was happy that she had puzzled out the trick behind mental communication, as she was sure her lungs wouldn't support any talk.

"Matt, why did Alcor do a western style bow with flourish while your friend, the prince, did an eastern style farewell salute?"

Matt seemed distracted as he said, "Alcor is and has been for many millennia a merchant of the first class. That means that in several cycles he's spent a significant amount of time in the west, either as a merchant and envoy or as a merchant and ruler. He is quite familiar with the western style of courtesy, and he practices it when I'm there. I assume he also uses the eastern style when it's appropriate."

Crystal considered that for a moment and then came back with, "Why are the eastern and western styles so different, and yet I get the sense that they are fairly constant through history?"

Matt continued, lecturing but distracted at the same time, "The obeisance practices of the east and west cultures have, over the years, been largely determined by two things. First, they have some history. Many humans die during each cataclysm, yet many others survive, and these humans can't help but pass along the practices they have to their offspring. That brings about the constancy you mention. On the matter of difference, practices of showing honor to your superiors really started with us gods forcing humans to do it a long, long time ago. The human rulers just copied us with their own subordinates. We western gods like bowing, scraping, and all that stuff, while the gods who began in the east have slightly different views on the role of humans in the world. It all just kind of played out as it has.”

“Oh. Well, that makes sense.”

“Yeah. By the way, you do realize that what he was telling you about a special cave with special waters was a line of bullshit, right?”

“I wasn’t sure, but it doesn’t surprise me.”

“Their secret is in how the silk is handled. They use fewer filaments per thread, and they also use slightly different colors in the warp and the weave of the loom in order to produce a more iridescent sheen. But there is no special cave under Atlantis that I know of. Anyway, let’s get back to the estate.” Their pace had led them quickly through and out of Atlantis and back to the opposite side of the hill. Sorscha was already there, lounging in her nude humanoid form on a set of rocks.

Crystal asked, “Doesn’t her butt get cold like that?”

Matt said, “Thrakkoni are cold blooded, dear. They have to be to change shape to and from the size that they do. I assume, though, that her butt will be the same temperature as the rock, and she really won’t care.”

Crystal mulled over why she had never considered how different the thrakkoni had to be in order to be able to become dragons. She looked closely at the wondrous creature as the couple approached and the thrakkon rose from her rock perch and wordlessly transformed. In the instant that Crystal and Sorscha facing each other prior to the transformation, Crystal noticed that something was missing—what was it?

Matt gripped Crystal from behind and leaped onto Sorscha’s towering back as she suddenly realized what had been missing. “Nipples,” she passed mentally to Matt, forgetting that he hadn’t been part of her initial curiosity.

“I’m sorry. Did I hurt them?” Matt asked, and Crystal chuckled and explained to her husband.

Matt responded by ordering Sorscha up in a terse voice. The

dragon spread her wings and was off without a word, also apparently appreciating the seriousness of whatever had happened. Crystal wondered if Sorscha knew more than she did.

"Teleporting now," was the only warning Crystal received, yet this teleport felt even smoother than the previous one. She supposed that she was getting used to it quickly, and she thought happily that it made her more likely to travel more frequently with Matt.

They had teleported to just over the courtyard at the estate, and as Sorscha's wings slowly guided her massive trunk to the ground Matt leaped off with Crystal in his arms. Matt gave his wife's safe landing a moment of concern and then spun and entered the estate, taking the path Crystal knew to lead to the chamber of sorcery, but she was surprised to see him turn to the right instead of entering the door. Matt pressed a differently-colored brick and Crystal watched in surprise as the bricks on the wall moved back and slid to the side. Lights on the other side of the new doorway flickered to life and Crystal peered in to see a dust-covered hallway curling a short distance, with two sets of footprints in the dust going each direction.

Matt knelt and touched the closest footprints, and then cursed softly.

"What's wrong?" Crystal asked out loud. Matt's only response was silence.

Crystal thought back to the times she had seen her husband this focused. They were very few and far between. Those few times had taught her that his silent intensity was not intended as rudeness, but was instead a sign of his own concentration on the danger at hand. Whatever it was that her husband, the god of war was focused on, a danger ahead frightened her greatly.

Matt's strides took him the length of the thirty-foot hallway in less than three seconds. Shoving open the door at the end, he went inside and swore angrily, louder this time. Crystal rushed in behind him, expecting in her horror to see dead bodies, and was instead greeted by a full-wall tapestry depiction of a heroic Matt—and Aphrodite.

Matt opened his mouth again, this time roaring in anger as he rushed to a desk in the corner of the room, looking carefully at figurines that he didn't touch. He then made a circuit around the room, examining the stacks of scrolls and the arms against the wall and nodding his head. Finally he came back around to the door, standing in front of Crystal, who was still looking at the tapestry on the opposite wall.

Crystal had heard his roar and had sensed but not followed his movements. She was immobilized by the scene in front of her, staring at it as a hollow feeling opened inside her. The tapestry had struck her an almost physical blow. Filling her sight was the image of her husband hand-in-hand with the woman—no, the goddess, she corrected herself—who had been doing everything Crystal could imagine to be mean and spiteful. They were standing atop corpses, posing in victory and, she was certain, love. She had known that they had been married, but she had decided that the past should remain in the past. The scene couldn't remain in the past, though, filling as it did the entire wall right in front of her. "That's not you, is it?" she heard herself ask, knowing that she already knew the answer but hoping that somehow she could be wrong.

"Yes, it is," Matt responded, his voice hard and tense. "We need to get up to the twins. Now."

At his mention of the girls, the tapestry's hold lessened on Crystal. "What's wrong with the girls?" she asked, her eyes switching from the picture to her husband. She stepped to the side to let him past and then following him closely as he stormed out. Matt's silence fueled a fear in the pit of her stomach, which in turn enraged her. She remained silent, though, her own anger boiling hotter and hotter with each step toward their chamber.

Sorscha awaited them outside the door to their suite. Matt swept past her without acknowledgment, flinging open the door. Crystal followed and heard him bellow, "Heidi! Linda! Come here!"

The twins shuffled in cautiously. "Yes, Daddy?" Linda answered, a quiver in her voice and a tenuous smile on her face. Her sister seemed to be trying to hide behind her.

Crystal stood rooted to a spot just inside the doorway, her emotions boiling over. She felt relieved to see the twins healthy, curious over what they had done, and angry that they had done it, while still seething over the picture on the wall hanging, all at the same time. She wasn't certain which inhabitant of the room she wanted to hug or scream at first.

Matt's voice cut through Crystal's indecision. "Why were you in the chamber with the figurines?" he asked quietly, his voice bearing a hint of steely hardness.

Linda's smile vanished, replaced instantly with an expression of terror. "We were trying to rescue a kitty, Daddy. It ran down there, and we just followed it to make sure it was okay."

Matt crossed his arms, face becoming darker. "A kitty?" he asked.

Linda nodded as Heidi cut in, "Yes, Daddy. We heard a kitty right out there, and we followed it out to the main entryway, and then down the sloping hall. There was a hallway full of dust, and we saw the paw prints at the end and the door opened, and then we were in that chamber. We thought we heard the kitty in the corner behind the desk, and on the way over we bumped it, and that's when the men came out and started fighting. They kept hitting the desk, and more of them appeared, till the whole room was full. The kitty must have snuck out while we were watching the battle, because we never saw it again."

Matt nodded slowly, a neutral expression on his face, as the story was recited in a rush. He stayed silent for several long moments after Heidi's storytelling had run down, and then pointed to her torn sleeve. "What happened to your arm?"

Crystal gasped. She had been so angry, had been focusing so much on the vision of that goddamn tapestry, that she hadn't seen the blood dripping down her daughter's arm. She started over to Heidi to look closer. Matt intervened with a sharp command, "Crystal. No." She drew up short, unaccustomed to her husband speaking to her in that tone, confusion cutting the link between her anger and her ability to move. She stood there, mutely looking from husband to daughter and back, at a loss for what to do for the first time she could recall.

"What happened to your arm, Heidi?" Matt asked, his voice once again flat and neutral.

"One of the soldiers' helmets, Daddy. It flew across the room, bounced off the wall, and cut across my arm when I wasn't watching."

"So that's your blood on the sleeve?" Crystal started to open her mouth. She wanted to shout at her husband. Of course that was her daughter's—their daughter's—blood on her sleeve! What game was he playing?

"Um—yes, I—I guess so." That certainly wasn't the type of answer that Crystal was expecting.

"Who healed your cut?"

Crystal's surprise turned to shock as Heidi's and Linda's faces went white with fear. The twins looked at each other for several long seconds and then finally, some decision firmly made, turned to Matt and as a pair began pleading.

"It was Aphrodite, Dad. She rescued us from the battling men, and then she healed me," Heidi said. "She told us you would be pissed, that you don't let her do anything but wander around the estate. Don't hate us, and don't hurt her, either. Please?"

Crystal saw the deception-laden story spinning out in front

of her. How dare Aphrodite, goddess or no, try to turn her own daughters against her? How *dare* she? The world began to turn red at the edges of her vision as her anger grew. Her fists clenched, and she felt herself gathering energy flows in her anger, unsure how to use them but looking forward to releasing her anger against something, anything....

"Crystal. Stop." Matt's voice again sliced into her mind, this time both through her ears and through their newfound telepathic link. She came back to reality in a snap, reeling a little from the transition, and looked at him. He was looking directly at her, through her, every inch of him now the commander, the god of war. He turned back to the twins.

"Back to this kitty, girls. Was it by chance a black and white cat?"

"Yes," Linda said, her demeanor confused.

"How many other cats have you seen here at the estate?" Matt asked.

"None, why?"

"Because there aren't any cats here at my estate, girls. None. Cats and dragons don't get along very well. One is fun prey for the other."

"Oh," Linda said, realization dawning on her face. "And you guessed the cat was black and white because Aphrodite likes that form?"

Matt nodded. "One more guess—you didn't really bump the desk all that hard, did you?"

"She caused that, didn't she?"

"Mm hmm. By the way, you can't get into the dusty hallway without knowing how to open the secret door, and a cat could never physically open it. Also, the door into my war room requires serious magic to unlock."

"Why would she lie to us, Dad?" Heidi asked.

"I haven't figured that out yet, Heidi. But I'm curious—why

would you believe her? About me, anyway, making her wander around the estate? When have you ever known me to be like that?"

"Well, you've changed, Dad. A few days ago you were Dad, the champion of the family. Now you're Dad, the god of war."

Matt nodded. "Yes, I have changed that way. But I haven't changed in here," he said, tapping his heart. "I still love all three of you the same way."

"So you're not pissed?"

Matt's stern visage melted. He held out his arms, offering an invitation that the twins rushed to take.

"I'm just glad you're all right," Matt said. "Most of this manor is perfectly harmless, but some of it is very dangerous, and I was so scared when I sensed the battle chamber being triggered." He pulled back from both and, looking each in the eye in turn, commanded, "Now, promise me you won't go exploring without me, your mother, or Sorscha along."

The girls nodded rapidly. "Go get ready for dinner, girls," Matt ordered. "Your mother and I have some talking to do."

Oh, boy, do we ever, Crystal thought.

The girls scampered off to their rooms at his words, and Matt led Crystal by the hand into their own room. Crystal noticed that Sorscha didn't follow them.

"So, your ex wife wants to turn your current wife's children against us," Crystal began as the door came to a close with a slam.

Matt rounded on her, his face an unreadable mixture of expressions.

"They're my children, too, remember?" Matt snapped back. "But, no, she doesn't."

"How do you know that?"

"She's crazy, but she's not stupid. She would know that I would see through the deception, would explain the circumstances to everyone involved."

"So what was she doing, then, sightseeing in her old digs and taking the kids along for the ride?"

"She was trying to piss me off. And it worked."

Crystal glanced down at Matt's fists. They were rapidly clenching and unclenching; that was bad, she realized. It was true that she had only ever seen him do that when he was infuriated. Idly she wondered if she should be worried now that he could shoot fireballs and summon flaming swords to his hands. At the moment, though, she was so angry herself that she didn't care.

"Piss *you* off?" she said, her voice rising. "You're not the one who just now realized that a goddess she hates knows her house better than she does, put her children into danger, has a great big tapestry picture with her husband, and probably slept in the very bed that she sleeps in, are you?" In the back of her mind, Crystal the language teacher frowned at the tossing around of pronouns, but she didn't care. Matt knew what she meant, and so did she.

As she spoke—ranted, she had to admit—she watched a transformation she would never have expected to see. As her voice intensity had swelled, Matt had *reacted*. She had watched his body surround itself in energy, his eyes going flat with rage, nostrils flaring against a sea of reddened face. For that moment, for the first time in her life, really, she had tasted fear. She'd thought the term was a case of personification before, of giving a sensation to something that really deserved none, but the small but present portion of her mind that remained logical and detached now noted that fear actually did have a taste—an acrid, burning taste that reminded her of bile. It was the reaction, she knew, to the realization that her husband easily could, and probably would, kill her. In that moment, Matt hovered on the brink between remaining a rational, loving husband, and becoming an angry god of war who could snuff a human's life force out at will.

"What are you talking about?" Matt replied, anger still radiating from his face. The logical and detached portion of her mind relaxed; Matt had chosen rational and loving instead of life-snuffing.

"I'm talking about *this*, Matthew!" Crystal said in a near-scream, arms waving wildly to point at all corners of the room. She raced over to grab one post of the bed, relieved that she was still alive to make her point. "How many nights did you sleep with *her* on this?"

Matt shrugged. "Well, none. I replaced the bed after she left. It had kinda been destroyed, anyway. I confess to being a little bit violently angry at the time. But—why?"

Crystal raced over to her closet and flung open the door. "You said some of these silk dresses were really old. How many were worn by her?"

Matt shook his head. "She cleaned it out when she left. The dresses are old, yes, but she left a *long* time before any of them were made."

Crystal stood panting, one hand on the door of the closet, knowing that most of the wind had been taken out of her sails. She still, though, had one thing that bothered her far more than who might have also slept in her bed or worn her clothes. Wrapping it around like a blanket on a cold winter night, she asked in a quiet, dangerous voice, "How long is she going to continue knowing more of my house than I do?"

Matt breathed in a long, deep breath, and then let it out slowly. "Is that what's bothering you? That she knew of the existence of a room you didn't ? Is that jealousy? Curiosity? What?"

"No!" Crystal screamed at the top of her voice, and then softened a little. "Maybe. Well, okay. Maybe a little. She's a goddess, the very embodiment of sexuality, at least in the only age I've been able to experience. I assume in other magic ages too, right?" When he nodded, she continued, "How can you expect me not to be a little jealous of the goddess who was in my place thousands—what, millions, maybe—of years before I ever came on the scene, who's *nearly as powerful as you,* who apparently knows every inch of this house, including the parts that are forbidden for me to know of, much less go into. She's got a goddamn tapestry with your smiling face on it right below us. How can you not expect just the teensiest eensiest bit of jealousy?" she finished, her voice crescendoing to the end.

Matt rose. "Fine, then," he said in a biting tone. "Let's go see it all, just you and me. But it must remain secret from everyone else."

Crystal shook her head, walked over to the bed, and sat down on it. "I don't want to."

Matt stood, openmouthed, and said, "You don't want to?"

"Am I going to see more tapestries like the one I saw?"

"No, I don't think so. I mean, it's been a long time since I've been in there, so my memory may be bad, but I really think the war room is the only room with a picture of Mars and Venus together."

"The war room?" she asked, her eyebrows arching in disbelief. "Aren't all your rooms war rooms?"

"Well, yeah," Matt smiled. "But that one is special. The weapons along the wall are all of the various types I've seen in all the battles I've watched or played in. The scrolls are the accounts of the battles, both my own and collected from whatever witnesses and scribes were available. The figurines are magical representations of the warrior types I've encountered, and are very useful for playing out various scenarios of battle. Much combat has been joined in that room. Thus, the war room."

"How many battles have you watched or played in?"

"I have no idea without going down and counting scrolls. Many. In the magic cycles I often start them, or lead them. The technology cycles I just sit back out of the way and observe when I can. People in those cycles look at you strangely when you get shot and don't have the decency to die."

"So why don't you want the mere humans in that room?"

"There's a method to teaching battle, Crystal. Keep in mind that I'm training battle mages, not any other kind. Of mages, I mean. My counterparts train as they do based on what they want. The guy the Greeks and Romans knew as Apollo trains his mages to be healers, mystics, and all that other touchy-feely stuff. His mages would probably already delight in the ability to study my ancient tomes for the knowledge they contain. I don't keep them for that, though. I train people for battle, and that means one step at a time, mastering each so that you know magic both as an offensive weapon and as a defensive shield." Matt shrugged and finished, "I didn't expect any of you to see that room in your lifetimes, really. It usually takes generations of mages to get to that point of development."

"So, has any other human seen that room earlier?"

"No."

"Has Aphrodite never taken anybody else to that room?"

Matt shook his head. "No, never."

"What's different about me, then? And our daughters? Are Heidi and Linda the only daughters you've had?"

"Well, no. I've had other children come through the apocalypse, and they've usually done just fine. They're always a little bit troublesome, of course, but that's just how my kids seem to be. You understand, I hope?" Matt finished with a sly wink.

"Uh huh," Crystal replied in a flat voice, leveling a disapproving look at Matt. "So, back to the topic. What's different about me, then?"

Matt's piercing gaze told Crystal she had lit a fire in his thoughts. "It can't be—I don't see why...." he stuttered before lapsing into a silence that ate at Crystal's patience. After several seconds, she had had enough.

"Can't be what?" she demanded.

"You're the first wife I've had in a very, very long time who could see flows of magic."

"The first one—like her, you mean?"

"Well, in that way, yes," Matt shrugged. "She was a powerful mage, and you also have the potential to become a powerful mage. But I still don't see why she would pick on you for it."

"Wait," Crystal said. "She was a powerful mage, you said. She was human?"

"Yes, a long, long time ago. Why?"

"A human can become a goddess?"

Matt's voice wavered as he answered, "Could, yes."

"Why could?"

Matt smiled. "There is no upgrade path from human to goddess. You can't just install Goddess 1.0 in your operating system."

Crystal ignored his attempt at humor, knowing that he always tried to smartass his way out of arguments. "So how did she do it?"

"You'll have to ask her."

"I'd die first."

"That's likely, actually," Matt quipped.

Crystal growled at him, then said, "I want to live forever with you."

"It's not everything it's cracked up to be."

"The living forever, or the living forever with you?"

"Both, I think. Living forever, you have to watch people you love grow old and die. And the latter, well—you know how grumpy I can be."

Crystal growled again in frustration. She knew her husband, though, well enough to realize the conversation wasn't going to go her way. "Fine."

"Now, weren't we about to collect the girls to go down to dinner as a family?"

"Sure, I guess. I'm ready. Let's go." The issue wasn't settled, but Crystal pressed it back behind her façade again. It would come back up, and some day she would win the debate. She always did.

The Battle Chamber, Explained

The family, served by Sorscha as usual, enjoyed a relatively quiet dinner. The remainder of the thrakkoni had proven Matt's words true and stopped serving the humans after the first couple of days. Instead they had helped the humans set up a work schedule for themselves under the oversight of Rellgll, who Crystal had heard was proving to be an excellent administrator. Birch, Phoenix, and Krista were indeed omitted from the work schedule as Matt had promised, but their spouses were not. Birch's wife Frieta, a dear friend of Crystal's from their school years, joined them. Her shift in the kitchen had ended, but Birch was, as usual, down in the chamber practicing magic.

As they ate in relative peace, Crystal was regaled with Frieta's tales of her experiences in the kitchens. There was a huge cooking complex underneath the dining room, easily large enough, Frieta said, to serve thousands of residents. The whole thing was run by one gruff old thrakkon, if thrakkoni could ever be described as old, who had a name that was impossible to pronounce. The humans on the kitchen staff had taken to calling him Chef Robert after a famous chef who starred on television before the cataclysm and who had been known for his no-nonsense manner. Frieta described Chef Robert in humorous detail, and Crystal had had to agree with her that the name was appropriate.

It was a compliment to the TV chef, really. The thrakkoni executive chef had apparently run the kitchen for close to as long as Sorscha had served Matt. It was said that you couldn't drop so much as a piece of bread on the floor at one end of the kitchen while he was at the other without him knowing it somehow. His insistence on perfect cleanliness and exacting order annoyed some of the staff, but Crystal found the knowledge of it comforting.

No one went hungry at the estate; that was certain. All three meals were still served family-style, and snacks were served to whomever wished them at in-between times, and there was always a buffet in the corner stocked with the everyday favorites such as meat loaf, roast beef, mashed potatoes, and steamed vegetables. Crystal found it funny that fried okra was always available. She was sure that others liked fried okra too, but everyone now knew that Matt, despite his lack of need to eat, loved to eat it like candy. Crystal smiled at the thought, noting that tonight Sorscha had seen fit to add a few of the deep-fried gems to Matt's plate.

Apparently Crystal was the only spouse who got out of being on the duty roster by virtue of her relationship. RJ had been put right to work, according to what Krista had told her on their occasional meetings. Due to his former position at the college, he was assigned supervisory status over the maintenance details, working side by side with the thrakkoni. It was he who had first confirmed to Crystal how amazingly strong the thrakkoni were, having watched one lift a marble statue that must have weighed well over a ton with one arm and move it to the opposite side of a path.

Under the administrative talents of Rellgll an entire organizational chart had quickly taken shape that was clear to all, because the chart was actually painted onto a large sign and hung right in the dining hall. Other than Chef Robert, the kitchens and associated pantries and dish closets were entirely staffed by humans. Now Crystal understood why the thrakkoni—dragons that devoured entire large mammals at a feeding—preferred their own dining facilities. He'd chuckled as he called them facilities and then explained that they actually flew out to the animal pens, selected an animal, and then carried their dinner up the mountain.

Other than the kitchen and the livestock pens, duties were shared equally between humans and thrakkoni and an easy-going friendship had emerged between the two groups. RJ, in particular, had taken to hanging out with some of the thrakkoni while Krista spent her hours in the sorcerer's chamber.

Crystal came back to the present and realized that her plate had been emptied. She had been so deep in thought she hadn't really tasted any of the food, which was a shame since she thought the kitchen food to be quite good. Sorscha gave her a warm smile as she reached around and took Crystal's plate away, saying, "I'll be right back with some dessert for you." Crystal sometimes thought it odd that, after their talk that second day she was there, Sorscha had been serving her as diligently as she served Matt. Sorscha had taken to serving their daughters, too, as she was now. Crystal wondered if Matt had said something to Sorscha, or if the conversation between Sorscha and herself had made the thrakkon decide to serve them. Or maybe, she thought, the thrakkon had just taken a liking to them. She wasn't certain, but whichever it was, she was glad for the change; she wasn't used to the jealous rage she had for Aphrodite and didn't think she could handle two targets.

Sorscha brought her dessert and took Matt's plate away. Crystal saw that the only thing missing from his plate were the fried okra nuggets, and that bothered her. He didn't need to eat, of course, so the only reason he ever ate was for the flavor of it. She had never, ever, seen him not eat all his okra, but the lack of other tasting meant that he was deep in thought.

Crystal took a bite of the Boston Cream Pie and moaned in delight. "Oh, that's so good!" she said, and Matt turned toward her, his face lighting up into a warm smile. "You should try some. It's your favorite dessert."

"No, I'm not really in the mood for dessert tonight," Matt replied through his smile. "It's been a long day."

"It has, hasn't it?" Crystal said, a rueful smile washing across her features. "It needs to be a little longer, you know. We still need to talk to the girls more about what happened today."

Matt nodded, but otherwise kept his thoughts to himself until Crystal and both twins were done with their pie slices and Sorscha picked up their empty dessert plates. "Shall we go?" he asked, rising and starting toward the door.

Crystal motioned for the girls to follow at Matt's brisk pace. All three women managed to follow him out of the dining hall and around a corner, in a direction that Crystal immediately realized didn't take them back to their suite.

Once through the secret door and the magical lock, Matt moved to the center of the room and then spun around, a motion that stopped all three girls in their tracks. He gestured, and the door shut behind them. "Alright, girls," he said, "we need to talk. You three are the only humans alive who know where and what this room is. I think that since you've seen it, I need to talk to you about it. Girls, neither of you is in trouble—much, anyway—but I need to know exactly what you did down here. Now, Heidi, what happened?"

Heidi stepped forward. "Well, we went over to the desk with all the figurines, having heard the kitty, and...." She told the story, battle by battle.

Matt nodded. "Thank you for telling the truth. Now, let me do the same. This is what I call my war room. It can only be entered through enchantment, which is why Aphrodite was able to let you in. She's very strong with magic. Now, these scrolls," he said, pointing to the wall covered in scroll shelves and cases, "detail every battle I've ever been in or witnessed. That's a lot of battles, of course. Over there," he said, pointing to the opposite wall, "is a collection of all the various weapon types I've seen used on the field of battle. Different cultures call them different names, but the basic implements of war are pretty constant."

Matt continued his lecture by pointing to the tapestry. He said, "This is me, in one of my earlier battle scenes. The woman in the image is Aphrodite."

Linda interrupted Matt, "Didn't we see a statue of her that you called Kallipygos?"

Matt said, "Yes! We saw the statue of Aphrodite Kallipygos on our trip to Naples not too long ago. In fact, I have the original here on my estate, just for the comic relief I get from seeing it. But anyway, I'll admit that I can't claim to have always chosen my consorts—um, my wives—well, though your mother is obvious evidence that I've learned my lessons finally." He sighed, looking at Crystal with a wistful smile, and continued, "In any event, Aphrodite was my wife a long, long time ago, and this tapestry in front of you was created to depict one of our greatest victories, when she and I together slew several thousand Amiotrites."

"Dad, what's an Amiotrite?" Linda asked.

"It's a nationality that died off long, long ago, dear," Matt replied, smiling at his daughter's curiosity. "Millions of years ago, for that matter. The details of the battle are too far gone for me to tell. I'd have to go through the old scrolls over there to recall, honestly. But it was a big deal at the time, and so that tapestry was created."

"That tapestry is millions of years old?" Crystal asked in an incredulous voice.

Matt shrugged. "Well, yes. My estate tends to preserve things for millions of years rather well, and that tapestry is an example."

"I was going to ask you to destroy it, but given its age I'm not sure I should."

Matt shrugged. "I'd honestly forgotten the tapestry was

down here. It's old, yes, but connected to a memory that no longer seems relevant."

Matt moved over to the desk.

"These figurines are actually magical replicas of various troop types that I've seen on the battlefield. Some—very few—troop types are truly unique. Most are the same, cycle to cycle. The lizard man you knocked over was a naga, a race that is based from Atlantis and is superior to humans in several ways. He beat the human mage, didn't he?"

Linda and Heidi both nodded. "So," he said, "this is the room where I play out various scenarios. Sometimes I pit one type against another, but usually I invoke several figurines several times each to see the result. It helps me consider strategy for battles."

Heidi interrupted, "So the naga and mage weren't real?"

Matt smiled at his daughter. "They were real for that time when they were out, dear. They can really cast spells and use tridents. They can also really kill teenage daughters. Yes, they were just figurines come to life, and after the battle they went back to being just figurines, but they were real in some very important ways.

"Look," he said after a deep breath, "the reason I brought you down here is to make sure you know that first, I'm not going to hide anything from you intentionally. Second, some things around here really are dangerous. Girls, if you'd stepped between the two duelers while they were out, or into most of the other contents later, you probably wouldn't be with us now. That scares both your mother and me. I need you both to promise not to go anywhere I haven't said is safe."

Both girls nodded and promised.

Going Home

Crystal woke the next morning with a start. Her body was telling her that she had slept beyond the time to be getting up, but she found herself alone in the large, dark room. Looking around as her eyes began to focus, she saw that she was indeed in her own bed, in her own room, but where was Matt? Why hadn't Sorscha opened the curtains as she always did? Crystal slid out of bed, intent on opening the curtains herself.

She made it a few steps before the door opened and Sorscha padded in wearing the usual silk slippers that made her footsteps nearly impossible to hear. "Good morning, Crystal," the thrakkon said. "Your husband instructed me to let you sleep in as long as you wished this morning, since your day yesterday was so awful. Now that you're up, though, let me draw the curtains and then a bath for you." In less time than it took to announce her intentions, Sorscha glided across the room and opened the curtains and then turned toward the bath.

"Where is Matt, then?"

"Up in the ruling chamber. There are quite a few reports he receives every week, and your friend RJ is becoming accustomed to giving one. RJ is bristling a bit at the reversal, but he's doing fine. I guess one instance of dying was enough for him." Sorscha huffed in the manner Crystal had come to recognize as thrakkoni chuckles.

"One instance of dying? What are you talking about?"

"Oh, you weren't there," Sorscha replied. "I suppose the master hasn't told you of it yet."

"No, the master hasn't. Why don't you?"

"I'm not sure...."

"Sorscha, dammit!" Crystal sighed, a long calming exhalation. "Look," she said once her temper had relaxed, "I've come to like you and trust you. Can't you do the same for me?"

Sorscha smiled and nodded after a second's consideration. In a conspiratorial tone, she described the events from the sorcerer's chamber.

"Oh," Crystal said after hearing of RJ's death and resurrection. "Wow. I kind of understand, though."

"I thought you would," Sorscha said, her warm smile making her feel like more of a sister than a servant to Crystal.

"So. Anyway. I'm sure the events upstairs are entertaining, but I think you're right that a bath would be best. I can draw it myself, though."

Sorscha's warm smile drooped. "I'd be devastated if you were to draw it yourself, Crystal."

"Really? Why do you serve me, when I'm just the master's wife?"

Sorscha's smile warmed again as she turned to the tub, talking as she adjusted the water temperature. "I like you. I like serving you, honestly. I was created to serve the master, and serve him I will, but when he has little need of me I am pleased to do the same for you, Crystal. My lady. And I call you that not just because I should, but because I wish to."

"Am I that different from Matt's previous wives?"

"I'm not sure how to answer that best," Sorscha said, turning to look Crystal in the eye. "The master has rarely arrived married. He tells me sometimes of some of his wives during the non-magical eras, but I don't see them. I've come to suspect he leaves most of them behind at the cataclysm."

"That's—cruel, though. I can't imagine Matt being that cruel."

Sorscha turned back to the water, continued her adjustments, and said over her shoulder, "It's not so cruel from my standpoint, and probably from his as well. Humans have it lucky, in a way. You live your lives, growing at a measurable rate, and you get to accomplish some of what you desire but always keep some in the future to be done. Then you die. To a thrakkon, thousands of years can become awfully tedious, and then that turns into millions. I can't imagine what it is like for an immortal. I suspect that he feels there's not a huge amount of difference in most of his wives passing away in the cataclysm or living another few quick years and then passing away. Clearly, in passing away during the cataclysm, they don't have to go through the doubt and emotional ups and downs that you have. You have to admit, your emotional ride has been rough."

Crystal nodded, despite the fact that Sorscha couldn't see her movement. She said, "I guess I can see the point, but humans come to treasure every year, and some of us even every hour and every minute on this earth, so ending a life early seems awful to me."

Sorscha stood up from her task, shrugging. "You'll have to ask him. I can only tell you what I suspect he feels. To be honest, I don't even know for sure that he leaves his wives there; he may just time it well. But your bath is ready, my lady."

"Can you please call me Crystal? I appreciate the title, but I really would feel more comfortable around you as just Crystal."

Sorscha nodded. "Crystal, then, your bath is ready."

Crystal slipped into the invigorating heat of the bathwater. "Sorscha, you really are wonderful at your duties," she said, sinking slowly into the perfectly-poured water.

"Thank you," Sorscha said and turned toward the door.

"So," Crystal interjected, trying to stop Sorscha without seeming too eager to ask the question. "What about Aphrodite? Am I much like her?"

Sorscha stopped but didn't turn around to face Crystal. "What about who?" She turned around slowly, forced smile on her face.

"Aphrodite. Venus. Whatever. Matt's ex-wife."

Sorscha's smile worked its way back to her face slowly. "You're nothing like her, Crystal," she finally said.

"I have to be something like her. Matt himself has mentioned an ability to do magic, and I've noticed that our red hair is similar. What else?"

Sorscha sighed deeply and tilted her head to one side appraisingly. "Well. You're prettier. You're also far, far nicer. She was rough when she arrived here, ticking off all of my brethren, but she got much worse after...." Her voice trailed off.

"After what?"

"You should ask the master about that. It's not my story to tell." Sorscha looked away sharply.

Crystal changed the path of the conversation, sensing Sorscha's tension. "How could I possibly be prettier than the goddess who pretty much defines beauty?"

"She's a goddess, Crystal," Sorscha said matter-of-factly. "You've seen the master change his appearance at a whim. She defines beauty because she can. But her natural face isn't—wasn't—the same one she goes around wearing now."

"Ah. Was Matt ever a human?" Crystal asked, changing the subject again, curious what she could get out of Sorscha by keeping her off-balance.

"Well, he made me, so I don't know how he was created. You'll have to ask him. But, speaking of the master, I should be attending to him now. Enjoy your bath!" Sorscha tripped in her haste to leave the room, a motion Crystal wouldn't have never expected to see from the graceful thrakkon.

Crystal watched the door close and then huffed aloud, imitating Sorscha's strange chuckle. She worked the sponge over her body, cleaning herself thoroughly as she thought about what she had learned in the conversation. It was obvious that the mere mention of Aphrodite angered Sorscha. Crystal wondered what the goddess had done to cause Sorscha such angst. Above that, and possibly more important, she'd learned that Matt, with his callousness toward human life—she'd known about that already, she thought, but now she had an inkling as to why—had still considered Crystal special enough to bring her through the cataclysm. As much as she wanted to be repulsed by the idea, she was pleased at the notion. She was different from all his other wives; she was special. That, she thought, was enough. For now.

****

Crystal drained the tub, dressed in the most comfortable tunic and pants she could find, and sauntered up the stairs to her husband's throne room. She kissed the side of his head and moved off to the side without comment. He acknowledged her with a playful smile and nod, but continued with business as Rellgll flushed slightly at the interruption and then continued plowing through the numbers in his report. Sorscha pointedly acknowledged her entrance, and then actively ignored Crystal as she made a show of listening to his discussion.

After a few minutes Crystal realized that her timing had been nearly perfect. Rellgll's report drew to a close, and RJ marched out with him. Matt brightened and asked, "Does anyone present have any further business to discuss?"

Greeted with silence, Matt rose and turned to Crystal. "Well, love, it appears that court is done. Shall we?" He gestured toward the door RJ and Rellgll had exited, rather than the curtain leading back to their chamber. Crystal jumped to the door, realizing she hadn't seen what lay beyond yet and excited to see another part of the estate.

Crystal was as unimpressed by the chamber beyond as she had been by the sitting room. For all the finery in the estate, this room had folding chairs and blank walls, in addition to a notice-able lack of the statuary so common elsewhere. "Matt, why so plain here?" she asked.

"Everyone who sits here is waiting to see me, to bring a grievance or other matter to my attention. Why should I enter-tain them while they wait?"

Crystal nodded, acknowledging the merit in the argument. They followed the path down the middle of the room between the rows of folding chairs, exiting the waiting room onto the second floor grand balcony.

As their feet cleared the threshold onto the balcony, Matt spun around, grabbed Crystal's hair, and kissed her long and hard.

When he pulled away, still gazing into her eyes, Crystal breathlessly asked, "Not—not that I didn't enjoy that, but what was it for?"

A twinkle gleamed in his eyes as Matt shrugged and danced away. "I felt like it," he said. She followed as he bounded down the stairs and back down the hall into their suite.

Once safely back in their suite, Matt plopped down onto the love seat in the sitting room, pulled Crystal onto his lap, and hugged her. "So, Love, what do you want to do today, now that the day is ours?" he asked.

"Mmmm. How about sit here and just be happy all day?"

Crystal loved hearing the resonance of his belly laughs, one of which he gave her now. "Okay, but won't you get hungry?"

Crystal pulled his chin around to look deep into his eyes. "Matt, I don't get hungry when I'm in your arms. Except, of course, if you're talking about *that* kind of hunger." She nipped at his neck playfully.

The two were interrupted by a young girl's throat clearing. Both twins were watching from the doors to their rooms.

"Mom, Dad," Linda asked, "can we go home sometime?"

"This is home, honey," Crystal said.

"We know that. But we were wondering if we could visit our old home, to see. You know."

Matt nodded, his expression grave. "Are you really ready to see the devastation that happened there, girls?" he asked, looking at each in turn. "That really was the apocalypse we went through. It's deadly, and what remains won't be pretty at all."

Linda and Heidi bobbed their heads quickly in response. "We wanna see what happened. We want to know what happened with our friends," Heidi said.

Matt shrugged and said, "Well, I suppose we can arrange for that. Crystal, how do you feel about it? Would you like to go back to Half Moon Bay today?"

"Um, it sounds okay," she said, not certain that was the most accurate answer. She really didn't want to see what Matt kept referring to as massive devastation, but she also didn't doubt the girls' sincerity in their desire to revisit the only home they'd known before their arrival in this palace.

She yelped slightly as Matt lifted her off the floor, holding her up still in a seated position. Responding to an unheard summons, Sorscha appeared in the door and said, "We can leave immediately, Master," before walking back down the hall and out of sight.

Matt motioned for the girls to follow, and then he followed Sorscha, still holding Crystal up.

"I can walk for myself, Matt."

"I know, but I was having fun carrying you," he said, setting her down gently and then continuing after Sorscha.

The family arrived at the now-familiar take-off patio to see Sorscha and one red-haired male thrakkon waiting. Both disrobed quickly. Sorscha changed as usual into her massive silver dragon shape, and the red-haired male transformed into a beautiful crimson dragon about half Sorscha's size.

Matt went to each twin, holding his arms around her and leaping, as he had with Crystal, up onto the red drake's back. Once both were deposited safely on the dragon, Matt gave some instructions that Crystal couldn't hear. He leaped down and slapped the dragon on the flank, and the drake bounded into the air, girls shrieking in excitement. At a few hundred feet in altitude he stopped his climb, circling in the airspace of the courtyard.

Matt grabbed Crystal and leaped onto Sorscha's saddle, yelling, "Let's ride!" at the same time. Sorscha's dragon form thundered up into the sky at a breathtaking speed. Soon they were in the clouds, the red following more slowly. They stopped and the red caught up, Sorscha turning her head to give the red what looked like it might be a playful grin for a dragon.

Ready to travel? Matt asked mentally. Crystal nodded in return, and then looked at her daughters over on the crimson dragon, a sudden knot of fear in her stomach.

"Will they make the jump safely?" she asked Matt.

"Of course. I'll just pull out my impressive god skills this once."

The girls both looked toward them so suddenly that Crystal knew Matt had to be sending mental instructions. Together they nodded, wide-eyed, and then turned their heads to the front again as Matt said in her ear, "Let's go."

The world shifted again in the queasy side-slipping manner that Crystal wasn't certain she would ever get used to. Looking nervously to her right, she spied the red with what looked like two girls on his back and exhaled in relief. *Ye of little faith*, Matt chided her mentally as Sorscha and the red both began a gentle dive through the thick clouds.

Crystal realized she was becoming more and more terrified with every few feet of descent. She had come to grips intellectually with the loss of their house; who could say no, after all, to moving up to a sprawling estate? She wasn't sure, though, whether she was ready for the emotional shock of seeing that their home was destroyed, as it probably was. She had been so proud when they had bought it. Her parents had been California public school teachers, and while they had managed well enough, she had grown up in a very modest home in Cupertino.

Moving into the million dollar house near the sea had seemed a dream come true. Over the past fifteen years they had made it their million dollar *home,* she thought, knowing how cliché the phrase was but finding it appropriate. They had painted the girls' rooms several times in several different colors, and had played around with coloring on several accent walls as well as different flooring types through the house. She had been particularly proud of what they had done in the back yard, building in a small pond and then putting up flowered terraces all around with a hidden hot tub in the back corner. She had always thought how much easier it was to accomplish projects around the house when your husband had a huge inheritance nest egg in the bank to draw from. Now, of course, she knew that he had never inherited any of it, but that bit of deceit didn't bother her. She wondered how she would've reacted if instead he'd come out and said, "Honey, I'm a god." Probably with a straitjacket, she acknowledged to herself.

Nervous as she was about the potential devastation, her trip through the memories of her home made her lean forward, pushing in her mind for Sorscha to go faster. Crystal wanted to see her home again.

Gradually, a landscape came into view, though it wasn't like anything she'd imagined. The line between land and sea was littered with shapes that slowly resolved themselves into remains of human existence. Boats of all sizes were laying, torn, at the water's edge, and littered between the boats were vehicles and— bodies. Looking back from the water's edge toward the hills that had backed their town, she saw row after row of flattened buildings, with more vehicles and smaller boats arranged in the most haphazard of sculptures in and around, with even more grisly displays of flesh that had once been people. There were thousands. No, tens of thousands.

The reality of the scene hit her, and the emotions made her heart sink. The grief was foremost, but lurking behind was shame at her previous concern over her own home as well as anger at the forces that had caused this to happen. Down there, resolving into ever-finer detail as the dragons' descent continued, was what remained of boats, houses, cars, stuff, and, most important, *people*. The past several days had seemed like a transition rather than a cataclysm to her. Her own losses that had been bothering her so much seemed laughable, comparatively. She had lost nothing, really, that hadn't been compensated for by a corresponding gain—god for human husband, estate for house. Who would care what happened to the Audi when you could ride flying dragons?

Many of the people who'd traveled with her to the estate had lost a great deal more than she had. She thought back on the times recently when she had brought Therapuppy to console the other residents. Yes, it had been a needed thing, the right thing, to do, but even that had been looking at the devastation of peoples' lives in a detached, third-person way. Now, flying down toward the crumbled, crumpled, and crushed litter that represented thousands of human beings, the devastation hit her in the face and left her feeling cold and empty.

She was surprised to see that Sorscha and the red weren't diving toward the land, but rather toward the water. As she came closer, she saw what she hoped to be her house, or at least the top floor of it. But either the land had moved west, or the sea had moved east. What had once been a sprawling community of well-to-do homes must now be beneath water level, and her house seemed the only structure still standing.

Is that our home? she asked Matt.

Yes, it is. Or was. That's our destination.

The dragons landed lightly on the rooftop, their claws destroying clay roof tiles as they grasped for purchase. Matt held out his hand toward the twins, levitating them down onto the roof on flows of air as he and Crystal also levitated to join them.

"Is this our house?" Linda asked, a catch in her voice.

"Yes, it is," Matt said.

Looking around, Linda said, "That means Cassie's house was right—over there." She pointed to a completely submerged spot.

"Yes, it does. All the homes in this area were obliterated when the first wave rolled through."

"Except ours. Why did ours make it, Dad?"

"I'm a god, dear," Matt's said as he shrugged, as though those four words were enough answer for any question. Linda just stood and looked questioningly at him over folded arms until he continued, "Everyone at the college had to be evacuated, and while the administrators were at it I teleported back here and warded it. I mean, yes, it's just a building full of stuff, but I know how important some of that stuff is to us."

Crystal stopped her scan of the horizon, sad that it was only bringing her more images of death and destruction, and started gingerly picking her way down the rooftop. She wondered briefly why Matt had teleported home and back but had made her walk through the strange magical doorway instead of teleporting with him, but the memory of the first teleport she had experienced answered her question.

"Love, why are you walking down?"

Crystal stopped. Good question, she realized. She kept forgetting that she was married to a god. She turned and walked back up to him. Crossing her arms, she said, "I'm not a god, dear," her tone mimicking his.

Kissing her forehead gently, Matt wrapped her in one arm and gestured for the twins to come to him. When they did, he put his other arm around both of them and then gently lifted the family out over the water where the front door must be, and then down. As they descended, a bubble formed in the water that forced it away from the wall of the house and the door it contained. Crystal watched closely, seeing the flows of energy Matt was using and wondering if she could manage them.

Some day, she thought. Some day she would be able to do this.

Sometimes she was awed by her husband, while sometimes she still thought of him as a mortal. Then again, she had always felt that way, even before he had revealed himself to be one of the most powerful beings in the universe.

Feet touching down lightly, Matt pressed the door and it opened. He smiled and motioned the family in, entering the house last. As they went through the door he turned and motioned it closed. Crystal watched closely, seeing the flows to close the door but not catching the intricate magic he used to remake his wards.

"Some day," she whispered as the twins ran up the stairs toward their bedrooms, "you'll have to teach me how to make those wards."

"No, I won't," he replied, his grin not quite reaching his eyes. "I might, or I might not teach you, but I won't have to. Kidding aside, those wards are quite beyond your abilities now."

"I know. I watched you put them up. Couldn't read the flows at all, unlike the ones where you used air and a little earth to push the sea away."

Matt looked at her appraisingly, and then smiled, the expression radiant in his eyes this time. "You are amazing, my love."

Shrugging, she replied, "I better be. Remember who I'm

married to," and then headed up the stairs to their own bedroom.

"Wait."

She stopped immediately, concerned over the gravity of Matt's tone. "What's wrong?"

"She's been here."

Crystal frowned, suspecting she knew who Matt meant. "Aphrodite?"

"Yes."

"How do you know?"

"I can sense not only flows, but also the remnants left behind when others change those flows. She was here fairly recently, and she performed magic."

"The girls!" Crystal started bounding up the stairs.

"Are fine. She was doing magic in our room, not theirs. And she's not here now, I can tell."

Crystal stopped a few steps up, and then rounded on Matt. "Why is she doing this?"

Matt shrugged. "Much as I hate admitting it, I'm not even really sure what she's doing. She's never plagued such visits on my family before."

Matt took the lead up the stairs and down the short hall to their bedroom door. Crystal saw the air around her sparkle with flows of elemental power. Out of curiosity, she looked closer at the elements of the shield that Matt had erected around her. It was quite colorful; she saw the deep blue of earth mixed with the yellow of water, primarily, but interspersed were threads of red fire energy and blue water energy, woven through in a complex oppositional pattern that she could see lent strength to the shield's elemental fabric. She also saw a hint of a new color, orange, and made a mental note to ask Matt about it when they had the time and the safety.

"Coming, Love?" Matt interrupted her examination of his spell, pushed the door open, walked in first, and then groaned in disgust.

Crystal entered after Matt. The furniture was all still in the state she had left it in. Nothing seemed to have changed except for the pictures. As she looked around, she saw that every picture in the room had been changed, and now Crystal was standing looking at a dozen replicas of the tapestry in the battle room.

"That's...." she said, spending several moments searching for the best term before adding, "childish. Especially for a goddess, I'd think. Why would she do it?" She moved over to the dresser, to the picture in the precious gold and silver frame that had been a wedding gift from her parents—one of the last gifts they had given her before their deaths. It had displayed one of Crystal's favorite images from their wedding day. As she picked it up she felt Matt touch the shield he had her cocooned in to strengthen it. She realized the potential for a trap of some sort, too late. The explosion wasn't what she expected it to be, though, just a puff of smoke and a flash that looked more like a firecracker than a trap from a goddess.

"Mom? Dad?" Heidi yelled as two pairs of feet pounded toward the door. "Are you okay?"

"We're fine," Matt's voice called out. "Don't come in, though. There's no telling what traps are set for you."

Two worried faces peered in the open door. Linda spied the change first. "Why are all the pictures changed?"

"We don't know, exactly," Matt replied. "Aphrodite Kallipygos is trying to send me a message of some sort, and obviously I'm just not getting it. Clearly I need to find her and talk it out a bit, but now isn't the time. Go back and get anything you want from your rooms. I don't want to hold back the sea too much longer."

Crystal's hand moved toward the jewelry box on the dresser. Matt strengthened her shield again and said, "Girls, move away from the door, please." The box opened uneventfully. Crystal sighed in relief as she removed a diamond necklace, several silver and turquoise rings, and a decorated hair clip.

"At least she didn't do anything to the jewelry my mother gave me," she said, relieved. "And this necklace—she took our wedding picture away, but not the crystal necklace pictured in it. Remember when you gave it to me that morning?" she asked, holding a voluminous necklace of cascading crystals up to her neck and pirouetting for Matt.

He smiled in return. "I do. It was a grand day, one of the absolute best in my long, long life."

Matt turned and looked at the two sets of eyes peeking around the door frame again. "Girls, please. Go get your stuff and meet us downstairs." This time, they obeyed.

Crystal stopped spinning. "I guess I need to get moving, too, right?" she asked with a rueful smile. "This bit of memory is really all that I want or need. Well, that, and your love, but I have that wherever I am."

Matt smiled, and she stepped back out the door. Once she was out of the room, Matt made a show of pointing to each picture individually and causing each to melt. This time Crystal saw clearly the simple flow he was using.

He stepped out of the room, and Crystal's shield winked out. "Interesting," he mused. "She only trapped the one picture. I suppose she guessed well which one you'd go to first, eh?"

"It was the only wedding picture we had up in the room, so I don't think it was a hard guess to make. And it wasn't trapped enough to do any real harm. It's almost as if she just wants to piss me off. But I'm curious. How did she know where our house was, Matt? Did you somehow know her during the last cycle, before the cataclysm?"

"No. She knows that I like to hang out near the ocean, though, in moderate climates, so I'm sure it didn't take much for her to figure out we were around here. Once she was in the area, my wards would glow like runway lights to another god. It would've been pretty easy. And I didn't think to protect the house from magical entry. It's just warded against physical attack by waves."

"You know, it's funny. Before all this happened, I was really happy with my image of god, or gods, anyway, as omnipotent, omniscient, beings who always knew the right things to do or say."

"Oh, great. So I fail your god standard?"

"No, not that, Love. It's just that I keep bouncing back and forth between being awed by your power and being surprised when you don't think of something."

Matt shrugged. "Well, yeah. All the different churches and temples over the centuries built up this massive image of gods as all-encompassing forces that knew everything and saw everything and did everything, except of course when it didn't fit in with their dogma, and when that happened their arguments were fun to watch. Most of the time it's fun watching people describe or debate their notions of what gods must be, think, or act like, because none of the debaters have any reality to base their knowledge on. Yet they persist, and god forbid if you try to suggest they might be mistaken."

He kissed her on the forehead. "But you're different, Love, and I thank god every day for that difference. Now, let's get downstairs to the kids."

She smiled and started following him, commenting to the back of his head as he walked, "You thank yourself, or somebody else?"

"Whoever," Matt replied with a shrug.

"How many gods are there, Matt?"

Matt continued his descent down the stairs, answering over his shoulder. "Thirty-three gods and goddesses. Thirty-one of us are active, by which I mean we maintain estates, go out and meet and get people all bedazzled, et cetera. Most of us are western gods with humans and thrakkoni at our estates, but some are eastern and stay over in their own groups."

"Who are the other two, Dad?" Linda asked, ears perked.

Matt smiled; he had always loved teaching. He replied, "Yahweh, or Odin, or Zeus, whatever you decide to call him, and Gaia. The Father hasn't been seen or heard from in a long time—a couple of cycles, in fact. Nobody really knows where he went off to, though frankly gods can be as bad as humans about speculating and gossiping. Anyway—Gaia, you met when we went to the estate. The Mother is still around, though usually she remains in her entire-world format and doesn't personify. That she did and came to my call was an honor to me."

"Aren't you the god of war, though?" Linda asked. "As in death, destruction, battle, and so on? Why would you be the earth mother's favorite?"

"That's tough to explain, dear. No, not really tough, so much as harsh. First, because I am the god of war, I have over the years built up a bit of a lead over my fellows in terms of power. I'm widely considered by my peers to be the third most powerful god, after Yahweh and Gaia themselves. As such, I take lead in many of our debates, and if there's a decision to be executed I am usually the one to do it. But you also have to understand, girls, that the earth is a delicately balanced system. Mother maintains the balance, but sometimes that's easier said than done. When the population or activity of the human race gets out of control, maintaining the balance becomes a great challenge. That's why sometimes she cherishes my activities."

"You make war to kill people off to make Gaia's job easier?" Linda asked, her expression doubtful and troubled.

"Well, yes, but—no. Look, I don't make war myself, though I have been guilty of causing it. I sometimes participate in the wars during the magic cycles, always with great effect, but I limit active participation in order to avoid direct conflicts with my peers, who tend to stay out as long as I do. But I cherish war, and I study it, and often I nudge it along, for the same reason farmers burn their fields between crops. The fire is destructive, true, but out of the destruction comes new growth."

Heidi and Linda both gave tentative nods in response. Crystal knew what they were thinking; she also was troubled, but decided to hold her thoughts. She had always known her husband to be pragmatic, but she had a hard time hearing him describe war in anything close to a positive light. Beyond that, to say that Gaia approved was incomprehensible as well as disturbing.

"So, do we have everything we need?" Matt asked, interrupting Crystal's conflicted thoughts.

Both girls nodded, and Crystal ran a mental sweep of the home. She gasped and said, "The girls' old pictures and baby stuff!"

Matt blinked out of sight and then blinked back into existence, and Crystal saw a few boxes from the attic had appeared at his side. "No need to fear. Those memories are safe right here."

"I don't think I need to fear much besides bad rhymes when you're around, Matt."

"Touché."

"Except Aphrodite, anyway."

Matt groaned and said, "Yeah, well, we'll see. I've got a plan for that, but we should talk it over later, once we're home."

"What's next, then?"

"Put everything you want in a pile there, first."

The girls and Crystal did as he requested, piling up precious family photos and artwork and small antiques as well as remembrances from family trips and heirlooms from Crystal's parents and grandparents. Matt waved and the stack disappeared. Crystal silently gaped; she hadn't even seen the flows this time; they were quick. Matt's quiet, wicked chuckle told her that he knew she hadn't followed his work and was proud of it.

"Okay, it's all safely teleported back in the estate, in the main room of our suite."

Crystal was bothered by a thought, and said, "If you can teleport that stuff into the estate that easily, what's keeping the other gods—or goddess, in this case—from teleporting something dangerous in?"

"My wards. Every god, actually, has a ward around his or her estate that prevents teleporting in or out without the presence of a god along for the ride. Doesn't apply to thrakkoni, of course, but it keeps packages from arriving unaccompanied. I also put up a special ward after yesterday's drama that will signal me if Aphrodite, specifically, teleports into the estate. I may not be able to keep her out without a major battle, but I can at least make sure I know if she's there."

Satisfied, Crystal nodded. "So, where to next?"

"The girls said they wanted closure. Didn't you, girls?"

"Dad, I think we have it," Linda said.

"Don't want to go see your old school, or anything else in town?"

"Is it going to look like what we flew over to get here, with the dead bodies lying in heaps?"

"Yeah, probably."

"I don't think so."

Matt nodded. "Probably a wise choice."

Crystal spoke up, "I'd like to fly over town, myself."

"Why?"

"To see if there is anyone else we can rescue."

Matt kissed her on the cheek. "There's the Crystal with the soft heart again. Sure, we can make a pass over the city. It's going to be gruesome, but there may be someone there."

The family walked back out the front door, and then Matt

spun on his heels and sprinted back in, breathing "wait a sec" to them. Moments later he reappeared from the dining room holding a small plate in one hand and a carved egg in the other. Crystal gasped. She had remembered these two ornaments, but had figured Matt would think her silly for going to get them.

"I couldn't forget these," he said. One was a simple white porcelain plate with their initials and "5 years" on it—Matt's 5th wedding anniversary present to Crystal, and one she suspected was worth far more than it appeared. The other she had always been scared to even bring out in company; it was the largest Faberge egg she had ever seen at nearly nine inches tall, and was a stunning gold, light blue and white enameled egg held up by lions with an elephant on top. Matt had presented it to her on a trip to Europe for her thirtieth birthday and had said only that he had found it in an antique store, had thought immediately and thoroughly of her, and couldn't have helped buying it for her. She was convinced it was worth a fortune, but the one time she had attempted to show it to an antique dealer to satisfy her curiosity, he had become visibly upset and told her to take it out of his shop immediately. As he physically ushered her out, he had muttered something about *lost Faberge egg* and *royalty*. No point, she had decided, risking further encounters of that nature. It was spectacularly beautiful to her, and that was that.

Matt handed her the egg, and she cradled it to her chest. He slipped the plate into his own tunic, seeming to find a spot for it to rest securely. "All right, now we can go."

"Are you ever going to come clean to me on where you found the egg?"

"I am clean on the matter of where. I bought it from a dealer of antiquities."

Matt had a peculiar way of phrasing things when he wanted to tell the truth while hiding something. "So," she countered. "What about the when?"

Matt smiled as he lifted his family back onto the rooftop on graceful columns of air. "When is a little sketchier. To be honest, I'd actually found that egg a few decades before I met you, and was holding onto it to give to the right person at the right time. It's not often one comes across a lost antiquity for purchase, after all. It cost enough to run a small country for a year or two, but it was worth it."

"So, how much is it really worth?" she asked, settling into her seat on Sorscha and feeling his arms wrap around her, holding her in place so that she could continue with her close hug on the egg.

"Not a lot, now. Not many people worried over collectible Faberge eggs these days. But I paid a few tens of millions for it back then."

"Tens of millions of what?"

"Hell, I don't remember. I think it was marks, but it might have been kroner. It was a long time ago. But it was a *lot* of money, I recall—somewhere around thirty or thirty-five million dollars worth."

"Wow. Just—wow."

Sorscha and the drake lifted off again, and hovered over the house as Matt called out loud to all three, "Last time looking at what was a good home for many years." Then he waved the wards released and the house sagged. She felt his head turn seaward, and as she followed the turn of his head she saw a massive flow of air and water pulled by Matt from out in the sea, creating a massive wave.

"Gonna destroy it yourself?" she thought to him.

"Don't want it standing out to be looted. It'd take a while for the sea water to degrade the structure enough to fall on its own, so I'm just helping." With that, he joined the wave as it reached the house with a flow of air directed downward at the roof, and the house she had called home for so many years toppled and sank into the sea.

Crystal heard the twins sigh as the same sound came from her.

"I'm ready. Let's go."

Rescue at the Library

The dragon flight circled in respect over the still-sinking house and then flew to the land. As they approached the beachfront, Crystal saw the girls engaged in an animated conversation. She looked over, and saw Linda looking back and pointing at the ground and then to her nose. She nodded. *The girls are saying how much it stinks here*, she thought to Matt.

Yeah, that's the smell of a battlefield, or of an apocalypse. You never forget it once you've experienced it.

Is it going to be like that for long?

Worse soon, when we fly over town. Lots of corpses, and not many living to take care of them. But we'll fly fairly quickly, and I'll use magic to sense ahead of us for surviving humans.

Fly over quickly they did, and she agreed that the smell got worse. They flew over mile after mile of lifeless ruins, turning north once they were over the town proper. It was difficult to recognize landmarks with most of them destroyed, but Crystal saw some still intact. The airport was an obvious one, she thought, but as Sorscha flew up and over the hills and toward the sprawling complex Crystal was amazed to see no signs of life whatsoever. Matt confirmed her fears.

That was an incredible tsunami, Crystal thought to Matt.

Matt's mental reply started with a sardonic chuckle. *The tsunami would have killed a bunch, but then several days of bitter cold coupled with a lack of utilities as well as no upper atmosphere to shield them from the sun's ultraviolet rays did quite a job of finishing off the rest. We'll find pockets of people, I'm sure, who found shelter from the wave and then the sun and fuel for warmth. Not sure if we'll really want to interact with them, but it'll be worth trying.*

Crystal shuddered again at Matt's callous tone, the same one he'd used to describe war's usefulness to Gaia. She shouldn't have been surprised that an immortal would be callous toward the deaths of so many human beings, but Matt wasn't just an immortal. He was her husband, and his cavalier way of dismissing mass death shocked her. *Matt, how can you be so matter-of-fact when you discuss the death of millions of people?* she asked. *You always seemed so caring, so—human.*

My attitude hasn't changed. We just have never really talked about it before.

No, I guess not. And you're right; nothing brings it to the mind quite like going through an apocalypse. It's just….

Look at it this way, Matt said. *When we went fishing for salmon, nobody seemed to have any qualms over it. The fish died to feed us, but they were also all going up the stream to die anyway. Right? If we'd been killing fish just to kill fish, it would've been different. Now, zoom out that time perspective a bit. Humans may not be swimming up a stream toward their imminent deaths, but they're certainly not going to live for any significant length of time when compared to an immortal. And while I would never be happy over someone killing humans for the purpose of killing them, this is—different.*

Crystal harrumphed in return. *You're comparing humans to spawning salmon,* she said.

Well, in a way, yes. It's a pretty weak metaphor, I admit, but it's all I've got on short notice.

Short notice? You've had millions of years to come up with your attitudes.

True, but this is the first time I've been asked to defend them. It makes a lot more sense to me when I just go with it.

Aphrodite didn't ask?

I don't think she cared.

As Crystal tried to digest the conversation, the dragons flew toward what had been downtown San Francisco. Crystal began seeing more structures still upright, owing their existence to the hills around them. She wondered how the flatter regions to the south had fared, and asked the question of Matt telepathically.

Not well, I suspect, he replied. *We're not going there to check anytime soon, but not only did they have a tsunami, incredibly cold temperatures, lack of shielding from ultraviolet, and no utilities to contend with, but there was probably also a nuclear holocaust.*

Nuclear?

The two nuclear power plants in California are both down that way, one near San Luis Obispo and one between LA and San Diego. The operators wouldn't have had time to shut them down without any electricity to run the administrative systems, and all of the cooling and backup systems are still based on electricity. I'm fairly sure they both melted down.

Crystal shuddered at the thought. *So, there's not much chance of any life remaining down there. Has this happened in previous cycles?*

Nearly every one. There's a reason why some areas of the world get marked as taboo, and why strange mutations happen early in the magical times.

Crystal lapsed into silence, thinking of the times she had been down to central and southern California, and wondering how they must look now.

As they flew over what had been downtown San Francisco, Crystal heard Matt chuckle. *I knew it. Every time. Can't blame them, I guess, since there's a ready supply of easily combustible materials.* They approached a large but squat rectangular stone building that was missing most of its windows but seemed intact otherwise.

What is that? she asked.

The main city library.

Of course. In a library, especially one as large as the edifice they approached, survivors would have access to a great many thousands of books, and possibly even wooden book shelves, as well as a collection of wooden and cloth seats to burn. Now she understood Matt's point. They circled over the building once and then landed on the roof beside a broken glass sky dome, out of which Crystal could see and smell smoke rising. Matt hopped to the roof and said, "I'll go down myself, ladies. The people down there might be happy to see us, and they might not."

Crystal said, "Wait, hon. I want to go with you."

"It's dangerous," he said.

"Can the god of war not protect his lady against a band of starving humans?"

Matt sighed and shrugged. "Okay," he said. "Change of plans. You two girls stay up here with Sorscha. Your mother and I will go down to meet the people in there." Matt levitated himself and Crystal through the largest hole in the glass dome and down into the darkness.

Daylight still streamed through the dome area at the top, Crystal saw as they descended, and the light was increased by the appearance of a glowing ball in Matt's hand. Crystal studied his flows for a moment and then held out her own hand, a glowing ball appearing there to her immense satisfaction. She turned and grinned at Matt, who bowed slightly to her prowess. *You do learn fast and well, Love,* he projected mentally to her.

They landed in the center of the library. Before them stretched what had been a sweeping lobby with information kiosks and what looked to Crystal to have been checkout stations, along with a strange glassed-in conveyor belt. She imagined that before the cataclysm the hum of activity would have been significant, but all was silent now. Too silent, she thought.

I don't hear anybody, Matt, she said. *Is that a bad thing?*

Probably not, Love. If they were hostile they would likely be screaming and attacking now. That they're hiding from us instead is a good sign. Crystal noted that he had put a shield up around her, anyway.

Matt turned to face a fire that was still burning brightly a few dozen feet away. Raising his voice, he said, "We come as friends, folks. We're here to rescue you." His gesture was greeted by continued silence.

Crystal stepped in front of Matt, raising her own voice. "It's been a tough, dangerous time. You must be hungry and thirsty. My husband and I have food and drink at our estate. All we ask is that you let us help you."

Crystal's words had the desired effect as a few dozen people rose, moved out from behind the cover of scattered furniture and library equipment, and shambled to the edge of the light ring caused by the sun's rays through the destroyed skylight above.

A regal gentleman—one who would have appeared regal, anyway, had his shredded black suit been intact—stepped forward slightly, staying back just out of the direct sunlight, and spoke. "Thank you for your offer, miss—whomever you may be. I hope you understand, though, that an offer like yours from someone who just impossibly floated down out of the sky makes us a little, shall I say, nervous? Now where did you say that heavenly estate was?" Crystal assumed from his tone and his white hair that the tall, gaunt man she faced was at least one of the most senior librarians, if not the head librarian himself.

"I didn't. It's up in the mountains, where it's safe, a long way from here." Crystal observed that Matt was standing back passively, letting her carry the conversation, and that realization pleased her more than she would have thought it might.

"I see. How did you get here, then?"

"We flew."

"We can't even get our automobiles to start, and you expect

us to believe that you started up and flew an airplane?"

"We didn't fly in an airplane."

"Oh. Well, that's even better. What would you have us believe, that you opened up your arms and took flight with your invisible wings?"

Crystal opened her mouth to reply but was interrupted by a middle-aged woman who also wore what had at one point been business attire—a fashionable skirt suit in her case, now torn completely down one side. "Give it a rest, Bob. I'm starving, and so are my boys, and if these strangers say they can take us somewhere there's food, I'm up for believing them."

The man identified as Bob turned to the woman as what sounded like expressions of approval were raised. "Natalia, I'm just...."

"Just wasting our time, Bob."

"Natalia, I'm still the boss."

Natalia looked around at the destruction, and then pointed at the roaring fire that had been built out of bookcases and the tomes they had held. "The boss over what? A destroyed library? A few hundred thousand books, all waiting to be burned to keep us alive? You expect me, a research librarian who can no longer conduct research in her own library, to worry over what the head librarian says I need to do? Should I go catalog something, you think? Are you really going to fire me because I say I'm hungry and that we should listen to these people?"

Defeated, Bob slumped. Shaking his head, he answered quietly, "No. I suppose there's no point, now, is there?"

"Our estate has a well stocked library," Crystal interjected, trying to smooth over the angst. "You'll all be welcome to enjoy it."

"I don't give a shit about that right now," Natalia said. "I only want food for my boys."

Two boys walked out of the shadow to stand beside her in

the gloomy edge of the central circle of light. Crystal groaned inwardly at the sight of two tall sandy-haired boys, both somewhere around fifteen or sixteen years old if her guess was good. She'd been hoping they found other teenage companions for Linda and Heidi, but—not yet. And not—well, boys. She knew her daughters' taste in boys, and these two were right in the danger zone. She could tell from the soft *Hmmph* behind her that Matt's opinion matched hers.

Crystal shrugged off her concern and called out, "Look, we're limited on time to bicker here, and I'm not of a mind to force anybody to come along. Those of you who want to stay here, stay. If you want to come with us, come into the center."

Several of the people in the dark hobbled up to the edge of the light, but then everybody stopped. "It's dangerous," one man called out.

"It was dangerous," Matt responded. "The earth lost its magnetic hold on part of the atmosphere for a while, so all the harmful rays of the sun were allowed to get to the surface with their full energy. But the reason we're here is that it's over now. A different type of power has stabilized the upper atmosphere once again, and so the sun's glow is back to where it used to be in strength. It's once again safe to walk in the sunlight."

Matt's words had little effect on most, but Natalia grabbed her sons by the arm and, boys in tow, marched up to Crystal. "I'm ready to go," she said, and then bent her head back, face to the sun, and smiled. "You know, it really is nice to be able to look at the sun safely again."

Natalia's actions broke the crowd's resistance. They all, Bob included, moved cautiously, gathering around the god and his wife.

Crystal looked around, pleased that she had succeeded in drawing the group out of the security of their hiding spots, but also horrified at what she saw when they came into the light.

The past several days had been brutal on these people, so much so that she felt a twinge of guilt at the luxury she and the others had been sharing at Matt's estate. The library's inhabitants' ragged clothes were dirty and smelly, but even worse were the burns. Several of them had obviously learned the hard way about the sun's intensity and now bore disfigured faces and blistered exposed skin. Some had body parts wrapped in wet yellowed cloth.

"Matt, can we heal those burns?" she asked softly.

"Yes, but better to wait till we're back at the estate, Love. The healing is instantaneous, but there will still be recovery issues, including weakness, and I'd rather not have them falling off in flight. Plus, once we get home, we'll have thrakkoni to help tend to them."

Crystal nodded. A quick count of heads told her there were thirty-five people in the new group. Half of those were in professional dress, while the rest wore everything from the rags of street bums to jeans and polo shirts worn by the boys.

"What's a thrakkoni?" Natalia asked.

"They're...." Crystal began but was cut off by Matt, who said, "My assistants back at the estate. They will help take care of you when we arrive." Crystal silently thanked Matt; she had been about to describe the dragons, but that would have been the wrong choice with this group.

Matt continued, "Alright, now, here's what's going to happen. We're all going to walk out the front doors. Outside, waiting for us, are the mythical creatures that you're going to find aren't really mythical at all. They're your transportation back to my estate, in fact. Let's go."

Matt led the group out of the door. Crystal looked up and saw several dots already descending in formation, as Sorscha and the red also flew down to the street. They landed about twenty feet away from the group, met by a chorus of gasps.

Just then, the fleet of dragons landed on the street, and the survivors from the library cringed. Some even yelped and leaped backward. Matt's voice rang out over the tumult, "Relax, all. The drakes are to be your transport to your new lives. Please be calm as I help you onto their backs so that we can fly home."

Matt helped the couple with the baby first, gently setting them on the back of a gold dragon and showing the husband how to wrap his hands around his wife's body and hold on. He had all settled into seats on dragon mounts within minutes, and then lifted Crystal back into their spot on Sorscha.

"Now," his voice boomed. "Please hold on tightly. The dragons will fly at their top speed, but it will take a few hours for you to reach my estate. Once you have landed, we will come out and help you further. Have a good flight, and remember that there are no seatbelts to keep securely strapped around you, so, well, just hold on tight."

Sorscha and the drake launched skyward and the rest of the flight followed. "Why aren't they teleporting with us?" Crystal asked.

"Many of them wouldn't survive the shock," Matt replied. "Their digestive systems are near to shutting down as it is due to several days of starvation and dehydration. Teleporting would kill them. Now, hold on, yourself." Matt broadened his mental voice to reach all three women, *Girls, tear your eyes away from the young men and stay with me. We're about to teleport, okay? Hold on.*

Crystal felt the sickening lurch again, and then they were flying over the estate once more toward the patio. She found it interesting to consider, as they spiraled down gently, how differently Matt reacted to different situations. He had no problem, it seemed, discussing the deaths of millions of human beings, and yet he was sensitive to the health of a small group containing a few dozen of them on their ride back to his estate.

What do you think about the boys? she asked.

Eh, I don't know. Their mom seemed a good, strong person, and they had the bearing of good kids themselves. At least it'll give the twins something to do all day besides sit in their rooms and wish they had someone to get in trouble with, right?

They landed, and Matt collected the girls to the side as the dragons transformed back. Sorscha slipped into her clothing and walked up to Crystal. "Crystal, I'd be pleased to put that egg in a special display for you if you'd like."

Crystal realized that she had forgotten she was holding the egg to her chest. "Oh, um, right. Here," she said, awkwardly handing the precious decoration to Sorscha. As the thrakkon took it, Matt handed the plate over Crystal's shoulder to her. "Please display this as well." Sorscha nodded and headed in.

Matt stood for a few moments looking at the twins, who were in turn staring up into the sky. "Four or five hours, Linda and Heidi," he said.

"What?" Linda said, jumping at the sound of Matt's voice.

"Four or five hours till the dragons arrive and deposit their human cargo, including the two young boys. You can stand here and watch, or you can just go back to your rooms and wait for me to let you know that they've arrived. I'm sure they'll want to eat and shower before getting to know the two most beautiful young ladies on the grounds, though."

"Dad, we're the only two young ladies on the grounds," Heidi reminded him.

"Well, yeah. Still, you are two very beautiful young ladies. If I know boys, and I think I do, they'll want to get presentable before seeking your companionship. Besides, you have all of your stuff from the old house to put away still."

"Okay, Dad." Heidi shrugged, accepting the inevitable, and the two turned and walked inside back toward their room.

Matt's grin sparkled, and Crystal chuckled. He pulled her face to his and kissed her long and deeply. "Young love," he said.

"Young love," she agreed, and then both returned to their chamber hand in hand.

The Early Years Explained

Crystal and Matt spent the next several hours laying around the room and talking. Crystal had to admit that the position of god had some perks that his employment as dean hadn't, one of which was the ability to spend an entire afternoon, any afternoon, lazing around in a huge comfortable bed with the lady who held the position of god's wife. She thought of a pun on the word position and snickered aloud, causing Matt to turn a questioning look her way.

"Sorry, was amusing myself in my own head."

"Ah," Matt said and settled back into a warm snuggle, only to perk his head up once again. "They're here."

"Who's here?"

"The folks from the library."

"Oh. Those folks. Of course. I was just wondering when they would arrive."

"Sure you were. It's time to go greet them."

"I'll go alert the girls," she said.

"Didn't we say they wouldn't meet the boys till later?"

"Yes, but they won't forgive you if we don't let them watch the boys arrive."

"Good point," Matt said, and got up and summoned tunic and pants from flows of magic. It was simple attire, Crystal saw, for a god and the lord of the estate, but she knew that he preferred to dress simply when he could.

Crystal also dressed simply, but her choices were made from fine cloth and well-embroidered. She shouldn't out-dress Matt, she thought, but she should still look her best. She hurried out and called for the girls, and then followed Matt down the hall and out onto the patio.

The flight descended in an orderly fashion, Crystal observed, starting with the gold drake carrying the small family. Their infant was now screaming at the top of its lungs, and Crystal sympathized, recalling her own first flight. Matt lifted them off of the drake with flows of air, and the dragon transformed back into a thrakkon shape. The couple gawked at his sudden transition into a naked humanoid, and continued staring as the thrakkon pulled on his clothes.

"Welcome," Matt said grandly, a chuckle finding its way into his voice. "Once everyone's down, I will introduce you all." Crystal saw that Sorscha had come out to stand to Matt's right, and Rellgll had joined them as well, standing a pace behind his master. The remaining drakes landed as smoothly as the gold had, and the process was repeated each time. The sixteen drakes that had flown the humans had transformed and changed quickly, and these thrakkoni now all stood to the side.

"Welcome, welcome," Matt said in his magically-amplified voice. "This is your home now for as long as you wish to remain and abide by the basic expectation of residents. You are safe within its protective shell. Don't consider the thrakkoni who brought you here to be your servants, but they will help you get to the rooms that have been prepared for you, and then to the dining hall where a meal has been laid out. Please, do not over-eat, as your bodies haven't had a good fueling for a while and will as a result reject it, and you will end up worse off. This is Rellgll, my primary administrator, who will be working you all in to the flow of maintenance and activities here over the next couple of days as you recover. For now, though, enjoy your newfound home, and take some time off to rest and relax. First, though, let me see to your injuries."

Matt walked through the crowd, touching each of the new arrivals on the head with his hand. Crystal saw with each exchange a delicate-looking, purple-colored flow that was new to her. Some of the new arrivals smiled warmly as he touched them, but the more badly burned gasped at the shock of healing. One of them unwound the cloth bandage that had been wrapped around her head, and a companion next to her exclaimed in joy and knelt on the ground in front of Matt.

Matt chuckled softly as he continued his healing round and said, "None of that. I don't do the groveling humans thing. Those of you being healed from severe burns will be quite weak for a while, so it's important that you get some rest. I will ask the thrakkoni who show you to your rooms to check in on you to see if you need anything while you do so. You will be welcome to join the community, of course, but only after you are well."

Matt nodded his head in a brief bow, then turned and went inside with Crystal at his heels. When the twins did not move to follow, Matt and Crystal each grabbed one by the hand and pulled them along. "We must let them rest and relax," Matt repeated once they were out of earshot.

Safely back at the room, Matt let out a guffaw.

Crystal asked, "Did you see the way the boys were sizing Heidi and Linda up? After, of course, they got done staring at the nude girl thrakkoni. I'm not sure which pair to be more worried for."

Matt sniffed. "Those are our daughters. They'd better not size them up too much. Besides, there are plenty of thrakkoni to play chaperone for us."

"Like the one did yesterday?"

"Hmm—yeah, valid point. By the way, it wasn't her fault. Aphrodite played a dirty trick."

"I'd been meaning to ask how that happened."

"There's one plant essence that puts thrakkoni to sleep, much like chloroform acts on humans. Aphrodite used it on Brrin, and then to keep her knocked out she cast a local extreme cold area to reduce Brrin's body temperature and put her into hibernation state."

"Why didn't she just use magic to knock her out or tie her up?"

"Thrakkoni are immune to magic, remember? We made them that way for this very reason, so that none of us could magically dominate any of the others' most trusted servants. On top of that, thrakkoni can communicate mentally with each other, and with humans as they wish, and there's nothing a god or goddess can do to block it. If Aphrodite's surprise hadn't been perfect, Brrin would have let every thrakkon on the estate know what was happening, and that would have become messy."

"Could the thrakkoni have killed her en masse?"

"I really doubt it. But they would also have alerted me, and—remember what I said about the battle that killed off the dinosaurs? Aphrodite is more powerful now than Hermes was then, and I have become far more powerful. Our battle would be epic, but could easily tear the world apart. More importantly, the truce would work to stop a major battle. The other gods would appear, join forces, and stop us by whatever means they had."

"Oh," Crystal said. "I suppose that means you won't be rushing over to her estate to ask her what the hell she's doing, eh?"

Matt shrugged and gave her a hopeless look. "Why would she tell me if I did?"

Crystal had to admit Matt had a point. "Right. So what does that leave us to do now? Just keep letting her pick at us?"

"No. I have an idea."

"Oh. I'm not certain whether to be scared of your idea or not."

"You'll like it."

"I'm sure," she said with a touch of sarcasm in her tone. "So what is it?"

"I'm taking you to Olympus."

Crystal froze briefly, her eyelashes batting in confusion. "Oh, okay," she said, "Olympus. A place mortals can't go. Right?"

Matt smiled, a mischievous twinkle in his eyes, and said, "A place mortals can't go on their own, yes. It's a place very, very few humans have ever visited. Think of it as an eternal godly palace mixed with that legendary bar scene from a certain space movie you and I watched. It's the hangout of the gods, and you just need godly transportation to get there."

"Oh," Crystal said, mind racing to catch up with the implications, and then continued, "so assuming you can get me there, which is a fine assumption, of course—how will that get us closer to knowing what Aphrodite is up to?"

"She is there. Frequently. Her human toys bore her eventually, so she likes to play games with her peers. That's part of the reason I don't go there much at all, and that, in turn, is how this is going to work out. Everyone will be surprised to see me there, and most will be shocked that I brought a human. Hell, many will be shocked that I'm together with a human in the first place, after the spectacular manner in which she and I split. Word will reach her, and she's bound to make an appearance, there or here, and either way, we'll be able to get a little face to face time with her."

"I guess," Crystal replied, still not certain she agreed with him on the likely outcome. "And what if she doesn't show up?"

"Then you get to see the mighty Olympus. And drink nectar and eat ambrosia, too. Even the worst case sounds good, no?"

"Right. Let's go, then. I'm just still not sure I see this ending well."

"It'll be fine. Trust me."

She nodded slowly, remembering the last time she'd heard that phrase.

"You'll want to dress up a little, though. My peers can be a little strange."

Crystal chortled. "Of course they can, dear, they're your peers."

Matt grunted in reply, saying to Sorscha as the thrakkon entered. "Sorscha, Crystal needs to be stunningly beautiful. Er. Beautiful-er, that is. More than she normally is, to me. She needs to be so beautiful that other gods' jaws will drop."

Sorscha's eyes widened at the last. "Mirrthra, Master?"

Matt nodded, and then explained to Crystal, "Mirrthra is the ancient name for Olympus. It came from a very early language for the word for gaiety. Which is, of course, what we're going to go participate in. Gaiety. Right?"

Crystal played along despite her misgivings. "Gaiety. That's what we're in for. Right."

Sorscha pulled Crystal into the dressing room, making short hissing sounds that Crystal guessed must serve as indicators of agitation. Closing the door, she sat Crystal down in a chair and began working on her hair.

"Very few humans have gone to Mirrthra, Crystal," Sorscha said.

Crystal swallowed, not certain what to say. Finally she blurted out, "I know. But I'll have Matt with me. All will be well." She wanted to believe it, herself.

In the mirror, she saw Sorscha's head bob once in assertive agreement. "Yes, all will be well. Just—remember, Crystal. The gods are fickle. Some appear in human form, and some do not. Some appear wise, and some do not. Some behave well, and some—do not. The least of them is powerful enough to snuff out the life of you or me. The master will protect you, of that I have no doubt. But you should take extra care to not need protecting."

Sorscha spent a few moments pulling a tangle out of Crystal's hair, and then continued, "Has he told you what happened between him and Ben'thra?" At Crystal's blank stare, Sorscha fumbled with the comb and with her words at the same time,

"Um, that's his old name. He was last called, let me see—Hermes?"

Crystal recognized that. "Yes, he did. When they tore open a canyon in the world and killed off the dinosaurs?"

"Is that what he said? A canyon?" Sorscha asked, chuckling despite her obvious concern. Crystal nodded, and she continued, "Did the human scientists in your era ever hypothesize about a single supercontinent in the past?"

"Yeah, sure," Crystal replied. "It was called Pangaea, if I recall, and they thought it broke up a couple hundred million—years—ago—oh." She blinked a couple of times, a new reality pummeling her mind. "It was Matt's battle with Hermes that broke Pangaea, wasn't it?"

Sorscha nodded, and Crystal objected. "But wait. The dinosaurs were extinct before Pangaea supposedly broke up. Weren't they?"

"Actually," Sorscha replied, "the dinosaurs were around as Pangaea broke up, and for many million years after."

"Matt said that his battle killed off the dinosaurs."

"It did."

"In his speech, he said that the battle lasted a while, but I figured a while meant, oh, maybe, a few days or so. Are you saying the battle between Mars and Hermes lasted for...." Crystal's mind was still working to do the math involved, "...over a hundred million years?"

Sorscha nodded. "It was quite a battle, Crystal," she said simply.

"Good god," Crystal breathed.

"The best, my lady," Sorscha agreed, a smile twisting her lips at the corner.

"No, no—and please, call me Crystal, remember? It's just that he battled with Hermes for longer than, well, for longer than it's been since the battle."

"That's why the gods have declared a truce, Crystal. Any two of them could easily cause the extinction of thousands of species as the Master did in his battle with Hermes."

Crystal yelped slightly as Sorscha pulled on a stray bunch of hair. She considered the thrakkon's words. The enormity of what she was going into hit her; her husband of fifteen wonderful years had spent over a hundred million years just in one battle, and with a god whom he was probably going to meet at Olympus.

"Sorscha?"

"Yes, Crystal?"

"I know you don't feel comfortable answering most questions about Aphrodite, but...." She saw Sorscha's face tighten in the mirror as she continued, "Was Aphrodite married to Matt before the battle?"

Sorscha answered quickly, "No, not before."

"When, then?"

She watched Sorscha's face as the thrakkon seemed to calculate whether to answer. Finally she said, "Well, you know that she was a human before she became a god, yes? There weren't humans before the battle. In fact, the dinosaur species were the gods' first attempt at mortal diversions for themselves, and they turned out to be too much like pets, so not many of the gods mourned their loss after they became extinct."

"Too much like pets?"

"Sure. The dinosaurs were a mighty and greatly varied group of species, but they exhibited no real conscious thought. Humans may not be as physically strong or as diverse as a species, but you, at least, show a fair amount of self-determination."

"You dodged the question well," Crystal said. When Sorscha looked confused, she said, "You know—when Aphrodite was married to Matt."

"Oh. Not long after the battle, actually. It was in the first few cycles."

"Sorscha, were you alive during that time?"

"I was. I was the first thrakkon created by the master to be in his service."

"So what did you do during the hundred million years of battle?"

"I fought by the master's side, just as Drragl fought by Hermes's side. Neither god, to their credit, ever asked us to fight one another. But we fought off all manner of attacks against our masters, and we fought, and we fought. It was exhausting, and I had to go away many times to eat and to rest. It hurt, at first, but after a few years it was just—normal, I guess. Strange to say, but we just settled into a rhythm."

Crystal looked at Sorscha with a new level of appreciation. This creature, who was incapable of a human's physical love, had stood beside Matt through battle for over a hundred million years, facing herself the possibility of death that he would never, could never, face. "Thank you."

"For what?"

"For being here for him for so long."

Sorscha hissed in what Crystal guessed was a dismissive tone. "He is worth every minute, as I am sure you agree. Yes?"

Crystal did agree.

Olympus

After nearly two hours of Sorscha fussing with hair, makeup, and gown, Crystal walked out of the dressing room resplendent. Matt turned from where he had been standing and whistled his appreciation.

"Very nicely executed, my ladies."

"You're not so bad yourself, my lord," Crystal said with a curtsy. And he *was* handsome. A crimson silk tunic loosely fit the curves of his muscular chest, its wide hems embroidered in gold dragons. It draped over black slacks whose trim down the sides of the legs was subtly enhanced in more gold threads that sparkled in the light. Black leather war boots completed the attire, strapped on with simple black leather strips that wound up from the instep to where they buckled on the sides of his calves. Over the outfit he wore a golden belt and diagonal sash. To the side where the sash and belt came together, he was attaching a bejeweled sword in its sheath. The sword completed the outfit, with a massive ruby-based and black-leather-wrapped pommel attached to a gold hilt. The sheath of red-glazed metal was impressive by itself, serving as home to several sizeable rubies at its tip.

"That's a broadsword, right?" Crystal asked. He had given her a lengthy monologue once on the different types of European swords, and how they were different from Asian swords, while touring a military museum. At the time she had been puzzled over how much he seemed to know of arms and armaments, but she had written it off then to him being a normal boy who had learned normal boy things.

Matt smiled. "Indeed. My favorite traditional combat weapon." To emphasize his point, he drew the sword and twirled it a few times. Crystal agreed it was impressive, but—*c'mon. What sword wouldn't be impressive when wielded by the god of war?* she thought to herself.

"So, just out of curiosity, what's your favorite nontraditional combat weapon?" Crystal asked with a smirk.

Matt sheathed his sword and scratched his chin. "That would have to be an artillery piece fired from the shoulder." She looked closer; he seemed to be serious.

"Can you do that?" She wasn't sure why, but the picture of a huge cannon being fired from atop someone's shoulder, even when that someone was the god of war, seemed impossible.

"I can." Matt's grin was impish. "It really freaks the other side out when you walk toward them carrying a cannon on your shoulder, stopping every few feet to fire it."

"I bet."

"Enough talk of war, love. You look exquisite. And radiant. Exquisitely radiant, I say."

Crystal curtsied again and spun around for him. On the way around, she caught her first glimpse of herself in the mirror and realized that she had to agree with Matt. Sorscha had done a very fine job. She wasn't sure if Sorscha had been lucky in her insistence on the gown she chose, or if she'd been secretly communicating with Matt, but the pair matched perfectly. Crystal's red silk gown had black slashes across the chest and down the skirt, and its hems, like Matt's, were also widely embroidered in gold dragons. The fabric clung to her curves perfectly, the low-cut bosom highlighting an exquisite ruby necklace that, to Crystal, felt like a museum piece. The gold chain was made of delicate thread-like wires woven in intricate, sinuous patterns around two carved onyx dragons. "How did you get us matching outfits?" she asked.

"Oh, I'm just good that way. Nice shoes. You are aware those are rubies?"

Crystal agreed that the shoes she was wearing were beautiful, peering down at the scarlet heels with straps gemmed in sparkling red crystals that wove up her legs to just above her knees. She loved the way the rubies sparkled through the thigh-length slits in the sides of her gown.

"Sorscha, my compliments on Crystal's hair and makeup. Very nice job."

Sorscha hissed softly at the compliment. Most of the two hours had been spent twisting and curling Crystal's locks into the sculpture she now wore. Split down the side, Crystal's hair flowed in waves of ringlets over her bare shoulders. Around her head were two braids, each starting in the front and going straight to look like a crown with diamonds and rubies attached to wires and woven in.

"I feel like a queen."

"You are a queen, Love."

Crystal smiled and curtsied low. "And you, sir, are my king."

"Careful. You're going to make Sorscha vomit."

Crystal turned to Sorscha. "Yeah, right. Do thrakkoni vomit?"

Sorscha chortled and shook her head. "No, not usually. And certainly not over the loving words of a god and his wife."

"See?"

"Whatever. Let's make like a tree and vanish."

"Okay, Mr. Broken Metaphor."

Matt chuckled and turned to the door. "C'mon. I haven't had nectar in a long time, and I can't wait to get you drunk and have your way with me."

Crystal smiled, thinking about how cute Matt had sounded the first time he'd broken that metaphor. It hadn't changed over the years. She followed him out into the dressing room. "I assume nectar, being the drink of the gods, is a bit alcoholic. Shouldn't I probably stay away from the drink tonight, considering our intent?"

Their conversation was interrupted as they entered the suite's sitting room and both girls whistled and clapped their hands while jumping up and down in excitement. "Mom! Dad! You two look unbelievable!" Heidi exclaimed, and Linda nodded her head in vigorous agreement.

Crystal spun again for the girls, showing off and loving the attention. Then she bent over and kissed each girl on the forehead. The girls promised to be good, and the pair left the apartment and paraded up the stairs. Everyone stopped and stared, and when the couple met Krista in the hall she gushed compliments over Crystal's regal appearance.

They kept going, following the path Crystal recognized that they had taken several days ago to get up to the glass cupola on the roof. Once they were alone, Matt continued the conversation from before. "When we get there, don't refuse to drink. To not partake in the refreshments would look bad. Nectar is quite stout stuff, though, so sip it very, very slowly. The same with ambrosia. It's quite delicious, and you'll want to eat it till you explode, but restrict yourself to a couple of bites, no matter how much you're offered."

Crystal nodded, nervousness surfacing for the first time. "Anything else I should know?"

"Follow my lead and you should be fine. There are some great old friends who will likely be there, as well as some old rivals. You've always been very good at reading me, though, so rely on that and don't worry much. Oh, and you'll probably feel all wide-eyed and awed, and don't be afraid to make that obvious. There are some gods who will likely feel affronted if a human doesn't get a little giddy over the grandeur of it all. Most importantly, be yourself and concentrate on having a good time. This is a date between you and me, first and foremost. Anything else we might accomplish, like confronting Aphrodite, is a bonus, but it's not why we're there, okay?"

Crystal nodded. "By the way, how will they look?"

"The gods, you mean?"

"Yeah. Will they all be dressed as finely as we are?"

"No, of course not. Olympus is our local pub. We go there to get away from humans, sit back and have some godly delights, and chatter amongst ourselves. To answer your question even more thoroughly than you meant it, I think, you need to be prepared for anything, visually. You've seen me shape change a few times, right? To a god, it's easy. They'll all likely be lounging in whatever shape makes them most comfortable, whether humanoid or not. Or, clothed or not. Or even the right gender or not. The eastern gods tend to appear as themselves more often, so they'll be recognizable for the most part. Like I said—go with your gut, follow my lead, and try to have a good time while doing it. The gods will know if you're faking."

Crystal nodded. "All right, let's see if I have this straight. Drink, but only sip. Eat, but only nibble. Follow your lead. Follow my gut. Gape and gawk, but don't be surprised. Gotcha."

Matt smirked and grabbed her hand. "Perfect. Just perfect," he breathed, looking at her from head to toe in a way that suggested he wasn't referring to her recital of the instructions. "Now, close your eyes and hold my hand tight. You've teleported before, but not to an entirely different dimension. We're going— well, I guess it would be called metaspace. It doesn't exist in the universe, and yet it exists everywhere in the universe. And in that one minutely tiny and infinitely large spot is the pub where the gods hang out."

She closed her eyes, expecting a now-familiar jumping sensation, but she felt a lurch as her body seemed to be trying to fit into a single atom and spread out to the stars at the same time. The strange sensation only lasted a tiny part of a second, though, and before she had time to analyze it she felt herself standing in an exuberantly noisy room.

"We're there, Love. Open your eyes and gawk."

She did, and turned away from him to face the inside of the strangest pub scene she had ever seen. He hadn't been kidding, she realized, that the gods and goddesses would be at their most comfortable. She saw Greek gods talking to kimono-clad Asian deities, and others lounging about in robes and even some in pajamas. A group in the far corner wore even less.

"Matthew!" a god clad in what appeared to be a lime green bathrobe yelled and sauntered over. "Been a long time, friend. Good to see you."

"Thanks, Helepatus," Matt replied in a dry tone. "How have you been, when you haven't been foolhardily attacking your betters?"

"What, is the almighty god of war going to whine about a little skirmish? You killed my best mage, you know."

"That was your best? Oh, my, that's too bad. You have my sympathies, friend, in addition to my recommendation that you seek better humans. Some who can actually do magic, perhaps?" Crystal saw a somewhat bashful smile on the face of Helepatus and wondered if he looked up to Matt as a mentor. Matt continued, "But I'm being rude. Helepatus, this is my wife, Crystal. Crystal, Helepatus, known to the Greeks as the god of—what was it again? Fertilizer and stuff?"

"I can understand the god of war confusing fertilizer with flocks, fruits, and bee-keeping."

"Oh, right. And husbandry, too, right?"

Crystal watched the banter, not sure how to react. Helepatus solved the problem by bowing, taking her hand, and kissing it. "The beautiful wife of Ares is always welcome in my company. The ancients know me as Helepatus, and the Greeks knew me as Aristaeus, but you can call me whatever or whenever you like."

"Flirting with my wife when we're out on a date? Shame on

you. I might forgive you, though, if you arrange a drink for us."

The three moved together toward the bar, a simple affair without any of the typical hardware Crystal had come to expect at Earth-bound drinking establishments. The barkeep, a stout dark-haired man with a weathered complexion who spoke with both the bluster and the accent of an Irishman, noticed her watching him and winked. "Matt?" Crystal said telepathically. "The barkeep looks and sounds Irish."

"Of course he does," Matt thought back.

"Isn't that a little clichéd?"

"So? Everybody knows Irish barkeeps are the best barkeeps, Love."

"How many varieties of nectar do you have in Olympus?"

"One."

"Doesn't look like the gods drink anything else," she said, noting that there were no bottles visible behind the bar.

"No."

"So why do you even need a barkeep?"

"Because he's Irish."

Crystal groaned quietly in frustration as they arrived at the bar and Matt motioned for a drink for each of them. A huge hand, easily a foot across, clapped Matt on the shoulder as a voice growled, "Well, well. Look who danced in."

Crystal turned to gape at the behemoth who had just assaulted her husband. The giant, towering well over seven feet tall, was scruffy from head to toe and was the only person in the room clad in armor. His boots appeared to be furs simply wrapped around his trunk-like legs and secured by leather thongs, and a massive hammer with runes inscribed on its head and along its shaft hung from a loop on his belt.

Matt brushed the giant's bear paw off his shoulder as he slowly turned to face him. "Silk, man. Why won't you ever try to be gentle with fabrics?"

"Real fabrics don't need the touch of a pansy."

"Your real fabrics aren't fabrics at all. How many bulls went into the making of your boots, Thor?" The giant snorted, and Matt continued, "Not that you ever bothered learning to count. Anyway, it's my honor to introduce my wife, Crystal. Crystal, this is—just call him Thor. He likes that name. A lot."

Thor leered at Crystal. "Tyr, I see why you never come here anymore. If I had a beauty like that in Valhalla, I'd never come here either."

"What he's trying to tell you, Crystal," Matt said in a voice that sounded intentionally slowed, "is that he thinks you are an unparalleled beauty, and I agree with him on that. But don't let him fool you. Thor keeps dozens of beauties in Valhalla, don't you, my gigantic friend?"

The barkeep interrupted by handing a glass to each of them. Speaking softly in a heavily-accented voice to Crystal, he warned, "Drink it lightly, lass. Ye've never had a drink with a smoother or more powerful kick than what's in that cup." He winked, and then went back to busily doing nothing behind the bar.

Crystal took her first sip of the nectar and realized quickly how important Matt's and the barkeep's warnings had been. It was delightful. It tasted of delicately honeyed fruit juice, and the warming sensation began at the top of her stomach and spread all directions through her body. She wanted to giddily down the rest of the cup and then ask for another, but she also felt the intoxicant already fogging her brain and turning the tip of her nose numb. One or two sips an hour, or maybe a day, were all that she could take.

Matt, for his part, raised his glass cheerily to the giant and drank a large pull. "Ah, nectar."

"Can you bring some home with us?" Crystal asked.

The giant exploded in peals of laughter. "Tyr, I see why you brought this one. A fine question from a fine woman."

Matt turned to Crystal and said, "I can, but it's not the same. Here, it's nectar. Back home, the different dimensionality makes it lose its essence, and it just becomes regular mead. Not that there's anything wrong with mead, of course, but why bring home another bottle when I have entire cellars full of it?"

Matt and Thor exchanged a few more jokes, and then the giant walked away and Matt grabbed Crystal's hand. "Let's go over there," he said, pointing with his chin to an unoccupied corner.

As they walked Crystal was able to take in more of her surroundings. The bar itself had been a simple slab of highly polished wood—mahogany, she thought. The walls were a little more difficult to figure out, the paint changing color as she moved around the bar. She was reminded of the holographic metallic finishes she had seen, but this appeared to be painted wood, and the only explanation her mind could fathom was that it was, after all, Olympus. The art was similarly chameleon in nature, each of the regularly-sized frames containing an image of a classic work of art, or a skyline of a city, or a landscape, some of which Crystal recognized, and the images moved with her body.

She noticed that there was only one exit from the room, a curtain hanging over the wall near the table toward which they were walking.

I presume everybody teleports in and out of here, she directed a thought at Matt.

Indeed.

I kind of expected it to look a little more—um....

Greek? he finished the thought for her. *Like in all the movies about the Greeks, where it was whitewashed and columned and the gods just stood there and argued?*

Well, yeah.

Now why would we have a retreat like that? We can argue anywhere on any of the existing worlds. But if you really want circular columned room for arguing, you go through that curtain.

I was just about to ask what the curtain led to.

I figured as much. Beat you to it, didn't I?

Why is the furniture so eclectic? Crystal asked. As they walked, she realized that every table was set in a different style.

Matt answered out loud, "What kind of furniture do you want, Love? We can go rustic Alaska bar scene, or posh New York City, or beach lounge chairs." As he spoke of each motif, the furniture shifted to match his words.

"I like rustic, really. But with cushions, please."

"Absolutely. Your wish is my command." The set transformed into a round plank-made table with three handmade birchwood chairs, each with several inches of cushion on the seat. As she sat, he sent, *Each god reworks the furniture to suit his or her needs, Love, and just leaves them that way for the next god to change.*

She should have known that. *I presume the room next door changes décor too based on what whichever god is in it wants, right?* she asked, relishing a long sip of her nectar to cover the pause in speaking.

Yep.

And the artwork is controllable, too?

Of course.

Why am I seeing so many different images then?

You're seeing all of our images. Each of us has the power to filter out the pictures from the other gods, but you unfortunately are stuck with what you can physically see.

Oh. And the barkeep is Irish because you like an Irish barkeep, right?

No, he's Irish because he likes to be an Irish barkeep.

He flashed a "gotcha" smile at her, and she playfully sneered back and stuck her tongue out at him.

"Lover's quarrel in the perfect house of Mars?" Crystal jumped in surprise as a sultry voice that she recognized came from behind her.

"Oh, how sweet. She jumps and looks all startled. Does she do any other of those cute human tricks you used to enjoy watching me do?"

"Nah," Matt replied, lazily stretching in his chair, "she's not into begging like you used to be. But you know, I was just hoping we might see you here tonight. Why don't you pull up a seat and share a drink with us?"

The third chair at the table morphed into an ostentatious throne and Aphrodite stepped seductively over to it and sat down. As she came into view, Crystal blushed. Aphrodite was naked.

Matt drank from his mug as Aphrodite sat, and then continued in his bored tone, "So, what'cha been up to, Kali?" Crystal appreciated Matt's refusal to give any notice at all to Aphrodite's lack of attire. She found herself working hard not to stare, in fact. Aphrodite was displaying an incredibly well-built physique, muscle tone perfectly enveloped in smooth skin. Her ample breasts hung perfectly, the complete lack of sag irritating Crystal more than she would have thought possible.

Aphrodite lounged in the throne, leaning back with her shoulders raised up and back, displaying her breasts to their greatest advantage, and replied, "Besides wishing you would quit calling me by that name?"

Matt dismissed her concern with a shrug, smile not leaving his face. "Fine. Would you prefer Venus, Aphrodite, or Stacy?"

Aphrodite leered back. "Stacy is fine, Matthew."

"Brings you back to old times, doesn't it?"

"You remember!"

"I said brings you back, not me. I'd just as soon not go back there."

"Well, if you're going to be uncivil," Aphrodite pouted, starting to rise.

"Wait," Matt interrupted her. He leaned forward intently, still looking at her eyes. Crystal was proud of her husband for holding his eyes level. "I need to ask you something."

Aphrodite made a show of settling back into her throne, pushed her breasts back up into the air, played sensuously with a thin silver chain that hung around her neck, and batted her eyelashes. Crystal fantasized briefly about being a goddess herself, perhaps even with the perfect, gravity-free, breasts. She was absolutely certain that if this creature in front of her could do it, she could too. She would just have to be patient, she told herself—she would wear Matt down on the topic, whether it took a month, a year, or even a decade.

"Well, then, ask away, my dear Matthew."

"Why have you been attacking us?"

Aphrodite feigned a shocked expression. "I don't know what you mean, dear. I haven't attacked anyone." The sweetness in her voice was disgusting.

Matt nodded, apparently prepared to concede the point. "You're right, of course. I'm sorry. I shouldn't have characterized your leading the twins down to my war room as an attack, should I?"

"Absolutely not, Matthew."

"So how should I have characterized it? Did you think you were teaching the girls something?"

"Of course not. But remember when I found your *war room?*" The sweetness disappeared, replaced by a venom that surprised Crystal. "It sparked a fight that lasted for days, remember? You never wanted to show me any of your tricks—outright refused, remember? I just wanted to make sure that your little one here had a chance to see the true God of War."

Crystal realized with a shock that the woman sitting with them—Aphrodite, of all people—gods, she corrected herself—was jealous of her.

Matt raised his glass with a smile. "You succeeded, Stacy. Didn't she, Crystal?"

Crystal thought it best to just nod while hiding behind her glass. She had to admit that she was out of her league. She had, just a couple of weeks ago, considered herself an equal and peer to Matt, but now she was sitting between two immortals.

"Besides," Aphrodite continued, "I was pleased to note that you still had our tapestry up, and it was wonderful to show that to the girls. I'm sure your little pet here saw it too, right?" Aphrodite asked, flashing a dazzling smile at Crystal.

"My wife saw it, yes. Stacy, if you're going to insist that I be civil, perhaps you could return the favor and call her by her name? It's Crystal."

"Crystal, then," Aphrodite said. "How nice to meet you so wonderfully formally, and finally, Crystal, wife of Mars."

"So." Matt ignored the sarcasm in Aphrodite's tone and said, "Why the parlor trick with the pictures in the bedroom?"

Aphrodite's laugh was clear and ringing. "Why, I thought that a mighty clever way to remind your cute little thing there— Crystal, right?—that you really do belong to me." Aphrodite again turned to Crystal and asked, "How'd you like my little surprise with the wedding photo, dear?"

"It was a blast," Matt replied for his wife, his voice making it clear that he wasn't impressed.

"Good, I thought it might be." Aphrodite flashed a toothy smile at Crystal. "See, dearie, you're human, as I'm sure you've already realized. Matthew there will have his way with you for the rest of your short little lifespan. And then he'll be mine again, forever. Forever is such a wonderful word, isn't it? Oh, but I shouldn't keep you two from enjoying your evening. You have such a short time with him, don't you, mortal?"

As Aphrodite started to rise, Matt leaned forward. "Stacy?"

Aphrodite leaned toward Matt in response to his beckoning. Crystal was envious of the way her perfect breasts leaned in as well, seemingly reaching out for Matt's pleasuring touch, but she very nearly jumped for joy when she saw that Matt kept his eyes locked on the Goddess of Love's face.

"Yes, Matthew?" Aphrodite asked, and Crystal couldn't help wincing at her tone. No wonder this woman was the Goddess of Love, Crystal thought. She had a bedroom voice that made Crystal want to sleep with her, and Crystal had never, ever, felt that way about a woman before.

Matt adopted his own bedroom voice as he replied, "We—you and me? Together? Forever?" He nodded along with Aphrodite, and then added in an abruptly harsh tone, "It's not going to happen. Ever. Got it?" He rose to his feet and leaned over the table, his tone growing even more menacing, the consonants hammered out drum beats, "And you know what? My family is my family. You touch them again, you set traps for them again, you interfere in our lives again, and so help me, the truce be damned. I'll blast you out of existence. Do you hear me?" Crystal worked hard to keep her composure, to keep from cheering out loud, as she heard Matt's tone change from merely harsh to the dangerous and commanding tone she imagined one must expect from an angry God of War.

Aphrodite was clearly surprised by Matt's vehemence, and though she only let it show for a brief moment, Crystal saw the depth to which Matt's words shook her. After a few moments she regained her composure, sneering as she replied, "I hear you, war god," and walked across the room to join a knot of other unclad celebrants on the opposite couch.

Crystal let out the breath she hadn't realized she was holding. "Wow."

Matt stared into his cup, his angry expression slowly relaxing. He drained its contents, and then spoke to Crystal without looking at her. "That wasn't what I was expecting to happen."

"What were you expecting to happen?"

Matt's angry face finally disappeared as he shot a grin her way. "Honestly, I wasn't expecting anything specific. But it sure as hell wasn't that."

She reached across the table and grasped his hand. "Want another drink?"

"That sounds good."

Crystal grabbed his cup and walked over to the bar. The barkeep saw her coming and was there before she was with a full cup to exchange for the empty. He winked at Crystal, motioning her head closer, and whispered, "You're a good lass for him, you are. Don't be lettin' Aphrodite and her venom get to you. All right?" Crystal nodded, and he winked and continued, "Those two were never right for each other, and they had some bad blood many eons ago. But he loves ya, and I can see that from here. Get back over there and love him back."

Crystal nodded again, and replied, "Thanks, um—what's your name?"

"Mike," the barkeep said simply. He winked again and then walked back down the length of the bar.

Crystal walked back to the table, trying to replicate the strut she had seen Aphrodite use earlier. Matt grinned in appreciation. She handed him his new drink with a curtsy, and then sat down and took another tiny sip of her own. Again, she was assaulted by an entire-body pleasure. "Oh, oh, oh my," she said, her words coming out as more of a moan than actual speech. "This stuff is really good."

Matt grinned evilly across the rim of his own cup, held to his lips. "What did I tell you about my plans for tonight?"

"I feel like you're having your way with me right now with

just sips. I'm scared if I drink more than a taste I'll fall down into screaming orgasm."

"That just might happen, actually, so be careful."

A new shadow fell across the table just then, and Crystal looked up to see a bearded man. His clothes were unremarkable; a white cloth wrapped around in the style of a toga was all that he wore.

Matt looked up and saluted with his glass. "My old friend Hermes. Have a sit, would you? This is my wife, Crystal. Crystal, Hermes. He and I go way back, Love."

"So I hear," Crystal said. With an impish grin she said, "Matt tells me he killed all the dinosaurs by flinging you around."

"Now see here, young lady, it was a mutual flinging," Hermes said, changing the throne back to a simple bar stool and sitting down with his drink.

"Yeah, that was pretty epic flinging, wasn't it?" Matt asked.

"Absolutely! But, ah, let's not do it again."

Matt held up his cup in response, and Hermes clinked his own cup against it. Crystal felt moved to join in, and her cup was eagerly met by both Matt's and Hermes' cups. Leaning in, the new addition to the table whispered to both, "Venus was really up and in your face, old chap. Now, if there's anything I can do to help, you'll let me know, won't you?"

"Of course," Matt replied with a smile.

Crystal smiled and asked, "Hermes?"

"Yes, m'lady?"

"What started the battle?"

"What battle?"

"The battle we were talking about. Between you and Matt."

"Oh that battle!" Hermes replied slowly, a little too much nectar evident in his system. He smiled. "It was—um—well...." Hermes sought an answer for several seconds by looking into his cup, and then met Crystal's eyes again. "Honestly, I don't remember."

"Ah. Matt didn't either."

"We were both young and brash then, I'm afraid," Hermes said.

"Young? That battle was measured in the millions of years, wasn't it?"

"Years were marked a little differently back then."

"But the battle was still pretty long, wasn't it?"

"It was. Lucky that we'll never see another, isn't it? And on that note, I must beg my leave." Hermes got up, staggered slightly, and then wandered back to the table where Crystal had seen him earlier.

"He gets a little drunk sometimes," Matt said quietly.

"How do gods get drunk, if you have no digestive systems?"

"We allow ourselves to. It's a decision on our part, just like tasting food is. And quite a pleasurable decision it is, too."

"Oh. Wow. Hey, how come a Greek god had a British accent?"

"He probably spent the last several hundred years hanging out in the Isles. During the technology eras, we kind of go wherever we're most comfortable, where the climate most suits us."

"Which is why you were in California with all the wine, right? Hey, didn't you promise me some ambrosia?"

"Oh, yeah," Matt said, and he looked up at the barkeep and motioned with his fingers held in a square. The barkeep nodded, reached beneath the counter, and brought over two plates, each with a small cube of white fluffy material on it. The barkeep set a plate down in front of each of them and then walked back behind the bar.

Matt picked his up and held it, watching Crystal. "Warning," he said, "this can be quite addictive."

Crystal smiled, picked hers up, and nibbled at a corner of the small cube. The flavor nearly overpowered her with an essence of every sweet she had ever enjoyed. In the one small bite, she tasted several fruits, honey, and a mélange of berry flavors.

"Wow," she said.

"Indeed," Matt replied, smiling broadly at her.

"That's intense."

"Were you expecting bland? Remember, gods only eat for flavor. This is what brings the gods back here cycle after cycle."

"I guess taking this back would get us simple cake, like nectar becomes mead."

"Styrofoam, actually, or at least something that tastes like it. I guess simple cake is appropriate, on second thought, if by simple you mean styrofoamy."

"Well, then, let's eat it here," Crystal said, taking a bigger bite and enjoying the flavors running rampant in her mouth.

Matt smiled, and then bit into his ambrosia. He chewed quickly, a satisfied look on his face, and then said, "The wines in California are nice, indeed, but it's the climate I most enjoyed there. Some of the gods, like Hermes there, enjoy the chill and the mists of the British Isles. Apollo spent some time there this cycle, too, I heard, but he's usually quite a traveler during the technology phases. Thor just stays up at his own estate, or at Valhalla, whichever he prefers at the time. He's not big on human interaction, unless it's a matter of watching a battle at some level or another. Artemis over there," Matt pointed with a nod of his head to a slender goddess with short-cropped sandy hair who was wearing sturdy, simple green and brown clothes, "usually runs alone, hermit-like, in the forests of Europe, but I heard she relocated to the western ranges of America last cycle because of the population growth on the European continent. She and her brother are a little strange."

Artemis, having taken note of the conversation, smiled and flicked her cloak around her. She disappeared from sight, and almost instantaneously reappeared in the spot where Hermes had stood and leaned down, smiling at Crystal. Where Aphrodite's movements had transmitted ravenous sexuality, Artemis's movements seemed the direct opposite—smooth, controlled, and dangerous. She said, "If you're going to talk about me, you should at least introduce us, Matthew."

"I would have, but I'm not certain what name you're going by, dear," Matt said. "In any event, this is my wife, Crystal. Crystal, meet the huntress. Artemis? Diana? Dionne? Which would you prefer?"

The goddess's smile brought a warmth that cut through the danger she seemed to pose. "Di is fine, dear. I see that you've met Matt's fabulous ex-wife, as well. For that, you have my condolences."

Crystal tried to make a demure joke, but it went flat thanks to the effects of the alcohol she had drunk. That, and she really was quite star-struck, she thought. Here, in one night, she was literally meeting the legendary characters of the planet's stories.

"So what brings you to Olympus, Di? You're not here very often," Matt said. Crystal couldn't tell if he was attempting small talk or was actually seeking information.

"I could ask the same of you, but I already know the answer," Artemis said. "You got what you wanted out of that little encounter, didn't you? Nice job. Anyway, to answer your question, I felt like coming. It's been a while, and I've spent a particularly long time out, and a drink sounded like a good way to wait out the cataclysm."

"It's been over for a few days, you know," Matt said.

Artemis nodded slightly in a muted acknowledgement. "I know. The forests and wildlife recover slower than the humans, though. I tried jumping back in right after it warmed up once. Won't ever do it again. Which you'd know, by the way, if you were ever up here yourself."

Matt's eyes wandered toward Aphrodite as he said, "For some reason Olympus just doesn't bring me the same effortless joy it used to. But—hey—how's your brother these days?"

Artemis snorted. "Last I heard, he was researching what they called dark magic in the British Isles somewhere. Haven't seen him in a while, but it would bring me great joy to let him know you asked about him next time he's in my presence."

The sarcasm in the goddess's voice was laid on thick enough to be unmistakable. Crystal was surprised to hear Matt return the tone when he said, "I'm sure it will bring him great joy as well."

Artemis snorted again, this time with a mildly humorous expression. "You two should have a drink together sometime. Yes, I know that'll never happen, but you should. Speaking of drinks, my own is getting warm over there, a situation in which I must intervene. Crystal, it was wonderful to meet you, and I wish you well in your efforts to take care of this big, brooding God of War you have suddenly discovered wrapped around your finger."

As the goddess returned to her table, Crystal tried to send her thoughts telepathically to Matt but couldn't find the flows. They were still there, she could see, but they danced away from her clumsy, alcohol-inhibited grasp. Resigning herself to actual speech, she leaned over and whispered, "Di isn't sarcastic at all, is she?"

"A little, but only toward humans and gods," Matt said, playing along.

"What else is there?"

"Animals and plants. I've never heard her be even slightly sarcastic to a cypress tree."

"Cypress trees probably don't take too kindly to that. Say, who is her brother?"

"Already forgetting your basic mythology? You have had too much to drink, haven't you?" Matt said. She responded by sticking her tongue out playfully, and he continued, "Apollo is her brother, sort of. Keep in mind that brother and sister is more of an assumed relationship among immortals than one dictated by any sort of birth. Those two are so closely matched in personality as to be brother and sister, despite the fact that none of us original deities ever had an actual mother and father, much less the same one."

"Yet you, and I presume others, call Gaia Mother. Is she not really your mother?" Crystal asked.

"No, we call her Mother because of her relative power and her role, not because of any physical birthing events. She's not *our* mother so much as she's *the* mother, to the entirety of what has been created."

"I take it she doesn't come here very often."

"Rarely, and then only on official business," Matt said.

"Official business? That sounds funny, considering the ambiance."

"Remember what I said is behind that curtain? We've had more or less regular meetings, once a cycle or so, since the early days. Gaia always attends those. It's the only time you'll see Apollo here, too."

"You and Apollo don't get along too well, I sensed," Crystal said, curious. Matt hadn't displayed a long-running bout of animosity with anyone she'd ever known of before; even RJ and he had coaxed out a convivial, if occasionally acerbic, sort of working relationship. "Wasn't he the god of healing and poetry and music and—stuff?" She thought back; how much *had* she drank, anyway? *Stuff?*

Matt caught it too and chortled softly. "No, no, dear, Helepatus is the god of stuff, remember? We'll have to wait and see what he picks this cycle. In any event, you're right. The wonderful and perfect and otherwise wonderfully perfect God of Light and Music and Everything Good has had a bit of a running personality conflict with me, the God of War. It can't be that surprising to you. Can it?"

"It is, in fact. You've always been good at mending relationships, even difficult ones. What's different about this one?"

"All the relationships you've seen me in are with mortals. No offense, but I have a bit of an advantage there, whether or not they realize that I'm a god. Apollo, meanwhile, is my peer, and he's a twit, on top of it. I have neither the desire nor the need to mend that relationship."

"Okay, Love, I understand," Crystal said in her most calming voice. She had, for a moment, watched darkness sweep over Matt's expression. It was clear that animosity ran deep between her husband and Apollo, and now wasn't the time to press the matter. She ate the last bite of her ambrosia, chewing slowly, and sighed wistfully when it was gone. "That was so good."

Matt nodded, smiling, the darkness gone. "I bet you want a lot more now, don't you?"

"Yes, I do."

"See? It's addictive. Best to just keep it to one small chunk a visit."

"Fine. I see how it is."

"Pout all you want," he said, "but it's for your protection."

"Well, hell." Crystal looked around the room at the assembly of gods and goddesses, none of whom were paying any attention to the couple. "Is it time to go, then?"

"I think so," Matt said. "We've learned something of use, and you've become the first human in a long, long time to taste both nectar and ambrosia. Ready to head back?"

Crystal nodded and took Matt's outstretched hand. The world lurched again, and she found herself back in the cupola of Matt's estate, looking out across a star-lit landscape, holding his hand. Acting on instinct, she reached up, grabbed his hair, and pulled his mouth down to hers for a long and passionate kiss.

His eyes twinkled when they finally separated. "I love you, God of War" she breathed to him.

"And I love you, Mrs. War." His sardonic smile was gentle. "Let's head downstairs and see about who gets to have their way with who."

"Whom, dear."

"Whatever," Matt said, leading her down the dark stairs.

She happily followed him back to their bedroom, and once there, had an amazingly satisfying night, learning a couple of new tricks of her own.

Mages, Meet Ka

Crystal woke the next morning pleased to feel Matt still snuggling beside her. As she stirred, he leaned in and kissed her forehead. "Morning, Love," he said, his voice radiating happiness.

"Morning to you," she said, her voice sounding the same.

"What did you think of your first visit to Olympus?"

"I want more nectar and ambrosia," she said, allowing the slightest touch of whine into her voice.

"See what I said? Small doses, Love. Maybe more in a year or two."

"A year or two? How do you expect me to wait that long?"

"It's easy. We won't go for a year or two, and then when we do go, you'll have waited that long."

She blew him a quiet raspberry, and he tickled her in response. Rising, Matt strode over to the curtains and swished them aside, letting an overwhelming amount of sun in all at once.

Crystal threw her covers up to shield her face a half-second too late. "Some warning, my lord, would be nice next time."

"Warning? Warning that it's beautiful outside? It's an incredible day, Love. I think today is a perfect day to move the magic outside!"

"Our magic? Outside? That's a little risqué even for you, Matt."

Matt turned and looked at her, confusion registering briefly before a grin took over. "Our magic? Oh, no no no no. That's a private affair, Love. I meant *the* magic. What you and the mages have been practicing. It's a great day to set up the practice area outside."

"You said what I and the mages have been practicing." Crystal's happiness in hearing that had been tempered by her suspicion that Matt had merely slipped in his wording.

Matt looked confused again. "Yes, I did say that. So?"

"It sounded like you have accepted that I've been practicing magic."

Matt shrugged. "You have been, haven't you?"

"And you've hated it."

Matt walked over and cupped Crystal's cheek in his hand. "Love, the last wife I taught magic to was Aphrodite. I've been scared that if you followed her path you would, well, follow her path. Last night, though, made it clear to me how silly that was. You could never end up like her."

"So—you'll teach me magic, then?"

"Yes." Matt punctuated his acquiescence with a light kiss.

Crystal was elated and showed it by throwing her arms around Matt's neck, pulling him down onto the bed in a cuddle. "Thank you. You have no idea how much that means to me," she said, breathing the words into Matt's ear.

"You're probably right. But I'll take the grand hug, anyway, and with pleasure."

Continuing with a thought from earlier, Crystal said, "One thing I don't understand is that when we first entered the sorcerer's chamber, you said the mages couldn't practice anywhere else because that room was specially protected."

"It is, but nothing says the walls have to be there in order for the mages to be protected. I can create similar wards anywhere, and it is good for mages to get a little sun sometimes. Have you seen how pale Birch and Phoenix have been getting?"

"Oh, I really didn't think of that. Yeah, they have been, and I confess I could use some sun myself. And now that Aphrodite is out of the way, there's nothing to hide from, right?"

Matt's face turned serious. "She's not out of the way, Love. It seems like over the past thousand or so years she's gone from being petty and mean to stark raving mad, and the madness is manifesting itself in an obsession for me. I'm not sure where it might be going, but as powerful as she is, it's of concern not only for your safety, but also for the sanctity of the truce among the gods."

"Has the truce ever been breached?"

"No, or at least not for long enough for the rest of the gods to become involved."

"What would happen if the gods had to become involved?"

"We would stop the battle, using any means necessary. There are thirty-two of us with the Father missing, and thirty on two makes for a pretty uneven fight."

"What if the fight resulted in the death of a god? Is that even possible?"

"The death of an immortal is so horrifying that we don't usually even think of it, much less speak of it, but yes, it is possible."

Crystal saw Matt's mood darken and changed the subject back to her curiosity over Aphrodite. "So how did you meet her?"

"Well, you already know she was a human first, right? It was a long, long time ago—several million years long ago, in fact. We gods had just established the truce framework, in fact, and then held discussions on how to keep humans from destroying the same thing we nearly had, and then we established the two thousand year cycles as a result of those talks. Of course, we started with a magic cycle, but in the next cycle, our first technology one, toward the end, I held the position of governor of the province that held most of the power reactors for the land mass you knew as North America. I hadn't been through enough cycles yet to know it is a bad idea for us to hold noteworthy political positions during the technology cycles. Anyway, Stacy was a pretty, and quite talented, reactor technician in the central headquarters complex where my own office was housed, and I ran into her many times before finally stopping to talk. She was an engaging conversationalist, and she intrigued me both with her intelligence and what I sensed of her enormous magical potential. We talked, we dated, and we married."

"Did the two of you have children?"

"No. She didn't want them. She maintained a trim figure that was the talk of the town, and she didn't want to risk losing it."

"That's an awfully selfish way to look at childbearing."

"At the time, I thought it was prudent. Remember, though, that I was already several hundred million years old, yet she was my first wife, and so I thought her attitude was normal."

"Wow. How long were you married before the cataclysm?"

"A year and a half. Boy, did Sorscha surprise me when I brought Stacy here."

"Oh? How so?"

"She did *not* like her, not at all. I attributed it to jealousy for a long time, and that mystified me because Sorscha and I had been together by then for hundreds of millions of years, yet we had never even thought of considering ourselves a couple. It wasn't until much later that she explained why she had reacted to Stacy the way she did, and by then I wished that I had been smart enough to follow her lead."

"Well, you know what they say about hindsight. When did Stacy become a goddess?"

"It wasn't till later. I had it in my plans to help her become a goddess all along, though I had no idea what that actually would mean in the end. I taught her to be a powerful sorceress first, and then began—well, it was silly of me. I can't, despite all my power, make someone into a goddess."

"But she got there anyway, right?"

"Indeed."

"How?"

"Through a transformation that is now impossible."

Crystal sighed. "I'm not going to be like her."

"So then why do you want to be a goddess?"

"Because what Aphrodite said to me last night hurt as much as any words could possibly hurt. Because I only have another twenty, thirty, or maybe forty years with you, and that's not enough time with the love of my life. I want to spend forever with you."

"It's impossible."

"Nothing's impossible when you have love. Isn't that what you've always told me?"

Matt leaned over and kissed his wife tenderly on the forehead, whispering as he rose, "I lied."

"Ohhhh," Crystal said, punching Matt playfully in the shoulder.

Matt rose and walked to the window, changing from his pajamas into simple linen garments with a deft twist of elemental power. "So, with all that settled, it's time to get out and have some fun today!"

Crystal rose and moved to her closet, selecting some comfortable clothes for herself for the day. "Settled isn't the word I would use, but we can drop the topic if you insist," she said.

Matt blinked across the room, appearing suddenly beside her. He lifted the back of her left hand to his lips, kissed it gently, smiled, and said, "I do."

The pair went down to breakfast with the twins, the girls asking along the way about Olympus. Crystal filled them in on most of what had happened, leaving the encounter with the naked goddess out of the story. They oohed and ahhed over the giant Thor, excited that they had studied him in their mythology class and saying how cool it was for their mom to have actually met him. The other gods they recognized as well, but Linda shot a confused look to Matt and asked, "Dad, why are Viking gods and Greek gods all jumbled together like that?"

"They're called Norse gods," Heidi corrected.

"Well, my teacher called them Viking gods. Which is right, Dad?"

As they took their seats, Matt said, "Both are right, I think. The Vikings and the Norse were the same people. I'm not sure what the linguists would say is the right term to apply to the deities, but it really doesn't matter anyway. I understand what you're talking about whether you say Norse or Viking. To answer your first question, Linda, the world only has one set of immortals running around. We take on different roles with different civilizations, depending on our preference. For example, Thor and I had a lot of fun running around in the Norse times, but he refused to involve himself with the Greeks. He thought they were pansies. Others, like Odin, Zeus, and Jupiter, were all the same immortal."

"Why different?" Heidi asked. "Why not just stay the same throughout time?"

"For one thing, it's boring to stay the same," Matt said. "You're talking about doing the same thing the same way for millions of years, and who wants to live like that? On the other hand, it wasn't always us who did the changing. Different cultures through time have had different filters through which they have in a general sense viewed actions and attributes. Take me, for example. I acted the same with the Greeks as I did with the Norse, and the Norse take on me came out as the deity representing justice and single combat and heroism, while the Greeks saw me as the God of War."

As she listened to her husband's explanation, Crystal noted that the dining hall was mostly empty. She had seen the magi seldom if at all recently, as their presence was excused from nearly everything in order to afford them as much training time as they could stand. She missed her friend Birch, and mentioned that to Matt.

Sorscha laid plates in front of them as Matt replied, "You'll be seeing him as soon as we're done eating. He's progressed nicely with his efforts. Certainly not nearly as much as you have, but he and Phoenix are doing quite well. One of the reasons I'm moving them to a training area outside, incidentally, is that I'm also bringing the new mage potentials into the room today to start their training, and I don't want Birch, Phoenix, or Krista—or you, for that matter—spending time teaching the newbies instead of practicing your own work."

"Makes sense. Reminds me, by the way, that I need to practice as well. I need to get as good as Stacy."

Matt stiffened slightly at the mention of his ex-wife's name.

"Who's Stacy?" Heidi, who was seated to her mother's right, asked through a mouthful of egg.

"An old friend and former pupil of mine," Matt replied, speaking up quickly before Crystal could respond.

"Oh," Heidi answered, more concerned with the plate in front of her than the glances to her left. "She must have been good."

"Very good," Matt said, at the same time as Crystal said, "Practically a goddess."

"So you'll be practicing a lot, Mom?"

"Probably, why?"

"I was wondering if today was a good day for us to meet those boys, since you'll both be pretty busy. We don't want to be bored, you know."

"I know," Matt said drily. "I'm sure you would absolutely die of boredom if they weren't around. Yes, you can meet the boys and hang out with them some if you'd like and if they're up to it. Just be careful, and remember that they haven't had the same briefings you have on safety around here."

"Okay, Dad," Heidi said, and she and Linda finished their breakfasts in record time. "Bye!" they each said as they waved to their parents and ran out of the hall.

Matt's long sigh echoed Crystal's. Eating in silence, the couple finished their breakfasts at a more leisurely pace than their excited children and then rose and walked hand in hand out of the dining hall. They passed again down the curved hall leading toward the magic practice room, and as they entered Crystal noticed a dozen new people standing in a circle, with Phoenix, Birch, and Krista lounging off to the side. Sorscha bowed as they came in.

"Ladies and gentlemen, welcome to the chamber of sorcery," Matt began, and then proceeded down the same lecturing path he had taken with the earlier group. Crystal saw that he even used the same tricks, making everyone dive out of the way of his fireballs with a wicked gleam in his eye. Crystal recognized most of the finer-dressed people from the library yesterday among the new cohort of mage trainees. It seemed strange to her how many library staff there were who could use magic. As Matt continued his talk, Crystal wondered if something about being a librarian made one more prone to be a latent mage, or vice versa.

"Birch, fireball me, please," Matt said, snapping Crystal's attention back to her husband. Birch looked confused for a moment, then shrugged and tossed what Crystal thought was a half-decent fireball Matt's direction. She was glad to see it explode harmlessly against Matt's chest, though she and several of the closer new students had to avert their faces from the heat. "Birch is one of my best students," Matt said, and Birch beamed at the compliment. "Many of you will never progress to his level, but those who work hard and have natural talent too will be able to toss fireballs like he does in a relatively short amount of time."

Matt completed his initial training session by distributing the rocks with instructions to practice lifting them. He exited calling the senior magi to follow him. As they climbed the ramp he explained, "I don't want you four always having to explain to the newbies how to lift a rock, and besides, I think I've kept you in the basement long enough. It's time to go outside."

Phoenix's reaction was neutral, but Birch and Krista both clapped their hands like children on Christmas morning. Krista had been very much of an outdoor enthusiast, Crystal remembered, which explained her glee. Birch, meanwhile, had called himself a practicing druid, one with the forests and nature, before the magic cycle had turned their lives upside down, and Crystal knew he prided himself on his rapid magical progress now.

They left the building, heading toward a copse of trees about a quarter-mile from the estate. Reaching it, Crystal saw a clearing a couple hundred feet wide surrounded by trees with a hillock in the middle. The trees and bushes around it formed a hedge thick enough to prevent most casual observation while being open to the sun overhead. It seemed a perfect haven for magic training, Crystal thought.

They followed Matt as he marched directly to the center, stopping on the little hill. He held his arms up and spun around. Crystal, used to seeing him manipulate wards by now, saw some of the flows he used. She was certain, however, that there was no way she'd be able to replicate the wards. Some day, she promised herself, she would be.

Birch and Phoenix both caught it, too, if their gasps were an indication. "What—what was that?" Birch asked, an awe-struck expression on his face. Krista, meanwhile, continued looking upward, a perplexed expression on her face.

"A ward," Matt said. As he walked back toward the edge of the clearing, he continued, "Several, actually. There was a ward against sound, so that you can cast your booms and your zaps without anyone overhearing. There was a ward against elemental flows of any type escaping with significant magnitude, so that none of you can accidentally set my forest on fire. There's a ward to blur the light rays to keep anyone above from seeing clearly who or what is going on down here. And there are other ones as well. I'll teach you wards, but not for a while yet. They're pretty complex flows, even individually. Together, and layered properly, they're quite difficult to get right."

Reaching the edge of the clearing, Matt stopped and turned back toward the center. He continued his speech, "You will be able to practice all your magic out here instead of in the basement, and later on this will make a good dueling location. Do you have any questions?"

It turned out they did, but mostly about wards and how to protect against the offensive spells they were learning to cast. Matt answered several before finally deciding he'd heard enough and telling them so.

Birch said, "Wait. I've wanted to show you what I can do." He beamed at Matt; Crystal knew Birch had come a long way and was zealously proud of it.

"Go ahead," Matt said.

Birch's display impressed Crystal as he sent several fireballs, each the size of a basketball, toward the middle of the clearing, with each exploding in an echoing and satisfying boom right on the hill. Birch turned and smiled at Matt, who looked impressed.

"Not bad," Matt said.

"Soon I'll be as good as you!" Birch said, using his right closed fist to physically beat on his chest. Crystal found it mildly amusing; she had never seen anyone actually beat on his own chest before.

Matt seemed to find it less amusing. "As good as me, hmm?" he said in a soft, dangerous voice. Birch's face slowly shifted from pride to panic as he realized what he had said. He began to cower while Matt spun back toward the hillock and let fly five balls in rapid succession, each easily three feet around and, Crystal could see, packed with an enormous amount of energy. The analytical side of her brain impressed itself by naming off the four elements as he cast them: earth, water, fire, and then air. The last, though, was unfamiliar to her.

Matt blinked, teleporting instantly to stand on the hillock at which he had directed the monumental surges. Crystal's pride in her recognition of the elements involved gave way to realization of dread as she screamed while the energy balls closed in on the center. First earth exploded in a spray of sand that showered them all, and then water splooshed with droplets coating the entirety of the clearing, leaving a wet sheen where Crystal had seen Matt put the warding barrier up. Crystal luckily didn't get very wet, herself, because she was diving for the ground in hopes of surviving the other elements. She had seen what fireballs and sonic balls could do, and had no idea about the last.

The fireball hit with the whoomph sound that she had heard before when lighting gas stoves out in a campsite, only magnified easily by a hundredfold. The sound was quickly overshadowed by the heat, though; she felt like she had dived directly into a pizza oven. It was over quickly, followed by the loudest sonic crack she had ever heard blasted through the clearing, pressing wave after wave of air with it, leaving her dazed and confused for a second.

Then the other ball hit, and it occurred to Crystal what she had seen as the energy hit its target and then expanded. She *had* seen it before, back in Dhri's study in Atlantis, and Matt had shrugged it off when asked. Now that she'd watched it spun into a ball, it seemed to be a combination of the other elements of magic, much the same as white light was a combination of other colors. The four elements she had worked with, she realized as the ball of destruction expanded, were really just aspects, specially-labeled portions of the magic that infused all the earth.

The energy which fueled the expanding sphere that was heading to kill them all, meanwhile, seemed to be an undistilled essence containing all four of its constructs. It was as though they had been playing with blue, and red, and deep blue, and yellow, and now she saw perfect white coming toward them. It was breathtakingly beautiful, and she also knew it was deadly.

She was going to die. She would die instantaneously and painlessly, most likely, but she was certain that there was no way that a human body could absorb the energy coming at them. This wasn't just a death ray, it was a death bomb. She had intellectually known that Matt was quite powerful, more powerful than all the human mages in the group put together, but that had been just an abstract thought. Sensing Matt's raw destructive power blew her abstract thoughts completely out of the water. Crystal was amazed and enraptured at his true display of power—and a little jealous, too, she realized.

Then it stopped. The energy had come at them quickly, but it had abruptly disappeared about six feet from the humans, whom Crystal saw were all lying on the ground. None of them moved or said a word.

Matt appeared beside her, bent down, and lifted her to her feet. "You okay, Love?" he asked with a tender grin.

"Did you almost kill me on purpose?"

"No. Well, sort of."

"Please explain, Matthew," she said, her irritation over her own near death and that of her friends, as well as his impish response, battling against the part of her that actually found it amusing.

"You should know I wouldn't—couldn't—put you in danger. The last spell was the most potent, but I had it blocked well before it could reach you. That said, yes, I did it on purpose."

He turned to Birch, who had climbed up from the prone and was now pulling twigs from his beard, and held up an index finger. "Lesson 1. Never challenge me." He held up the middle finger of the same hand to take its place beside the already-raised index finger, and said, "Lesson 2, always remember lesson 1. Okay?"

"Yes, sir," Birch said, jumping up and down to shake the dirt, mud, and grass off himself.

"What was that last explosion?" Phoenix asked, then said, "I didn't see any flows." Crystal was surprised; she knew her old friend wasn't catching on as quickly as she was, but the answer had seemed so obvious to her.

"That was *magic*. The essence of magic, anyway. It's the force behind life, behind creation itself. It's called ka. It's what you get when you wield the flows without allowing their character to separate into the four elements. You can't do it, by the way. Only the gods have the ability. It's dangerous, too. Had the energy reached you, it would have removed every ounce of life from your bodies."

"So this ka is the life force?" Birch asked.

Matt nodded, a pleased quirk to his lips. "That's right, in a nutshell. It's more complicated than that, of course, but you're close enough. And with that, I leave you to your practice. Enjoy!"

Crystal moved with her husband as he walked away, mind still racing on the magic essence and her ability to recognize it. Did it mean that she was a quicker study than Phoenix, or possibly that she was a suitable candidate for god-hood? She had to find out.

The pair crossed the field holding hands. They walked in silence at first, Crystal bluntly breaking the silence halfway back with a question. "Why could I tell what the essence of magic ball was, and Phoenix couldn't?"

"You're a faster study," Matt replied quickly—too quickly, it seemed.

"So all magicians eventually learn to at least see this ka?"

Matt stopped and turned to look at her, his expression unreadable. "No, Love. Very, very few do. Maybe one in a million. I'd say it's only the precocious few who ask too many questions, in fact."

"Too many? I thought you wanted me to ask questions."

"I do. Just not about that."

"Why not?"

"It's complicated."

Crystal gaped at him, shocked. In all their many years of marriage, she had never heard Matt short-circuit a question like that. Other husbands had, she knew from talking to her girlfriends from before the cataclysm, and often following serious attempts at conversation like, "What were you thinking when you cheated on me?" or, "Why does your mother seem so much more important to you than I do?" But not Matt—he never shied away from questions, especially the ones that were hard to answer.

Matt turned and started walking, though, so Crystal got over her shock quickly and ran a few steps. Catching up to him, she said, "So I'm not supposed to ask any more questions about it, right?"

"Right. At least, not now. I do plan on explaining to you, some day. I just don't know how to right now, and besides, I'm curious what the twins are up to."

She continued trotting along behind him. That was it. He was preoccupied with his protectiveness over the girls. Made sense, she thought. He had always been jovial about the girls' interest in boys before, but that was before they were seemingly the last teenage girls on the planet put together with what seemed to be the last teenage boys on the planet. A dangerous combination, and the mental image that went along with it made her own quick steps seem slow. Then again, the twins' father was the head of the estate, and the God of War too, so surely that had to count for something in teenage boys' decision-making processes. They did have decision-making processes, didn't they?

Rescue at Stanford

Matt quick-stepped directly to the library with Crystal right behind to find the four youths engrossed in a board game under Sorscha's watchful eye. The group of teenagers looked up as Matt and Crystal entered the room. "Hi, Mom and Dad!" Heidi called out, apparently delighted to see her parents, and waved them over.

"Sorscha showed us this really cool game," Heidi started, but Linda cut her off.

"Mom, Dad, this is Steve and Corey. Steve and Corey, Mom and Dad."

The two young men rose and held their hands out. Matt and Crystal each shook each young man's hand in turn.

"You're the guy—the god, rather—who rescued us, aren't you, sir?" the youth introduced as Steve said.

"Indeed," Matt replied. "I was glad, and a little surprised, to find as many of you alive as I did."

Steve and Corey both paused, confused expressions on their faces, and then Steve asked, "Aren't you omnipotent?"

"Omniscient. Omnipotent is all-powerful, and I must admit there are limits to my power, though you'd be hard pressed to ever see them. Omniscient means all-knowing, and no, gods don't know everything," Matt replied. "You should probably be happy that I can't easily read teenage boys' minds."

Steve grinned and nodded.

"So, what were two teenage boys doing on a weekday at the public library?"

"Our mother worked there as a research librarian. But you already knew that, didn't you? She was helping us look up college choices when...." Steve's narration stopped as both boys' faces clouded over.

"When disaster struck, right?

"Right, sir," the other boy said.

"Can we go out sometime on your dragons to see if our dad and sister are alive?" Steve asked.

"That can be arranged. Where were they?"

"Our dad was at work at Stanford. He's a physics professor there. Our sister was at school in Cupertino."

"Do you know where the school is?"

"Yes, I do."

"Well, we should probably go sooner rather than later. How healthy do you feel?"

"Fine, sir."

Crystal saw Steve's use of the word sir was impressing Matt. Then again, she thought, not many young men in California used honorifics in conversation anymore, so it even impressed her.

Matt looked at Sorscha. She nodded, then turned and walked out of the library. Matt motioned for all of them to follow in the thrakkon's footsteps. Crystal joined in the small procession.

When they arrived at the launch patio Steve turned and asked whether they should bring their mother, but Matt explained that she probably wouldn't be physically able to travel yet. Sorscha had summoned another thrakkon, a male with gleaming bluish hair who transformed into a glistening blue drake. Crystal hadn't seen that color before, but found it especially beautiful.

Matt got them all seated, the boys on the blue, the girls on the red, and he and Crystal on Sorscha. The girls seemed to have assumed that they should go, and Crystal was glad they had. She had thought Aphrodite a neutralized threat earlier, but after Matt's words this morning she doubted her assumptions. It was best, then, for all to remain together for a while.

The dragons circled over the estate a couple of times as Matt looked over at the boys and relayed information mentally. Soon they nodded, just as the girls had nodded on the earlier flight, and Matt broadcast to them all, *Ready?*

The world shifted briefly, and then they were flying over clouds. Crystal could feel Matt's head shifting back and forth between their destination and the boys as they descended, coming out of the clouds and floating down wing beat by wing beat toward what Crystal guessed based on the horizon and the coast lines in the distance was a destroyed Cupertino.

They landed in a deserted school yard—elementary, she guessed based on the quantity of destroyed play sets. The swing sets were mostly serviceable due to their structural lack of resistance to flowing water, but it appeared that the teeter totters and the spinning wheel had been stripped away by the force of the wave that had hit. A mangled piece of tin draped across the steps to the partly-downed building appeared to have been a slide at one point in the past. Matt helped everyone down from their drakes, shaking his head. Crystal could tell from the set of his jaw that he had bad news.

As the boys started to run off, Matt stopped them with a flow of air and said, "Before we go in, let me tell you all that I don't sense anyone alive in there. Boys, I know you need to find out what happened to your sister, but you need to prepare for no news, or—well, worse than no news."

Matt released the flow and the boys ran toward the school building. Crystal could tell that Heidi was torn between sprinting to follow and staying with her parents. Linda's restraining arm helped Heidi make her mind up.

Crystal strode forward and grabbed the girls by their shoulders, marching all three as a single, somber unit toward the building into which the boys had disappeared. Inside, they found the boys kneeling, sobbing, beside a body that lay next to a large group of corpses.

Crystal held the girls back, her own eyes filling with tears. Matt's voice was soft as he said, "I'm sorry. We're sorry."

Crystal, the girls, and Matt all stood silently for several minutes as the boys mourned their dead sister. Corey was the first to break the silence, looking back over his shoulder, straightening his spine, and asking through his slowly-dwindling sobs, "Can you—can you help us bury her?"

"Of course," Matt said, his tone still gentle. "Bring her outside," and motioned for the boys, and then everyone else, to follow as he walked back down the hall past what Crystal now saw was a scattered mass of hundreds of bodies. She'd missed them on the run in, being intent on finding the boys, but now she was appalled at the number of the dead.

They all followed Matt silently outside, the two boys carrying their lifeless sister, the girls trudging just behind, and Crystal bringing up the rear. Exiting the building, Matt bent his head in consultation with the boys, and then turned and pointed to a spot in the playground. As they watched, a circle was cleared from trash and debris using flows of wind, and a small hollow was carved in the earth now bared.

"Lay Ellen down in her cradle," Matt said, his voice soft and caressing.

The boys laid their sister's body down in the hollow as instructed, and Matt used flows of air to float up above their heads. His strong voice carried for many hundreds of feet as he boomed, "Ellen, your brothers have presented you to me, Mars, an ancient nearly as old as the earth to whose bosom you return, as one worthy of remembrance. May your journey to the afterlife be easy, and may you be remembered for many, many centuries."

As Matt spoke, Crystal watched a dome build over the young body. At first it seemed to be soil, and Crystal could identify the flows as primarily earth-based, but then both the dome and the flows changed and became more complicated. Crystal saw flows of air, earth, and water all interacting, and then she recognized a flow of magical essence enveloping the crypt, strengthening the dome that had been formed and making it glisten. The flow of ka increased till it glowed so brightly Crystal had to avert her eyes, and then the glow disappeared.

Crystal turned back. The young body that had been Ellen now lay entombed in a translucent crystal monolith. The crystal displayed the body not as they had found it but rather as Ellen must have been as a vibrant and vital young girl. Crystal heard the boys sob as they fell to their knees.

"This tomb will withstand the flow of weather for thousands of years," Matt told the boys. He walked over to several bare bushes, picked dead branches from each, and then walked back. Crystal gasped as another flow of ka surrounded the twigs, causing them to spring to life and then bloom. Matt handed the flowers to Steve and Corey, wordlessly motioning toward the tomb. Once the boys had placed the bouquet ceremoniously and returned to the group, all fell into a tight embrace.

Several minutes later, the three dragons approached the group. Matt silently helped everyone onto the backs of the dragons, and then took his own seat behind Crystal on Sorscha. "Let's go to Stanford," he said.

The dragon-bound trio lifted off and flew a farewell loop over the school, and then turned toward the northwest. Crystal asked Matt mentally, *So, are the boys in for two heartbreaks today?*

Tough to say, he replied. *The Stanford University campus has some nooks that are just about as survivable as anywhere else on the planet. There are chambers below ground there that are insulated from nearly every possible disturbance, and temperature would have remained fairly stable that many feet under the surface. Their problem will have been food and water, and I can't believe a bunch of otherwise smart people wouldn't have solved that problem satisfactorily. It's a good bet that we'll find somebody alive. Whether that somebody is the boys' dad, we won't know till we get there. There's an additional factor, though. It's been a few days now since the atmosphere returned to relatively normal, and so it's entirely possible that any survivors from Stanford will already have left the campus, headed toward who knows where.*

Oh, Crystal said, seeing the dilemma. *Well, given all that, where are we going to start looking first?*

The campus. Specifically, the Varian Physics Building there. It's well built, has some underground nooks of its own, and is very likely still standing, and it's most likely that the physicists are still in the physics building if they're still on campus at all.

The dragons swept over an oval grassy area then landed a little to the west in front of a large building that seemed to have withstood the ravages of the cataclysm fairly well. It, like most of the buildings on campus, was covered in light-colored blocks and topped in red tiles. Matt helped everyone off of their dragons, and Steve asked, "Is Dad alive in there, sir?"

Matt shrugged and replied, "The function has an Eigenvalue greater than zero. We'll have to observe the cat."

"What?"

"Dad never taught you any quantum theory, did he?"

"I think he tried, but we were never really interested."

Matt sighed. "Too bad. Physics, specifically quantum mechanics, can really be pretty funny stuff."

Crystal's curiosity was piqued. "What's a cat got to do with it?"

"I'm glad you asked," Matt replied, a wicked grin on his face. "A central theme of quantum mechanics is explained to newbies through a thought experiment in which an imaginary cat is enclosed in an imaginary box and maybe or maybe not killed. The point is that you don't know whether the cat is dead without opening the box and observing it. Then, you have the fact that sometimes the difference between velocity and acceleration is explained by another thought experiment in which a cat is dropped off a building of either more than or fewer than six stories. At six stories the cat reaches terminal velocity, stops accelerating, feels the shift into now-constant velocity, and relaxes, thus getting hurt less. The physics is irrelevant right now, but the only way to explain the stories at all is a general hatred for felines, right?"

"Hmm," Crystal answered, unconvinced.

"So is anyone alive in the Varian building, sir?" Steve asked. Crystal admired Steve's focus.

Matt turned back toward Steve and nodded, saying, "I do sense life down there. Can't tell who, though, so we'll need to go in and find out."

"Down there? Why down?"

"The Varian building has labs a couple of floors down below ground level to minimize vibrations. If I were a smart human scared of dying in a cataclysm, it sure seems like where I'd go to. I sense that somebody had that same idea."

The group made their way into the building and to the landing of the stairs. Crystal noticed that Matt seemed to know exactly where he was going, and asked him how he knew so much about the building. He smiled and winked back at her from his spot leading them down.

"Been here before a time or two, I guess," he said.

"Teacher or student?"

"Student. It was quite a while ago."

"Of course it was."

The family made their way without talking down a flight of stairs. Suddenly they were greeted by a gruff, "We're armed, so stop right there! Who are you, and why are you here?"

Matt stopped abruptly, causing the rest to pile up behind him. Motioning for everyone else to stay put, he continued walking and said, "I could tell you, but you wouldn't believe me any more than I believe you that you have weapons."

A second person sighed out loud and said, "Shit. See, Brian?"

The boys' faces lit up. "Dad?" Corey said.

"Corey?" the second man's voice called out at the same time a metal bar clanged on the floor. Moments later a large bearded man rounded the corner in front, taking two steps at a time. Matt and Crystal both stepped aside to let him pass. He scooped both boys up in an athletic bear hug.

"Steve, Corey," the man said, relieved tears running down his face as he set them back down on their feet. "I didn't think I'd ever see you again. Thank God you're okay."

"You're welcome," Matt interjected drily.

The man glanced Matt's way, briefly displaying confusion and irritation at the same time, and then turned back to his sons. "Where's your mother? Wasn't she with you at the library? And how'd you get here from there?"

Steve pointed to Matt. "Mom's fine, Dad, back at the estate. And Dad, he really is a god. Mars, meet Dr. Ben Phillips, one of the best experimental physics researchers on the planet."

"One of the only ones, now, you might wish to add," Matt said, extending his hand. "Nice to meet you, Doctor Phillips."

Ben looked at the hand and took it slowly while eyeing Matt from head to toe. "A god? Forgive me if I'm not entirely versed on protocol. And—Mars? Did I hear that right?"

Matt shrugged. "He did. Most of my friends these days call me Matt, though. Protocol with me is pretty easy. I'm not one of those gods who wants to see you snivel and whine and proclaim that you're lower than dirt."

During the reunion several other men had climbed to the bend in the stairs and were silently watching the exchange. Finally the large man in front, who Crystal noticed was holding two four-foot long, one inch thick rods of some sort of metal, cleared his throat and said, "You really want us to believe that man is Mars? Mars is a myth."

Crystal sensed Matt's glee as he shot *Oh, goodie* mentally at her, and she watched as he roared and turned toward the assembled group on the landing below. His body suddenly transformed into a nine-foot-tall giant, his head slanted sideways along the bottoms of the stairs above and his torso a mass of knotted muscles under a Greek-style tunic. In his right hand he brandished a flaming sword that seemed as long as Crystal was tall. The humans on the landing shrank back, a few in the rear turning and running for the labs beneath.

As suddenly as he had changed, Matt changed back, laughing as he did. Looking directly at the man who had called him a myth, who was now cringing behind his two metal poles, Matt asked in a sweet voice, "I'm—sorry, I'm afraid I didn't hear you well. What did you say I was?"

"A—a—a g—g—g—god?" the man stuttered, obviously shaken to his core.

"Excellent!" Matt said, smiling and turning back toward the father-son reunion that had been interrupted. The father and sons were all staring at him. "And now, Professor, I have transportation back to my estate for you and all of the rabble below whom you wish to bring along. I just need to know how many."

Ben's face focused for a minute, his lips moving as he counted to himself. "Twenty-six," he finally announced to Matt.

Matt nodded, seemed to stare off into space for a minute, and then said, "Get everyone up to the oval on Palm Drive. We leave in ten minutes."

Ben nodded and leaped down the stairs, his twin sons by his side as he ordered his colleagues up and then went down further into the basement. Matt, meanwhile, motioned Crystal and the girls up the stairs.

"Shouldn't we follow them to make sure everything's all right?" Linda asked.

"Everything will be okay, Linda," Matt said. "Leave the physicist to the task of rounding up the physicists."

The girls, disappointment painted across their faces, followed Matt and Crystal up the stairs and onto the road. The physicists who followed them up gathered in the oval and eyed the three dragons warily. Walking forward, Matt said in a loud voice, "Oh, this is stupid." He motioned over Sorscha with one hand, and the silver dragon trotted toward the knot of humans. They all gasped and moved back against the curb, and Matt said, "Oh, come on. I thought all of you were respected Stanford physicists. The creature over there is big and fierce, to be sure. But if she had wanted to kill you, she would have killed you. Right?"

The terrified crowd of physicists looked at each other and nodded reluctantly.

Matt looked up, and Crystal followed his gaze to the spot in the sky where a couple of dozen dots had appeared and were now approaching out of the sky. Soon the dots resolved into flying creatures, and then it was clear that they were dragons. One of the physicists asked out loud, "We're not going to be flying on those, are we?"

"BART's not running much anymore, and it's a bit too far to walk, so—yeah, I guess you are," Matt replied. "Or you can stay here."

"What about our families?" the same physicist wondered.

"Those of you with families can ask your dragons to allow you to guide them to check on those family members whose location you can pinpoint, and once you find them you can tell the dragons to return home to my estate. Those of you who don't have anyone to check on can fly back with the main group. How's that?"

Murmurs of ascent rose from the crowd as the dragon flight came to a landing at the other edge of the oval and the group was joined by more from inside the building. Matt approached the boys' father as the large man led the new group toward them. "Ben, how are you feeling? Are you up for an internally jolting flight?" he asked, a smile on his face.

"I suppose so. The boys told me we get to ride on dragons, and they also told me about the teleporting. You shouldn't be able to do that, you know. Violates the theory of relativity."

"Yeah, well, there's plenty of new violations for you to learn, Professor. Would you rather sit down now to discuss the actual physics involved and find out what Einstein didn't know, or get back to my estate to see your wife?"

"You make a valid point. Let's go."

Matt nodded, and then turned to address the entire assembly with a grin on his face. "Ladies and gentlemen—and physicists—you will now be given a rare opportunity for humans to fly on the back of a dragon. Please note that the dragons who have come to help carry you all back to the safety of my estate are doing you a favor in letting you ride on their backs. Be very nice to them. If you have loved ones to check on, let the dragon know how to get to wherever those loved ones might be and they will help you search. Keep in mind, though, that some humans all over the planet survived the cataclysm, and some of those are not as well behaved as you are. Tread with caution, then, as you search. Once your search has been satisfied, let the dragon know and he or she will fly directly back to my estate. Don't keep them away too long, though, because they do get hungry, and you really don't want to know what they eat. Understood?"

As Matt spoke, the dragons fanned out, and after he was done the physicists made their way to the line of dragons and each selected a mount. Matt demonstrated how to use an outstretched hind leg to climb up and onto the back, and then he helped the family and the boys and their father onto their three dragons. They launched quickly, soaring up into the sky. This time Matt didn't warn them as the world shifted and they began their descent toward the estate.

They landed in the same courtyard they had used, and were greeted by a high-pitched scream of "Ben!" Ben leaped down from his dragon's back and was immediately engulfed in his wife's arms. The boys joined their parents as the family walked inside.

Linda grabbed Heidi's arm and prevented her from following. She responded to her sister's glare with a hissed, "They need time to be together." When Heidi looked unconvinced, Linda continued, "Neither their mom nor dad knows about Ellen yet, remember? I, personally, don't want to be around when that announcement is made. Do you?" Crystal smiled, proud of Linda's sensibility, as the twins walked back inside.

A cleared throat near them caught Matt's and Crystal's attentions. RJ stepped forward and said, "Matt, some of the college folks have heard about your trips for survivors, and were wondering if they could take part."

Matt nodded. "Absolutely, yes. Much of my flying contingent is away right now bringing back the Stanford survivors, but I'll ask the ones who are here to help out, and as soon as the others return and rest and eat a bit we'll send them back out with more college folks."

RJ nodded and retreated. Crystal was still amazed at the change in demeanor he displayed ever since Matt had killed and then revived him.

More Magic Lessons

The next morning dawned as bright and clear as the previous mornings had. Matt was once again out of bed seated at the end of the room by the windows, reading an ancient manuscript on something that had to do with Loki, when Crystal woke. After a stretch and a grand yawn, she rose and joined her husband, sitting in the other chair and reaching for his hand.

"Hon, if it's always this bright and sunny here, how do the plants get any water to grow?"

"Once a week, the thrakkoni transform into dragons, drink a lot of water, and fly around spitting everywhere. You should probably stay inside on those days," Matt replied, not looking up from his book.

"So how do the plants really get any water to grow?" Crystal had always thought Matt's sarcastic humor was really quite funny, but part of the game was her refusal to give in to it.

Matt shrugged and turned a grin toward her. "It rains, when I want it to. Usually that's when I'm away from the estate, or when I feel like running around outside in the rain. You know how much I enjoy that sensation."

"Yes, I do, Mr. Streaker," she said, remembering a time when touring Greece that she had thought they would likely be arrested. "Does the lack of law enforcement here mean your daughters will get to see their dad running around naked in the rain?"

"Oh, there's law enforcement here."

"So will your daughters get to see the law enforcement person running around naked in the rain?"

Matt chuckled. "I'll try to avoid having the law enforcement person's daughters see things that might upset them, my love."

Crystal smiled and lapsed into silence, enjoying the moment. She thought back to when they had first met, her a grad student in a master's of the arts in teaching program looking forward to her first job as a sculptor of young peoples' minds, looking up to the guy who was a strikingly handsome college teacher, her science education professor. She'd been delighted to find someone who shared her passion for education and fascinated at his breadth of knowledge of the sciences, but more importantly to her, she'd been overjoyed to find someone who could keep up with the verbal jousts she enjoyed so much. She couldn't quite remember the topic of their first conversation, but she vividly remembered the path of discussion going much the same as the one they had just finished.

She remembered presenting Matt to her friends, and how heartily they had approved of him. She thought briefly of their wedding and her amazement at how significant a college teacher's financial resources could be. That was, of course, when she had learned of his extremely large inheritance.

As she ruminated on their past, she was reminded of her earlier fantasies of growing old with this man. She had, once upon a time, enjoyed imagining herself and Matt, both old and grey-haired, sitting on the back deck of their home together and enjoying long talks about whatever old people talked about. She tried to recall one of those imaginations again, but the realization that she would be alone in growing old struck her and gripped her heart.

It took significant effort, but she shook off the dark thought, not wanting to destroy the serenity of the moment. Knowing Matt, he had caught the dip in her emotional state. Before the cataclysm, he'd always seemed to know when something was troubling her. Now, though, he said nothing about it.

"Well," he said, breaking into her reverie, "are you ready for some breakfast?"

She nodded, still not able to completely shake off the dark emotional cloud. She rose and dressed, and they left their chamber silently.

They had just seated themselves when Ben and Natalia and the boys entered the dining hall. Matt looked at Sorscha, who hustled over to the young family and spoke quietly with them. Ben nodded to whatever Sorscha said, then guided his family up toward the main table to sit to Matt's left.

As the family sat down, another thrakkon entered and began serving them. Crystal recognized him as the thrakkon who had served that end of the table their first night here. Matt was giving the family special consideration.

When they were done ordering, Matt nodded to Ben. "Good to see you all up and about this morning."

"Thank you, and thank you for the nice seats," the physicist said. "The boys told me what you did for Ellen, so thank you for that as well."

Matt nodded. "I'm sorry for your loss." Crystal turned and echoed her husband's words.

"Aren't you the god of war, though? I'd think you're probably used to loss," Ben said.

Matt shrugged and replied softly, "There are different kinds of losses. When men and women are engaged in the art of war, they expect to die. A big difference between me and some of my peers, though, is that I've always held the death of innocents to be a special sort of loss. The one is glorious and part of the battle, while the other is disgusting."

"But didn't you say before that this is all part of the gods' method, or Gaia's plan, or whatever it was?" Heidi asked from down the table.

Matt sighed and then answered in a distant voice, "Yes, I did, and it is. And there's a huge portion of the human race that I really don't miss each time it happens. But there are also exceptions. Many of my fellows really don't consider any human worth caring about, but I've seen otherwise. I've fought wars. Hell, I've started wars, and I've ended them. I've gone through entire cycles in one long, brutal, war. Nothing thrills me quite like a noble clarion call for battle, trust me. But along the way, I've also come to know those who don't deserve to suffer and die. It is something that will always bother me."

"Ah," Ben said. "Well, it is comforting to know that a god can be bothered by the state we humans are in, but in any event, thank you for what you did."

Matt nodded and then switched subjects, pulling information from the physics professor regarding his most recent experiments and displaying a vast knowledge of physics. Crystal found little of the discussion interesting, though, so she turned to her right and asked the girls their plans for the day. When their answers that they didn't really have any plans proved even less interesting, she finished her food in silence.

Sorscha cleared away their empty plates as Matt broke out of the physics discussion to explain the estate rules to Ben, pointing out that Natalia, as a promising battle mage, was expected to be in the chamber of sorcery practicing most of the time. Ben was in his first day, a period when nobody was expected to join in the work efforts, so he would likely have the day to himself. Assuming, Matt pointed out with a wry grin toward both ends of the table, that the teenagers decided to hang out together again. Matt suggested some ancient works in the library to Ben, pointing out that the translation might be rough, but the description and methods of physics through the cycles hadn't changed much.

Ben's family rose, Ben promising to send Natalia straight away to the sorcerer's chamber and then to seek out the library at his first opportunity. They left as a group, the boys bringing a smile to Crystal's face when they turned and motioned to the girls in the familiar, yet now obsolete, gesture for calling them later. They both turned back and hastened to follow their parents. Linda leaned closer to her mother and asked, "Mom, how are they going to call us with no telephones?"

Crystal chuckled and tousled her daughter's hair. "They'll find a way, I'm sure. It's what boys do when they're around girls. They find a way."

The family rose and left the dining hall. As they set a course for their suite, Crystal asked, "Why the great interest in physics, hon? I never knew you enjoyed it so much."

"Physicists are some of my favorite people, Love. Along with philosophers they share a spot in the center of my stage of interest, physicists because they're always trying to understand the physical world around them, and philosophers because they're always doing the same for the spiritual and intellectual world. But the physical world is as complicated as the other one, and yet physicists as a group diligently work to explain its complexities only to be physically proven wrong when they screw it up. Granted, they get it wrong most of the time, a fact most of them acknowledge, by the way, but at least they make a concerted and repeated effort at it."

"But don't engineers and mathematicians also seek to explain the physical world?"

"In terms of the span of human knowledge about the physical world, everyone plays an important role—physicists, engineers, mathematicians, carpenters, brick layers, cement shufflers, everyone. It's the nature of the role that makes a difference to me. Mathematicians, you gotta love them, but they spend their time studying—well, the methodology and structure of mathematics. Problem is, there's no mathematics in the world. When I drop an apple and watch it hit the ground," he emphasized his point by making an apple appear in his hand and then dropping it, "do you think, 'oh, what a nifty integral you get when transforming velocity to acceleration', or do you wonder how long the apple takes to hit the ground, and perhaps where it will hit, and even whether it will hit with enough force to splatter? Math is as important to understanding the physical nature of the world around us as your knitting needles were to you when you were in your afghan creation phase. Remember that?"

Crystal nodded, remembering a time many years ago when she was pregnant with the girls and, after knitting one baby afghan, she had learned she would be having twins and so she knitted another. But she had found that making two identical ones bored her, and so she made another and then a few more. Matt had been awfully supportive, bringing home skein after skein of yarn in various colors. She remembered wondering back then why he was so intent on supplying her new hobby. After all, she had convinced herself at the time, she was so much less bitchy than all those other expectant mothers. She had been certain about that. Now she chuckled at her own expense and then turned her attention back to the conversation at hand.

Matt's eyes had been watching her in her travels down memory lane and so she grinned and said, "Sorry, Love. I do remember that. You were so sweet to bring me all that yarn. So, anyway, you're saying that math is just a tool for physicists to use."

"Exactly."

"So what about engineers? Weren't you one, yourself, for a while?"

"Ah, yes, those were some fun days back in the RF lab." Matt wiggled his eyebrows in a humorous gesture.

Crystal was struck by a thought. "RF was like magic back then, wasn't it?"

"Oh, sort of. Actually, RF *was* one flow of magic. I was just as powerful then as I am now. It's just that instead of flows of magic, I had flows of the four atomic forces to play with."

"Four, Dad?" Linda asked from behind. They had entered the sitting room of their suite and stopped to talk, and Crystal hadn't noticed Linda standing to listen while Heidi went on into her room.

"Four, dear." Matt motioned their daughter over into his lap and continued, "Electromagnetic, gravitational, and strong and weak nuclear forces."

"I thought electricity and magnetism were two different things."

"Most people do, sweetheart. That's part of the reason physicists have had to work so hard getting past that in each of the technology phases. It doesn't make sense that two differently-appearing phenomena are actually the same force, but they are. Usually in the cycles humans do really stupid stuff, like trying to deliver electrical power over long distances with a steady voltage, before they finally figure out how the two are interrelated. But again, it's the domain of physicists to figure that out, while the engineers just take that knowledge and implement it. Back to the afghan metaphor, your mom was the physicist who created it, using the needles that, in this case, are like the mathematics involved. Then the engineers would be the people who used those blankets to cover up two sweet little girls."

"I think I get it," Linda said.

"I'm not sure I do," Crystal said, a doubtful look on her face.

"I did kinda stretch the metaphor past the breaking point, didn't I?"

"Uh, huh," Crystal agreed. "So, in the magic periods there are four elemental flows with one overarching essence. What's the force in the technology phases that corresponds to the essence of magic?"

"You're not supposed to know about that, remember?"

"So arrest me, Mr. Law Enforcement."

Matt laughed a loud belly laugh and then bowed. "It's actually easier to figure out that the essence is there in the technology cycles, which is why I sometimes enjoy those periods more. In the last cycle they called it Unified Field Theory, or Universal Field Theory, or one of several other equally-magnificent sounding names. It's there, alright, but it's the domain of the gods."

"Oh, I see." Crystal didn't see the physics, she admitted to herself, but she did see how it connected to the flows.

"This estate is physically impossible to get to without the ability to fly, and then it takes a long time if you can't fly the speed of a dragon, which is well beyond the speed of any airliners ever made by humans. How do you think I got here in the technology phases? I can manipulate the unified field to appear nearly anywhere in the space continuum I want."

Crystal had taken basic scientific courses in college on her way to the general teaching degree, and so she knew about the work done combining electricity and magnetism, and she had taken Matt's courses on teaching science, so she also knew about gravity and some about Unified Field Theory. She had no idea what the nuclear forces were, but she decided to let it go.

"So what about biology?" Linda asked, remembering her trauma over having to dissect a frog earlier that school year.

Matt shrugged. "Life sciences bore me. Living things, like your frog buddy, are made of cells. Cells are created, they live, and they die. Different cells do different things, granted, but it's all in the same basic way. And the study of it has never really changed in any of the cycles. At first everybody agrees that some mysterious force is driving the creation of life in organic matter, and hundreds of thousands of so-called scientists are all happy with agreeing that physical activity is generated by something they can't see, can't touch, can't point to, can't even prove exists. Then along comes somebody with a microscope and proves them all wrong. They spend the next one, two, or several hundred years describing and cataloging the various types of cells until all their methods and documentation are lost in the next cataclysm."

"So you're saying we don't really have a soul?" Linda asked. Crystal smiled, impressed with her daughter's mental jump.

"No, I'm not saying that. But I'm not ready right now to go into the intricacies of how the Underworld, or the Heavens or whatever you want to call it, really works, especially in conjunction with your physical existence here on the Earth. Right now, I need to get down to the sorcerer's chamber to see if anyone can lift a pebble yet."

Matt turned to Crystal. "Are you coming with me, Love, or doing something else? It's going to be a beautiful day for a ride."

Crystal nodded, sensitive to the mild castoff. She thought she understood, though; Matt was probably going to be as hard on this group as he had been on the last, and she was certain that neither of them wanted her to be seen as his little shadow minion. Besides, she thought to herself, she really did want to take an unfettered spin around the estate on the magnificent dappled mare she had ridden the other day. "You're right. I think I'll go for a ride," she said and then walked into the master bedroom to find some suitable riding clothes.

A Truce, Broken

Lady seemed to remember her, Crystal thought, her hair streaming behind as the pair galloped as one across the field in front of the estate. She loved to ride at a gallop, the horse's fastest pace. The gallop, she thought, was the one hundred and eighty degree opposite of the canter. When a horse switched from a canter to a gallop, all the vertical motion smoothed out into a rhythmic series of forward surges that merged as the horse gained speed. A full gallop was as beautiful to experience as a canter was painful.

As she galloped, she practiced jumping over any obstacles that presented themselves, whether logs or the streams that rolled down the gentle slope toward the center of the valley. Lady was the most amazing creature she had ever ridden, she thought, and then hastily qualified her opinion to include 'without wings.' She smiled to herself, knowing that Sorscha would not be pleased to know that she had been compared to a horse.

Nearing the point in the valley farthest from the estate, Crystal saw a girl walking with a basket of flowers toward the buildings. She smiled at how cute a scene it made, and then wondered idly where the girl had come from. Krista's children were the youngest, other than the baby, that had been brought to the estate in all three of the groups she had been with. Maybe one of the physicists had a daughter who had already made it back?

Her thoughts were interrupted when the little girl suddenly stumbled over something and pitched forward, her basket tossed several feet and its wildflowers flying everywhere. She saw the girl hit the ground hard and heard the impact and then the little girl's sobs welling up.

Lady didn't need prompting to change course. It was as though the horse was actually reading Crystal's mind. Within seconds, the powerful mare had covered the dozens of yards between them and the girl and abruptly halted, allowing Crystal to leap out of the saddle and rush over to the fallen girl.

Reaching down, Crystal asked, "Are you okay? That was a tough fall."

The girl's juvenile sobs suddenly changed into adult laughter, causing Crystal to recoil in confusion. Out of the corner of her eye she saw Lady, behind and to the side, whinnying and rearing as the little girl's body elongated and transformed as she stood up.

Crystal now found herself looking into the face of Aphrodite. The goddess, still laughing loudly, advanced on Crystal, who was suddenly unable to either move or breathe due to the flows of air and earth that wrapped securely around her.

"Silly girl, getting away from your protector like that," Aphrodite teased. "You knew I would come for you. Some day soon, or some day later, but some day nevertheless. How about today? Today's a fine day to die, isn't it, silly girl? You think you deserve him, but you don't. You're just a silly human girl, weak and worthless."

Crystal fought through the red haze that was clouding out her sight, her body's supply of oxygen running dangerously low. She grasped flows of air, beating futilely against the goddess and trying to push her back. She tried to weave a flow of flame around her foe, but Aphrodite's flow of air lazily flicked Crystal's gathering flows apart so that they never coalesced. Panicking, Crystal reached deeper, trying to summon ka to do her bidding. She knew it was there, knew she could touch it. Some day....

But not today. Crystal couldn't touch the essence of magic. She acknowledged that she was going to die, leaving her husband to finish raising their daughters. Their faces came unbidden to her hazy vision, and she felt a sob well up at the thought that this memory would be the last she saw of them. Through the sight of her daughters' faces, she also saw Aphrodite's sneer, her enjoyment in slowly killing her rival etched plainly on her face.

Both women were so absorbed in the conflict that neither saw the assault until its force hit. A flow of air suddenly spun around Aphrodite, lifting the goddess and flinging her away from Crystal. It was followed by a dazzling column of magical essence that hit the goddess at the same time that a gout of searing flame landed at her feet. Crystal's ability to breathe returned abruptly as she felt Matt's power wresting Aphrodite's flows away from her and then surrounding her in the god's own protective shield. As she gasped much-needed air into her lungs, she saw a massive silver dragon explode onto the scene violently attacking the goddess, Sorscha's wings flapping wildly and her serpentine head jabbing in, sharp teeth seeking any opening in the goddess's attempts at mounting a quick defense.

Within seconds Aphrodite had regained her wits. By then, Crystal was safely ensconced in Matt's magical orb of protection. He was advancing wordlessly on Aphrodite, flaming red sword summoned magically to his hand and raised for battle. A terrible anger radiated from his face. Aphrodite, meanwhile, easily flicked Sorscha away with a simple gesture and then summoned her own swords, one in each hand, and took up a defensive stance.

"I disabled your wards, Matthew. How did you know to come?" Aphrodite asked, her words sounding impossibly calm as her body shifted to match his stance.

"You missed one," Matt growled, and then charged. The resulting impact shook the entire valley, forcing Crystal to her knees as the god and goddess exchanged powerful sword and magic blows at the same time. It was over in a second, though, and both god and goddess maintained ready poses as they circled like cats, each looking for weakness in the other.

Crystal felt powerful arms curl around her as Sorscha came up from behind and pulled her away from the combat. "This is between god and goddess," the thrakkon said. "You need to get away, or else Aphrodite will be able to finish what she came for."

Crystal saw Sorscha's logic and allowed herself to be dragged away, her heart breaking as she did. She knew her husband had to be at least an even match for Aphrodite, and that she could do nothing but get herself killed, but her gut told her to stand beside him and help fight or—well, do something.

Sorscha seemed to read her mind. "You can't do anything, Crystal. He's fighting to keep you alive. You need to help him by getting back, away from the battle."

As Crystal continued backing away, she watched Matt and Aphrodite trade physical and magical blows. Intellectually, Crystal was thrilled at being this close to such a display of raw power, despite the danger she knew she was in. She was also reminded of the story of Matt's battle with Hermes. Was this going to end the same way? He couldn't kill Aphrodite, and she couldn't kill him. Would they battle until Crystal eventually died anyway of old age?

Matt summoned a flow of ka, throwing it in a beam at Aphrodite's face and then coming in low with a two-handed swing of his sword. Aphrodite somehow leaped over the low swing while ducking the energy bolt, and returned the attack with a double attack of her own. Crystal, who had watched some sword fights played out at fairs she had attended, was amazed at the fluidity Matt showed in blocking Aphrodite's dual-wielding flurry, moving his own sword with unbelievable speed. Aphrodite finished her counterattack with a blast of ka directed at Matt's face, a bolt that Matt brushed away carelessly. It sailed into the trees to the side, exploding with a vigor that sent splinters showering over Crystal and Sorscha.

"Who's going to win?" Crystal asked Sorscha, the pair still backing away from the battle.

"Who knows? Probably neither. The master is stronger physically, but Aphrodite has one of the strongest commands of the flows of any of the gods. I'm surprised she hasn't attacked purely magically yet."

As if Sorscha's words were a cue, Aphrodite summoned flows of all four elements, sending several huge balls of energy at Crystal, and then followed with a ball of ka that was far larger than the one Crystal had seen Matt use.

"Duck!" Crystal yelled, realizing as she said it how absurd that order was, there being nothing to duck behind. She dropped herself toward the ground anyway. Sorscha was faster, though, pressing Crystal's body to the ground and landing on top of her just before the explosion.

Crystal wondered if the sensation was similar to what being in a nuclear blast felt like. Sorscha's downward press had knocked the wind out of her, and so now she was struggling to catch her breath while at the same time trying to deal with entirely new sensations running along her skin and down the nerves to her brain. Matt and she had been caught out in an electrical storm once, she recalled, and the tingly feeling from that memory was similar to though far less severe than what she was feeling now. All over her body reactions were happening— reactions she couldn't categorize or describe.

Sorscha rose and helped Crystal up as they continued backing rapidly away from the battle. Crystal looked down at her hands and arms and saw that her skin glowed faintly. Stifling her curiosity, she turned her attention back to the battleground where Matt was once again dueling with the goddess. He struck several deadly blows, slicing through Aphrodite's guard and into her torso while knocking her back. She leered at him as her nicks healed, her body growing whole again before his eyes.

Matt adopted a defensive pose, and then looked back toward the retreating human and thrakkon and pointed. Once again a magical cocoon enveloped Crystal.

Aphrodite saw the motion and lashed out viciously to take advantage of his distraction. Her sword swings came in both high and low, catching Matt across the neck and the torso and slashing deep into his flesh. Crystal wailed in horror at the sight, and Aphrodite smiled and stood back, swords still at the ready.

Matt shrugged, his deep wounds becoming scratches and then disappearing altogether. "That the best you got, Stacy?" he asked, his voice calm.

Aphrodite sighed, watching the fatal wounds she had inflicted close and heal with a sour expression. "Yeah, I guess it is," she said. "Battling an immortal is kind of pointless, I guess."

Matt nodded and flung his massive sword down to the side. "Let's talk about this," he said, folding his muscular arms over his chest. "Neither you nor I can fatally harm the other. I can, however, prevent you from harming my wife, which is what you came for, right? So this little battle is going to go on either forever, or until our brethren decide to intervene since we're violating the long-established truce. Either outcome doesn't seem like much fun to me. How about you?"

"All I want is you," Aphrodite said.

"That's a bridge you burned long ago," Matt said.

"I can build new bridges. I'm pretty good at it," the goddess said, her body and attire settling back into a human-sized seductress.

"I'm sure you are. But no."

"She'll die some day, and then you'll want me back."

"No, Stacy."

"No, she won't die, or no, you won't want me back?" Aphrodite asked, a teasing lilt in her voice.

"Both."

Matt's response reached Crystal's ears, stopping her in her tracks. Both?

Aphrodite apparently had as much trouble grasping what Matt had just said as Crystal did. "What do you mean both? You can't show her the way to becoming a goddess."

"I didn't show you either, but you managed."

"I was different."

"Yes. And special. Just like her."

Aphrodite's expression changed, a panicked look spreading across her face. "Matt, you can't. It's not fair. Not fair to her, not fair to me, not fair to you."

Matt shrugged. "She can make her own decision. Me—I'm sure I can handle it. And you? Why would I care anymore about being fair to you?"

"But—no...." Aphrodite advanced sinuously on Matt, reaching out to touch his face.

"No," he said, batting her outstretched hand away. "It's over, Stacy. Has been for a long time. Didn't seem to bother you for—what? A million years? Give or take a few eons? Give it up. We're done. I've moved on. I have a family now, and they make me happy. Their love is a given, an absolute, without either demands or consequences."

Aphrodite snorted. "There's no such thing." Suddenly the world lit up around Crystal as a ball of ka energy engulfed her. The ground rose and then dropped away again, by how many feet Crystal couldn't tell. A great wind seemed to blow the energy ball away from her, allowing her to see again just in time to realize that the earth was moments from slamming into her in its tumultuous rise. She gasped, unable to produce words, as four great silver-scaled legs wrapped around her body, holding her above the heaving soil. Looking down through a tiny gap between Sorscha's legs, she saw the spot where she had stood was now burning. She looked forward, to see that Matt had moved directly in front of her. Sorscha was hovering several feet off the ground, buffeted by winds to every side yet holding her position unsteadily behind Matt. Aphrodite, meanwhile, stood across the field, radiant in her fury. The goddess was, apparently, pulling out all the stops to end the threat that was Crystal.

Crystal heard a loud clatter and glanced up. A shield Matt had erected was effectively bouncing away hailstones that were as big as baseballs. How many attacks could Matt defend against simultaneously? As he deflected one attack after another, Crystal thought to Sorscha, *Can't you get us farther away from here?*

Away to where? You can't run from a goddess. At best, you'd make it a moving battle, and at worst, you'd run away from the master's defense. I've got you....

Sorscha's mental voice was drowned out by the bray of angry claxons. Crystal couldn't tell whether the noise was generated telepathically by magical alarms or physically by actual horns, but she was stunned by the volume. They stopped as suddenly as they had begun, though, leaving an eerie almost-silence in the midst of the maelstrom of wind, rain, ice, and earth slamming against Matt's shields that were steadily expanding, pushing the attacks farther away from Crystal and Sorscha.

Her eyes caught a glimmer at the edge of the field, and as she focused on its source she realized the cause for the alarms. There, suddenly, was Gaia, dressed the same as she had been on the day Crystal had met her, standing as tall as the trees with a stern expression on her face. Crystal saw others teleporting in. Artemis, gleaming golden bow held at the ready, appeared at Gaia's right, and next to her a man in white robes with a raven perched on his shoulder stood haughtily, the life-or-death battle scene laid out to his front clearly beneath his consideration. To the Mother's left stood Thor, holding what could only be Mjolnir, his legendary war hammer, ready for battle. A black-haired god with a scowl that was as dark as his hair appeared, a three-headed dog to his side, and next to him was a god whom Crystal recognized as Poseidon from the trident he was wielding like a weapon.

The gods kept coming as Aphrodite's rage crashed against Matt's shields. Next to the raven-god—Apollo?—stood Hermes wielding a winged staff and a goddess wearing a golden helm with an owl familiar. Crystal felt her curiosity splitting; most of it remained on the ongoing battle designed to either end her life or save it, but she had never imagined an opportunity to see the world's gods arrayed in front of her. They stood watching the conflict like moving, glimmering statues as the circle filled in around Matt and Aphrodite. Toward the back she saw deities who represented the eastern pantheon. She had never studied any of those gods and goddesses, and as a result she had no idea who the tall god in green robes or the goddess with four arms, or any of the others, were. She would have to ask Matt later.

If she lived.

The cavalry is coming to protect me! Crystal said to Sorscha, glee and relief both lightening her mental voice.

The cavalry doesn't care about you one way or another, Sorscha corrected. *They're here to protect the truce.* Sorscha's mental voice was tense, and the images that slipped across the link were of Matt, himself, being judged, Matt being found, Matt's immortality being ended.

Crystal's heart skipped a beat. *But she started it!*

The master is the reason the truce exists in the first place.

Crystal's chest went cold with dread as, battle forgotten, she watched the last couple of gods glimmer into place in the circle around her, her love, and Aphrodite. Surely they wouldn't punish Matt for this....

"CEASE THIS!"

Gaia's command was echoed over and over again from the

nearby mountains. Crystal's ears rang, an especially eerie sound in the silence that now lay over the glade. It was an effective command, though. Matt still stood in a defensive posture, shields around Sorscha and Crystal intact, but he made no attempt to move. Aphrodite's stormy demeanor blew away, replaced by an angry look that relaxed itself into surprise as she took in the gathering of gods and goddesses that surrounded them.

"This is unbecoming, Stacy," Gaia admonished.

Aphrodite looked at Matt, an appeal plainly written across her face. "There is no such thing as true love, Matthew. Please, come and enjoy immortality with me."

"Yes, Stacy," Matt said, "there is. Really, there is. Remember how much it pained you to come here with me and leave all your friends and home behind when the cataclysm hit? They followed without fear, without complaint. They followed me because they love me. And I love them. Where I am is their home, and where they are is my home. And Crystal, my wife—well, she's going to have the same opportunity you did."

Aphrodite, visibly crushed, nodded once and then disappeared. Matt watched the space she had vacated for several long moments before turning and teleporting over to Crystal. He picked her up off of the ground and held her tight.

"You're—actually going to show me how to become a goddess?" Crystal stammered.

"No. She was right. I can't show you. Nobody can. I wasn't lying when I said there's no upgrade path from human to god. But you were right when you said it's possible, and I think you are one of the very few humans ever with a decent chance of making it."

"So when do I start?"

"Well, right now, your skin is glowing."

Crystal looked down at her body, reminded of the fact that her neurons were still firing rapidly over the tingling sensation.

"I shouldn't have survived the first blast, should I?"

"You wouldn't have without Sorscha. She shielded you. At least, she shielded you as much as she could. Her body is immune to magic, but she can't block magic otherwise. My shield helped dampen the effect too, but Aphrodite held nothing back, and so that was a damn powerful spell. The ka that was intended to suck the life out of your cells still got through. What you're seeing is the energized cells left behind by the buffeting your body took. It'll dissipate over time, and there's nothing really unhealthy about it. You're fine, Love, just—kinda pretty and sparkly, in a magical sort of way."

Crystal turned and gave the still-nude thrakkon a tight bear hug. She began weeping slightly as she said, "Sorscha, thank you. Thank you for everything. You saved my life."

Sorscha stepped out of the hug and nodded gravely. "I couldn't allow anything to happen to you, ma'am."

"Since when did I become a ma'am?"

Sorscha shrugged and grinned. "Since we survived that, I guess, Crystal. Many beings perished in the battle between the master and Hermes."

"Speaking of Hermes," Crystal said and looked around. The circle of deities had disappeared, crisis averted, and only Gaia remained. As Crystal met the Mother's gaze, Gaia smiled and blinked up to the group.

"I'll heal her, Mother," Matt said, irritation in his voice. Crystal looked down at where wounds she hadn't realized she had were now disappearing. She tried to observe and analyze the flows that were being used, but she was too exhilarated after winning the encounter. She was surprised Matt wasn't as happy as she was.

"I can see that, Matthew. Relax. You deserve no censure for this battle. The truce is still intact, and I think you won't hear from Stacy again for a long time."

"That's good, isn't it?" Crystal asked Gaia. As much as she hated to sound naïve, she had to admit that she was in this case, and she wanted to know what lay ahead.

Gaia smiled tenderly and touched Crystal's face. "Good indeed for you two young lovers." Matt snorted, and she admonished him with, "You're still younger than me, young one, as measured by both years and actions." Turning her attention back to Crystal, Gaia said, "You undertake a rough and dangerous road. Are you sure you want this?"

"I am, Mother" Crystal said.

"Well, then best of luck, child. One thing you humans have that we immortals sometimes covet is that you have room in your lives for dreams of the future," Gaia said, and then vanished.

"Thank you," Crystal said into the empty space where a moment before the Earth Mother had stood.

A thought suddenly occurred to her, panic welling up. "Lady? Where is Lady?"

Matt whistled loudly and pointed to the opposite end of the valley as the large mare emerged from the tree line and galloped toward them. Sorscha said, "Lady wisely ran off when I showed up. Horses don't like dragons much."

"Somebody must've told her what dragons eat," Crystal said, a wry grin on her face.

Sorscha returned the grin with a toothy smile, lines of sharp teeth showing fully.

"That was intense," Birch's voice sounded from behind. Crystal spun around, seeing the trio of senior mages walking toward them. "Matt," he continued as they drew nearer, "the bolts of elements I got, but what was it that felt like a nuclear bomb going off?"

"That was the core, the essence of magic," Matt said, switching easily back into his lecture style. "Ka. You've seen it once before, remember? What I used was a very small taste of it, just enough to kick you in the pants. Aphrodite, though, meant to harm Crystal and me with it, so the power she put into her attack was a little more generous. You can't really learn anything from it, since humans can't touch ka. Other than Lesson 1, anyway. Remember what that lesson was?"

"Don't piss off a god?" Birch chirped.

Matt nodded, and a laurel wreath suddenly appeared atop Birch's head. The man grinned, touching the laurels.

"So is she coming back?" Phoenix asked.

"Probably not," Matt said. "I think I finally impressed upon her the real odds of the two of us ever getting back together. Which are zero, by the way, in case you were wondering."

"I wasn't," Phoenix replied. "It's obvious how you and Crystal feel about each other."

As Lady cantered up, Sorscha reached over and surprised Crystal with a kiss on the cheek. "I should probably get back to the estate," the thrakkon said, "and get some clothes on," she finished, pausing to direct arched eyebrows at Birch. Birch averted his eyes, his face turning red.

"Sorry. You have a pleasing figure," he muttered.

Sorscha's laughter trilled as she ran off toward the manor. She covered the ground quickly, her strides easily reaching ten and twelve feet each.

"The thrakkoni never stop amazing me," Crystal said.

"Yeah," Birch breathed, his lusty tone causing Crystal and Phoenix both to giggle.

"What?" Birch said, spinning around in mock agitation. "Even happily married as I am, I find it hard not to enjoy a beautiful work of art."

Crystal and Phoenix responded by breaking into peals of laughter. Matt also chuckled and slapped Birch on the shoulder. "Indeed," Matt said. "Millions of years, and the male half of the species still hasn't changed much."

Matt hoisted Crystal onto Lady's back, and the group set off after Sorscha, walking at a relaxed pace. Crystal, feeling the tingling in her skin, was delighted after brushing so close to death to still be alive and able to catalog the sensations. Her hips rocked in rhythm to Lady's walk. As they walked, she heard her friends' light-hearted banter, and smelled the musky scent of her horse combined with the fresh aroma of the grass and the wildflowers growing nearby. Most significantly, she looked at the back of her husband, leading the group down the hill. The man she loved, she thought, who had swooped in to her defense, powerfully protected her, and agreed to help her achieve what she had only ever dreamed of achieving.

She wondered as they walked what it would take. Aphrodite had said it was too difficult, wasn't fair to her to try, and Matt hadn't contradicted her. But whatever it was, whatever it took, she knew she would do it for him, and for them. She would find a way to live forever with her husband, the man—the god—that she loved.

About The Author

Dean by day and writer by night, Stephen H. King grew up being asked whether he was "that Stephen King." "Not the author," he'd say until his writing addiction took hold and made that into a lie. Now he writes and reads and blogs as The Other Stephen King—you know, the one who writes fantasy and science fiction. When he's not writing, he enjoys thinking about writing while going on hikes or long road trips. When he's not thinking about writing, it's usually because he's fishing.

Find other Stephen H. King works at:
http://TheOtherStephenKing.com

Read his ongoing thoughts about writing, authorpreneurship, and other key parts of life at his blog:
http://TheOtherStephenKingOnWriting.blogspot.com